Advance praise for Pintip Dunn's
MALICE

"Like a virus that takes over the world, my love for *Malice* replicates with every page. With its shocking twists and to-die-for romance, I dare you to put this book down!"
—**Kristin Cast**, *New York Times* **bestselling author**

"A pulse-pounding, big-stakes romance that warms your heart. *Malice* belongs on the keeper shelf."
—**C.C. Hunter**, *New York Times* **bestselling author**

"Unexpected in all the best ways. It has everything—twisty time travel, an impossible romance, and intrigue—wrapped up in an #ownvoices story. Entertaining to the last page!"
—**Lydia Kang, award-winning author of** *Toxic*

"A riveting story full of mind games, deception, and romance that had me holding my breath from page to glorious page."
—**Brenda Drake**, *New York Times* **bestselling author of the Library Jumpers series**

"A gripping read from beginning to end. The twists will keep you on the edge of your seat while the romance will make you swoon!"
—**Meg Kassel, award-winning author of** *Blackbird of the Gallows*

"Buckle up! This is time travel like you've never experienced before!"
—**Marissa Kennerson, author of** *Tarot*

MALICE

PINTIP DUNN

NEW YORK TIMES BESTSELLING AUTHOR

Entangled Publishing, LLC
10940 S Parker Road
Suite 327
Parker, CO 80134
rights@entangledpublishing.com

Entangled Teen is an imprint of Entangled Publishing, LLC.

Visit our website at www.entangledpublishing.com.

Edited by Liz Pelletier and Heather Howland
Cover design by L.J. Anderson
Cover images by
grandfailure/depositphotos and
oxygen64/depositphotos
Interior design by Toni Kerr

ISBN 978-1-64063-412-1
Ebook ISBN 978-1-64063-411-4

Manufactured in the United States of America

First Edition February 2020

10 9 8 7 6 5 4 3 2 1

entangled teen
an imprint of Entangled Publishing LLC

For Atikan, my blue-haired bear

CHAPTER 1

Blue ink spreads like ants across my brother's skin. He moves the pen over his palm, dipping into the hollow of his hand and rising up again. Never stopping. Never slowing.

"Archie—" I start to say.

"Hold on," he mutters. He doesn't say any more. He doesn't need to. I learned long ago not to interrupt when his genius strikes. He needs to write the equations down—fast—before the insight flees, lost forever in the ether of his brilliance.

My brother and I are opposites. We have the same pale, nearly translucent skin, the same unruly dark-brown hair... but that's where the similarities end. He's a bona fide prodigy, while I gained admission to our exclusive STEM-focused private school only by virtue of being his younger sister. I spend a good part of each day fantasizing about the banana pudding from Magnolia Bakery. Archie forgets to eat half the time. I've been known to plan my outfits a week in advance, but my brother wears the exact same thing every day: khaki shorts and a Marie Curie T-shirt.

Still, I wouldn't have him any other way. He is my family,

and he loves me deeply, even if he doesn't always show it.

I sink onto the grass, cross-legged, dropping the pig-and frog-shaped bento boxes. Across our high school's grassy field, my best friend, Lalana, is jumping up and down to get my attention, her black hair flying and her sneakered feet bouncing. I can't tell if that means Reggie finally asked her to prom or didn't. Either scenario would have her fidgeting through our lunch hour.

I give her a quick wave. I'm dying to hear her news, but Lalana's just going to have to wait. Same as me. I'll find her after I make sure my brother eats his lunch.

Finally, *finally*, Archie lifts the pen to his mouth, chewing on the tip. His lips will be partially stained for the rest of the day, but at least his inspiration is safely recorded.

I shove the box toward him and throw a napkin onto his lap. "You know...I have paper. You don't need to write all over your hand."

My brother blinks behind his black-rimmed glasses. "Well, yeah, but that's *your* paper," he says, like that explains everything. Maybe to him, it does.

"Half of lunch period is already over." I take the lid off my bento box to reveal rice balls arranged in the shape of a caterpillar, complete with bell-pepper antennae and string-bean legs.

He arches an eyebrow. "You cooked for me? Should I have the number for poison control ready?"

"Very funny." Okay, so maybe I'm not the world's best cook. Something to do with burning the food every. Single. Time.

But I was so careful today. Just look at this gorgeous caterpillar!

"There's chicken teriyaki inside the rice," I continue. "You'll love it."

He makes a big show of picking up a rice ball and squinting at the eyes I punched out of nori. And then he takes a bite.

A strange expression crosses his face, and quickly, he shoves the entire thing in his mouth.

"What?" I ask, alarmed. "What is it?"

"Nothing," he says, chewing as fast as he can. "It's delicious. Best thing you've ever cooked. You should make it every week. Every day!"

I cringe. Archie couldn't lie convincingly to solve the Riemann hypothesis.

Snatching up my own rice ball, I sample it. A bitter, acrid taste spreads across my tongue. No question about it. I burned the chicken.

"But how?" I moan. "I only took my eyes off the pan for a second, I swear. One tiny, little second. There was this fascinating article in this week's *National Geographic* about the authenticity of these nine-thousand-year-old masks from the Judean desert—"

Archie bursts out laughing, and I join in grudgingly. Maybe one of these days I'll stay focused enough to make the perfect meal. Just not today.

He eyes another rice ball. "My sister. The only foodie account holder on Instagram who can't actually cook."

"For your information, the caterpillar post has already gotten a hundred likes!" I grab his arm as he reaches for another piece. "Don't. Really. The chicken's disgusting."

"I kinda like it," he says loyally, even as he grimaces. "The flavor's…interesting."

I rock back onto the grass, shaking my head even as my cheeks go soft. What am I going to do without my brother? He leaves for Harvard in a few months, and already I'm dreading my final year in high school without him.

It's bad enough that I'm the only student here who's

not a science wiz. My dream is to take photos for *National Geographic*, not solve world hunger with a well-placed equation. My fledgling foodie account is a poor facsimile of what I hope to one day achieve.

But more than any of that, Archie *gets* me.

Losing a parent will do that to siblings.

He's the one who picks up a pint of cookie dough ice cream for me on the rare occasions he remembers to go to the store. He listens to me agonize over whether to use "yesterday" or "the day before" when I'm posting on social media. He even watched *Thor* with me thirteen times in a single weekend because he knew I needed to forget the anniversary of our mom leaving.

My brother understands, without me saying a word, the hole in my heart that Mom created when she abandoned us. Maybe because he has one, too. Maybe because he's the only one who ever comes close to filling mine.

Dad doesn't have a clue. Since Mom took off six years ago, he only talks to me when he has to—about dinner, the plumber, my allowance. It's almost like I lost both of them that day, instead of just her.

My stomach tightens at the thought of my absentee parents—one literal and the other in practice. But I push away the sensation and toy with the carrot slices I carved into flowers this morning. "You…um, you didn't come out of the basement for dinner last night."

"Oh." Archie's grimace morphs from distaste into guilt. "I was working on a proof. Sorry."

"With Zeke?" I ask.

He frowns and looks away. "No. Just me."

Zeke is a year below Archie, a junior like me. Since middle school, he and Archie would sit in our basement for hours, heatedly debating hypotheses with names as complicated as one of the old languages that dies approximately every fourteen days.

Zeke makes me laugh. A lot. We share a mutual love of Emily Dickinson, and we're both obsessed with the Avengers. But more importantly, we both love my brother.

He hasn't been around as often as he used to, and I can tell that's bothering Archie. "So…how is Zeke?" I ask carefully. "I haven't seen him at our house lately."

"He's busy," Archie grumbles.

"Oh. Okay." I chew on my cheek, wondering how to continue. "It's just that you don't talk as much anymore, not even to me. I thought maybe if you and Zeke—"

"Don't worry about it," Archie says gruffly, dropping his eyes. "It's not your job."

Damn it. I've embarrassed him. He might spend the bulk of his days in a science-induced daze, but that doesn't mean he likes admitting that his little sister takes care of him.

Just as he takes care of me.

Pointing that out won't make him feel any less awkward, however.

"You're right. It's not my business." I pause. "Dad didn't show up, either," I say, just to change the subject. That particular fact isn't exactly groundbreaking. Dad never has dinner with us. Too busy running the biotech company he founded when he graduated from Harvard at nineteen. "I had to eat the lasagna by myself."

Archie tilts his head. "You could've called Lalana. She would've been happy to have dinner with you."

"It's not that." The backs of my eyes heat. I blink rapidly, chasing away the warmth before it can materialize into something ridiculous like tears.

What's wrong with me? I've eaten countless meals alone. Archie and I have always fended for ourselves, and each other, even when Mom was around. She'd get caught up in her studio so often, my childhood growth spurts were practically fueled by microwavable pizza rolls.

"Could you…come out for dinner tonight?"

"Sure," he says, but by the way his eyes travel back to the writing on his hand, I can tell he's done with the conversation. He picks up his pen and starts scrawling another row of numbers, as if determined to fill the last few centimeters of free space.

Sighing, I shove the bento boxes into my backpack and make my way across the lawn, toward Lalana. The sun reflects off the squat brick buildings, and tiny purple flowers bloom under the oak trees. A basketball court covers one end of the neatly shorn grass, and picnic tables are strewn across the other.

Closing my eyes, I lift my face to the sun, soaking up the warmth. April in Maryland can either be freezing or scorching. Thank goodness the weather is finally cooperating, with spring break two days away and prom a week after that.

Yeah, I know. What kind of fresh torture is that timing? The dance is earlier than usual this year—something about exam schedules and budget constraints. Which means, my friends will spend every moment of our vacay consumed by their outfits and accessories and hair. Ugh. Good thing I'm not going—

A streak of electricity zaps through my head.

My eyes pop open. What was that? I swear I felt my brain short-circuiting.

Cautiously, I glance around. A couple of my classmates are biting into fat, foil-wrapped burritos, and a girl with a feather tattoo is stretched on the lawn, using her girlfriend's stomach as a pillow. A group of guys throw a basketball around on the court, and Lalana is frantically scrubbing at her pants, as though she might have spilled something.

Not a single person looks at me. Clearly, no puff of smoke billows around my head.

Okay, then. I was probably just imagining it. Lack of sleep and too much fatigue from carving all those veggies. That combo's enough to make anybody hallucinate.

Giving my head a firm shake, I start walking—

Zapppp.

My breath hitches.

The synapses inside my brain sizzle, as though they're being held over an open fire. I grab my temples between my hands, but it doesn't help. The pain intensifies, as though my brain is slowly being brought to a boil.

My vision blurs, and I lurch behind a tree, dropping to my knees. A muffled voice rumbles. I don't pay attention. I have more pressing concerns, like keeping the brain inside my skull. The voice rumbles louder. *FLAMING MONKEYS. Can't you see a girl is dying here? Go. Away.*

"Maybe I would if you would listen a moment," the Voice snaps, much more clearly this time.

What? Disoriented, I look up. But there's no one around other than a butterfly flitting by my head.

"I'm in *here*," the Voice says, as though I'm a wayward two-year-old. "In your head."

The pain dials back a notch, but my stomach is still swirling with nausea. A voice…in my head? No way. I'm hallucinating. I've got to be. The chicken tasted worse than normal—maybe I have food poisoning. Any second now, I'm going to vomit or pass out. Probably both.

"Focus," the Voice barks. She sounds feminine, but I can't tell if she's young or old. "Do you want this pain to stop?"

The flames roar back, burning even hotter. This is the worst food poisoning *ever*. I'm never cooking again. "Yes!" I moan. "I'll do anything. Just make it stop."

The pain shuts off like a door being slammed, and I collapse against the tree trunk, panting.

"Good. I'll go away, once and for all. You won't have to deal with this pain anymore. You just have to do one thing for me." She pauses, as though gathering her thoughts. "Tell Bandit that you love him."

"Huh?" The electricity must've fried my hearing. "Who?"

"Bandit," the Voice bites out. "You know. The Thai boy playing basketball across the field?"

Pushing myself off the tree, I peer around the trunk. Across the courtyard, a guy with electric-blue hair raises his hands to shoot the ball, and his shirt rides up, revealing nicely defined muscles.

That's right. Now that I can string two brain cells together, I know exactly who she means. Bandit Sakda. We don't travel in the same circles, but his reputation precedes him—he's as smart as he is aloof.

I should know. We had Visual Studies together last year. The one—and only—time I tried to talk to him, I complimented him on a photo he'd taken of an older woman holding a garland of jasmine and roses. Instead of responding, he just pressed his lips together and turned away.

"You've g-got to be kidding," I sputter. "I'm not listening to some voice that I'm probably just imagining. I don't even know him! I'm not going to profess my love to some random guy."

The Voice sighs. "You're not imagining me. And yes, actually. You are."

The sharpest, most intense lightning bolt yet sears my brain. The world fractures into a dozen glowing stars, each one bigger and brighter than the last.

When I can see again, my heart rate has tripled and

I'm heaving in air. This can't be happening. If it's not food poisoning, then I must be dreaming. Or maybe I'm having a bona fide break with reality. Better still, I've been kidnapped by aliens who are putting me through a sick simulation.

Voices don't randomly appear in people's heads. They just don't.

Except…this one keeps talking.

"Well? I'm not sure how much more you can take, but I'm willing to find out."

I'm not. I may not know what's real anymore, but apparently I'm going to confess my infatuation to a stranger.

Coming out from behind the oak tree, I put one foot in front of the other. Bandit's blue hair glistens under the sunlight, and he's passing the basketball from one hand to the other, his movements quick, his hands nimble. His rudeness notwithstanding, he's certainly…attractive.

Not that it matters. He could be the best-looking guy in the world, and he still wouldn't be my type. I have very few rules, and this is one of them: no romantic entanglements in high school. My parents were high school sweethearts and look what happened to them.

I take a deep breath. This is going to be harder than I thought. My heart is racing at the idea of telling this guy *anything*. Bandit's an unusual blend of jock and genius, making him one of the most popular kids at our school. Both girls and guys swarm his locker in between classes, and his ego must be through the stratosphere. It's got to be, 'cause only a boy with supreme confidence could pull off that blue hair. He's pretty much everything that I'm not. Entitled. Self-assured. *Accepted.*

This is a guy who's never had to question his parents' love *or* his classmates' approval.

I hate that part of me is jealous. For me. For Archie. I hate that another part feels less than. And for those feelings... I kinda, sorta hate him, too.

Before I know it, I'm a foot away from the basketball court. The players are taking a break, and Bandit stands at the edge of the concrete, taking long pulls from a water bottle. Up close, his brilliant hair looks almost purple, and his T-shirt sticks to his back in sweaty patches, hinting at his solid muscles.

Now what? Do I clear my throat? Tap his shoulder? Going for broke, I do both at the same time.

He turns and lifts his eyebrows, as though wondering how a mere mortal such as myself dares to approach him. He's tall—really tall. Almost a head above my five feet five. His jaw is chiseled, his shoulders broad. I'm so close that I can feel the heat rising off his body.

My brain scrambles. I forgot to check if I had any food in my teeth! Did I brush my hair this morning? Put on clothes?

Okay, so clearly I'm not naked, but for the life of me, I can't remember what I'm wearing. Please don't let it be the navy T-shirt with the faded splotches on the shoulder, from when I accidentally added bleach instead of detergent to the laundry.

I glance down. Jeans and a white tank top—my favorite shirt because it has *Lin-Manuel Miranda's* autograph. More than passable.

"I, uh..." My entire vocabulary chooses that moment to flee.

His lids lower, and he looks at me, decidedly bored. "Yes? Can I help you?"

Three, four, five of his basketball friends angle their towering bodies toward us, probably wondering what the interruption is about.

Sweat gathers at the nape of my neck, and electricity

hums along my skin. The Voice is about to zap me again. I just know it.

"Running out of time," the Voice pipes up, as if on cue. "Tell him."

Say the words and be done with it. Say the words. Say. The. *Words*.

"I love you," I blurt. "That is all. Goodbye."

I wheel around, ready to sprint, when a hand snags my arm. *His* hand.

"Wait a minute," Bandit says, his eyes 2 percent less bored. "Are we in third grade? Do you want to give me a note asking if I love you back, so I can circle *yes* or *no*?"

My cheeks burn hotter than the sun assaulting my skin. Hotter, even, than the flames that got me into this mess.

I could really use that alien abduction right about now.

The object of my supposed affection smirks. "We can skip the note. Can't say I blame you for falling for me. I mean, I'm a lovable guy. But have we actually met?" He lowers his voice. "Outside of your wildest dreams, that is."

I gape. Is he kidding me right now? How does a person live with this much arrogance?

An earsplitting whistle slices through the air, returning me to my senses. I jerk back, away from Bandit. Away from my disgrace. Without looking at him, I crash through the crowd. There couldn't have been more than half of these students here before. Where did they come from? The seams in the concrete?

Worse, they're all smirking and laughing. At me.

Nobody else was supposed to have heard. I was willing to embarrass myself, but only in front of a guy who couldn't care less what I say to him.

The double doors of the school swing shut behind me, taking with them the excited laughs, the wild chatter, the indistinct *whir* of speculation.

"Don't tell anybody about me, Malice," the Voice warns.

Malice? Did the voice just call me *Malice*? That can't be right. The evilest thing *Alice Sherman* has done all year is make sure her brother's fed.

"And whatever you do, don't fall for that boy," she says. "It'll only make what you have to do later harder."

My mouth drops open. *What* will I have to do later? As in, this voice thing is going to happen again? More to the point… "Of course I'm not going to fall for him," I snap. "He's the most obnoxious person I've ever met."

But the Voice doesn't respond. Instead, there's a popping sound in my head, like a shoe escaping the mud, and the space inside my brain is still and quiet.

As though she was never here at all.

Maybe…she wasn't.

CHAPTER 2

My cell phone pings with an incoming text message. *Again.* For only the hundredth time this hour. From acquaintances I haven't spoken to in months, from classmates I didn't even know had my number. All pumping me for details: What did I say, how did he look, why did I do it?

I had no idea the junior class was so preoccupied with Bandit Sakda. I'd welcome the infatuation, as it draws the attention off *me*. Except the texts are accompanied by snarky comments like, "You poor thing! Just how long have you been crushing on Bandit?" and "Too bad he doesn't feel the same way about you."

Which kinda makes me want to sink into the quicksand at Mont Saint-Michel. At least then I'd be in France.

Gritting my teeth, I transfer the beef and broccoli that Dad picked up from the takeout cartons to a serving platter. The whispers followed me from period to period, as faithful as a watchdog. Add to that, you know, *the alien in my skull*, and this day can't be over soon enough.

I refuse to think about the Voice. Because it either means

I'm slowly but surely losing my grip on reality…or someone really did hack into my brain and can now force me do anything she wants. Both options make me feel nauseated.

"Aren't you going to see who sent the text?" Lalana asks from where she's sitting at my kitchen table.

"No need. They're all the same." I focus as hard as I can on distributing the broccoli evenly among the beef so that nice pops of green show up against the rich brown. I then press jasmine rice into small bowls and overturn them onto the plates so that the scoops come out domed and pretty. Perfect for a photo for my foodie account.

Idly, Lalana picks up my phone and glances at the screen. "It's from Bandit."

I drop my tongs with a clatter and snatch up the phone. "Give me that."

124.087.3562: Tell me. How does a person fall in love w someone they've never met? Is it my good looks? My rock-hard body? Or my big, big…brain?

My mouth drops. His sheer arrogance takes my breath away. "This is Bandit's phone number?"

"Yep." Lalana drums her fingers on the table. "He's had the same number since he was thirteen."

As luck would have it, my best friend actually *knows* Bandit. Lalana is also Thai, and their parents have been friends since she was a little girl peeling layers off her *kahnom chun* and eating it piece by piece. Most of their interactions are during family events, however, which is why I've never hung out with him.

"Tell him the truth," Lalana says. "I don't mind."

I gnaw on my cheek. Marching up to Bandit was completely out of character for me. Lalana would know. I mean, she knows that I once accidentally killed my goldfish because I fed it freshly baked cookies. Of course she's going to figure out when I'm confessing to a nonexistent crush.

Fortunately, she automatically assumed I was looking out for her. Right before my confession, she'd spilled water on herself—in the exact spot that made it look like she had wet her pants. She thought I made a scene just to distract our classmates so that she could slip away unseen.

"Announcing that you're crushing on Bandit *is* a little over-the-top," she said, her eyes shining. "But I love you for it."

"It's what we do," I responded faintly. "What we always do."

And it's true. From the day we met, Lalana and I have been covering for each other—literally. On the first day of my brand-new middle school, I ripped my jeans, revealing my Sonic the Hedgehog underwear. Even though we'd never spoken, Lalana took off her sweater and handed it to me. We've been inseparable ever since.

I hate lying to my best friend. *Hate* it. But the Voice said not to tell anyone, and until I find out more about who—or what—she is, I'm not sure I should disobey.

"Are you going to respond to him?" Lalana asks.

My fingers are already scrambling across the screen. I'm not going to sell her out, though, even if she did give me permission. I would never do that.

Me: The only thing big about you is your head! Listen. I don't know you. I don't like you. I was dared to tell a stranger that I loved him. End of story.

Most Obnoxious Boy Alive: Even if that's true...which it's probably not...u picked me. How come?

Me: Because you happened to be there?

Most Obnoxious Boy Alive: Nice try. The lawn was filled

w people. U could've picked anybody. But u chose me. &
I know why

Me: Really? Well, enlighten me, O Wise One. (This ought
to be good.)

Most Obnoxious Boy Alive: Cuz of my big, big...toe

    I stare at the screen in disbelief. And then I let out a bark
of laughter.
    "What is it?" Lalana asks.
    "Nothing." I shake my head, resolutely tucking the phone
in my back pocket. "He's just being…"
    She lifts her eyebrows knowingly. "Cute?"
    "Definitely not," I say quickly. "Annoying. Obnoxious. Full
of himself. Did I say annoying?"
    A small smile crosses her lips, but it doesn't quite reach
her eyes. "Listen," she says. "I know he can be charming or
whatever, but I don't think you should get to know Bandit
any more. Trust me—striking up a relationship with him will
only make things harder."
    My breath lodges in my throat. That's almost…*exactly*
what the Voice said. Wasn't it?
    No. I'm not thinking about what happened, remember?
And I'm certainly not going to draw parallels where none
exist. Voice who?
    "I promise I'll never speak to him again." It's a small
concession for the girl who gets up an hour early on the
weekends to make pastries people will actually eat for me
to photograph. "Happy?"
    Her lips twitch. "Drama queen."
    "Enough about me," I say, vowing to forget that I ever
knew a boy named Bandit. I peer at my best friend. There's
a dullness to her expression. A sheen of…sadness overlaying

her features. "Lalana, are you okay? You seem a little down. Is this about Reggie?"

She straightens, flipping her hair over her shoulder. "Nah. Just some family stuff I can't really talk about."

"O-kay," I say slowly. "But I'm here for you. You know that, right? Any time at all."

She smirks. "Even two thirty in the morning?"

I grin. "Even then." In eighth grade, I snuck out my window at two thirty a.m. with a box of mochi under my arm because Lalana was convinced she couldn't survive the night without the green-tea ice cream. Made perfect sense to me. Unfortunately, I slipped and broke my arm in two places. It did *not* make sense to my father.

"I made something for you," I continue.

She wrinkles her nose. "Please tell me you didn't bake."

"Ugh, no." I shudder. I measure ingredients by, you know, scooping up a bunch of flour and dumping it into a bowl. Who knew that in baking, a cup isn't really a cup? Instead, it's this precisely measured amount that involves scraping a knife across the top to get rid of the two excess grains. Who has that kind of time?

I cross to the drawer and pull out the masterpiece I created this afternoon. "Ta-da!"

A printout of Chris Hemsworth's face is taped to the end of a chopstick, with a cartoon bubble coming out of his mouth that says, "Will you go to prom with me?"

Lalana cracks up. "Oh, Alice," she gasps, holding onto her belly. "I can't even."

I smile like a proud parent. "Who needs to go to prom with Reggie when you've got Thor?"

"Who's going to prom with whom?" A male voice drifts into the room. Lalana and I both freeze.

Before we can recover, a tall African-American boy with

a disarming smile strolls into the room. Zeke, a prodigy whose genius rivals my brother's—and my brother's only friend outside of me.

"Nobody," I say. I didn't know Zeke was here, even though I'm secretly glad he is. Archie needed this. "We were just goofing around."

Lalana picks up the Chris Hemsworth replica and strokes his cheeks possessively.

For a few moments, he blinks confusedly at Lalana. She proceeds to plant a kiss on the two-dimensional face.

"Well, *that's* disturbing," he says, his eyes bright. Although, let's face it. Everything about him is bright, from the light reflecting off his cheeks to the glow that radiates from inside him. What's more, as smart as he is, he's not arrogant in the slightest. Unlike other people I know. Other people I've *forgotten*.

Now, if *Zeke* asked me to prom, I would actually consider it. Maybe. Probably.

Archie walks into the room, still in his Marie Curie shirt and khaki shorts. Contrary to popular belief, my brother's not actually dirty. Instead, he bought a dozen of the same T-shirt and shorts after reading an article about decision fatigue and highly effective people.

"Barack Obama and Michael Kors wear the same outfit every day," he'd explained to me. "It's one less decision they have to make so that they can focus on more important things."

I gaped at him. "But President Obama wears power suits. And Michael Kors wears all black. Not…" I gestured helplessly at his decidedly unfashionable getup.

He pushed the glasses up his nose. "Are you seriously asking me to wear tight pants when I sit in the basement all night?"

I guess not. But his insistence on comfort does make him

the target of hushed and not-so-hushed snickers at our school.

"Hi, Lalana," he says now, oblivious to my scrutiny. "Nice cutout." My best friend is currently dancing Thor over the tabletop. We all stare at his bobbing head, transfixed.

Damn. Chris manages to look hot even on a stick.

"At the risk of interrupting…" Archie says drily, as though he expects nothing less from my friends or me, "do you mind if Zeke and I grab some food? I know I said I would have dinner with you, but we're in the middle of a project. Besides—" He glances slyly at the acrobatic Thor head. "It doesn't look like you need any more company."

"Oh, sure." I shove the perfectly arranged beef and broccoli platter at him. "Here, take this. I'll eat the tofu. It's my fave anyhow."

Oops. I haven't taken any photos of the beef and broccoli yet. But the foodie account can wait. Zeke and Archie's friendship is way more important, and I'm thrilled they're hanging out again.

With one last smile from Zeke, the boys leave.

Lalana and I take one look at each other and dissolve into laughter.

"Did you"—she wheezes—"see the look…on Zeke's face… when I was fondling Thor?"

"And Archie!" I gasp. "I think he was wondering if I was somehow switched at the hospital!"

We laugh until we're doubled over, panting for air, tears running down both our faces. Which, in my opinion, is the best kind of laughter. The kind I like to indulge in at least once a week. The kind I have only with Lalana.

When we're sufficiently recovered, she rises to her feet in one boneless motion. "I have to take off," she says regretfully. "I promised the Wat Thai I'd update their website tonight. Thanks for my prom date, though." She winks. "I'll keep him close by my side, where he belongs."

She tucks Chris's face into her purse, kisses me on both cheeks, and floats out of the house. I look at her retreating figure. After the recent hilarity, the empty room feels…quiet. Almost too quiet. *Otherworldly* quiet.

Shaking off the sensation, I begin arranging the *ma-po* tofu on a plate, humming to myself. This is going to be a challenge. Despite the fiery red sauce, tofu does *not* photograph as well as beef.

I'm repositioning some of the cubes when a streak of electricity flashes across my brain. A very familiar streak of electricity.

My eyes open wide, and every residual ounce of amusement drains from my body.

The Voice is back.

CHAPTER 3

My breath comes in quick, shallow pants. I brace myself, preparing for the pain that's about to follow.

But it doesn't come. The zap doesn't return, the electricity doesn't intensify, and my brains don't feel like they're being boiled. What's going on?

"Move away from the sink," the Voice says evenly. It's the same one as before, but she's not impatient and angry this time. Instead, she sounds quite calm.

I perform a quick calculation. It's been seven hours since she last visited. What happened? Did she take a nap—or whatever disembodied voices do to rejuvenate—since we last talked?

I take a step back. Our dishwasher is broken, so the counter is piled high with recently cleaned plates that have yet to be put away. "Who are you?"

Which is a nicer way of saying: *damn you, you made me think I had lost my* ever-loving *mind!* But Mom raised me to be polite to strangers, even if she's not around to enforce it. Even if said strangers take the form of unexplained beings.

The Voice ignores me. "That's not far enough. Walk at least fifteen feet. To the very edge of the kitchen, where the tile meets the carpet."

I scrunch up my nose. "Why?"

"No time for questions," she says, sounding more like her original self. "Do it. Now."

There's no corresponding zap of pain. Compared to my earlier torture, this request is downright courteous. I'm not prepared to accept whatever this is as my new reality. I sure don't like being told what to do by a *voice in my head*. But I comply, more out of curiosity than any desire to obey.

"Okay," I say from the doorway. "I'm here, but I have questions. Lots of them. And if you think I'm just going to—"

BOOM!

The entire pile of kitchenware crashes to the floor. Pots, pans, cutting boards, knives. Plates, dishes, cutlery, and a wineglass filled with a deep-red merlot from Dad's dinner last night. It hits the floor at just the right angle and shatters, spraying drops of wine all over the kitchen.

The epicenter of the crash is exactly where I was standing.

I stare at the blue linoleum squares in front of the sink. My heart gallops, and the rain of wine all over the counter, stove, and cabinets echoes in my mind like the ringing of bullets. I sag against the doorframe, sliding down until my butt hits the floor, half on the shaggy carpet, half on the cold tile.

The Voice… She just saved me. From being drenched with wine, if not cut by the shards of glass. How did she…? The words refuse to form. Instead, images flash through my mind, like a movie sequence on fast-forward.

Drops of wine fly through the air, splattering my skin. Up and down my bare arms, my cheeks, my forehead. My white tank top. Splashing against the fabric, staining it in a random starburst pattern, right next to Lin-Manuel Miranda's autograph. The liquid flows down my body, drip-drip-dripping like the steady trickle of a faucet.

Me, gaping at my tank top. The surprise gets stuck in my throat at first, but then it shakes free in a shriek so loud that Archie vaults up the stairs, taking them two at a time.

Archie's disgust when he realizes I'm crying over spilled wine. The hurried swipes of my finger on my phone screen as I try to figure out how to neutralize the red liquid. For an hour, I dab at the stain. Sprinkle it with salt. Add boiling water. And then I run an entire load of laundry, just to save the shirt. But it's no use.

My favorite tank top, made special by the black Sharpie scrawl of my idol, ruined. Forever.

The events fly through my head like a reel of memories. Just as vivid as if they actually happened. But they're not memories. They can't be.

I stare at the white fabric of my shirt, unmarred by a single stain. And I'm jolted by clarity so deep that it must be true.

This is what my future would've looked like if I hadn't moved.

All of a sudden, fine tremors roll along my skin like choppy ocean waves. For my birthday last year, Archie bought me the autographed tank from eBay…and a pair of earplugs for himself. Can't really blame him. I *might* have been singing about not throwing away my shot from dawn to dusk. But more than the prospect of my nearly ruined shirt, I'm freaked out because of what this vision implies. About the Voice, about its presence in my head.

"Who are you?" I ask again.

The Voice takes a breath, a fluttering of air inside my brain. Or maybe that's me. Or the both of us together. I have this eerie sensation of breathing with this being, of our lungs (if she has them) rising and falling as one. Me, on this floor.

And her…wherever she happens to be.

"I always loved that top," she says musingly. "Maybe it was silly to pick this moment to prove a point, but I might as well save our favorite shirt, if I could."

I shake my head. "What…what are you saying?"

"It's nice to meet you, Alice," she says gently. "I'm you from the future. Ten years older."

CHAPTER 4

My mouth drops. Air wheezes in and out, but it's like I've grown gills in place of lungs. The room dips and spins so violently, it's all I can do to hang on to the doorjamb and not slide across the linoleum.

She… Me… Well, flaming monkeys. We. Us.

Is it possible? The Voice is me? An older Alice Sherman?

"Ticktock," the Voice says. Or maybe I should refer to her as "me." But I can't. Not yet. I can't wrap my head around this new reality so soon. If ever. "We only have a short amount of time. Our consciousness can travel for a few minutes during each visit. Go ahead. Ask your questions."

"What questions?" I croak. It's a wonder I can still talk.

"All the things you've never told a single soul. The answers to which only you—or your older self—would know. My knowledge of the wine spill should tell you I'm from the future. The questions will prove that the rest of it is true. I am you, and you will one day become me."

A puff of oxygen slides into my chest, and the room begins to right itself. She knows me so well. She knows exactly what

I need to get over this shock. Exactly what will push me into the realm of believing.

Proof. In the only form available to me.

"Who did I crush on in the first grade?" The question spills out of me like a geyser.

"Easy. Steven Chu. You pretended you thought he was disgusting, but you were giddy every time he pulled one of your braids."

I make a face. So sue me. I was six years old and clearly had a lot to learn.

"Did I ever cheat on a test?" I ask.

"Seventh grade. Mrs. Miller's class. You went to turn in a history quiz and saw that the test on top had a different answer. Panicked, you changed yours, but karma isn't kind. Turned out, your original answer was the right one after all."

My cheeks flush. Four years ago and the shame still rises in my chest. I was all emotion that day. All fear and self-doubt. The monster was so big, there wasn't room for anything else.

I take a deep breath. One more question. I almost don't want to ask. But I have to know, once and for all, if she's me.

"What's the worst thing I've ever done?" I whisper. "The thing I'll never confess to, as long as I live?"

She laughs so hard that my brain seems to vibrate. But unlike her earlier amusement, soaked with nostalgia, this laughter has no real mirth. "Oh, Alice. You're so…*idealistic*." She says the word like it's a sour candy. "I'll answer the question, but I gotta warn you." Her voice lowers. Thickens. "You'll do much worse before you become me."

I wrap my arms around myself, yearning to dive into the comforting sand dunes of the Arabian desert.

"Let's see. The worst thing you've ever done…Alice, at seventeen…" she says slowly. "Okay. At seventeen you were the Goodiest Two-shoes who ever lived."

Derision lives in the space between her words. Gone is her light teasing. Gone is the warm remembrance. She's angry with me. At herself, at this young age. But why? What did I do? More importantly: *What will I do?*

"Last year, Archie was being recruited to attend college a year ahead of schedule," she says. "By Harvard, MIT, Cal Tech. They all wanted him, and they wanted to lock him down early. You were the messenger between Dad and Archie. Most days, Dad couldn't even bother to talk to you, but that didn't stop you from inserting yourself. You took it upon yourself to act as mediator."

I close my eyes. I know all this, of course. Still, each word slices at my heart. Every sentence stings like a thousand paper cuts.

"But you lied. You told Archie that Dad wouldn't let him graduate early. Then you told *Dad* that Archie preferred to stay home another year, when the truth is, Archie can't wait to leave. Dad would've burst with pride—*he* did the same thing, after all—but you cut off your brother's dreams without a second thought."

"No," I whisper, defending myself even though she must know all my excuses. "I didn't take away his dreams; I only delayed them. The schools will still be there next year. And in the meantime, I get to keep him here. With me. So I can make sure he eats." The pressure builds behind my eyes. "You should remember this. You know he isn't ready to be on his own yet. Beyond the basics like food and laundry, he gets lost in his research. If I'm not here to draw him out, who knows how long he would go without talking to anyone?"

"I'm not judging you, Alice." Her voice softens. "In fact, I'm here to tell you that you don't need to feel guilty anymore. Turns out, that was the best thing you could've done for Archie. The more time he spends with you, the better."

"Really?" I could weep. My middle-of-the-night prayers answered right here, in this moment. I just never dreamed it would come from my older self. "You're not saying that to make me feel better?"

"Really," she says. "Pinkie swear, on the hair of a bear, with a cherry on top." The rest of the solemn promise I used to make as a little kid.

All of a sudden, I'm aware of the snores coming from the back of the house. My dad, after pulling an all-nighter at the office. Four rooms separate us. Any less, and the indistinct rumbling would sound like a faulty lawn mower.

"Is that Dad?" the Voice asks.

"Yep. Delivered the food. Reminded me about the awards banquet Sunday night. And then stumbled to his room."

I don't even blink at the fact that she's calling him "Dad." And that's when it hits me. There's no longer any doubt in my mind. She's actually my older self.

"Whose memory was that?" I blurt. "The one where I *didn't* move from the center of the crash. The one where drops of wine splattered everything."

"Mine," she says. "From my original timeline. But since I've shared my consciousness with you, as you take actions that diverge from the original thread, your memories will splinter into two timelines—what *just* happened in your life and what *did* happen in mine."

"But that's…that's absurd," I stammer. "Are you saying I'll constantly be bombarded with every difference from your life?"

"Of course not. Remember, I'm a lot older than you. I no longer have memories of every moment. You'll only experience the memory reel from my life during the big events, the ones that made an impression on me."

That's a relief. At least my mind will be my own. Mostly.

"One last question," we both say at the same time.

I shake my head, and I feel her performing the same motion, sometime in the future. This is weird. This person is undoubtedly me...but isn't.

"Why are you here?" I ask.

She hesitates. The silence is so abrupt that I think she's disappeared. So drawn out that my mind has time to race through several possibilities.

Maybe she's here to tell me that getting a tattoo of a star on my belly is a colossally bad idea. Or to impart the winning lottery numbers so that I'll be able to cross-country ski around Antarctica. Or maybe—

"I'm only allowed to tell you what you need to know," she finally says. "Time travel is tricky. One wrong move, one detail too many, and we could create ripples that will change the future in ways we never intended."

She stops once more.

"I'm trusting you here. Trusting that you'll keep what you learn to yourself. Trusting you won't let an immature need to confide in someone ruin the future for millions of people. Saying too much to the wrong person could result in a disaster of unknown proportions."

"You have my word," I swear. "Besides, if you can't trust me, then who can you trust?"

She sighs, as though she's asked herself the same question. "We need you for a very special mission," she says slowly. "In the future, a person will invent a virus that will wipe out two-thirds of the world. It's your job to stop them now, in the present."

A blast of cold hits my core, and my mouth opens and closes, opens and closes. Seconds loop around to eternity and back again.

A fatal virus? Two-thirds of the world's population? *My*

responsibility?

It's…it's too much to process. Too much to comprehend.

Faintly, I hear myself asking, "How am I supposed to do that? It's not like I know many mass murderers hard at work in their lair."

"Wrong," the Voice says. "You already know this person. The Virus Maker is a student at your school."

CHAPTER 5

5:58 a.m.

Most Obnoxious Boy Alive: Black flannel shirt, sleeves rolled up. Black jeans. White canvas sneakers

Me: *???*

Most Obnoxious Boy Alive: Ur imagining what I'm wearing, amirite? Don't lovesick girls fantasize bout this every morning?

Me: Hate to break it to you, Bandit, but the only "sick" I'm about to be is all over my phone.

Most Obnoxious Boy Alive: Could u plz not call me that?

Me: What? Bandit? But it's your name.

Most Obnoxious Boy Alive: Yea, but when u say it, w all ur proper spelling, it sounds like ur scolding me

Me: What should I call you, then?

Most Obnoxious Boy Alive: How bout babycakes?

Me: How about Most Obnoxious Boy Alive? That's how you're listed under my Contacts.

Most Obnoxious Boy Alive: Ur giving me pet names already? Aww, honey oats, that's sweet. Not sure I'm ready 4 this level of commitment tho

Me: You started it!

Most Obnoxious Boy Alive: Ur rite. I did. Ok fine. 2 eggs over easy. Bacon. Toast. What I'm having 4 breakfast

Me: Told you already. Utterly uninterested.

Most Obnoxious Boy Alive: Chrysanthemum tea too. Cuz it reminds me of my khun yai. She used to make it 4 me every morning w loads of brown sugar

My fingers hover over my cell phone. I can't bring myself to shut him down. Not now. Because I know from Lalana that "khun yai" means "grandmother." And…he spoke about her in the past tense.

I remember, too, that Lalana attended a funeral last year. And I'm pretty sure it was for Bandit's grandmother.

Me: Of course you would like your tea super sweet.

Most Obnoxious Boy Alive: I don't. But that's how my khun yai liked it, so that's how I drank it

Me: And that's how you still make your tea?

Dots appear. And then disappear. And then appear again, as though he can't decide how to respond. I meant the question as a throwaway, but now I'm gripping my phone like our very future depends on the answer. Finally, his response pops up.

Most Obnoxious Boy Alive: yea. that's how I still make my tea

Ninety minutes later, I stifle a yawn as I pull our beat-up Honda Accord into a parking space in front of our school. It's early still, a half hour before first bell—but the real problem is that my eyes didn't close for more than a few seconds last night.

I'd just learned that the Voice in my head is my *older self*. Who traveled *ten years* into the past. Because she wants me to stop the person who will *destroy the world*.

That's enough to give anyone insomnia, right?

Turning off the ignition, I glance at my brother in the passenger seat. He's staring out the window, probably still half asleep, unaware of my emotional turmoil.

I'd give up my brand new Canon Rebel if he would give me some much-needed words of reassurance. That I'm up to this task. That I didn't imagine the Voice. That I haven't completely lost my mind.

Of course, Archie can't comfort me if I don't confide in him. And I'm not going to do that. Not yet. Not when the Voice was so adamant about keeping the knowledge to myself.

"Archie," I say when he doesn't budge. "We're here."

He sighs and grabs his backpack from the floor. As smart as he is, my brother never wants to come to school. He'd much rather be down in the basement, his mind busy operating on another plane.

As he turns, however, I spy something sticking out of his bag. Something that looks remarkably like the cutout of a head...attached to a chopstick.

"What's that?" I blurt.

"Oh. I forgot." Archie glances over his shoulder sheepishly and then pulls out the object and hands it to me. "Zeke helped me make this last night."

I flip the head over, and my mouth drops. It's Tom Hiddleston—aka Loki—complete with flowing black locks, high forehead, and piercing stare. A cartoon bubble reads, "The Golden Apples of Idunn. It's what's for dinner."

"I thought you could eat with him the next time I have to bail." Archie snickers. "Since no one else seems to like you."

I shake the chopstick, and the Loki head vibrates. I'm grinning so hard, you would think that both Chris and Tom were here in the flesh. I can't believe my brother made this for me. "That's not true. I have tons of friends. *Loads*. And they all *adore* my cooking."

He arches an eyebrow above his glasses. "Who are these so-called people? And what's wrong with their taste buds?"

"Well, Lalana, obviously. And, you know, Thor." My lips tremble with the effort not to laugh. "And now I have Loki. Perfect. We'll double date. I'll make my specialty, pork and chive dumplings."

"Just don't burn the bottoms like you did last time," he says. "That would just be embarrassing."

"Maybe Loki will love them so much, they'll trend on Instagram. Blackened dumplings!"

He shakes his head. "My sister the optimist."

I'm still smiling as I grab my backpack from the trunk. I can always count on Archie to make me feel better.

My bright-blue nails glint under the sunlight, and my glow dims just a tad. I painted them an hour ago, after I finished texting with the most obnoxious boy alive. But now, I'm second-guessing my decision. Why, oh why, did I choose this particular shade?

It was a whim. One that had absolutely nothing to do with Bandit.

I round the car to the sidewalk and stop short, nails forgotten. Archie's been accosted by Lee Jenkins, a beefy, red-faced senior who's almost as wide as he is tall.

My mouth goes dry. Is Lee the one I'm supposed to stop? Will he grow up to destroy the world? Or is it one of his buddies loitering on the grass, Scotty or J.J.?

More importantly, will I now be suspicious of everyone who crosses my path?

Lee slaps Archie on the back, so hard that my brother stumbles forward. "Dude!" Lee says, ten degrees warmer than I thought him capable. "You're awake! I can hardly believe it!" Behind him, Scotty and J.J. shove each other, snickering.

I cringe. My brother's so smart that he can pull straight A's in his sleep. Literally. Archie has the unfortunate tendency of dozing in his classes, partly because he stays up all hours and partly because the material bores him. The impromptu naps may not affect his GPA, but they do affect his coolness factor. Add to that his habits of wearing the same clothes and scribbling formulas on whatever's handy, and…well, let's just say neither my brother nor I are challenging Bandit for his title of Most Popular.

Archie swallows hard. I can almost see him withdraw, like a turtle retreating into his shell. He puts on a brave front, but on more than one occasion, I've glimpsed a suspiciously red tint to his eyes. Allergies, he always says. As if you can get springtime allergies in the winter months.

Lee slings an arm around my brother's shoulders. "Listen." He lowers his voice conspiratorially. "Maggie Falk is newly single. You should ask her to prom."

"Maggie?" Archie repeats cautiously.

"Yep. She's super hot. *And* she's on the honor roll. Exactly your type." Lee gestures down the sidewalk, where a girl is just disappearing inside the building, her lustrous mane of brown curls bouncing. "She'll say yes in a heartbeat. I have it on good authority that she has a crush on you."

Archie looks from Lee to his friends. Their faces are neutral, relaxed—maybe even genuine. My brother clamps his lips together, as though a battle is raging inside him. "Is this a prank?" he asks calmly.

"What? No!" Lee widens his eyes. "Come on, man. We're not in seventh grade anymore. I have no reason to make this up. She really does like you." He pauses. "Think about it. Just…don't wait too long, okay? Prom's in only eight days."

He catches my gaze over Archie's shoulder and winks. "I've already got a date myself. But if you want to join us, Alice, I never say no to a threesome."

I roll my eyes. "Gross."

"Is it because I don't play basketball?" he asks innocently. "I heard how you have an affinity for tall, blue-haired players."

My ears burn. Okay, sidewalk. You can split open and swallow me anytime now. Better yet, maybe I can squeeze beside my brother inside his turtle shell.

Without waiting for a response, Lee saunters off, his buddies trailing behind him.

Archie turns to me, frowning. "What was that all about?"

I don't know whether to laugh or sigh. My brother may have been on the lawn yesterday, but he probably got lost in his equations the moment I left his side. For once, I'm glad he can be so oblivious. One less person to witness my humiliation.

"Nothing." Quickly, I change the subject. "Are you going to ask Maggie?"

"I'm not sure." He shifts his feet, as though he does *and* doesn't want to have this conversation. "Do you think Lee was telling the truth?"

I gnaw on my lip. Maggie's supposed to be a nice girl, and I'm Archie's biggest fan. He may be a little on the strange side, but he's also kind, caring, funny. He's got that smart, serious vibe, too, which lots of girls find attractive. I couldn't ask for a better brother. Why shouldn't Maggie have a crush on him?

At the same time, I trust Lee about as much as I trust koalas. As cute as they are, these "drop bears" have also been known to drop from trees in order to knock people unconscious—and eat them.

"I don't know, Arch," I say hesitantly. "Lee doesn't strike me as the most upstanding person ever."

My brother shrugs. "He could be telling the truth." He *wants* to believe Lee. That much is obvious. Hell, *I'd* like nothing better than if Lee were sincere.

"It's just that this has happened before," Archie continues quietly. "At the Johns Hopkins program last summer. There was a girl there. She liked me, but I blew it. I was too much of a wuss to ask her out." He looks up, a pained glint in his eyes. "I sometimes wonder what would've happened if I had."

I stare, my heart sinking. Oh. So *that's* why he came home from the program so moody and withdrawn. *That's* why he locked himself in the basement for two days straight. That might have even been why I heard strangled sobs coming from his bedroom—although he assured me that was just the soundtrack from one of his science podcasts.

"If I ask Maggie and she says yes, could you go with me to the tux shop?"

My cheeks soften. "You know I will, Arch."

Satisfied, he sails down the sidewalk.

I look at his retreating figure, in the white T-shirt and khaki shorts, getting farther by the moment. And wish, with every cell in my body, that Maggie Falk is my brother's perfect match.

CHAPTER 6

I bound up the main staircase inside the school. The sun blazes through the oversize windows, highlighting every footprint and scuff mark on the worn linoleum. Plastered on the walls are posters advertising this year's prom theme, *Love Through the Ages*, and a clock displays the time in big red digits.

Bandit of the blue hair himself is standing in front of the first locker in the corridor. Lalana's locker.

He looks up, and our eyes clash. My cheeks heat like they're being warmed by the sun over Dallol, Ethiopia, the hottest inhabited place on Earth. This is the first time I'm seeing him since I told him I loved him. Since our text messages. What, exactly, is our status? Certainly not friends, although I have to admit, our last exchange makes me wonder if I misjudged him. And yet, we're not strangers, either. Not anymore. Not after being paired up in this week's juiciest gossip.

A pang shoots through me. I was so preoccupied with *my* humiliation that I forgot to think about *his*. Has Bandit also been the victim of endless inquiries and crude remarks?

Sadly, he's used to having his name on people's lips. Last year, all anyone could talk about was the undivided attention his parents "bought" from the school's guidance counselor. Before school, during lunch — Bandit was always seen exiting her office, while the rest of us had to wait weeks for a measly five-minute appointment. It paid off, apparently, as Bandit scored a research position at a prestigious lab at MIT.

His popularity might make him immune to the worst of the social ramifications. Still, it's no fun being the topic of widespread rumors. And here I am, making him go through this particular brand of fresh torture — again.

The least I can do is apologize. I just really, really wish I had any other color on my nails.

Time slows to a crawl as we stare at each other. My skin goes hot and cold, and I'm aware of every nerve, every cell in my body. I have to be, since they're popping and sizzling all over the place.

And then, out of nowhere, a heavy weight slams into my back, and I stumble.

"Sorry!" a freshman calls as he sprints down the hallway.

Too little, too late. I pitch forward, and Bandit rushes toward me to break my fall. My hands end up splayed on his pecs, on that black flannel he so generously told me about, our lips a few inches apart. For a moment, neither of us breathes.

His chest feels so…solid under my hands. His muscles so…firm. He definitely spends as much time on the basketball court as he does in the science labs.

Get ahold of yourself. This is the most obnoxious boy alive, remember?

Snatching my hands away, I take a deliberate step back. We look at each other for a few confused moments. Then he lifts those straight eyebrows, giving me his bored face. "You know, if you're trying to get my attention, there are subtler ways of doing it."

My mouth drops open. "Who said I want your attention?"

"*You* did, yesterday. And today." He looks meaningfully at my fingers hanging by my sides, their tips glistening with the sparkly blue polish. "You painted your nails after our texts this morning, didn't you?"

I grind my teeth so hard that I can almost feel the enamel flaking off. "I most certainly did not." I don't care that I'm lying. He deserves it for being the most presumptuous, conceited boy on the planet. To think—I was actually starting to give him credit for being a human being! "Look, you don't have a monopoly on the color blue."

"Good thing," he says agreeably. "I like blue on you."

I blink, taken aback by the compliment. But if he's trying to be nice, maybe I should, too. "I wanted to apologize for yesterday. Like I said, I was, uh, dared to tell a stranger I loved him. I'm sorry if it brought you any unwanted attention."

"No problem. I imagine you're suffering the worst of it." He lowers his head. "Let me know if anyone gives you a hard time, okay? I'll talk to them."

The corridor tilts lazily to the side. Is this the same guy who listed all the reasons why a person might have a crush on him?

"What would you say?" I manage. "That I couldn't help falling in love because you're so irresistible?"

His mouth quirks. "Something like that." He checks the time on his cell phone. "I have exactly ten minutes before I need to make up a quiz. So whatever seduction you've got planned, make it quick."

I bang my hand against Lalana's locker, making the curling peels of paint vibrate. And…he's back, ladies and gentlemen. The most obnoxious boy alive.

"For the last time, I have no interest in seducing you," I

say between clenched teeth. "I don't date, okay? I'm not even going to prom. If you knew me at all, you would know that. But you don't know me. Hence, the whole stranger bit."

He tilts his head, considering me. The bored expression has returned, but he only looks up-to-his-ears tedious now, instead of out-of-his-skull. "Why don't you date?"

I frown. I'm not about to tell him the truth: that the last thing I want to do is follow in my mom's footsteps. "None of your business. All you need to know is that it's not happening in high school. Not with you or anyone else."

"Got it," he says lightly. "So no dating for another decade, huh? I can just see you, ten years from now. Living on a beach in Ko Samui, sipping from a fresh coconut, and falling in love with the first charming guy who comes along."

The back of my neck prickles. I never said anything about being a decade older. That's the same age as the Voice. Why is he picturing what I'll be like ten years from now?

Flaming monkeys. What if *Bandit* is the Virus Maker?

I suppress a shudder. Ridiculous. I can't go around suspecting every student at this school. My brain will explode before lunch.

Except…part of me feels like that's exactly what I should be doing.

"What makes you think I'll settle in Thailand?" I ask, struggling to keep my tone casual.

A grin bisects his face. "Because we have the best-looking people. Didn't you know?"

I snort. Right. Should've seen that one coming.

"Okay, easier question." He gestures to my backpack. "Why do you have a map of the world on your bag?" He moves closer and squints. "And what are those? Stars that you've inked in with a pen?"

"Those are all the places I want to visit." This is better.

Dream travel I can always talk about. "One of these days, I'm going to backpack across the world, to see firsthand all the animals and natural wonders and cultures featured in *National Geographic*."

"There must be a hundred stars on here!"

"I add a few more every week," I confess. "Sometimes I worry that's all they'll ever be: just some symbols on a backpack."

I regret the words as soon as they come out of my mouth. A couple of volleyball players walk by, ponytails swishing, and a gangly guy, more limbs than torso, sends Bandit one of those head nods. The buzz of conversation swirls around us, more excited than usual because it's the last day of school before spring break.

Our ten minutes must be nearly up, but I don't want him to leave yet. My skin feels itchy, like I've given up too much of myself. I need to even the scales, if only for my own pride.

"Your turn," I say quickly. "Tell me something you've never told anybody else."

He lifts his brows in what I'm beginning to think of as his signature look—superior and oh so uninterested. "I don't know who taught you about conversation, but that's not the way it works."

"Oh, come on." I extend my arm, intending to punch him lightly, but he closes his hand around my fist in midair. And holds it.

My heart flutters, and my head is rather…floaty. His hand is warm. And big. He hangs on to my fist for another beat and then releases it. I'm having a difficult time finding enough oxygen.

"Tell me about your name," I whisper. "You said you didn't want me to call you Bandit. Why?"

"I was named by Khun Yai." He shifts forward. "Bandit is

a Thai name, you know. It's actually pronounced *bun-dit* and it means 'one who is wise.' Unfortunately, it has a different definition in English."

"Did your khun yai know that when she chose it?" I will not think about how close he is. How less than a foot separates us. How that distance could be erased in a fraction of a second.

"No." His lips flatline. "She had no idea she was essentially calling me a robber. My mom was out of it at the hospital. My dad was working. They left Khun Yai to fill out the paperwork, and by the time they bothered to find out what name she picked, it was too late."

"I like your name," I offer. "It's different. Unique."

"I got into more trouble because of it. Teachers automatically assumed the worst when it came to me."

"Really?" I shouldn't be surprised, but I am. Would I be the same girl if I were a Darcy or a Meg? I'm not sure. Like our appearance, like our demeanor, names can affect the way people perceive us. The way we see ourselves.

"Yeah." He shrugs. "I think of my name as a challenge. Every day, in every interaction, I can fulfill people's first impression of me and become the Bandit of the English language. Or I can live up to the Thai definition." He looks straight at me. "I don't want you to call me Bandit until you can believe in my name's true meaning."

My mouth parts. He's not what I expected. He's not just a basketball player with blue hair. Not just a really smart guy who thinks he's better than everyone else.

Instead, I'm beginning to think he's exactly who he says he is. He's…Bandit. The real one, who is wise beyond his years.

Beep! Beep! Beep!

He lifts an eyebrow, silencing the alarm on his cell phone. "Gotta run. Try not to stalk me too much, okay?"

My cheeks, my neck, my ears—everything is burning. *This*

is why I swore off relationships in high school. Because clearly my judgment of people is impaired. Male praying mantises (whose female partners eat them after sex) probably have better instincts than I do.

"I am. Not. Stalking. You!" I shout at his rapidly retreating form.

He doesn't retort. Instead, he just looks over his shoulder... and winks.

CHAPTER 7

Thirty seconds later, I'm at my locker down the hall, still fuming. Seriously? If I wanted to stalk someone, I'd photograph them. And do you *see* my beloved Canon Rebel in my hands? No, you do not. It is safely tucked in my backpack, where it belongs.

Shoving my hands into my hair, I look up to see Lalana in front of her locker, gaping at me. Perfect.

I dodge a skateboarder flying down the hall and skirt around a couple devouring each other's lips for breakfast. Huh, maybe humans are more similar to praying mantises than I thought.

"Hey," I say, moving into my best friend's perfume-scented airspace. No matter how early or late, Lalana always smells like jasmine. "What's up?"

She snaps her mouth shut. "Were you just flirting with Bandit Sakda?" She picks up my hand. "And you painted your nails *blue*. With sparkles! Why?"

"Not you, too." Groaning, I pull my hand back. I knew the nail polish was a bad idea. I'm taking it off the minute—no, the second—I get home. "The color was next in the rotation, okay? And we weren't flirting. He was just antagonizing me."

"Why?" Her high voice becomes shrill. "I thought I asked you to stay away from him."

I run through our previous conversation. I *did* promise never to speak to him again, but I was joking. I also never expected it to be an issue. "You never explained why."

Her dark eyes flash. "I shouldn't have to. I'm your best friend. Shouldn't my wishes be enough?"

Yes, of course. But this isn't how our friendship normally operates. I stopped talking to her ex-boyfriend Julian after he cheated on her. I even disinvited Abby Moore from my birthday party when she made fun of Lalana's "paper-slit" eyes. But both were *my* decisions. Not once has Lalana ever asked me to excommunicate someone for her sake. Until now.

I look at her more closely. Her face is pained, and she's holding her shoulders so tightly, they vibrate. "What's going on?" I ask. "What aren't you telling me?"

"Nothing." Sighing, she turns to her locker and begins to load binders into her backpack. "Forget I said anything. I'm just in a bad mood. Probably because of *that*." She gestures to the top shelf, where a blown-glass butterfly sits. It's stunning, with delicate wings swirled with colors that should clash but don't—purples, reds, turquoises, yellows.

"Apparently I have a secret admirer," she says shakily. "All week, things have been showing up in my locker." She bites her lip. "It's kinda creeping me out."

"Really?" I ask. "I think it's sweet that someone's leaving you little presents."

She groans. "You would, Betty Crocker."

I flush. Okay, so I *might* have a bit of experience being the gift fairy. Last year, for Valentine's Day, I baked a yellow cake with chocolate frosting for my mega crush, Dev. He was so thrilled, he proceeded to eat it during lunch…with someone who wasn't me.

Which pretty much cured my infatuation with Dev.

"That was the best cake I ever made, too," I mutter.

"It came from a box!"

"Yes, and I measured everything perfectly. They ate every last bite."

She snickers. "Meghan came to fifth period with crumbs on her lips."

"I still have her thank-you card," I say mournfully. "Tacked up on my bulletin board, in case I ever get another urge to bend my no-dating rule."

"Oh, Alice," she says, her voice warm and amused. "It's just like you to keep the card." Her gaze falls back on the butterfly, and her smile falters. "Too bad my secret admirer isn't anything like you."

Something in her tone makes me swallow uneasily. Lalana doesn't get creeped out. We could be staying over at her house, alone, and hear a strange noise. I would dive to the bottom of the sheets, squealing, while she'd just shrug and say that's what old houses do. They settle.

Now she wiggles free the square of paper underneath the butterfly and raises her perfectly tweezed eyebrows. "Read it together?"

I nod, tucking my chin into her shoulder. Together, we scan the paper.

I love you, Lalana. But you don't see me. Instead, you waste your time with other people who will never be worthy of your mind and soul. But hope must be strongest when hope appears lost. I believe in us, Lalana. So please. Open your eyes. See me. Before it's too late for us both.

I read the letter again and then a third time, my stomach sinking. Because the secret admirer can only be one person.

"It's Bandit," I blurt. "I saw him in front of your locker this morning."

There's a hollowness in my chest, a churning to my insides. Is that…disappointment? It can't be. So what if I was beginning to think Bandit was more than a cocky jock? I don't like the guy. I barely know him. A few text messages and a single conversation don't change that.

Lalana barks out a laugh. "No way. I saw him at the Wat Thai last weekend, and he traded me the *bua loi* his mom made for my psych notes. You know I have a weakness for warm coconut milk. I told him to put the notes in my locker when he finished copying them."

"He could've returned the notes *and* left the butterfly," I insist.

She squints, probably wondering why I'm pressing the issue. I'm not sure myself. Except the Voice targeted Bandit for a reason. She threw me in his path in the most embarrassing way possible. Why? Could he—or this "love" letter—have something to do with the mission?

"Look." I point at the note. "He says you never notice him, even though he's around. It fits. You two have been friends forever, but you don't see him in a romantic light, the way he wants."

She purses her lips. "I don't know. It could be anybody. Like your brother's friend, Zeke. He's always staring at me in history class."

I sigh. "You're stunning, Lalana. Everyone stares at you." I read the note again. "This last line here. *Before it's too late for us both.* Is that a threat?"

She fiddles with one of her chandelier earrings. "Isn't that just an expression?"

"Not one I've ever heard."

A charged silence descends, filling the space between us. My mind whirls, trying to connect the dots. What could Lalana's secret admirer have to do with the future? And how can I do anything about it if they're just that—a secret?

Lalana glances over my shoulder. I turn to see Reggie striding down the hall, his powerful legs eating up the distance, his brown skin as smooth as river stones.

Reggie. Maybe the Virus Maker is Reggie. He certainly has the confidence. He struts around school, secure in the knowledge that someday, some way, he'll be *someone*. He'll do *something*. Could his legacy be a biological weapon of mass destruction?

"Let's talk later," Lalana says quickly. She kisses me on both cheeks, and her floral scent wafts around me. "Reggie is *this* close to asking me out. I can feel it."

"Maybe you should make him a cake." I try to curve my lips. I don't like this. Not the fact that there might be a mass murderer walking in our midst. And not the possibility that my best friend might somehow be involved.

Lalana's already heading toward the heartthrob of the senior class, but she turns and flashes me a brilliant smile. "Only if you promise to help me bake it."

The final bell rings. Lalana and the rest of the students clear out, leaving me with the dirty-gym-socks scent of the corridor. My head aches. My nerves buzz. I can't possibly sit and listen to Ms. Carlyle drone on in my next class, so I shove my cell phone and car keys into my back pocket.

But I don't leave. And I groan when I realize why. I really

am a Goody Two-shoes, since I've never actually cut class before.

Instead, I loiter at my locker. Darn it. I forgot to tell Lalana about the Loki head. It shouldn't matter. I can show her the cutout face at lunch. But for some reason, the omission feels like a huge loss.

Electricity flashes across my skull.

I jerk my hand up, rapping my knuckles against the underside of the locker.

"Ow," I mutter. "At least you could give me a warning."

"The current *is* the warning," the Voice says nicely. She's in a good mood today, just like last time. Thank goodness. I don't miss the ragey woman from the first visit.

"Pay attention," she continues. "We don't have much time. I got access to the school's facility records, and they're upgrading to a new security system. From precisely 7:54 to 8:05, the cameras will be off-line. That's two minutes from now. The second that clock hits 7:54, I want you to go to locker number 247. Use the combination 32-9-28 to open the lock and remove the Ziploc baggie from underneath the gym bag."

I glare at the large red numbers blinking at me from the end of the corridor. "What? Why? You tell me I'm supposed to stop some future mass murderer from our school and now you want me to steal someone's lunch? What's wrong with your priorities?"

"Would it help if I said please?" she asks. "Or reminded you that lives are at stake?"

"Would it help if *I* reminded *you* that you haven't told me anything *useful* about my mission? I suspect everyone right now. Paranoia isn't a good look."

"So stubborn," she murmurs. "I remember that well."

"Do you really?" I look into the eyes reflected by the rectangular strip of my locker mirror. "Or are you just pretending so that I'll believe you're me?"

"I *am* you! That's what you don't seem to get. Any trouble you're giving me now is trouble you're causing yourself later on. Do us both a favor and stop arguing, okay?"

She's agitated, but so am I. My pulse is racing; my breath is short. I don't know how she's feeling in the future, but I imagine it's pretty much the same. Ten years can't have changed our visceral reactions *that* much.

"Listen," she says gently. "I know you've put off certain decisions to the future, such as dating. You believe an older Alice would make better choices. Well, here I am. This is exactly what you've always wanted. An older *and* wiser you, telling you the right decision. You don't have to worry about following your gut. I *am* your gut, with the extra security of knowing how things turn out."

I exhale slowly. She's right. She's the guidance I've been seeking ever since Mom left. All I have to do is accept her advice.

"7:54," she says. "Move. Please."

"Fine." Shutting my locker door, I walk to the end of the row—and freeze when I realize whose locker is number 247.

Lee Jenkins, the jerk who was messing with my brother. He cuts class more often than he attends, and I often glimpse him in the woods behind school, a halo of smoke around his head.

I'm supposed to retrieve a plastic baggie from the bottom of *his* locker? Three guesses what the baggie contains.

I go to work on the lock, my heart galloping, my mind sprinting. *Oh, please. Let the contents be weed.*

Not that I *want* to handle marijuana. I would just prefer not to touch—let alone move—a more serious drug.

My hands are so sweaty, they slip off the combination lock twice, but I finally get the door open. Just as the Voice predicted, underneath the gym bag, I find a Ziploc. It's filled with dried green buds. The skunky smell drifts up, the same scent that had me scrambling out of a darkened den at a party last month.

Weed. My shoulders sag, even as my stomach flips. I'm grateful I found the lesser of possible evils—but why is my older self embroiling me in something illegal?

"Now what?" The question is rougher, my tone harsher, than I intend.

"Proceed to locker number 200. Open the combination. Put the baggie inside."

I don't have to guess. I don't need to, because I was just there. I know exactly who uses locker number 200.

Lalana Bunyasarn. My best friend.

CHAPTER 8

The hallway suddenly darkens, as though the sun has ducked behind a cloud. In the distance, the intercom crackles while Ms. Bui, our principal, reads the morning announcements. I can no longer swallow. My throat's blocked by a lump the size of the Samoan Islands.

Clearly, the Voice knows the locker belongs to Lalana. That's why she didn't bother giving me the combination. She knows I've been using my best friend's locker as overflow storage, and vice versa, since freshman year.

"No," I whisper. The word is hardly audible, a syllable shaped more in my mind than on my tongue. But my older self hears me anyway.

"I get it, Alice." Her voice is as soft as mine. "This is as hard for me as it is for you. Maybe even more so—you've only had Lalana a few years; she's been by my side more than half my life. She's a true sister to us both." My older self stops. Takes a breath. "But we have to put our feelings aside. I swear to you on everything we hold dear—the hairbrush Mom used to brush our hair, the penguin Archie won by calculating the number of jelly beans in a jar. This action is integral and necessary to preventing millions of deaths."

"How? What does putting weed in Lalana's locker have to do with anything?" I ask, my voice shrill. "Are you trying to frame her? Get her kicked out of school?"

She doesn't respond, which is answer enough.

Last year, Lalana's dad moved to the West Coast. Her mom agreed to stay with her in Maryland so she could finish high school, on the condition that she behave perfectly. One lousy B or a single detention, and her parents promised she would be shipped to California quicker than she could pray to the Phra Buddha Chao to forgive her.

I don't know what the Voice has planned for Lalana. But I have no doubt what would happen if she was caught with a bag of weed in her locker.

"No way," I say. "I don't care if you're me. My loyalty to the future doesn't extend to betraying my best friend. Sorry, not the slightest bit sorry."

I march to my own locker and toss the baggie on the shelf, next to Loki. For what comes next, I'll need my hands free.

Tightening my stomach, I dig my toes into the bottoms of my sneakers. "Bring it."

She laughs. "Bring *it*? What is *it*?"

"You know," I say. "The electricity. The pain. I can take more than you can dish out."

"I'm not going to hurt myself." She has the gall to sound horrified. Seriously? When half my brain cells are still strewn across the school's back lawn like ash from the Kilauea volcano? "We're on the same side here. We're the same *person*. What will it take to convince you of that?"

"I want answers," I say immediately, even though there's nothing she can say that will make me double-cross my best friend.

But for once, I have the advantage, and I'm not going to let this opportunity pass me by. "I want to know everything. This person I'm supposed to stop. How Bandit figures in. Lalana's involvement, if any. Also, if I'm married in the future, I want to know if my future husband is cute."

"Oh, your hubby's adorable." Her tone is a cross between amused and exasperated. "Just who we've always wanted, even if we didn't always know it. You broke your wrist last year, and he braided your hair for six weeks."

"Nice. I think I'll keep him. What about the rest?"

She pauses. A senior guy appears in the hallway, bopping his head to the beats in his earbuds.

I slam my locker door shut and hurry down the hall. Normally, I'd say hello to a fellow student in the hallway. But I also wouldn't normally have a plastic baggie of marijuana in my possession.

"All in good time," my older self says. "Come on, Alice. I know you've thought about this. After that last Avengers movie, you developed a fascination with time travel. In fact, you watched every movie they referenced in *Endgame*. Surely you understand that one wrong move, one detail too many, and we could create ripples that will change the future in ways we never intended. For the sake of humanity, you'll have to trust me."

A feeling of déjà vu washes over me, one that has nothing to do with the fact that we apparently have the same memories. Lived the same life. I push the feeling aside. "How am I supposed to trust you?" I ask. "You just ordered me to hurt my best friend."

"I know." Her voice drags with regret. "But I also knew you would refuse. I knew you would demand answers I can't give. That's why I'm offering you an alternative."

The senior exits the hallway, and I'm alone again. Or

at least as alone as I can be with a voice in my head. I stop walking and lean my forehead against a locker, hoping the surface will cool my skin. But the metal is hot and sweaty, increasing rather than decreasing my agitation.

"I've run a marathon in your shoes, but you've never taken a step in mine," she continues. "I told you that a decimating virus will wipe out the world, but you need to see for yourself. Only then will we stop having this separation of minds."

I go perfectly still. It doesn't matter if this locker door might've been forged in hell. She can't possibly mean…

"Are you taking me to the future?"

"Exactly. And don't worry. I'll get you back in time to put that baggie in Lalana's locker."

Adrenaline spurts through my veins. Flaming monkeys, she is! The future. Time travel. A chance to glimpse across a ten-year window.

"How do I get there?" I ask, my heart quivery.

"We have to latch our consciousnesses together," the Voice says. "You need to reach up, link your mind with mine. Once we're connected, I'll be able to bring you forward. Got it?"

I swallow hard. "Maybe?"

"Try." The word is wrapped around a smile. "Reach for me. I'm waiting."

Okay. Here goes nothing. Closing my eyes, I stretch up, up, up, as far as my mind will allow, looking for the older Alice's consciousness.

Nothing. All I can see is the darkness of my own eyelids. Pinpricks of light that my imagination probably willed into existence.

"Stop using your vision," the Voice commands. "Don't look for me the way you search for the perfect angle of a photograph. Instead, *feel* me."

"How?" I run my tongue over the bumpy ridges of my

teeth. "Do I touch you? Taste you?"

"Sense me, with your mind. Feel the contours that are nearly identical to but not quite yours. Find the indentations into which you can fit yourself."

She's speaking gibberish. The more I attempt to understand her words, the less sense she makes. I want to pull out my hair, particularly frizzy today because of the humidity. But she gave me one instruction that was moderately clear. I cling to that. *Don't look for me.*

I squeeze my eyes shut again, but this time, I'm not blocking my vision of the physical world. This time, that world is just…gone.

The split-pea lockers disappear. The black scuff on the walls, created from a generation of skateboarders, fades. Even the solid linoleum tiles that hold up my feet melt away, so I'm left floating in space.

Kinda. If I don't think about it too hard.

I let my mind drift…and there she is! This is really happening!

Her consciousness shimmers on top of mine, calling me like a beacon even if I can't technically see her. But once I sense her, it's as easy as pulling a zipper to fit our jagged edges together.

Click.

I feel in my teeth our consciousnesses snapping together. And then I'm hurtling forward through the blank nothingness of time.

CHAPTER 9

shoot through a black void, floating in ether, my limbs weighing nothing. No, that's not right. I have no limbs. I have no body. I have no head or mouth or lips. I'm just a consciousness, existing in the realm between times.

Panic scrambles my mind, making my thoughts both sharp and fuzzy. But underneath the shock and fear is an overwhelming sense of wonder. I'm here. This is real. This whole new dimension exists, has probably always existed, and I'm just now discovering it.

A bright line wavers in front of me. At least, I think it's in front. There's no direction here. No up or down, no left or right, no front or back. There's only the meaning my mind supplies to make sense of the nonsensical.

And so I think the line is in front. I think I'm moving along it. I think it's connecting the present and the future? I'm not sure.

All I know is that I'm drifting, drifting, drifting in a space that shouldn't be. A realm outside my comprehension. A dimension unlike any I've encountered before…

. . .

I come back to myself as though I am waking from a long sleep. Disoriented, foggy. I blink as I get used to my new surroundings—a black underground cave, its walls slick with water. Bandit couldn't have been more wrong. Wherever I am in the future, it's definitely not a beach in Ko Samui.

Except—that's not me blinking. That's not me splaying my hand against the cool cavern walls, soaking up the wetness. That's not me inhaling the mossy, dank scent of my new location.

Instead, it's the older Alice performing these actions. I can see, hear, smell, taste, and touch everything she does, but only she has the power to control her body—our body. I'm just along for the ride.

It's…weird. Panic surges through my consciousness again, and now that I have a mouth, I try to scream. Try to unhinge my jaw and let loose the terror that permeates every unit of my being.

But nothing happens.

"You okay in there?" my mouth asks.

I jerk. Or at least, I *would've* jerked, if I had control over my body. The person speaking is my older self. Except she's not some disembodied voice anymore. She has a mouth and vocal cords, while I'm the one who's been relegated to a corner of her mind.

Well, flaming monkeys. This time, *I'm* the Voice.

"Alice," my mouth says a little louder. The sound bounces off the walls, and I detect an outline of a door in the rock. We must be in a private room within a network of caves. "The first few minutes are always disorienting, but don't freak out. We don't have time. Are you with me?"

"Yes. I'm here." That's me! Not even a voice, technically, because I make no sound.

And neither did she.

Holy moly. I must've been interpreting the Voice all along, translating her into an entity my mind could understand, when she's never existed as something audible. Something spoken.

"Where are we?" I ask, getting used to the way my words turn into thoughts instead of speech. "Is this where you live? Do you have children?"

"This is my friend's residential unit," she says. "I'm just borrowing it for a while."

She doesn't elaborate, but she does glance around, a quick flick of the eyes. I leap at the opportunity to see more of the space.

A twin mattress lies directly on the ground, next to a long metal tube, big enough to fit a human body. Above a washbasin, a small mirror is attached to the cave wall—and I'm dying, *dying* to see how I look ten years older.

Before I can make such a frivolous request, however, older Alice places our hand on the rectangle etched into the rock and pushes it open.

We hurry through the opening, entering a low, narrow tunnel. Wall sconces light the way every few yards. She takes a hoverboard from a compartment set into the rock. The platform of the board is a fat oval, and she hops on expertly. We fly down the tunnel, so quickly that the light from the sconces elongates into blurry flames.

We bend and curve with the board, my body adept even though I've never ridden before. A low humming fills our ears, and I spy a constant stream of people walking along the tunnels that branch off from ours.

So many twists, too many turns. I try to keep track, but after a while, I give up and just enjoy the experience. The hot air whistles through our hair, and our stomach dips and floats with the path. I haven't had this much fun since Lalana taped a full place setting, complete with a paper plate and plasticware, to my bedroom ceiling, just for the hell of it. I'd break out into a huge grin if my host body would let me. As it is: not even a twitch.

Still, a thought niggles in the corner of my consciousness. I don't get this place. We're ten years in the future. Why are we underground? Shouldn't I be dazzled by technology I can't begin to fathom?

And I am. Kind of. I mean, this hoverboard is awesome, but the rest of the surroundings feel sort of primitive. It's like modern society was lifted up and plopped inside these caves in a hurry, so people didn't have time to bring their gadgets and toys.

Eventually, we touch down in a dimly lit clearing. A couple of people wearing gray jumpsuits greet us as they pass through the open space. The ceilings are still low, just a couple of feet above our head, but the extra width suggests this room is a transfer station of sorts. We nimbly descend from the board, stowing it in another compartment set into the wall.

"The boards are solar powered," the older Alice whispers reluctantly, as though every piece of information has to be pried from our throat. "The boxes take the boards to the surface to recharge, without exposing us to the solar rays."

"Why would the sun be dangerous?" I ask.

"Because of the virus," she responds. "It was manufactured to be highly contagious, and it renders the infected allergic to sunlight."

If I had command over my mouth, it would be hanging open. Seriously? Somebody made a virus that makes people allergic to the *sun*? This is worse than life versus death. This is life versus being buried alive.

Suddenly, a hand lands on our shoulder, and our entire spine stiffens.

"Not. Now." My older self's voice is low and controlled, each word a precise and deliberate bite. She turns away, tucking our chin into our chest and closing our eyes, as though she doesn't want the intruder to see her face.

No, I realize with a flash of clarity. *As though she doesn't want* me *to see the interloper's face.*

My thoughts jam into one another like bumper cars. This person must be important. They must reveal answers to questions I don't even know to ask. I strain our eyelids, struggling to crack them apart.

Lift, lift, open. Just a slit, just a centimeter. *Come on, eyelid! You can do it!* But it's like trying to move my neighbor's limbs with the force of my mind alone.

The hand squeezes gently. It's large and warm, comfortably spanning my shoulder and part of my biceps. Probably not an enemy, given the affection behind the caress. My older self's husband, maybe? Or someone else?

I'd give anything to know the older Alice's thoughts, to feel her emotions. But she seems to be shielding from me, erecting a barrier between her past and present selves.

The stranger's breath rustles against our ear. There's something familiar about it, but I can't figure out what. Or maybe I'm not acquainted with the breathing at all. Maybe it's older Alice who recognizes the sound, and I'm just confused about where she ends and I begin.

The hand lifts off our shoulder and footsteps retreat. A wave of disappointment floods me, one I don't fully understand. Older Alice waits ten whole beats before lifting our head, allowing me a view of the cavern once again.

Steadier now, I soak up the details with a vengeance.

Who knows when she'll deprive me of my vision again? Only a few sets of footprints mar the dirt, suggesting that traffic in this area is light. Glow-in-the-dark strips line the top and bottom of the cave walls, and three tunnels branch off from the clearing.

"Let's go," my older self says brusquely, as if *I'm* the one dawdling.

We set off down the left-most tunnel. A hundred feet later, we come upon a glassed-in room. Older me steps right up to the glass, so close our nose brushes against the cold, hard surface. She's not trying to obscure my vision this time. In fact, she wants me to see. All of it.

I look—and wish I hadn't.

CHAPTER 10

Cots are crammed together inside the room, in lines so twisty they can hardly be considered rows. Each narrow mattress holds a writhing mass of protrusions and limbs. Bodies, naked—but unlike any I've ever seen. Red splotches cover the skin like a rash. The center of each splotch is an open, gaping wound surrounded by pustules, some exploded and some intact.

That's why they're not wearing clothes, I think faintly. The wounds must hurt too much to come into contact with any material.

Horror and sadness rise inside me. The patients behind the wall are in tremendous pain. That much is obvious. Although no sound leaks through the glass, their mouths are open in varying degrees, caught between a moan and a scream. I could count the number of teeth in each mouth—but I don't. I'm too busy mourning their loss. These people may still be alive…but not for long.

"What's wrong with them?" I ask, even though I don't want to hear. Even though, on some level, I already know.

"Sunburn," the older Alice says. "In the most literal sense. Their skin became allergic to the rays of the sun, and they weren't able to take cover soon enough."

"How many?" I brace myself for the answer. A part of me would like to dive behind the veil of my ignorance, so that I can stay safe and insulated in the past. But it's too late for that.

"The virus has spread all over the world. The US was hit the hardest because that's where it originated," she says, her voice hollow. "Two-thirds of our population has perished, even as we speak."

Two-thirds of our population. That means eight hundred kids at Silver Oak High, dead. Two out of every three mothers and brothers and best friends, never to take a breath or give a hug or push their glasses up their nose ever again. More than two hundred million people in the US alone. Just gone.

"The rest of us are stuffed into caves like this one, some natural but most hastily man-made," she continues. "Bulldozers are working around the clock, digging new tunnels. If the human race still exists in a year, we'll have entire cities underground." Our throat moves as she swallows. "Every sick bay in every network of caves is filled to capacity."

She doesn't speak for a moment, and neither do I. Instead, we breathe together. Our eyes sting. Our heart shudders. Our nose twitches with the sanitized smell of the glass.

Something wet drops onto the back of our palm. We're crying. Or rather, *she's* crying. These are her visceral reactions. Not mine.

"This is your mission, Alice." Our throat is thick with emotions that belong to her but somehow feel like both of ours. "This is what you have to prevent. I don't want to hurt Lalana, either. But what's a single person when you could stop all this suffering?"

"I..." The sentence dies in my consciousness. Given

the scene before us, I want to promise her my unwavering obedience. I would do anything to stop the future from arriving here, at this moment.

And yet... And yet... Can I trust her to make the right decision? She still hasn't explained how framing Lalana could stop this atrocity. She hasn't even told me *who* I'm supposed to stop. Can I put my faith in her logic and reasoning and methods just because she happens to be the future version of myself?

Something bangs on the wall, and our head snaps up. A little girl is pounding her fist against the surface. Her mouth moves, but no sound penetrates the glass.

Her skin is no more burned than the others, her wounds no more festering, and yet our heart melts at the sight of her. Her dark hair is shot through with gold, springing into ringlets by her ears, the way mine used to as a kid. The eyes staring deeply into mine are fully lashed, bark brown, and glinting with a too-familiar expression.

Our breath hitches, and our kneecaps evaporate, flinging us forward into the glass. "You're not supposed to be here," the older Alice says, her voice pitching wildly. "You're supposed to be in the middle bay. I arranged it myself."

The little girl can't hear, of course. Her mouth keeps moving, shaping the same syllable over and over again.

"Get out." Older Alice claws at our head. The skin at our temple smarts as one of our fingernails scratches a deep groove. "Go back to your own time."

My consciousness rattles around, and I fall, even though I have no physical body, half in and half out of this time. She's unzipping me, detaching her consciousness from mine. Boomeranging me back to the present.

Not yet! I'm not ready! I have so many questions. Not enough answers.

Frantically, I latch onto her physical body, her five senses, trying to ground myself in this time. The acidic taste of fear in our mouth. The granular pebbles pressing through the soles of our shoes. The distant *whir* of a hoverboard traveling through the tunnels. And the mouth of the pretty little girl, opening, closing, shouting, screaming.

ZIIIIP.

With a final, desperate yank, she separates her consciousness from mine, and the scene around me vanishes.

As I'm hurled through a blank, empty void, I finally figure out the word the girl was saying. So obvious and yet so unexpected. So natural and yet so earth-shattering.

Mom.

CHAPTER 11

'm in the locker corridor. In my body, which I can feel *and* move. *I* stumble backward until my heels bump into the plaster wall. *I* slide down until my butt hits the linoleum tile. *I* shove the hair out of my face, as though that will help me understand. What just happened?

8:01.

The digital clock at the end of the hallway blinks at me. Eleven minutes past final bell. Four more minutes until the security cameras turn back on. However long I spent in the future, very little time has elapsed in the present.

Did I really travel forward ten years? Did I witness all those dying, sunburned victims? Did I actually see my future daughter?

I gasp at the air, my breathing hard and labored as though I've traveled a great distance. Which, in a way, I have.

Flaming monkeys. In the future, I have a *daughter*. And she's *dying*.

A shudder overtakes me, from the top of my head to the base of my spine. I sit on my fingers, pressing them into the dust-covered tile to keep them from trembling. What do I do with these feelings? This fierceness. This resolve. The determination to stand by my child at all costs. These sensations feel too big for my body, as though they're fighting to break free of my physical skin.

Squaring my shoulders, I beeline for my locker and spin the combination. 8:03. Two minutes until the security cameras reset. Remember the writhing bodies and the open wounds.

Do not, whatever you do, DO NOT think about Lalana.

Do not imagine her dancing the Thor head across the table.

Do not picture her orange-peel smile when she stuck a slice of fruit inside her mouth to make me laugh.

Do not conjure up the time I accidentally gave myself too-short bangs, and she whacked off her hair, too, so that I wouldn't be the only one with a microscopic fringe.

I brush my fingers along the baggie, and the scent of cannabis swirls in my nose. I love Lalana. I could live to be a hundred, until my teeth start falling out one by one, and I'll never find another friend like her. But a truth settles inside my soul, one that is as unshakable as the sun rising majestically over Mount Bromo in Indonesia.

I can't abandon my daughter. Not the way my mother left me. I have to do everything I can to save her. Even take this leap of faith.

Gritting my teeth, I open Lalana's locker and throw the baggie on her shelf. I slam the door so hard that my bones tremble.

8:04. There. It's done. I followed the Voice's orders, with a minute to spare.

And maybe, just maybe, she doesn't intend for Lalana to get caught. Maybe she just wants my best friend to *smoke* the weed.

Oh, please. Don't get in trouble, Lalana. Don't let my actions mess up your life.

I walk away from her locker, swaying and lurching all over the place. Little wonder. My head's spinning...with what? Revulsion. Self-loathing. Sorrow. All of the above.

Clank. Tap. Rattle.

I jerk up my head. Mr. Dan, our school janitor, enters the hallway, a doughnut-size circle of keys in his hands, his silver hair puffed out around his head. I like the guy, always have. When he sees me standing in the middle of the hall, his eyes go as wide as his key ring.

"Alice! Why aren't you in class?"

"Oh." My hands are empty. No books, no hall pass, nothing. "Just, uh, admiring the pea-green view?"

"Didn't you hear the announcements?" he continues, as though I haven't spoken. "We're on lockdown, and I'm doing a final sweep before we let in the drug dogs. They'll be searching the premises for contraband today."

My heart leaps into my throat. Spring break starts tomorrow. It's just like the administration to surprise us with a drug raid the day before freedom.

Oh, Lalana. No. Nooooooo.

"Off to class you go," Mr. Dan says, gently but firmly. "You've always been such a good student. Wouldn't want you to get detention for wandering the halls."

I flush. If he only knew. I try to smile, but the nausea anchors down both sides of my lips. "I don't feel so well."

Mr. Dan turns the same shade as the linoleum. "On second thought, let's go to the nurse's office."

He marches me down the corridor, past my locker. Past Lalana's.

My stomach rolls. There's nothing I can do now to grab the baggie, to stop the course of events. What's done is done.

I made a decision. I took an action. And the future will be forever changed because of it.

CHAPTER 12

An hour later, the lockdown is finally lifted, and I leave the nurse's office. Just as I open the door, however, three people cross in front of me: a uniformed police officer with a yellow Labrador on a leash; Ms. Bui, with a perfectly coiffed silver-streaked bun; and Lalana, tears streaking down her face, her eyes darting around as though she's looking for assistance.

As though she's looking for me.

I'm the one who always helps her. *I'm* the person who has her back, forever and always. At least...I used to.

Every cell in my body screams at me to go to her. To take her hand. To make this right.

But I can't. The lives of millions are at stake.

I back away before she can see me and get outside just in time, scrambling behind a tree and emptying the contents of my stomach into a scratchy bush. The toasted onion and sesame seed bagel is considerably less appetizing on the way up. Oh, man. The excuse I gave Nurse Hoyle is coming true. Funny, so not funny.

What's happening to Lalana now? Ms. Bui will call her

mom, who will call her dad in California. There will be no excuses. No second chances. Lalana will be packed up and shipped to California by the end of spring break.

I did this. Me. With a simple action, I single-handedly ruined my best friend's high school career. She'll have to spend the rest of junior year *and* all of senior year at a new school with people she doesn't know. Without the friends she's relied on her entire life.

Because of me.

I gag over the bushes again, but nothing comes out. My hair falls into my face, and impatiently, I shove it back. Magically, the strands stay, as if caught by a barrette—or someone's hand.

Oh. A person must be standing behind me, holding the hair off my face. But I'm too numb to be surprised. Too utterly wretched to care.

I hate myself. So much. If I could seep into this hard-packed ground, along with the vomit, I would. Then, I wouldn't have to live with my betrayal.

The person who has a hold of my hair clumsily pulls it into a loose ponytail, securing it with some kind of band. I hear the zipper of a bag being pulled, and a few moments later, a hand shoves a crumpled napkin under my nose.

I take it, wiping my mouth, and turn to thank my helper.

Concern is etched on Bandit's face, and his broad shoulders nearly block the crisp blue sky.

Perfect. The most obnoxious boy alive just watched me throw up. He held the hair off my face. Stab me now.

I reach for my hair and discover that he's tied it back with one of his wide terry-cloth sweatbands.

His ponytail-tying abilities could use some work, but the gesture is kinda...sweet.

"Um, gross," I say to cover up my confusion. "Is this

sweatband still damp?"

He lifts his eyebrows. "My sweat can't possibly be any grosser than your vomit."

Okay, so he has a point. I'm pretty nauseating—literally. Spying a water hose at the side of the building, I squeeze past him. He turns sideways, but my shoulder still brushes against his chest. He really shouldn't be so warm. That slight contact really shouldn't make me shiver.

He's not my friend. Not my ally. Instead, his labels are much less appealing. The potential secret admirer of my best friend. Someone I'm afraid is wrapped up in the devastating events of the future. I can't forget those things. Not even for a moment.

I walk over to the faucet and aim the hose into my mouth. After I rinse as well as I can, Bandit hands me a bottle of sanitizer, which I pour into my hands.

"You're prepared." I give the sanitizer back. "I'm impressed."

He grins, and I know I've said the wrong thing. Never, *ever* give the cockiest boy in school this kind of ammunition.

"Oh yeah?" he murmurs, his voice low and seductive. "You should see my first aid kit. It's very…thorough."

My cheeks warm, which might be even more ridiculous than our conversation. Only Bandit could sound arrogant about a box of bandages. "You're kidding," I manage to say. "You don't actually carry around a first aid kit."

He holds my gaze, steady and unflinching. "Actually, I do."

"Why?"

"Well, the sanitizer is because I know entirely too much about the germs that get passed between people." As if to demonstrate, he douses his hands, rubbing the formula over each and every finger, so thoroughly that I wonder if I should feel insulted. "And what would-be doctor doesn't carry around a first aid kit?"

Plenty, I want to say. A quarter of our class must be premed, and I don't see anyone else with emergency supplies.

But I don't. He'll make a good doctor, with or without the advantages that his parents can buy him. He has the brilliance to pioneer medical breakthroughs, a superior but utterly engaging bedside manner. He'll have legions of patients in love with him.

I can just picture it—maybe *too* clearly.

"What are you doing here?" I blurt before I can dwell on the image.

His lips sober. "I heard the news about Lalana. I was looking for her, to see if she was okay, when I saw you running past, your face as green as the frog I dissected in bio last year."

I grimace. Yep, that's me. An American tree frog, small and green and easily frightened. More to the point, why does he care so much about Lalana? Because they're family friends? Or because…he's the one sending her creepy love letters?

"You followed me because you thought I would lead you to Lalana?"

He blinks. "No, Alice," he says slowly. "I followed you because you looked like you were going to throw up. And guess what? You did."

He takes a flat white box out of his backpack. Aw, hell, he wasn't kidding. He really does have a first aid kit. I watch, mesmerized, as he rips the corner of an alcohol wipe. And then he reaches for my collar and proceeds to rub at a stain.

I go perfectly still as my brain scrambles. Do I smell like vomit? I must. Does he notice?

Awareness snaps into the air. I register every motion, every nuance. The crease between his eyebrows. The way his fingertips scrape against my collarbone. The mere inches that separate us. He's standing so close that if I lifted my mouth, we could be kissing.

As soon as the thought pops into my head, I have to force myself *not* to look up.

I clear my throat—almost desperately. "You, uh, you don't have to do that."

"I can't have you walking around with these pathogens on you." He continues to scrub at the spot. "You're like a first-class incubator for germs."

Right. Pathogens. Germs.

This is not a seduction of any sort. Wooing me is the furthest thing from this guy's mind.

"Maybe I'll just burn the shirt," I say weakly. "Scorch these germs out of existence."

He looks right into my eyes. "I don't want you to get any sicker."

Seconds pass, and the air between us thickens. If you ignited a flame, I swear it would spread like the fires devouring the Amazon. I don't get this guy. Not in the slightest.

And I *really* don't understand why my older self set him in my path. If it weren't for her interference, he and I would've traveled down our separate roads, happily unaware of each other's existence.

Why? Why throw me together with the most exasperating guy in school?

Think, Alice. Be smart. My older self made me confess to being in love with Bandit.

She said my mission is to stop the person who will one day decimate the world.

She believes that framing Lalana will help us with that goal.

Bandit *might* be in love with Lalana.

Therefore…what? What is the answer? I don't know.

Problem is, I have too few puzzle pieces—and none of them are adjoining.

One thing is clear, though. Until I have more answers, I need to stay away from him.

"Thanks for the sanitizer." I step back, stumbling over my own feet. "I've gotta go. Errand, you know. Or a test. Something. See ya!"

With this incoherent bit of dialogue, I run away from Bandit. For the second time in two days.

Oh well. I can't dwell on what he must think of me. I need to find out what happened to Lalana.

CHAPTER 13

My triumph at cutting short my interaction with Bandit lasts, oh, about three minutes—the time it takes me to leave him and get back to class. Everybody everywhere is gossiping about Lalana. She wasn't the only student pulled out by the principal. The dogs also found contraband in the locker of Lee's smoking buddy, Scotty Spellman. If there were ever a candidate for a world-ending villain, Scotty would be it. The curl of his lip, the way his eyes rake over my body, never fail to give me the heebie-jeebies.

In contrast, Lalana is…was…a model citizen. I should know. She's only had one sip of alcohol ever, and that was a spiked punch at her parents' *Loi Krahtong* party. One day, Lalana promised, we'll celebrate this holiday in Thailand together. We'll launch banana-leaf boats into the water on the full moon of the twelfth lunar month. She'll pose, I'll take photos—and we'll publish the images in *National Geographic*.

Now it's looking less and less likely that particular dream will ever come true.

"Did you know Lalana was smoking up?" Gabi asks as soon as I slide into my seat for history class, her eyes taking up half her face.

"It's always the quiet ones." Isabelle flips her frizzy hair over her shoulder.

Micah looks up from his notebook. "I heard she's been covertly dealing for years."

"Stop it." All of a sudden, Zeke is next to me, his comforting hand on my shoulder. "She clearly doesn't want to talk about it, so why don't you leave her alone?"

Isabelle nudges Julie, who shoots a look at Trevor, who elbows Ethan. They all stare at Zeke's hand on my shoulder. I can hear the whispers now: "Zeke likes Alice! Are they dating? I thought she loved Bandit! Drama!" Instead of commenting, however, they all back away and face the interactive whiteboard.

My hands shake as I pull out my notes. They have no idea. They think I'm upset because Lalana's my best friend. They don't know I'm responsible for her downfall.

For the rest of the day, I call and text my best friend, desperate to find out what her parents said.

Right before seventh period, I hear the ping of an incoming text. I promptly drop my armload of books and grapple for the phone. But the message isn't from Lalana.

124.274.3567: Alice, this is Mrs. Bunyasarn. Lalana is grounded. Please stop reaching out to her. She will contact you when—and if—she is able.

My stomach sloshes uneasily, although the bushes could tell you there's nothing left inside. *If* she is able? What does that mean? She wouldn't go to California without saying goodbye, right?

My heart sinks to the vicinity of my toes. For the first time since I betrayed her, an unimaginable thought occurs to me.

What if I never see my best friend again?

A few hours—and ten thousand years—later, the dismissal bell rings, and I trudge outside. The air is cool, as though winter is digging in its nails for one last hurrah, but the bright sun takes the edge off.

Instead of feeling comforted by the rays, I shiver. How many times have I lifted my face to the sky and let the light caress my skin? In a decade, the sun will no longer be the source of sustenance and life but the origin of sickness and death. The virus will turn our most basic natural resource into a weapon.

And then what? How can the resulting scenario—most of the population dead, the rest stuffed into underground tunnels—be any way to live?

I wrap my arms around myself as my fellow students scurry about, oblivious to the future. As I'd like to be.

They don't harass me about Lalana. Maybe word's gotten out that I have nothing to say. More likely, my scowl is unusually effective at warning them off.

Ow.

Electricity. Brain. The Voice.

For once, I don't even mind the quick zap of lightning. I'm dying for a conversation with my older self.

"Climb the tree," she says without preamble.

I look at the intersecting branches and leaves of the elm tree above me. The first limb is a foot above my head. Perfect for climbing. "Okay."

"You're awfully accommodating all of a sudden," she says.

"That's what happens when you travel ten years into the future and meet your dying daughter." I swallow hard. "I…

don't want to fight anymore. I just want to save her. That's it. So tell me what to do, and I'll do it."

"You weren't supposed to meet her." Genuine distress fractures her voice. "My goal is to save myself from pain, not cause it. But if it gets you up that tree so we can have a private conversation, then I'm not complaining."

Sighing, I plan the spots to put my hands and feet. And then, I leap up and grab hold of the branch. The wood bites into my palms, and my feet scrabble against the bark. It's been ages since I climbed a tree, but as muscle memory takes over, I slowly but surely pull myself up, my feet walking along the trunk. I've only done this a hundred times. Maybe even a thousand. I was taught by the best, after all.

"Alice is climbing trees again," Archie had tattled to Mom when I was eight and he was nine. "She's going to fall and break her neck, and then you'll be left with one child instead of two."

Instead of lecturing me, Mom just smiled. "Let's make sure you do it properly, then."

Every afternoon for the next week, she spent hours with me, observing my technique and offering suggestions. I memorized her every critique, my heart swelling with each word of praise.

She wasn't like other mothers in the neighborhood. She didn't cook or do laundry. Reading bedtime stories wasn't her thing. Forget baking cookies. Once in a while, however, something we did would catch her attention. Tree climbing was one of them.

By the time I hoist myself up several branches and the budding coverage of leaves shields me from the passersby below, my eyes are dry but my soul is drenched. With the memory of my mother. With the tears I didn't shed every night as I went to sleep.

This, too, is intentional, I realize with sudden and complete clarity. My older self doesn't just want privacy. She wants me to remember Mom. To be thinking of her during this conversation. Why?

Older Alice might say she cares about me. I even believe her. And yet her motivations are a mystery. Her agenda her own. I have to remember that.

"Why did you make me screw up my best friend's life?" I plant my feet on a thick branch. An occasional person walks by underneath, but no one looks up. From this vantage point, the tops of their heads look remarkably similar.

"Doesn't matter because it didn't work." Her words bump into each other. "We've tried *everything*. And nothing's worked."

I brush away a scratchy leaf poking at my jaw. "What didn't work?"

"Getting Lalana out of the Maker's life!" she screeches. "We thought if they never got involved, we could alleviate the betrayal. This would be one less way for the Maker to lose touch with reality. But we were wrong. They don't even have a relationship, not yet. But the Maker's already betrayed. Already angry."

I shake my head. Is she talking about Bandit? She must be. And yet...Bandit and Lalana *do* have a relationship. They've been friends forever. Does the Voice mean a romantic relationship? Or is she referring to someone else altogether?

"Are you talking about her secret admirer?" I ask.

"Yes." She pauses. "I thought that was clear. Lalana's secret admirer grows up to become the Virus Maker."

Finally. A concrete piece of the puzzle. I open my mouth to ask her to explain, but she rushes on. "I already told you—I'm not going to reveal this person's identity, so don't ask."

Damn. It's like she can read my mind. Predict my every move. And maybe, disturbingly, she can.

"There's a good reason I can't tell you. Please trust me on that," she continues. "For now, all you need to know is that framing Lalana didn't accomplish what we intended. It didn't stop the future. All those people still died."

The half-formed demands leak from my mind. "So I betrayed my best friend for no reason," I say dully. If only a branch would detach from the tree and impale me now.

"It wasn't for no reason." Her voice feels quieter. Before, I would've thought she was speaking more softly. Now, I know she's simply thinking her words with less force. "Framing Lalana may not have taken us all the way to salvation, but it's a step in the right direction. It can contribute to the future in ways you can't understand. So don't you dare try to undo your action!"

I blink. That's *exactly* what I was thinking. Man, she's good.

"We can't have you fessing up that the weed was yours. Dad will ground you as quickly as Lalana's parents, and we need you free and unencumbered for the rest of spring break. Got it?"

I lick my lips. I don't like it, but for the sake of those suffering people, for the sake of my daughter, I can wait. "Okay. But if I don't see a tangible effect of pinning the weed on Lalana by then, I'm going to the authorities."

"She's just one person," the Voice says, exasperated. "With the kind of stakes we're facing, the life of one person is an acceptable sacrifice."

I close my eyes. She might be right, but damn. Why is it so hard to accept?

"How was the tree climb?" the Voice asks suddenly. "Did the technique come back to you?"

I tense, and the wood scrapes against my skin. She doesn't fool me. My older self doesn't ask idle questions; she has no time for small talk.

"Fine," I say shortly.

And still, she pauses. Still, she hesitates. A drop of sweat rolls down my neck, and an ant crawls off the bark and onto my knuckles.

"I didn't want it to come to this, Alice." The sentence dips in and out of focus. "But we have no other options." She sighs. "Maybe you'd better sit down."

I obey, settling my butt in the V of the branches and anchoring my back against the trunk. My heart ratchets up with each passing second that she doesn't speak; my breath wheezes in and out like a punctured tire.

My future self remains annoyingly silent.

"What is it?" I ask impatiently, and when she doesn't respond immediately, I can't stop myself from repeating them. *"What is it?"*

"It's simple, really," she finally says. "In order to save the world, you must kill a person. Now, in the present, before the Maker has a chance to invent the virus."

I shake my head. And then shake it again. There must be gnats in my ears, 'cause there's no way I heard correctly.

"I'm sorry, what?" I attempt a fake laugh. "It sounded like you said I had to kill someone."

"I did," she says quietly.

"No." The gnats push into my brain and buzz around my bloodstream, scattering my thoughts, mocking my protest. "There has to be another way."

"I promise you, there isn't." She sounds weary, as though she's not just ten years older but a hundred. "We've spent the last six months exploring every other avenue, but nothing has worked." She enunciates her words carefully and oh so deliberately. "I know this is hard for you to hear. The last thing either of us wants is to kill someone. But we have to make this impossible choice. It's either us. Or them."

CHAPTER 14

I sag against the trunk, every knot digging into my spine. Did I think the temperature was cool? Ha. The air I'm swimming in is as thick and hot as soup. I can't breathe. My eyes dart from branch to twig, from a tattered bird nest to the disappearing tail of a squirrel. If my feet weren't braced against two branches, I'd slide right off and crash to the ground.

"Alice. Say something," the Voice pleads.

"I'm not a killer." I squeeze my eyes tight. If I can't see the world around me, maybe I won't have to know what I know. Feel what I feel. "I'm not. And you're not, either. I don't care how much you grew up. How wise you've become. You can't have changed this much. I know me. And we don't have that inside us. We just don't."

The wind whispers against my ears, saying words too low for me to comprehend. Humming a verse too lonely for me to ignore.

"Tell me I'm wrong," I continue. "Go ahead. If I become a monster, I want to know it. Right here. Right now. I want to know if everything I've ever believed is false."

"You're asking an impossible question. One I don't know how to answer." There's a weariness in her voice that makes me certain that something…happens in the future. Something so painful that it will shred my soul. Something so excruciating that it will turn me into *this*. Into her.

"When you grow up, you'll see that the line between good and evil isn't so clear." Sorrow strangles each syllable. Despair drips from every word. "We all have goodness inside us, but we're also capable of doing monstrous things. Especially when we're pushed against a wall. Especially when all that's left of our hearts is a deep, gaping hole." She lowers her voice. "The lacerations in your heart have already begun, Alice. At seventeen, you've already experienced loss. And that's what will give you the strength to act. To do what you previously thought undoable."

My eyes drift open. Of course. This is why she had me climb the tree. This is what she wanted me to remember. My mother. She's talking about our mother.

When Mom left, she sliced out a piece of me the size of the Grand Canyon. Most days, I tiptoe around the emptiness, pretending it doesn't exist. But when I least suspect it, I edge a little too close. My footing slips a single inch. And the void sucks me in and swallows me up with the force of a black hole.

"Think of the teenagers around the world, some just like you. Others, not so much. If you don't change the future, untold numbers of them will lose a parent, a brother, an aunt, a friend. Maybe all at once. They will suffer what you suffered. Hurt like you hurt. And you can prevent it all with a single action. Will you do it?"

She knows me so well. Better than Lalana, better even than my brother. She knows exactly what to do in order to sway me. Show me firsthand the torture that the people will have to endure. Then, relate it to my own pain.

This is manipulation at its finest. If my emotions weren't wrung to the last inch, I might even be impressed.

"Why does it have to be me?" I protest weakly. "There are twelve hundred kids at our high school. Millions more in the US. Why do I have to be the one to stop the Maker?"

Seconds pass, one melting into the next seamlessly, if not quietly. In fact, this is the loudest silence I've ever heard.

"You aren't the only one being visited by the future," she says finally. "There are several missions taking place simultaneously. All of you have been chosen because you have special access to key moments of the target's past."

I think immediately of Lalana. Of her evasiveness, of the secret she won't share with me. Is she, too, on one of these missions?

Suddenly, I miss my best friend like I'd miss my left arm. Every adventure, every scheme I've had since sixth grade has been with her. From devising a plan to get back at the resident mean girl to drafting a blueprint for our very own tree house. Even if she's *not* on a mission, I'd still like to talk to her. Brainstorm and analyze with her. Laugh because of her.

But that's no longer an option.

"Fine," I say abruptly. "But I guess now you'll have to tell me. Who do you want me to kill? Who will one day invent the virus?"

"I stand by my decision," she says. "You're going to have to uncover the identity for yourself. Not because I'm being coy. Goodness, no. The future is much too important to risk on games. But because I know you, Alice. And I know, unless you convince yourself beyond a reasonable doubt, you'll never be able to follow through with this mission. You'll never be able to kill this person."

I take a deep breath. "Are you talking about—?"

"Don't guess," my older self interrupts. "Not yet. You still have a lot you need to learn."

My stomach sinks. *Please don't let it be Bandit*, I whisper to the universe.

"How will I figure it out?" I grip the branches on either side of me. "How can I be sure I have the right person?"

"You'll know," she says. "You'll feel the unshakable truth directly in your soul. Soon enough."

"When? We don't have school for a week. What if I don't even come across this person?"

"Oh, you'll come across them, all right." Her voice is already fading away. Already leaving me here, in the present, to my own devices. "And you'll get the clarification you need at the Newhouse awards ceremony."

The spaces inside my mind are quiet. Empty. And she's gone once again.

I shiver, lowering myself from the branches, scraping my exposed ankle against the bark.

Because if she's right?

In approximately forty-eight hours, I'll come face-to-face with the person I'm supposed to kill.

CHAPTER 15

T wo nights later, on the evening of the awards banquet, I'm no closer to figuring out who the Maker is. I'm supposed to get clarity tonight, and at this point, I need it. No one from school has shown up at my door looking suspicious. No students were skulking through the store when I ran out to pick up dinner for Archie and me. There have been zero flashing neon signs in my soul, blaring, *This person is a future mass murderer!*

I watch as my father pulls the wide end of a tie under and over the narrow end, up into the loop, and down through the front hole. I have no idea how to knot a tie, and neither does Archie. He'd just as soon wear a clip-on, but that is *not* happening tonight. *Not* at the ceremony hosted by Newhouse Information Systems, honoring him as one of the brightest young scientists in the country.

So asking Dad for help it is. Even if he can barely tolerate my company.

As I wait, I glance at my cell phone and reread Bandit's latest texts. It's like the black letters encased in gray bubbles have cast a spell over me.

Most Confusing Boy Alive: Swishy blue dress. Bubblegum pink lip gloss. Hair curling @ shoulders

Me: Interesting. Did your hair grow twelve inches since I last saw you?

Most Confusing Boy Alive: Not me. Just guessing what ur wearing

Me: Oh, really? Someone once told me that's what lovesick people do. Are you lovesick, Bandit?

Most Confusing Boy Alive: Nah. Ur vomit missed me by a few ft so I didn't catch ur virus. Thx for asking tho

Me: I'm not lovesick!!!

Most Confusing Boy Alive: 3x in 2 texts? I'm flattered, honey oats. but u've got to stop using luv in connection w me. People r already talking bout us

I've only read these words nine, maybe ten times. And I still don't know whether to laugh or scream.

"Here," my dad says, pulling me back to the present. He takes the loop off and hands it to me.

"Thanks, Dad." I accept the tie and tuck the phone in my pocket, where I'm resolved it will stay.

I survey my father. He's clean-shaven, and his newly cropped silver hair contrasts nicely with his navy suit, giving him an air of elegance. Dad's a handsome man, no doubt. I just wish we had more to say to each other.

It wasn't always like this. Our relationship during my childhood was warm, loving. He would forge me letters from Harry Potter and leave them under a snowy-white owl.

For more than a year, I faithfully wrote Harry once a week. Without fail, "Harry" responded, in a messy block-letter script. I was devastated when I found out I had been corresponding with Dad all along—but I treasure those letters now.

He started distancing himself right after Mom left. At first, I thought he was just depressed. Like me. Like my brother. But six years later, he still talks to me only when necessary.

In contrast, he's fully and completely focused on my brother. Archie's grades and Archie's future. Archie's moods and Archie's desires. It's like he's forgotten that he also has a daughter.

"Tell your brother to get a move on. And ask him if Zeke still needs a ride." Dad hooks a finger in his own necktie and adjusts the already perfect knot.

That should end our conversation. I'm lucky he even gave me two sentences. But I can't make myself move away.

Maybe it's because I'm still rattled by my conversation with the Voice. Or the fact that someday, soon, I'll have to take an irrevocable action. Or maybe, just maybe, six years is too long for *anyone* to receive the cold shoulder.

"Why don't you talk to me anymore?" I blurt.

Dad's fingers freeze on the tie. "We're talking now."

"Not really. You can't look at me. Every word comes out like it hurts." I lick my lips. "Did I do something to make you mad? To make you...not love me anymore?" I mumble the last words, half hoping he doesn't hear them.

"What? *No*, honey. No." He massages his temples. "This has nothing to do with you. Of course I love you. I always have."

Funny way he has of showing it.

"Your mother—" He stops, shaking his head. "I've been doing this all wrong, haven't I? Okay, Alice. What should we talk about?"

Anticipation flutters in my chest. It's probably unwise to wish after so many years. Definitely naive to yearn for the way things were. But I can't help but hope that he might actually be back, if only for a moment. The dad who loved me.

"Anything, really," I say. "Are you excited about tonight?"

"Yes, for sure," he says. "I'm hoping to run into someone at the banquet."

Me too.

"Really?" My heart pounds so hard, the beats blend together. No. I won't ruin our first real conversation in six years by thinking about the Voice. This is too important. We're talking. Maybe not like we used to. Maybe we'll never get back to the place where I crawled into his lap and cried for forty-five minutes over Harry. But at least he doesn't look like a male Sydney funnel-web spider is dangling over his head. "Who's that?"

"My old lab partner from college." He rubs his chin. "I heard from a colleague that he'll be attending the ceremony. We…had a falling-out senior year and haven't spoken since. I'd like to make amends, if possible."

"What did you fight about?" I prompt so that he doesn't retreat.

"Back in those days, we thought we could change the world." He meets my eyes in the mirror, which is the closest we've come to direct eye contact in weeks. "Charlie had some wild ideas, but it was exciting stuff. Stuff no one had ever dreamed of, much less seen."

Suddenly, he drops his face, as though our connection is too intense. Too honest. "When you're on the knife's edge of discovery, sometimes it's hard to know what's right or wrong. Hard to see how much is too far—or not far enough. Mistakes were made. Leaving me with regrets that span a lifetime."

I tremble from my shoulders to my toes. Because I've

heard that same tragedy-soaked tone before. I've listened to similar despair-drenched words. At this moment, Dad sounds eerily, coincidentally, like the Voice.

But I'm just being paranoid. Right? The future has invaded my present so thoroughly that I'm seeing parallels everywhere I turn. Clearly, Dad and his former lab partner are too old to be the person I'm looking for. Even if they'll both be at the awards ceremony tonight.

And yet, that doesn't mean they're not involved.

This feels like my first break in my mission. Is this why the future chose me? Is my "special access" to the target through my father?

Taking a shuddering breath, I turn up the corners of my mouth. "That must be a heavy burden to bear."

"No heavier than the responsibility to the future."

The smile freezes on my lips. There it is again. So many parallels. So many coincidences. They keep adding up.

"One more thing, Alice." My dad's eyes are bright, alert. As intense as I've ever seen them. "Please don't blame yourself. For my actions or anybody else's. You are as good, as innocent, as they come. It's the rest of the world that's messed up."

I don't know what he means. I'm not sure to what he's referring. But I can tell that this moment, this sentiment, is important to him. "Okay, Dad." I turn to leave, think better of it, and then fling myself into his arms.

Startled, he pats me awkwardly. When was the last time we hugged? Not in the last year, that's for sure. But maybe I've been too complacent in letting him take the lead. Maybe it's my responsibility, as well as his, to repair this rift in our relationship.

I leave the room a few minutes later, my heart as buoyant as my feet, anticipation—and a little dread—buzzing through my veins.

Not two steps later, a current zips across my brain.

Oh no. Not now. Not when I just had a real moment of connection with Dad. Not when I feel like I might have had my first breakthrough. The last thing I need is the Voice with another demand.

"What do you want?" I ask before she can say anything.

"I remember that dress," the Voice says, her tone soft and nostalgic.

I stop in front of the mirror in the foyer. Bandit wasn't too far off. I'm wearing a pale-blue dress printed with seahorses, one that cinches in at the waist and then flares out. My curly hair is swept up in a high ponytail, and my lipstick is a soft coral. Coral, mind you. *Not* bubblegum pink.

Still, his prediction makes me shift uncomfortably. Lucky guess? Or can he, I don't know, *see* me somehow?

I shake my head, pushing away that creepy thought. When I meet my eyes in the glass, however, they widen, as though I'm surprised by my appearance. Or more accurately, as though *she's* astonished to glimpse my younger face.

My mouth dries. Her emotions don't typically leak into my body, but the barrier between us feels flimsier than usual.

"You're beautiful," she whispers, awed. "Funny, I never noticed back then. There was always something wrong with my looks—I was too heavy, or my hair was too frizzy. I hated my nose, the gap between my front teeth." She pauses, and the silence balloons with her wonder. "All those years I wasted feeling less than. Never good enough. And all this time, I was perfect. Just perfect."

"Oh, please." I've never been comfortable with compliments, and they're not any easier to receive just because they're from an older me. "You clearly have middle-age goggles."

I feel more than hear her snort out a laugh. "I am *not* middle-aged."

"Fine, but your opinion is still compromised. I'm hardly perfect."

"You are," she says firmly. "Even though you just called me old." Now she's laughing at me...at herself...at us both. "I wish you could see what I see."

Part of me wishes that, too. But then I'd have to live through her tragedies. I'd have to suffer the experiences that made her so hard, so desperate. And I'm not sure I'll ever be ready for that.

I swallow. "We need to leave soon, or we'll be late for the banquet."

"Don't worry, Alice," she says pleasantly. "Today's task is easy. Do you have the tickets?"

"Yes." I pat the envelope I left on the foyer table, so we could grab it on our way out.

"Open the envelope," she says. "Make sure everything's accounted for."

I sift through the stubs carefully. Cocktail reception: three. Banquet dinner with awards ceremony: three. Parking voucher: one.

"Got 'em," I say.

"Good. Now destroy the tickets for the cocktail reception."

My mouth falls open. "Wh-What?" The reception is being held for the Young Scientist Award contenders and their families, right before the banquet. Not all the attendees are invited, so it's an incredible honor for my brother. "But Archie—"

"Rip them up. He doesn't need to go."

"Um, okay?" I close my hand around the tickets, crushing them. "I mean, I'll do it, sure. But can you tell me why? Archie might seem indifferent, but he *does* care."

She sighs. "I doubt it." A prickly sensation forms on my scalp and moves along my face. It's not painful like the electric current but almost…soft. As though my older self has reached back ten years and caressed me. "I can't explain any more than that. It's dangerous for you to know too much. One wrong move, one detail too many, and we could create ripples that will change the future in ways we never intended. Please, Alice. Trust me on this. You'll thank me for it later. The whole world will thank you."

I exhale shakily. She's definitely said those words to me before, but maybe I needed to hear them one more time.

Quickly, before I can change my mind, I rip the reception tickets into a hundred little pieces. When the confetti falls into the trash can like discarded snow, the Voice speaks again.

"One more thing. Whatever you do, keep Dad away from a man named Charlie."

I freeze. Charlie. Dad's old lab partner. The person he's hoping to run into.

I have my work cut out for me tonight.

CHAPTER 16

After I get rid of the evidence of my ticket destruction, I descend into the basement. The air smells musty, like it's circulated the room too many times, and the temperature must be ten degrees cooler down here. Archie is sitting at the scratched-up ping-pong table that he's converted into a work desk. Every inch of the surface is covered by three oversize computer screens, several microscopes, piles of papers, and a box of slides.

Behind him, largely ignored, is Mom's old gun cabinet. I don't know if it was fascination or paranoia, but she began a collection a few months before she left. No locks on the cabinet door, of course, because she was never much for child safety. All those gates and outlet covers? Just another way for corporations to scam money from overprotective parents, she claimed.

Not that Archie or I need the deterrent. Hell, I don't even know how many weapons are inside. Even after she left, we haven't so much as opened the door. I doubt Dad's taken a peek, either.

"Hey, Arch. Does Zeke need a ride? Dad wants to know."

My brother's hands fly over a keyboard, and he's wearing—wait for it—his uniform of khakis and the T-shirt with the Marie Curie head.

Which reminds me of the Voice in *my* head. *You'll get the clarification you need at the Newhouse awards ceremony*, she said.

I blanch. I haven't seen Zeke since before spring break. If he's going to be at the awards ceremony tonight, does that mean he just entered my pool of candidates for who might become the Maker?

I shake my head forcibly. No. Zeke is one of a hundred students who'll be attending, several of whom are from our school. And the Voice said I'd feel the unshakable truth in my soul when I figured out the target. My soul doesn't feel anything when I look at Zeke—except maybe that he gets better-looking every time I see him. Zeke is too kind, too good. There's no way he's the Maker.

I wrench my attention back to the present.

Archie continues to type a billion words a minute.

"*Brother.* I'm talking to you. Can you listen, please?"

Still no response. I jab him in the shoulder. "Archie!"

He leaps out of his seat, and I jerk back before his head slams into my chin. We reenact this scenario at least five times a month.

"Don't sneak up on me like that." He rubs the head that definitely missed my chin. What, does he have a phantom ache? "And yes. Zeke needs a ride."

I stare. "If you heard my question, why didn't you answer?"

"I was in the middle of a thought?" The sentence tilts up at the end, as though even he's not sure if this is a reasonable excuse.

I sigh. The house could be in flames and he'd take his

chances with the fire extinguisher, so long as he could finish a proof. "Never mind. Lookee, I brought you a present." I hand over the knotted tie, which is covered with elements from the periodic table. I found it online during one of my stress-shopping sprees and couldn't resist.

A smile spreads across his face. "It's perfect. How do you always find just the right gift?"

My annoyance melts away. Archie spends a lot of time with his head in the theoretical clouds, but when he does come down to earth, there's no one more appreciative.

"One of my many talents," I say modestly.

"You should put it on your résumé," he says, "right next to Uncanny Ability To Burn Anything—Even Water."

"Oh, be quiet." I shove his shoulder. "Or I'll never make you burned water again."

"Speaking of your unparalleled flair for fashion..." His body is all at once in motion: knees bouncing, fingers drumming, elbows vibrating. "I asked Maggie to prom. She said yes."

I blink. "That's great."

Maggie Falk said yes. I can't believe it, but I'll wish on every star I find that she'll be able to see past my brother's eccentricities. That she'll be the one who makes him happy.

"Are we, uh, still going shopping?" he mumbles.

I smile. My brother is always brilliant and sometimes vulnerable—but hardly ever shy. "One hundred percent. Now, can you please get dressed—in something other than Marie Curie's head? Dad's waiting."

He grabs the tie and stands up. An object falls from his lap and rolls along the concrete floor, bumping against my bright-blue toenails. I pick up the cylindrical piece of wood—and the blood drains from my face. "What...?"

"It's a spindle that forms the back of a chair." Archie

pushes the glasses up his nose.

"I know *what* it is. Why do you have it?"

When my mother still lived with us, she made and sold furniture with inspirational quotes carved into the wood. Once, she was written up in a big wedding magazine, and for a year, our house was swarmed with would-be brides and grooms searching for the perfect manifestation of their love.

Personally, I wouldn't want other people's butts parked on my declaration of forever. But maybe that's just me.

"Give it back," my brother says, ignoring my question.

"In a minute." For reasons I can't explain, I curl my fingers around the rod. Maybe it's because I didn't know we had any remnants of my mom's old furniture. Or maybe I just want to hold something of hers again. Since her hand is out of the question, this piece of wood is the next best thing.

"It's mine," Archie says roughly. Without warning, he plucks the rod right out of my grasp.

I gape. "What, are we two years old?"

He runs his thumb along the etched letters. "It's mine," he says again, more softly.

When he looks up, his eyes are glossy.

"Mom left us six years ago next Saturday," he says, as though I didn't know. As though the date isn't already tattooed in my mind. "Six years that we've had to think about what we did to make her leave. Six years we've had to crave the smiley-face pancakes she made once a year…and wonder if we'll ever taste them again. Dad has his rituals to get through the day. I have mine."

I frown. Dad holes up in his office around the anniversary of Mom's abandonment, but my brother's never adopted a similar habit. Or so I thought.

I stare at the piece of wood, at the way it fits in Archie's hands, horror dawning. This rod isn't just a spindle from one of my mom's furniture pieces. This is *the* spindle. From *the* chair.

The breath wheezes in and out of my lungs. "Archie…" I reach out, but there's no way I can possibly comfort him when I'm about to collapse myself. "This spindle. It's… It's…"

I can't finish the sentence. In all these years, we've never talked about it. Not once have we ever discussed or referred to what happened on that terrible day.

"Yes," he says, lifting his chin. Clutching the piece of wood as though it causes him great pain—but he'll bear it anyway. "This spindle is part of the chair that Mom threw at us, right before she left forever."

CHAPTER 17

Archie exits the room. I hardly notice. I had no idea he kept this piece of Mom for the last six years. For what? As some kind of sick souvenir? Isn't the gun cabinet enough?

A tremble moves through my entire body. Mom was so hard that day. As unyielding as the wood with which she worked. As cold as the rivets that held together her furniture. I don't know what she wanted from us during that last conversation. I'm not sure we could've said anything that would've made her stay. But when we didn't give her the answers she was looking for, she flung the chair at us...and took off. For good.

My brother was never the same after that. Me neither. How could we be? The situation was twisted enough to mess us up for life. Luckily — or not — Dad put us both in therapy.

In my sessions, I learned my mother's actions were not my fault. I learned that I couldn't have stopped her. She was an adult, and she made her own decisions.

All this I grasped with my head. If anything, I should be angry at her betrayal. But in my heart, in the deepest, most desperate part of my soul? I still miss her. I remember the good times. And I yearn, with every cell in my body, for just five more minutes of her time. So I can understand *why* she left. So I can figure out what was so bad that she couldn't call us, even once, to wish us a happy birthday.

I wrap my arms around my torso. I don't know how long it's been since my brother left the room, but surely he's almost dressed by now. Surely it's almost time to go.

I trudge up the stairs, wondering for the millionth time what Archie discussed in his therapy sessions.

Did he find a way to live with the loss? Or is he, too, still trying to fill the hole of Mom's absence?

The lobby is teeming with people: women in sparkly dresses, men in elegant suits, and teens who tug at their hemlines and neckties as though they're wearing their first formal attire.

A beautiful chandelier, spilling diamonds like fountain water, hangs from the ceiling of the two-story hall. The carpet is plush, and even the air smells fancy, like it's been lightly scented with a floral perfume.

I make my way through the crowd. The bile rises in my throat, and I push it back down. There will be plenty of time later to think about the spindle. Such as next Saturday, six days from now. The anniversary of Mom's abandonment. For now, my focus has to be keeping Dad, Archie, and Zeke away from the cocktail reception—and Charlie—while keeping an eye out for hints about the person I have to kill.

I timed our entrance perfectly. A steady stream of people flows from the double doors opposite the grand ballroom. The cocktail reception must've just concluded, right before the awards banquet as scheduled.

The three men walk in front of me. Dad's eyes search the room for either his lab partner or a waiter with a tray of champagne flutes. Archie, who looks rather dapper in an actual suit and his chemical elements tie, appears uncomfortable in this room full of people, but Zeke has his hand on my brother's shoulder, seeming to guide him through the throng. Every ten feet, Zeke looks over his shoulder, checking to make sure I'm still behind them, and sends me a smile or nod.

I smile back. I can't help it. I don't *need* anyone to look after me. But it's nice that he cares. Nice that he pays attention. Doesn't hurt that he fills out his navy suit so well, either.

All of a sudden, a large middle-aged man lumbers into my path. I stop abruptly. His shirt is untucked, and his pants are baggy. His jacket, if he ever had one, is long gone. Dark hair sticks out all over his head. And is that…? Yes, that's a *leaf* in his hair—green, crumpled, with a tender new stem. His gaze jumps all over the spacious lobby, and he upends a flask to his mouth.

My spine tingles…with what? Recognition? Familiarity? And yet I'm utterly certain I've never seen this man before.

Without warning, the sequence of memories slams into me, the images rolling through my mind like a movie.

Wineglasses clinking. Smoke curling in the air. Archie pushes through the crowd, wearing a necktie patterned with the chemical elements. Zeke follows, his shoulders broad and powerful in his crisp navy suit. They park themselves against the leather-padded wall, the epitome of man-cave decor, and chat with each other.

A large man with wild brown hair—complete with a leaf— steps menacingly up to my father. Dad visibly swallows and gestures with a tumbler filled with amber-colored liquid. He says something I can't hear, and the man snatches the glass from

Dad's hand and hurls it against the wall. The tumbler bounces off harmlessly, but the ice and liquid drench the shoulder of a white-haired woman.

The room falls quiet, and the man shoves Dad's chest.

"Apologies would've been inadequate twenty years ago," he snarls. "But now? They're nothing but an insult."

He stalks away, and Dad sags against the wall next to Zeke, right where the tumbler hit.

The reel ends. The man moves along. And I'm shaking, shaking, shaking, despite the warmth created by a couple hundred bodies.

This. This is the future I avoided. This is the future I changed when I tore up the reception tickets.

My older self isn't here right now. How am I seeing an event that must've come from her timeline, before I destroyed the tickets? Her consciousness must have somehow blended with mine. Maybe now I have the power to access both timelines.

More importantly: Who is that bushy-haired man? Dad's old lab partner? He's got to be.

A million goose bumps pop up along my skin. Dad spoke of cutting-edge research; he talked of a lifetime of regrets. All of a sudden, I'm very sure that this man is instrumental in helping the Maker invent the virus.

It's just like the Voice said. It's looking more and more likely that I'll get some much-needed clarification at the awards ceremony.

Swallowing hard, I begin walking again, keeping the disheveled man in my sights while searching wildly for my family. There! Archie, the present-day Archie, scribbles on a napkin he must have grabbed from a passing waitperson, his brows drawn so closely together, they almost touch. Dad has a champagne flute, and he's chugging the contents, oblivious to the bushy-haired man. Thank goodness. Half a crowded lobby separates them, but I rush up to Dad anyway so that he'll focus on me and not the rest of the room.

It's Zeke, however, who watches me with an intensity that creates all sorts of lines on his smooth skin.

The creases disappear the instant our gazes connect. *Are you okay?* he mouths. Three simple words, and yet they're the best antidote for my nerves this entire night.

I nod gratefully, and we enter the ballroom. I grab Dad's arm and start chattering about the size of the room, the menu planned for tonight—anything to keep him from looking around. For a moment, I lose track of Charlie. Still talking, I dart my eyes from the round tables covered with heavy linens to the partitioned stations set up along the side of the room. Where is he?

When I finally find the mass of dark hair again, my heart stops. Because Charlie is no longer alone. Now a younger guy is removing the leaf from Charlie's hair and trying to smooth the wrinkles in his shirt.

A guy who has been flirting at the edge of my consciousness this entire day. One with brilliant blue hair.

Bandit Sakda.

CHAPTER 18

cut off mid-sentence. Luckily, Dad just tips back his champagne. He's probably grateful for the reprieve.

My head's spinning, but it shouldn't be. Bandit is the Archie Sherman of the junior class. He's as brilliant as my brother; I've heard talk that he might even be more innovative. It makes perfect sense that he's also a finalist in the Newhouse science fair.

Especially since he teased me about what I was wearing.

I groan as the pieces click together. So that's why he guessed that I was wearing a dress, even though black leggings and a tank top are my uniform during the weekend. He knew Archie — and, by extension, I — would be at the banquet tonight.

Always one step ahead of me.

Bandit is a lot of things. Stern and cocky, athletic, and maybe even a tiny bit sweet. But at this moment, what I care most about is: he's here. At this ceremony.

Was this the clarification I was supposed to find? I was already worried that Bandit is Lalana's secret admirer. But seeing him with Charlie, a man I feel certain is connected to my mission… I can no longer deny the possibility.

Bandit could be the Maker. He could be the one I'm supposed to kill.

I watch Bandit and his companion weave through the tables and find a seat.

"Let's sit over there!" I blurt, pointing to a table on the opposite side of the ballroom. It's all the way on the right and has a dubious view of the stage, but Dad, Archie, and Zeke follow me without protest. Over the years, they've witnessed me doing things like put ketchup on everything — pizza, waffles, even soup. I guess they no longer question my eccentric decisions.

We arrive at the table, and I stumble on the slick floor. Just my luck, Lee Jenkins and our classmate Cristela Ruiz are already sitting there, along with a gorgeous woman with glossy black hair and big brown eyes who must be Cristela's mother.

With an effort, I shape my lips into a smile. According to Principal Bui's brag over the intercom, Silver Oak always has a good showing at the Newhouse awards, so it's fitting that our top female student is also present. Lee Jenkins, on the other hand? School bully and most likely to be expelled? As much as I hate to admit it, the guy's probably smart, since he's a student at our prestigious school. But judging from the arm he's slung around Cristela, he's more likely her date.

Two more students from my school. Two more people to add to my candidate pool.

"Well, well, well," Lee drawls. "Look who's here, and out of his smelly clothes! How's it hanging, Archie? Couldn't get a date other than the little sis? Nice tie, by the way. Where'd you get it? The dollar store?"

Archie fidgets with his sleeves, not meeting any of our eyes.

I'm not a violent person, never have been. But for once, I feel like I could be. I almost hope that Lee *is* the Maker.

How hard can it be to kill someone this nasty? Zeke and I move toward Archie at the same time, but Zeke gets there first and places a reassuring hand on my brother's shoulder.

Cristela knocks away Lee's arm. "Stop it," she says sternly. "*You're* here with *me*. An old family friend. And only because my girlfriend dumped me last week. So it's not like you're doing any better."

Lee opens his mouth, probably to say something offensive. Before he can respond, Cristela jumps up. "Are you sitting with us? How fun!" To her credit, her voice shakes only a little. She gives us a tentative smile. "Archie, I think you look dashing. So lovely to see you in a suit. And I'm so glad you're here, Alice. It's always nice to have another girl at these events."

I look around the ballroom and realize what she means. The men outnumber the women at least two to one.

Zeke starts talking loudly to my brother, angling his body to block Archie's view of Lee. I shoot him an appreciative look. I swear, if he and my brother weren't such good friends, I'd fall in love with him in a hot second.

There are four empty seats. Dad heads toward the one closest to him, which would give him a direct line of sight to Charlie's table. Can't have that.

I leap forward, and my elbow kinda accidentally goes into his side. "Do you mind if I sit next to Cristela?" I pant. "There's, uh, something I wanted to discuss with her."

Dad raises an eyebrow, but he agreeably settles down next to Cristela's mom, which puts his back to Charlie. Whew. Crisis averted for the time being.

Cristela turns to me with an expectant smile. "What did you want to talk about?"

Aw, crap. Now I need a topic of discussion. She seems nice enough, despite her poor choice in dates, but we've never really spoken.

"What's your area of research?" I ask politely.

Her cheeks, her eyes, even her teeth—everything about her suddenly glows. I silently congratulate myself for a smart conversation choice and reach for my oversize purse, where I've stashed my camera. This face, this expression *needs* to be captured.

"Time travel," Cristela chirps. "I know, I know. It's out there, and I get teased constantly. But it has a foundation in actual science, you know. In fact, Einstein theorized that if mass is zero, then time travel is possible. Which means that even if we can't push physical bodies through time, we might be able to send a consciousness. That is, a soul." She leans forward. "This is my dream. That one day, I'll make an earth-shattering discovery, and time travel will be possible."

I freeze, my fingers on the zipper of my purse. I'd been prepared to tune her out, but her first words are like a dash of water to my sluggish brain. Time travel. Consciousness. A soul. A *voice*.

That's what my older self is, isn't she? A consciousness that has been sent back from the future for a few minutes at a time. Which means Cristela—or someone else—succeeds. Ten years from now, the mechanism that allows people to time travel will exist.

Hell, maybe I've got this all wrong. Maybe the Maker isn't the nastiest person in the room. Maybe instead, it's his cute, cheerful companion, the one who nobody would suspect in a million years.

They both could feasibly be Lalana's secret admirer.

Swallowing hard, I consider my next move. The Voice's words come back to me, that sentence she is so fond of repeating. *One wrong move, one detail too many, and we could create ripples that will change the future in ways we never intended.*

I can't let on that I know about the future. Not only am I unsure of Cristela's role, but if she *is* fated to invent time travel, then that knowledge might make her overconfident, less hungry. She might *not* invent the machine as the result of my words. That's exactly what the Voice feared, right?

On the other hand, Cristela might just tell everyone that I'm hearing voices, and I'll get sent away for some much-needed mental assistance.

So no bizarre declarations to a virtual stranger. And yet I'm supposed to do *something*. I feel it in my gut. But what?

My fingers trembling, I sift through my purse, finding an old receipt and one of those stubby pencils you get at mini golf to keep track of your score. Good enough.

I scrawl my full name and every contact identifier I can think of. Phone number, email address, social media handles. If Cristela's not the Maker, then she'll need to find me in the future. And if she is…well, then I'll have to kill her before she grows up, so it hardly matters if she has my deets.

"Time travel? I'm all in!" I say with feigned excitement. Leaning forward, I press the note into Cristela's hand. "Keep this." I lower my voice. "In case you ever need to get in touch with me. Next week. Or ten years from now."

A waiter leans between us, taking away the wineglasses and plunking down baskets of dinner rolls covered with cream-colored napkins.

When I can see Cristela again, she nods. "You never know," she agrees, tucking the note into her pocket.

She doesn't ask why. Does she think I'm hitting on her? Maybe she's one of those people who simply go with the flow. Or maybe *her* older self has told her to keep my contact information safe.

She just might need it someday.

CHAPTER 19

"Ladies and gentlemen," a man in a tuxedo booms from the podium. "It is my honor to welcome you to an evening celebrating the brightest minds of our future, the finalists of the Newhouse science fair!"

One sentence in and my eyes glaze over. I poke at the gravy-drenched quarter chicken on my plate. The anchovies swim through a sea of dressing in my Caesar salad. This food is so unappetizing, I'm not even tempted to take a picture of my meal, even though I've been woefully neglecting my foodie account.

"Don't bother eating that. I've got something much better," Cristela whispers, reaching under the table and producing a box of cupcakes. "In honor of my fellow Young Scientist nominees." She starts handing out the cupcakes. "May the brightest mind win."

Now, this is more like it. Decorated with elegant swirls and precise crisscrosses, these small purple cakes are almost too pretty to eat. But absolutely perfect to photograph.

Lalana loves cupcakes. Over winter break last year, we

not only spent an entire day learning about the ancient art of tea making (my choice), but we also had a cupcake bake-off (her choice). She was in charge of the timer—so there would be no danger of me burning them—and Archie was our judge. He awarded her the win. Mine were "marginally edible," he proclaimed before dissolving into laughter. I don't think I've ever seen him laugh so hard. But Lalana brought out the fun in him. She did in all of us.

Heat pricks behind my eyes, and there's a lump in my throat that has nothing to do with the food I haven't eaten. It's only been two days since we've spoken, but I miss her. Terribly. How am I supposed to get through the rest of spring break—let alone my life—without her?

I stare at the cupcakes that Cristela's doling out and make myself hope for the striped one with the delicate pearls. She places that one in front of my brother, however. No matter. The moment she turns away, I switch our cupcakes. Archie doesn't even notice. He's abandoned his notes and appears to have nodded off. Looks like my brother's true to form, anyway.

There's one cupcake left in the box, which Cristela says she's saving for her "good friend Bandit."

My mind whirls. So Cristela and Bandit know each other. They're also both involved, in one way or the other, with the future. The question is: how?

More importantly, are they my ally...or my enemy?

The speeches of the other award recipients drone overhead, with their incomprehensible talk of space debris, cloud tracking, and mutations in cancer development. Barely listening, I move my newly acquired cupcake an inch to the right and snap a photo in an attempt to settle my roiling nerves. Another inch, so the pearls catch the light, and another picture. A quarter rotation. On the plate. Off the plate. Next to the fork. Behind the glass. *Click, click, click.*

Zeke leans forward. "Um. You do realize you've taken a hundred photos in the last two minutes? Of an *inanimate* object?"

I take a picture of his hand hovering near the cupcake. "I need to get the perfect shot."

"Just in case the cupcake blinks?" he asks, amusement dancing in his eyes.

My lips twitch. "She's having a good frosting day. Gotta capitalize on that."

I raise my camera just as Zeke breaks into a grin.

There. The light falls across his face perfectly. His features are chiseled, his expression warm. I can't believe it. An Instagram-worthy shot in just a single frame. It's a miracle.

Just then, a willowy African-American woman ascends the stage. Murmurs of excitement zip around the ballroom. The Young Scientist Award. The one we've all been waiting for, the one that will distinguish one student scientist above the rest.

Archie has always downplayed his chances to win this award, but he's a shoo-in. I know it. There's no one smarter than my brother. I put down my camera and poke my brother in the side. Archie jerks awake. His glasses are askew, and there's a crease along the side of his face where it was pressed against his arm. Honestly, he looks awful. Just how little sleep did he get last night?

"And the Best Young Scientist Award goes to…" The presenter pauses dramatically as a drumroll is piped over the loudspeakers. "Zeke Cain for his cutting-edge research on cell modification!"

Zeke. Not Archie.

Our tablemates stand and cheer. Stunned, I push to my feet, clapping even as I try to puzzle out how he managed to beat my brother. But that's selfish of me. If Archie can't win,

Zeke's the next best choice.

Zeke shakes hands with Archie and Cristela, then heads around the table. As he passes my seat, I grab his arm. "Congratulations!"

"This moment is pivotal," he says, his voice dazed. He looks into my eyes a moment longer than necessary. "For the rest of my life. For the future. Everything changes because of this."

My excitement teeters just a bit. Is it just me, or is everyone suddenly fixated on the future?

Zeke continues his path toward the stage, and I shake off my uneasiness. Words. Just words. They don't make him any more likely to be the Maker. He's still the same Zeke who's constantly looking out for my brother. But then he walks by Bandit and Charlie's table. And stumbles. Or—more accurately—*trips*.

I swear that Charlie stuck his foot directly into Zeke's path. That flash of movement couldn't have been anything else. But *why*? He's a grown man, not a little kid.

Zeke catches himself on the edge of Charlie's chair. The moment is over before I can take my next breath, and my friend continues toward the stage.

I shiver. The Voice told me to keep Dad away from Charlie. *Dad*. Not Zeke. And yet, in the original timeline, Zeke watched the altercation between Dad and his old lab partner from the sidelines.

Did I just mess up? Does Zeke and Charlie's "accidental" meeting mean that I failed?

Everything changes because of this, Zeke said.

If he's right, what will be the consequences?

• • •

Finally, the ceremony ends. As soon as the lights brighten, our tablemates take off, leaving Archie, Dad, and me.

I jump to my feet. "Let's go." Zeke may have crossed paths with Charlie, but maybe I can still prevent disaster. If I get Dad out of here without seeing his old lab partner, I would've technically followed the Voice's order. "I'm not feeling very well. I want to go home."

"Can you wait a few minutes, Alice? The banquet's not over." Dad gestures at the people still milling around the ballroom. He looks at my brother, who's back to scribbling on that napkin. Guess his nap revived him enough to continue being brilliant. "I know you're disappointed, son, but you shouldn't miss this opportunity. Some of the most renowned scientists in the country are in this room. The connections you make tonight could be vital to your future."

"What if I don't want to talk to anyone?" Archie glances up, thunderstorms on his face.

"I implore you to try," Dad says.

My brother stares back for a few breathless moments. And then he slams his palms on the table and stalks away. Right in the direction of Charlie's table.

Crap! "Don't go anywhere," I say to Dad and hurry after my brother. "Archie, wait." I grab his shoulder as we squeeze between two unoccupied tables, darting my gaze around. I've already slipped in allowing Zeke to cross paths with Charlie. I won't make the same mistake with Archie. The seats are clearing quickly as people make their way to the long dessert tables, but there's no wild mane of brown hair. No Charlie.

My shoulders droop just as Archie spins around, snarling. "Zeke didn't even mention me in his speech. Even though I was instrumental in helping him with his research. And now Dad's getting on my case. He's just mad I lost that stupid trophy."

"That's not true." I wrench my eyes from the scene over

his shoulder and focus on my brother. I can still see the line on his face from his dinnertime snooze. "Dad loves you. He's proud of you." Which is more than I can say for his feelings toward me.

Archie scoffs. "The only thing he loves is the prestige my success brings. He's only concerned about what will take me to the next level. Advanced courses. Science fairs. Olympiads. He doesn't actually care about *me*."

"He does! It's just that you have a gift. Dad wants to make sure he does right by you."

He dodges a waitress as she walks past with a bin of empty glasses. "Don't you dare take his side."

The anger hangs between us. His conflict with Dad has been simmering for months. Sooner or later, it's going to blow up—and I don't want to be in the middle of the detonation.

"I only want what's best for you, Arch," I say softly.

His eyes sharpen, assessing me as thoroughly as a scientific equation. "Do you?"

I wet my lips. It's a weird question. Why would he question my loyalty? And why now, when he never has before?

"Of course," I say. "I've been rooting for you since the day I was born."

But he's already taken off, weaving deftly among the tables.

I stare after his retreating figure. He'll be okay. He always is.

At least, that's what I used to think. But maybe I've been wrong. Maybe this fissure between him and Zeke is more serious than I thought.

But I can't worry about him right now. I've left Dad alone for entirely too long. I need to get back before he does something stupid—like get in a fistfight with the man who will help the Maker invent the virus.

CHAPTER 20

When I get back to the table, however, Dad's no longer there. Where did he go? I was only gone for a minute! I look around wildly, prepared to slide across the floor, leg-swiping anyone who gets in my way, if it means preventing a meeting between Dad and Charlie. But I don't see either him or his bushy-haired ex-friend.

Maybe it's just as well. The Black Widow I am not. No matter how much I admire Natasha's red hair. Or her black jumpsuit. Or her badass moves. I'd as likely knock over the chocolate fondue, which would just be embarrassing (and sticky).

I'm about to go search for Dad when my attention is caught on the sad cupcake pieces strewn across the table. Bites, big and small, have decimated the spirals that once stood so proudly. Only crumbs remain, with splotches of buttercream frosting flung here and there.

Sighing, I pick up the only intact cupcake, the one with the shiny pearls I photographed, and bring it to my mouth.

Before I can take a bite, however, electricity flashes across my brain.

"Don't eat the cupcake!" the Voice screeches.

I startle so hard, I nearly drop the dessert in question. "Did you really travel across ten years to scare the crap out of me with *dietary* advice?"

"You're such a brat sometimes, you know that?" the Voice snaps. "I don't know how I've made it this far without wringing my own neck."

Oh. So it's this version of my older self tonight. The ragey one. "Calm down, jeez. I was just kidding."

"Do you have any idea how condescending that is?" she asks. "You don't know what I'm going through. You can't even begin to guess what's happening in the future. So do *not* tell me to calm down!"

An electric jolt zaps my brain. It's not a signal of her arrival but a punishment for my quip.

"Owwww! Stop that! Aren't we beyond this?" I cradle my head between my hands as stars explode in my vision. This is ridiculous. My older self is so erratic, it's like I'm dealing with two different people.

"When you've had enough," she says icily, "give that cupcake to Bandit."

I blink. "What? Why? He has his own. Cristela was saving one for him."

"Don't argue, Malice. I'm the one doing the thinking here. Not you."

Lightning fries my brain again. I pant as sweat bursts from my skin and drips into my eyes. Did it hurt this much last time? It couldn't have. And why is she calling me Malice again? She hasn't done that since our first meeting.

"Make him eat the cupcake," she demands. "Every last bite. Whatever it takes, make sure he finishes. But for heaven's sake, don't talk to him any more than is necessary."

I prop myself against the back of a chair, spent. I can

hardly string a sentence together. I'm not sure how I'm going to walk around an entire ballroom, searching for a blue-haired boy. "How am I supposed to make him eat if I'm not allowed to talk to him?" I'm not trying to be contrary. Really. It's just that my older self isn't making any sense.

"I don't know!" the Voice says as if she's speaking to an exasperating child. "Figure it out. Shove his face in the frosting if you have to."

The pain lashes out again, this time in slow, undulating waves.

"I'm going, I'm going!" I yelp. "You don't have to hurt me. I would've listened without the pain. We're on the same side here, don't forget." I shake my head. I was supposed to be keeping Dad away from Charlie. Do I have a new mission now, one that supersedes the previous one? I can't do both at once.

The Voice didn't mention her previous directive, but I guess she doesn't have to. She's used to me doing what she wants. When she wants. How she wants.

Good thing she's my future self. Otherwise, this total control might scare me.

At the dessert bar, people jam around the chocolate fountain, the cascading platters of macaroons, and the rotating displays of raspberry tarts. I hold the cupcake gingerly as I walk, trying not to crush the wrapper. As usual, my older self has issued a command with zero context. I'm willing to give her some leeway because I do want to save the future. I don't want to abandon my daughter. But my patience is wearing thin.

Why does she want me to give Bandit this cupcake? To

impress him? Or is it because he's the Maker, and she has a deeper, more sinister motive? I almost drop the cupcake.

But that doesn't make any sense. If she were going to *trick* me into killing someone, she wouldn't have gone through all that trouble to *convince* me. Right?

Feeling better, I weave through the throng. With my luck, he's already left. Maybe tall, athletic boys have no use for sinfully rich desserts. Maybe that's how they maintain their washboard abs.

Someone snags my arm.

Disoriented, I glance up and see well-shaped lips, intense brown eyes, hair the same shade as a peacock's feather.

"Looking for me?" Bandit asks, a dimple appearing on one cheek.

Since when did Bandit have a dimple? And how come I never noticed before? "Um. Yes, actually." The truth slips out in my distraction. Oops.

He smirks, and for once, I can hardly blame him. The Voice's demands have turned me into the person he assumed I was all along: a lovesick girl begging for his attention.

He skims my outfit. "So I was right," he says, his voice low and a little rumbly. "You *are* wearing a blue dress. I like it."

I blush. Does he think I chose the dress on his behalf? I didn't! I've had this outfit planned for weeks, way before I ever spoke to him. But his eyes are knowing—and more than a little appreciative—and I just don't know what to do with that look.

"I brought you a cupcake," I burst out. "You know, as sort of a consolation prize. For not winning tonight."

He raises his brows. "You do know that laid out behind you is thirty feet of every dessert known to humankind?"

He has a point. Maybe I should've thought through my

strategy more carefully. "But this one's special," I barrel ahead. "Homemade."

Too late, I remember that Cristela was saving one of her cupcakes for Bandit. If he catches me passing off her cupcake as one of my own, I'll never live it down. "Did, uh, Cristela already give you one tonight?"

"Nah," he says. "She's been too busy charming her many admirers."

This would be the appropriate moment to hand him the cupcake. It's the easiest thing in the world. All I have to do is lift up my arm, offer him the dessert.

Except…I don't. I'm not sure why. Something feels…off inside me. I can't explain the what or how of it. But something in my gut is screaming, *Don't do this. You will regret this action for the rest of your life.*

Bandit tilts his head, probably wondering why I'm still clutching his gift.

And then my arm shoots out of its own volition, thrusting the cupcake at him.

No, *not* of its own volition. Of the *future's* choice. Holy crap, that's the older Alice controlling my body. I didn't know she could do that!

Bandit takes the cupcake, forehead creased.

I try to smile, but it's like I've lost control of those muscles, too. I feel like I did when I traveled forward in time—except I'm in the present. In the body that should be mine.

There's not enough oxygen. I can't breathe, even as my lungs rise and fall in an even rhythm. How is she doing this? How is she controlling my physical movements?

She flees my body in an instant, and I sway, almost falling to the floor.

With lightning-fast reflexes, Bandit shoots forward and gathers me in his arms. "Alice!" he says urgently. "Alice, are you okay?"

I want to respond. I do. I want to reassure us both that I'm myself again, that I have control over my own body.

But when I open my mouth to say the words...I black out.

CHAPTER 21

I come to standing on my own feet but not bearing any weight. Instead, strong arms are wrapped around me. Cradling me. Keeping me safe.

"Alice, you're awake," Bandit says, his voice weak. "You fainted for a second. Do you want me to call the ambulance? Find your dad?"

"No!" I practically shout. The last thing I need is someone poking around in my head. Taking a deep breath, I lower my voice. "Please. I promise I'm fine. Can you just get me away from all these people?"

"Done." He glances at the throng bunched up against the dessert bar. "I'd like to carry you, but that will attract too much attention. Can you walk?"

Can I? My legs wobble like Jell-O, but even gelatin can stand when it has the proper support. "I think so."

Keeping an arm tightly around my back, he guides me to the exit. A few heads turn in our direction—but nobody even blinks. What do you know? Apparently, one of Bandit's many talents includes putting on a front to deceive other people. Interesting.

We exit the ballroom, cross the grand lobby, and enter a small conference room, which is thankfully empty. The breath rushes from my lungs.

Bandit doesn't let go until he eases me into a rolling chair at the oval-shaped board table.

"Don't move," he says in a low voice. "I'll be right back."

I lean against the chair and close my eyes. I'm tired, so tired. All the energy seems to leak through my feet into the plush carpet. Maybe this is what happens when not just your mind but also your body is occupied by another being.

Seconds or minutes later, I hear the squeak of the door and quick, steady footsteps. I creak open my eyelids. Bandit places a bottle of water on the table, along with a heaping plate of dessert. To my immense relief, he also puts a whole cupcake next to the plate.

"You'll feel better if you eat and drink." He glances at the plate, piled high with cheesecakes and cookies, pie and cake. "I wasn't sure what you liked."

"So you brought one of everything?" I ask incredulously.

He shrugs, red tingeing his cheeks. "What else can I get you? A wet washcloth for your head? Tylenol?"

"I'm fine, really!" I protest. "Just hang out. Talk to me."

He sits across from me and picks up my hands, holding them between his. "Your hands are freezing."

He rubs them, and slowly but surely, my fingers begin to tingle with warmth.

Confusion swirls inside me. It's been so long since anyone's taken care of me. Even longer—by which I mean never—that the person might one day be responsible for wiping out two-thirds of the world.

How am I supposed to feel here? What am I supposed to do?

"Um…" I cast out my mind, struggling to focus, to remember who he is and who he might become. "Are your parents here?"

I have no idea what they look like. Actually, I don't know much about them, other than the fact that they were rumored to have bribed the guidance counselor.

"They were too busy to attend, so they sent my uncle instead." He gently kneads my fingers between his thumb and forefinger. "Charlie's not my real uncle, of course, but in Thai culture, you call all your parents' close friends 'aunties' or 'uncles.'"

Charlie. Finally. Confirmation that the bushy-haired man is Dad's old lab partner.

"He was the obvious choice, since he's a scientist, too," Bandit continues, still massaging. "He used to be one of great renown…well, until Harvard kicked him out a few years ago."

"How come?" I could float away on this sensation. His fingers are so capable. I wouldn't complain if he massaged me for the rest of the night. Week. Year…

Gah! Focus, Alice. He might be the enemy. I pull my hands out of his grasp, smiling to soften the gesture.

"It's a sore subject. We don't talk about Charlie's dismissal much." Not at all insulted, Bandit kicks back in the chair. "From what I understand, he was into some really fringe stuff. Harvard didn't approve, so they parted ways."

Fringe stuff? My dad described his former lab partner's research as "wild." Sounds like a virus that could wipe out the human population to me.

As I'm pondering, Bandit picks up the cupcake and opens his mouth.

"Wait!" I yelp.

He blinks, the dessert an inch from his lips.

"Are you, uh, allergic to nuts? I'm not sure what's in the cupcake."

He bursts out laughing. "I thought you said it was homemade."

"By Cristela," I say, refusing to feel ridiculous. "Not me. You wouldn't want a baked good by me. Unless you like burned desserts."

"You *stole* the cupcake to give to me?" A smile spreads across his face—a real one, maybe the first I've seen from him. It changes his face, turning him from merely handsome to...devastating.

My stomach flips. Maybe it's a good thing he doesn't smile more often. A very good thing.

"I'm even more flattered," he says. "But don't worry. No allergies here."

He takes a huge bite, leaving a few crumbs on his mouth. Whatever my gut was trying to tell me, it's too late now. The Voice made sure of that.

And see? He's fine. He hasn't collapsed to the floor. He's sitting there, all tall and muscly and solid. The crumbs cling stubbornly to his full, well-shaped lips, just waiting for someone's fingers to brush them away...

Do. Not. Stare. At. His. Lips.

"Are you and Charlie close?" I ask, sitting on my fingers.

"Not really. He lives in a remote cabin in the middle of nowhere, and he doesn't surface all that often." He takes another bite.

"Maybe I can meet him sometime," I venture. After all, the Voice said to keep Charlie away from *Dad*. Maybe my family by implication. But she didn't say anything about *me*. What better way to find out about Charlie than to go directly to the source? "He seems like an interesting guy."

"Sure," Bandit says easily. "We can do it now, if you're

feeling better."

Yes! I pump a mental fist in the air, my energy returning in waves.

I'm about to get to my feet when Bandit crumples up the rest of his cupcake and tosses it in a nearby trash can. My heart lurches. How many bites did he take? Two? Nowhere near the entire thing.

The Voice isn't going to be pleased. She said to make sure he ate all of it. But what can I do? Short of fishing the dessert out of the trash, I can hardly make him finish it.

"Don't tell Cristela I threw away the cupcake, okay?" Bandit grins. "It was a little sweet for my taste."

"Your secret's safe with me." I force up my lips. "Let's go meet your uncle Charlie."

"Are you sure you're up to it?" His forehead creases. "No pressure. You can meet him some other time."

"I feel a 110 percent," I assure him.

But as we walk from the room, I can't help but wonder: What other secrets does Bandit have? Is he the arrogant and easygoing boy he appears to be? Or is his blue hair hiding dark secrets—a creepy obsession with my best friend, a hand in his uncle's "fringe" research?

The Voice put him in my path for a reason. I don't care how cute he is; I'm going to figure out his role in the future apocalypse—and hold him accountable if it's bad.

I just really, really hope I don't have to kill him.

CHAPTER 22

Bandit casually wraps his arm around my back, if there can be anything casual about his bare skin touching mine, and guides me back into the ballroom.

We walk to the corner farthest from the dessert bar as my mind whirls. What do I say to Bandit's uncle? *So, Charlie, tell me about this fringe research of yours. Does it have the potential to wipe out two-thirds of the world in, oh, about ten years' time?*

Ugh. That's about as smooth as the Drake Passage, which—spoiler alert—is where the Atlantic, Pacific, and Southern seas meet, resulting in the choppiest waters on earth.

Before I can come up with a better approach, I see Charlie, huddled with two students. Except…those aren't just any two students. The older man's bushy brown mane is bent toward Zeke's closely shaven head and Archie's wild mop.

My heart stops. I was willing to put myself in danger by talking to Charlie. But not Zeke. Not Archie. They shouldn't be anywhere near that man. Even if the Voice didn't mention their names, my gut tells me I need to keep Charlie away from my family, my friends. From everyone I care about.

Why, oh why did I have to faint? Damn the Voice for asking me to do two missions at once!

I take a shaky breath. This is okay. They're just talking. Disaster hasn't struck yet. No harm in a few exchanged pleasantries.

Charlie looks up as we approach, cutting himself off mid-sentence. "Ah. Chubbs. I was wondering where you'd gone off to."

Bandit wipes a hand down his face. Chubbs, huh? Interesting. Now where did that nickname come from?

"Zeke here was telling me about his research," Charlie continues, beaming at Zeke. "Fascinating stuff. Do you know each other?" He waves his hand among us.

"We go to school together," Bandit says smoothly, giving a nod to both Zeke and my brother. "Congratulations on the Young Scientist Award," he says to Zeke, then turns to me. An awkward pause descends, as though he's not sure who should introduce me to his uncle. Him, because he brought me over to the group? Or my brother, because we have the closer relationship?

Ha. Little does he know that Archie's about as likely to perform such niceties as Chris Hemsworth is to show up at this banquet. Shirtless. Proposing marriage to me on bended knee.

Not that I've ever entertained that particular fantasy.

"This is Alice," Zeke jumps in. "Archie's sister. We came to the banquet. *Together*," he emphasizes ever so slightly.

Bandit arches an eyebrow. "She just gave me a purple cupcake." A note of challenge creeps into his tone.

"We *all* got cupcakes," Zeke says, deep grooves in his forehead. "They're from Cristela, not her."

I blink. What is happening here? Are they actually…

competing over a cupcake? Over *me*? Yeah, right. When the god of thunder swings his hammer through a tray of petit fours, maybe.

"I'll bake cupcakes for everyone!" I say cheerfully. "Just name the time. Place. Flavor—"

"Don't mind her excitement," Archie interrupts. "No one—*literally* no one—has ever asked her to bake before."

I slap my brother's shoulder, but before I can retort, Charlie groans. "You've got to be kidding me. This is what we're talking about at the Newhouse awards? Cupcakes?" He levels me with a glare.

Every last drop of hilarity seeps from me as sweat breaks out on my neck. The older man's attention has turned to me. Finally. Here's my chance to change the subject to his research. "Oh, um. I have lots of interests besides cupcakes. I'm not a scientist myself, but I love hearing about it! What's your field of study, sir?"

"So you're one of *those*." He ignores my question, his temple twitching. "I never did understand you liberal-arts types."

He skims his gaze over the crowd, dismissing the subject. Dismissing me. I haven't felt this small since the admissions officer of our school deigned to interview me.

"Not long ago, I was a science fair judge, too," Charlie says tightly. "Students would line up around the table just to have a word with me. I was more popular than the chocolate fountain! And now look at me." His tone is so bitter, it makes the acid rise in *my* throat. "The only way I got entry to this banquet was as someone's *guardian*."

"It means a lot that you came with me, Uncle Charlie," Bandit ventures.

The older man sighs, not sparing his nephew a glance. "I'm done, Chubbs. Let's ditch this joint." He turns to Zeke.

"You have my contact information. Use it."

No! He can't leave yet. I've barely had a chance to talk to him. I haven't received any evidence that he's involved with the virus.

"It was an honor to meet you, sir," Zeke says, oblivious to my growing panic.

I need more from Charlie. More interaction, more information. More pieces of the puzzle. And I won't stop until I get them.

"Wait!" I shout as Bandit and Charlie turn to leave. All four men look at me, and I give Charlie my most charming smile. "It's not often we meet someone of your esteem. The other students don't know what they're missing. Before you go, could you…give us some advice?" I gesture at Zeke, my brother, and myself. "We'd be so grateful for any wisdom you're willing to share."

Charlie tilts his head, assessing me. My smile wobbles, but I fix it in place.

"You remind me of me when I was your age," he says thoughtfully. "Drifting along. My head in the number-saturated clouds. That was before I understood the cruelty of the human race. The indignity of the intellectual."

He looks from me to Archie to Zeke. "You want my advice? Here it is. All the people in this ballroom? The ones who pretend to nurture your talent, to advance your career? They don't care about you. They only care about themselves. Only the fittest will survive—and your number one priority? To make sure *you* survive."

His lips curve, but it's too serene. Too peaceful. A misty, dreamlike expression crosses his face. Instead of reassuring me, it makes me feel like I have grasshoppers stuffed under my skin.

"What…what do you mean?" I stammer. "How do we

make sure we survive?"

"There are two sides to every equation," he says. "A dark side and a light inside us all. Find your own way, Zeke. Archie. Malice. Figure out what's best for *you*. Don't let anyone else, even a voice of supposed wisdom, tell you what to do." He directs the last sentence at me.

I go perfectly, absolutely still. My blood turns to snow, my nerves to ice. There it is. The proof that I've been waiting for. "You called me Malice."

He lifts his eyebrows. "Excuse me?"

"My name is *Alice*," I say. "Without the 'M.'"

"You must've misheard me," he says smoothly. "It's quite loud in here."

My teeth want to chatter, but I slam them together. I'm desperate to scream, but I lock the wails inside. I didn't mishear. I couldn't have. Because he also mentioned a voice. One of supposed wisdom. To me.

"Who are you? Are you from the future?" I blurt before I can stop myself.

He laughs, so loud and deep that it could span a decade. "Of course not, my dear. Time travel is only possible when mass is zero. And this?" He grabs two handfuls of his belly. "Unfortunately, this doesn't qualify as zero."

The breath lodges in my throat. He referenced the premise of Cristela's research, which establishes one more connection with the future.

My vision narrows. Archie's blinking consideration, Zeke's assessing gaze, even Bandit's solemn lips fade into the background. All I see is Charlie. Disheveled clothing. Bushy brown hair. All-too-knowing smirk.

There's still so much I don't know. Still so many dots I need to connect.

But the Voice said I would get the clarity I needed at the

awards ceremony. I mistakenly assumed that the person I have to kill is the Maker. But now I realize that the Voice never said that. She only stated that in order to stop the Maker, I had to kill *someone*.

Someone who is inextricably linked to the future. Someone who might serve as a mentor to the person who will grow up to invent the virus.

Someone exactly like Charlie.

CHAPTER 23

The next morning, buckets of water, soapsuds, and big yellow sponges are strewn across the school's parking lot. A girl in a bikini top and white shorts washes the roof of a car while her friend aims a hose at the fender. Two guys attack a newly washed sedan with clean towels, leaving their unfortunate friend scrubbing at a bird poop stain.

Silver Oak Academy might be populated with STEM geniuses, but they sure know how to host a car wash.

I rub my temples. I barely slept last night, the events of the banquet looping through my mind. By four a.m. and the forty-fifth iteration, I was utterly convinced: Charlie is my target. He is the man I have to kill.

Now, the only question is: how?

I haven't quite figured that out yet, but it's pretty clear that my access to Charlie has to be through Bandit. It all fits. That must be why the Voice threw the blue-haired boy in my path, only to order me to keep him at arm's length. He is a stepping-stone, a means to an end—but nothing more.

I still don't know which of my classmates has a crush on

Lalana. I still don't know who invents the virus…but maybe that doesn't matter. If I eliminate the mentor, then I stop the Maker. Right?

That's my working theory, anyhow.

Now, I just need to "accidentally" bump into Bandit, and the fundraiser is my best bet. As president of the junior class, he's *always* at these events.

Zeke trots up to Archie and me as soon as we arrive. "Wow. You're here."

"Only because Alice bribed me," Archie grumbles. The sky is a cloudless blue, the sun warm and invigorating on my neck. My brother's back in his khaki shorts and T-shirt, but he's acting like I've dragged him to a deep, dark cave rather than a fun outdoor activity.

"How?" Zeke asks. "Did she promise not to cook anymore?"

"Close," my brother says, so casually that I can tell he doesn't want Zeke to guess the actual truth: that he capitulated only after I reminded him that I was accompanying him to the tux shop later this week. "She said I could choose the car's music for the rest of spring break."

Ah, so that's the story he wants to tell. I can play along. Especially since I snuck a handgun from Mom's cabinet into the glove compartment without him knowing.

After all the buildup, when I finally cracked open the cabinet, the result was underwhelming. Two lone weapons and a whole lot of dust. I haven't settled on *using* the weapon, particularly because the feel of that cool, heavy metal freaked me out for a good ten minutes. But given the nature of my mission, it makes sense to have a gun. Just in case.

"It's a heavy price to pay," I say mournfully, squashing my guilt. I'm not taking advantage of my brother's obliviousness. I'm not. More like I'm protecting him. The less he knows about my future crimes, the better. "I mean, I'll be listening to Taylor Swift's greatest hits for an entire week! But anything for the junior class, right?"

"Hey!" Archie protests. "I don't like her songs."

I blink innocently. "But you're a die-hard Swiftie. I heard you singing 'Trouble' in the shower the other day. And don't you have that 'I heart Taylor' pennant in your room?"

My brother glares, and I hold back a smile.

"I have no idea what she's talking about," he tells Zeke stiffly. "Why would I sing a song that came out when we were in elementary school?"

"Oh, I don't know. Maybe because you know exactly when it released?" I tease.

Archie huffs out a breath and glances toward the entrance of the parking lot, where a cash station with a small table and umbrella has been set up. "Oh, look. I think they need my help collecting money. Which I'd better do before I give in to temptation and *strangle my sister*."

I giggle as he stomps away, happy to be out of my head, if only for a moment. His anger's just for show. He may or may not care if Zeke knows that he has the musical taste of a teenybopper, but he'd for sure be embarrassed if anyone found out he needed his sister to choose a tux.

"Love you, Arch!" I call after his retreating back.

Turning, he kisses his fingertips and then slaps them onto his butt.

I pretend to catch the kiss in the air and smack it onto my own butt. Ever since we were kids, this has been our smart-aleck version of the French double-cheeked kiss. Not as classy but uniquely us.

Casually, I look around the parking lot, but there's no brilliant blue hair. No superiorly arched eyebrows. No Bandit.

Did he sleep in? Or is he already huddled up with Charlie,

plotting the demise of the human race?

Zeke shifts forward, pulling my attention back to him. "I know for a fact that he listens to 'Blank Space' on repeat whenever he gets stuck on a proof." He lowers his voice conspiratorially. "Says it helps him think."

I smile up at him. He's so close that I can see the bob of his Adam's apple.

His gaze flickers down to my bare legs under the hem of my cutoff jean shorts. Just like that, awareness snaps into the air. At this moment, Zeke's not just my brother's buddy. Instead, he's a really attractive guy standing six inches away from me. And I don't have the first idea what to do with that information.

"Did you have fun last night?" he asks.

"I did," I say. "I'm so excited that you won!"

"I still can't believe it." He shakes his head. "I had tough competition—your brother, Cristela, Bandit. And those are just the finalists from our school." He pauses, as though carefully selecting his next words. "I heard about what happened at school. When you, uh, said you loved Bandit. Is it true?"

"Oh, no," I babble. "That was just a joke. I barely know the guy. We've talked two, maybe three times?" That might be understating it just a little. But the last thing I need is my brother's only friend grilling me about something I don't even understand, especially when he's looking at me like my answer means way more than it should.

"Okay, good." Zeke lets out a breath and smiles at me. "Do you want to be on my wash team?"

I nod, caught off guard by how pleased he seems. It doesn't help that I'm also ashamed for being less than honest with him.

He hands me a sponge and a bucket of water, and we begin to suds up the windows of a Toyota Camry. His forearm slides against mine—wet, soapy. I take a shaky breath. I'm not sure what's going on. He's my friend, and I enjoy his company. But he's Archie's friend, too. He's Archie's friend *first*.

Is there a sibling code that covers this? Not sure. But I know that I don't want to take any of Zeke's time away from Archie.

Sighing, I step to the left so that we're no longer touching. I wish Lalana were here. Not only would she have a plan for bumping into Bandit, but she'd also know how I should handle Zeke. More than that, I just want to see her. We always used to volunteer for community service together, from sorting books at the library to cleaning up the park. And now we're not. Both my shoulders and heart droop to think that I might never pick up trash with my best friend ever again.

Zeke turns to me, an indecipherable expression in his dark eyes. "Lalana says hello."

I almost drop my sponge. "Wait, what? Are you a mind reader?"

His eyebrows crease, and I hurry on. "Never mind. When did you talk to her? I didn't know you two were friends…" I trail off, remembering Lalana saying that he stares at her in history class. Could *Zeke* be her secret admirer?

"Well, I always saw her at your house, but I didn't get to know her until last summer, when I ran into her at the superstore. She was ripping down a poster advertising Father's Day, and I ended up helping her shred it into a million pieces." He shrugs, and now that I've dropped my guard, I can't help but notice how wide his shoulders are. Zeke may not be a jock like Bandit, but he clearly gets his exercise in other ways. "Not my best moment, but, uh…" He clears his throat. "I don't know if you know this, but my dad passed away a few years ago."

My heart pangs. "Oh. I didn't know. Archie never

mentioned it." I touch his elbow with my free hand. "I'm really sorry."

"Thank you." He meets my eyes. "You know what they say. The death of a parent is the ordinary tragedy, while the birth of a child is the ordinary miracle. Both extreme events for the individual but so commonplace that they're ordinary in the context of the universe."

The emotions gather in my chest. "Is that supposed to be uplifting or depressing?"

"Both, I think," he says with a small smile. "Tragedy doesn't cease to exist just because it's common. At the same time, there's comfort in knowing that you're not the only one to experience such devastation."

We don't speak for a moment. I run my sponge along the window frame, and Zeke angles his so he gets at every cranny and crevice. Whoever owns this Toyota Camry is going to be one satisfied customer.

"Anyhow, I wanted to check on Lalana, so I called," he finally says.

Oh. I guess Mrs. Bunyasarn wasn't screening *all* Lalana's calls. Just mine. "How is she?" I ask, suddenly desperate to hear any news about my best friend. "Did she sound okay?"

"No," Zeke says in his direct way. "She seemed depressed."

Damn it. I'm a terrible person—a terrible friend. I didn't expect Lalana to be doing *well*. But hearing Zeke's assessment slices open my wounds all over again.

He steps closer to me, and my breath catches until I realize he's just moving on to the next window, since I'm standing here, immobile.

Miserably, I lift my sponge to the side-view mirror.

"How come you don't know how she's doing?" he asks. "Isn't she your best friend?"

"Yeah." I scrub furiously at the same spot on the mirror.

"But her mom won't let me talk to her or see her. So I can't send her photos of us with cat-ear filters to make her laugh. And I can't sneak her romance novels with sticky notes marking the kissy bits. I…I miss her."

Zeke shoots me a concerned look. I bite my lip and move all the way to the front of the hood. I will not cry. Not here, at the class car wash. Because I don't deserve any sympathy, not from Zeke. Not from anyone else.

Shouts ring out across the lot. Distracted, I glance up. Did Bandit finally haul himself out of bed? A group of kids have abandoned their hoses and towels and are bunched together at the front entrance, around the umbrella and cash box.

Oh no. Not Bandit after all.

"My brother," I blurt, my eyes darting to Zeke.

That's all I have to say. "Let's go." He drops the sponge and grabs my hand. We sprint across the parking lot.

I don't have time to worry that we're holding hands. We push through the crowd, and then I'm faced with a scene from my worst nightmares: my brother, frozen in the center of all those people.

"Archie, will you go to prom with me?" Tessa Jones lays a sultry hand on his shoulder, blinking fake lashes that are completely inappropriate for a car wash.

"No, me! Archie, be my date! Please!" Nikki Ferris bounces up and down like an overexcited puppy.

"Um…" My brother darts his glance from one girl to the other. "I already have a date."

Shayla Allan saunters forward, and the people part for her as though she's royalty—because she kinda is. Queen of the junior class, that is. "No way, ladies. He's mine."

Archie shakes his head. Something's not right, and he knows it.

He reaches behind his back, and sure enough, there's a

paper taped there.

ASK ME TO PROM is written in big block letters. I'd bet all the money in my savings account that the handwriting belongs to Lee.

For a moment, my brother stares at the words, stricken. And then his face crumples.

A sharp pain lances my chest. I hate this. So much. If I could redirect those jeers toward me, I would. I'd suffer a million cuts, a million rejections, a million heartaches, if I could save my brother from this moment.

But it's too late. Archie's skin pales until he's the color of the soapsuds. He gets shakily to his feet and walks rapidly through the bunch, his head held high.

I start after him, but Zeke stops me. "Let me," he says. "He's not going to want to face anybody, not even you. I'll distract him with a science conundrum. Luckily, I'm in a snare with one of my experiments, and I could really use his help."

I bite my lip. Zeke's right. As hard as it is for me to admit, there's nothing I can do for my brother at this moment.

"Okay," I say. "Just tell him… Tell him I'll make a cutout of Taylor to hang with Thor and Loki. And that he doesn't have to hurry home for dinner, because I'll be in good company. But whenever he's ready…I'll be there."

He creases his forehead, as though not sure what to make of my strange message. But then he places his hand on my cheek. "Don't worry, Alice. We'll get him through this."

I cover his hand briefly with mine. Because he makes me feel like I'm not alone. More than ever, I appreciate having someone by my side, even if it's not Lalana.

The group dissipates, and Zeke easily weaves around the students wandering back to their posts. I'm lucky he's in our lives, watching out for my brother. Especially because it gives me time to confront the biggest jerk at our school.

Lee Jenkins is already leaning his butt against a shiny red Honda Fit, arms crossed, while Cristela dries the bumper.

"Finally, one thing you aren't good at!" Lee says to her as I approach. This guy is unbelievable. He goes directly from making fun of one person to insulting another. "How bad does a cupcake have to be to flatten a tall dude like that?"

"Shut up." Cristela blows the hair out of her eyes and attacks the hood of the car with her towel.

My steps falter. Flatten a tall dude? Cupcake? Is this why Bandit isn't at the car wash? "What are you talking about?" I demand.

Lee turns to me, his eyes dancing. "Didn't you hear?" he crows. "Bandit's been throwing up all night after eating one of Cristela's cupcakes."

"He ate a lot of food last night," Cristela mutters, not meeting my eyes. "It didn't have to be my cupcake."

"He texted Cristela and told her the cupcake had tasted funny." Lee grins so widely you'd think he'd won the Best Young Scientist award last night. "About five minutes before he puked all over the floor!"

Now it's my stomach that churns. My stomach that's about to empty its contents, right here on the parking lot. At least they'll have a bucket of water to wash away the sickness.

Because Lee's revealed exactly who he is: a guy whose soul is fed by terrorizing other people.

Because Cristela's far from innocent, if she baked the cupcake that made Bandit sick.

Because it was *my hand* that gave the dessert to Bandit. Even if I didn't have full control over it. I'm a direct link in the chain of events that led to him throwing up all night. Why didn't the Voice tell me the cupcake was poisonous?

She'd been so adamant that he eat the whole thing.

I stumble backward. Away from Lee and Cristela, two

people who have just climbed my list of suspects for being the Maker. Away from the doubt and confusion that are suddenly chasing each other round and round my midsection.

But I have one more thing to do before I can leave.

"Lee, you're an ass," I call out. "You're going to pay for what you did to Archie."

"Wasn't me, dude," he says. But the laughter in his eyes, the smugness in his smile contradict his words.

"Watch your back," I say darkly. "Someday, when you least expect it, justice will be served."

And I'm really hoping it's me, or at least my older self, who doles out that justice.

In the meantime, I have bigger concerns. Same side or not, the Voice *tricked* me. She made me hurt someone against my will.

And I'm not okay with anyone deceiving me. Even if it's myself.

CHAPTER 24

Half an hour later, I'm ringing the doorbell to an unfamiliar house. Bandit's, to be precise. My older self wouldn't approve. She warned me not to fall for him. To avoid talking to him any more than is necessary. I'm pretty sure visiting him at home crosses the boundary she wants to erect between us.

Well, I don't care. I'm sick of doing what I'm told just because my older self said so. Bandit is so far my best—and only—access to Charlie. The fact that I feel guilty as hell about poisoning him is only a secondary concern.

Even if it gives me a perfect excuse to visit.

Determinedly, I press the buzzer again, faintly sick at my own deception. Is this what the future has turned me into? What's an acceptable price to pay for saving the world?

Bandit opens the door. He's not wearing a shirt, and his sweatpants ride low. If I looked, I could probably see his hip bones. Not that I'm going to look.

My throat goes dry. Resolutely, I fix my eyes on his face. He's gaping at me, his skin sallow, his eyes fatigued.

His hair flops onto his forehead. Instead of its usual

brilliant blue, the color's faded to a tarnished silver, with bits of bleached blond scattered throughout.

He must use a shampoo to maintain the color, I realize. And last night, he was too busy vomiting to apply it.

"You're here." He shakes his head once, twice, as though I'm a mirage in the archipelagos of the Mediterranean.

"I know it's unexpected…" I begin.

"Forget that." He touches my elbow, his fingers lingering. "Come in."

Abruptly, he turns and walks inside the house. I follow him down a wood-paneled hallway, into a spacious kitchen with stainless steel appliances and an island with a marbled green countertop. The sun drifts in through several oversize windows, casting everything in a warm, cheerful glow.

Bandit grabs a T-shirt from a chair and pulls it on. At least I can look at him now.

After he's dressed, he heads to the induction stove and stirs a pot. The aromas of fried garlic and fish sauce waft around me, and my stomach grumbles. Yikes! I press my hand against it, hoping Bandit doesn't notice, but he just laughs.

"You want breakfast?" he asks.

I flush. "You don't have to feed me. I heard you were sick, and I wanted to see how you were doing. Help you the way you, uh, helped me. I got your address from your friend Anthony at the car wash."

My words are simple. Basic. They're all my tangled-up tongue can handle. But Bandit blinks as though I've confessed to discovering the last number of pi. "Really? That's why you're here?"

"Yep. Cue the stalker jokes." I cross my arms, bracing myself for his ego. But he just stares wordlessly, and I drop my arms. "What? No witty remarks?"

"No," he says, his eyes solemn. "That's really nice of you,

Alice. No one's ever visited me because I was sick before."

"Oh, come on." I'm more than faintly disgusted with myself now. The self-revulsion roars to the surface: *liar, liar, LIAR*. And yet…I do care about him. My worry *is* genuine, no matter the true motivation for my call. "I'm sure your parents would visit, but, you know. You live with them."

"I wouldn't bet on it." He moves his shoulders. On Bandit, even a shrug looks elegant.

He ladles boiled rice into a bowl. "In Thai cuisine, each person seasons to their own taste. But my friends get a little overwhelmed at the thought, since they haven't grown up doing it. May I?" His formal tone unnerves me. This is a Bandit like I've never known, outside of a few concerned moments last night. But I was so freaked out by the Voice controlling my body that I didn't take proper notice of the shift.

I nod. "If you wouldn't mind."

Lalana always seasons my food at her house. She knows exactly how I like my noodles, too. Dry, without broth. Heavy on the vinegar, light on the sugar, just a dash of red chili flakes.

I don't tell Bandit any of this, though. As evidenced by my conversation with Zeke, I can't talk about my best friend without choking up.

He moves assuredly, adding fish sauce, jalapeño vinegar, garlic oil, and chili pepper to the rice. He then garnishes it with chopped cilantro and spring onion and places the steaming bowl in front of me.

I perch on a stool, feeling absurdly touched. "This is so fancy. What is it?"

He laughs again. The warm sound pulses through the room. "*Kao tom pla*," he says. "And it's the opposite of fancy. Basically, it's just rice soup. The dish can be made with pork, shrimp, tofu, anything really. I used sea bass, which they don't really do in Thailand. Kinda my own American twist." He stops. Pushes the hair off his forehead. "You like seafood, right?"

"I love it." I take a bite. Oh, wow. I've never made anything even half this delicious in all my years of trying. Where's my camera when I need it? My followers would be panting over this dish. Especially if I included a photo of the chef.

"Are your parents home?"

"Nah." He slides onto the stool next to me. "They work so much, they're never around. My khun yai used to live with us before she passed away. I made *kao tom* for her every morning during the last couple of years. She cooked for me when I was a kid, so it was only right." He shrugs again. "The cycle of life, you know."

He's different here, in his house. In this kitchen. Warmer, more open. It's like he's shed the armor that keeps out the rest of the world.

I like it, I realize. I like *him*.

"Are you eating?" I ask.

"Maybe later. I'm still trying to keep down water."

I drop my spoon, my appetite suddenly gone. For heaven's sake. I'm sitting here, scarfing down his food. Trying not to sneak glances at his broad shoulders. Completely forgetting that I poisoned him, that I have an ulterior motive for visiting. What is wrong with me?

"Listen, Bandit." I look down into the soup and let the steam heat my face. "I'm really sorry about the cupcake."

"Why? It wasn't your fault. Cristela probably left the frosting out too long."

Jumping up, I pace the gray tiles. Each seam I step on makes me more agitated. It's like the crack that breaks your mother's back. But Mom left a long time ago, so the only thing breaking is the tenuous sway my older self has over me. "I should've known. I could've pressed harder. Asked more questions."

He shakes his head, mystified. "It was an accident. I don't see how you could've known about it."

He's so earnest. So quick to absolve me of any wrongdoing. And the last of the Voice's control just snaps. "Don't you see? She wanted you to eat the whole cupcake. You only took a couple of bites, and look how sick it made you! What would've happened if you'd finished it?"

He frowns. "Who wanted me to eat all of it? Cristela?" The lines on his face deepen. "She played a prank on me? No way. Although I wouldn't put it past her buddy Lee. I have no idea why she puts up with him."

I sink onto the stool, pushing the bowl aside. I've revealed too much. Said one thing too many. He deserves an explanation now—one I'm not allowed to give.

"It wasn't Cristela," I say as the numbness pours into me like concrete.

His eyes turn blank, as though he's sliding his shields back into place. "So that's why you're here. *You* were conspiring with Lee? For what? Seriously, Alice? I thought you were better than that."

"I am!" I shout and then scrub a hand down my face. "I mean, I don't know. I just don't know anything anymore."

He laughs, and the sound is so hollow, it makes my insides twist. "Well, that's convenient."

A strained silence falls between us. Thirty seconds pass. And then a minute. Just when I don't think I can take any more, he pushes himself off the stool. "You'd better leave now. I have enough people in my life who make me feel worthless. I don't need any more." The edge of his sweatpants brushes against my knee, and that slight touch makes me want to cry.

I finally lift my eyes to meet his.

They're no longer blank. No longer bored. Instead, the expression I see in them is achingly familiar. It's the same pain I saw in the mirror for weeks after my mother left.

I don't want to be the cause of that pain. I can't stand the thought of making anybody feel the way I felt.

He turns and strides down the hall. He's all the way at the front door, opening it, before I can make my feet move.

"Bandit, hold on." I push the door closed, even though I shouldn't be so presumptuous. Even though I have no right to another minute of his time. "I'm sorry. I wasn't conspiring with Lee, okay? I never meant to hurt you. But even if I did, you shouldn't let what I do affect you. I'm just some girl you barely know." I lean against the door, my breath coming too fast. "Who else? Who else makes you feel worthless? Because they don't deserve you. You're too…" I stumble over an adjective. Smart? Caring? Sweet—who I'm beginning to suspect is the sweetest boy I've ever met? "Good. You're too good to waste an ounce of energy on them."

He stares at the chipped wood. "That's not any of your business."

"You're right. It's not." I take a deep breath, collecting myself. "I can't explain any more, but…I promise I didn't know the cupcake was poisoned. Do you believe me?"

"Yeah." He nods slowly. "Yeah, I think I do. This prank doesn't fit in with what I know about you."

Relief rushes through me, and I have the urge to confess everything. But the Voice's warning flits through my mind: saying too much to the wrong person could result in disastrous consequences.

At the same time, I'm pretty sure Bandit's not my enemy here. He might be connected to Charlie, but judging from his all-night vomiting session, he's just as much a pawn in this process as I am. Just as manipulated by a future that we don't understand.

"Do you think time travel is possible?" I ask.

The air around us seems to shiver, and Bandit squints at the two-tiered chandelier that flickers above our heads. "I'm a dreamer." His words are careful, reluctant, as though he's being drawn into the conversation despite his better instincts. "I believe that innovation—like the universe—has no boundaries. So, do I believe in time travel?" He moves me gently to the side so he can open the door. "Yes."

"You're right," I blurt. "Time travel exists in the future, at least for a person's consciousness, if not the physical body."

His hand drops from the handle. Two, three, four seconds pass, and he continues to gawk at me. "You're being serious right now?"

I nod, fixing my eyes at the hardwood floor. I can't look at him. If I look at him, I'll tell him the rest of it. How my future self has been visiting me, how she's been making me do things I wouldn't normally do.

"How do you know?" he persists.

I peek up. Just a glance, for one infinitesimal instant. The action should've been safe—it would've been safe—but his eyes catch mine and hold them as surely as any prison.

Helplessly, I look into those bottomless eyes, and my mouth parts...

Nothing comes out.

I shiver. Does my older self have control over my body again? Or have I just finally regained my sanity?

I don't know, and it doesn't matter. Because the moment passes and I didn't do anything stupid, like blurt out the truth to a person whose involvement I'm still unsure about.

"I don't *actually* know." What's one more lie to add to the pile I've already told? "Time travel is Cristela's research project, and she's convinced."

He nods, accepting my answer. "I thought you were going to say that you've traveled to the future…and that you're *still* obsessed with me, all those years later."

I blink. And then the giggle rattles free. I sag against the straw wallpaper, probably getting stray fibers all over my clothes. I don't care. I'm so happy he buys my story that his ego doesn't even bother me.

Instead, I smack him across the shoulder. "You are the most arrogant boy I've ever met!"

Smacking leads to yelping, which leads to tickling, which leads to collapsing onto the floor in fits of laughter.

The situation's not even funny. Not really. But we're rolling on the hardwood floor, grabbing our sides, shrieking like little kids who stayed up past our bedtime. Maybe my near-confession and his night of vomiting have scrambled our brains. Or maybe we both just need the stress relief.

After a minute or ten, I push myself up on one elbow. As much as I'd like to lose myself in our mirth, I can't. I have a mission to accomplish. A person to kill. And I can't forget why I'm here.

I take a deep breath. It's now or never. He'll either go along with my request—or toss me out for my manipulation. But I won't know until I try.

"Hey, I thought your uncle was really intriguing," I say as casually as possible. The tension builds in my stomach and begins to climb up my esophagus. "Are you, uh, planning on seeing him again? If so, I'd like to tag along."

CHAPTER 25

For a moment, he just stares.

My heartbeat is a drumroll of palpitations. Does he suspect me? Was I too forward, too…obvious?

"Are you asking me out on a date, Alice?" he asks slowly.

My mind races. What is the proper move here? Should I—*gulp*—try to flirt? Problem is, I have no idea how to do that. And even if I did, he probably wouldn't buy the act in a million years.

"No!" I say, letting my natural instincts take over. "I told you, I don't date. But, um, I was asked to do this other dare…"

"Sure you were." He's full-on laughing at me now. "Let me guess: and I just happened to be here?"

"Maybe I like hanging out with you," I mumble to the floor.

He slides a finger under my chin and gently tilts up my face. Our eyes meet—and hold. "Maybe I like hanging out with you, too. Did you ever think of that?"

My mouth parts, as though I have an answer. But I don't. My brain cells are too busy firing signals to my nerves, my heart, my stomach. Sending everything dancing and flying and flipping.

"I'm actually supposed to go to Charlie's cabin today," he continues. "He's got an errand for me to run. Do you want to come with me?"

The sparks fade, and I sit up, instantly wary. I was picturing seeing Charlie in a common area, like last night. A coffee shop, maybe, or the park? Sure, the public aspect will make Charlie harder to kill...but it also gives *me* a measure of protection. "You want me to go into a remote forest with you?" I repeat numbly.

"I'm not luring you into the woods to get revenge, if that's what you're worried about." He nudges me, the dimple winking in his cheek. "You can trust me."

"Do you trust me?" I counter. It's a legitimate question. I mean, I don't even know if *I* can trust me, since all I've done is poison the guy and lie to him.

He looks at me for so long that I want to scrape the question out of the air. "Yes," he finally says.

"Why?" I whisper.

He crawls to where I'm sitting and leans back against the wall. Our shoulders touch. My skin sizzles like water dropped in a hot pan, but I don't move away and neither does he.

"I trust you because I noticed you long before you ever approached me on that basketball court," he says quietly. "Because you bring two lunches to school every day, one for you and one for your brother. Because when I talk to you, sometimes you forget to blink. And so help me, that makes me feel like the most important person on the planet."

He turns his head so that he's looking right into my eyes. "But even if none of that was true, I would still trust you. Do you want to know why?"

"Yes." The word is a puff of air that barely leaves my mouth.

"Because we had Visual Studies class together last year. And Mrs. Bryce hung up your photo on the bulletin board the second week of school. You'd captured the image of a five-year-old boy pushing his grandmother in a wheelchair. The little boy was Asian, just like me. And the grandmother's hair was dyed ruthlessly black, just like Khun Yai's. They were smiling like the sun rose and set with each other."

He drops his gaze to his fingers. "Khun Yai passed away around that same time. I felt like the oxygen had been sucked out of my lungs. But I walked past your photo every day, and for that one moment, I was able to breathe a little bit easier. Because of it." He raises his eyes. "Because of you."

He lifts his hand, and it hovers in the air, as though he's not sure where to put it. And then he cups my cheek, holding it as though it were Lalana's blown-glass butterfly. "Thank you, Alice. Thank you for helping me breathe when I needed it most."

I don't know if I can speak. The tears coat my throat, drowning my words, stealing my vocabulary. I've always hoped someday my photos would mean something to somebody. I never dreamed that it had already happened without my realizing it. "Thank *you*," I finally manage. "That's the best compliment I've ever received."

"You have an unbelievable talent," he says. "Don't let anyone convince you otherwise. Don't let people like Uncle Charlie belittle you for your art. And stop wasting time on your foodie account!"

I laugh, shocked. "What? How do you even know about that?"

He crinkles his eyes. "Don't get me wrong, your food photos are great. And if I ever need inspiration for what to make for dinner, I know just where to look. But your talent lies in capturing movement, in showcasing emotion. Not food. That's what's going to get you closer to reaching your potential. Photos that reveal your true heart. Not ones that hide your talent behind dinner."

My jaw's hanging open. Bandit follows my account? He must, since he wouldn't be able to offer such sound advice otherwise. Advice that I've known in my gut—but have been too scared to follow.

He slouches against the wall, his eyes glowing with amusement. But he appears to be laughing at himself, rather than me. "I'm @ThiefOfYourHeart."

My mouth clicks closed, only to open again.

@ThiefOfYourHeart religiously likes all my photos. He comments at least once a week. "Now who's the stalker?"

He grins. "Only of the cyber variety. You're the real-life kind." He fiddles with the sleeve of my shirt. "So will you come with me to Charlie's? It's a two-hour drive. I could use the company." He pauses. "Unless, uh, you have a boyfriend? Someone like Zeke?"

"I told you, I don't date," I say, even though I'm struggling to remember why. "Zeke and I are just friends."

I'm aware that I just had a very similar conversation, with a very different boy, not two hours earlier. It's...unsettling, to say the least.

This outing to Charlie's cabin is exactly what I wanted. What I've been hoping and planning for this entire day: a way to access my target. And yet, I hesitate.

There are so many reasons to back away from Bandit's invitation. My own personal security. The fact that I feel entirely too much for Bandit. Even now, the Voice's words echo through my head. *Don't fall for this boy. It'll only make what you have to do later harder.* She may want me to save the world, but she wouldn't want me to get closer to Bandit in the process. She'd suggest that I follow him instead. Find out where Charlie lives and return at a later time.

And then, there's the pesky detail that I'll have to kill a person. I'm not ready! Not now; not today. It would be so much easier, so much safer, to put off this task for another day.

There's only one reason to proceed: because I refuse to abandon the future for another second.

I feel like I'm on a precipice. One decision would take me back to the Alice I've always known, the one who opts for the sheltered path, who follows without question the advice of someone older and wiser. The other decision would make me topple down unfamiliar terrain. It would forge a course to a new Alice, one whom I don't know but whom I've glimpsed in sharp, vivid flashes in the last few days.

To tell the truth, I started making this decision the moment I rang Bandit's doorbell. And now his fingers are brushing the skin below my sleeve. Now he's giving me his trademark smirk, the one that no longer looks arrogant to me, only confident.

I'm more certain than ever that my older self and I are not the same person. We don't have the same agenda. We may not want the same thing.

Which means I get to choose. Me. The present Alice. I get to decide how best to accomplish my mission.

"Let's do it," I say. "Let's go to Charlie's."

But what I really mean is: Let's embrace the present to save the future. Let's journey deep into the woods, to the cabin of the man I'm supposed to kill.

CHAPTER 26

Two hours later, we pull off the paved road. We've been climbing into the mountains for a few miles, twisting and turning with the contours of the range. But now the dirt path onto which we've plunged is barely wide enough for Bandit's navy Tahoe. A sudden dip causes the seat belt to bite into my shoulder, and a branch scrapes against the side of the car, creating a loud screech.

"Your poor paint job," I moan, white-knuckling the bar on the passenger door. "These trees are wrecking it."

Bandit fixes his eyes straight ahead. "Now you know why I don't get out here more often."

These are the first words we've exchanged in the last five minutes. He's silent because he's concentrating on the road. Me, on the other hand? I'm tense because there's a gun in my backpack, and the closer we get to Charlie's cabin, the more aware I am of its heavy weight against my thigh.

Earlier, however, I was able to forget my mission for long minutes at a time. I told Bandit about my passion for exploring the world—and all the nature, animals, and people in it. My mom lived in only one town, I explained. She only ever knew one group of people, one way of life. Maybe that's not why she left; maybe my need to take a divergent path is only one factor contributing to my career choice. But I'd be lying if I said that her abandonment didn't play a role.

He told me he used to be nerdy as a kid. He wore thick black glasses and was constantly teased. That was why he wasn't nicer when I confessed that I loved him on the basketball court. He felt the scrutiny of all those eyes—and he resorted to the role he knew best, the one that's protected him all these years: arrogant jerk.

Of course, it didn't help that he was the victim of rampant rumors last year, the ones that claimed his parents were bribing the guidance counselor.

"Do you want to know why I was really seen leaving her office at all hours?" he asked, his eyes dark and vulnerable. "I was receiving counseling for Khun Yai's death. But I suppose the truth is nowhere as juicy as the gossip."

I reached across the console and squeezed his arm. Because I was as guilty as the rest of our classmates in my perception of him. Entitled, universally admired Bandit, without a worry to darken his painfully perfect life.

Yes, he's popular. Yes, he has a high opinion of himself. But though we may be different in some ways, we're achingly similar in others. In our values. In the cores of who we are.

Presently, we stop in front of a cabin, and my vision narrows to a single pinprick. The gun feels like it's burrowing a hole in my leg. I think I'm going to black out.

Breathing deeply, I relax my fingers on my backpack straps, one by one, and focus on the scene in front of me. The cabin is unlike any I've ever seen. Elevated ten feet in the air, the grown-up tree house is complete with balconies, windows, and sliding doors. The entire structure is perched on three thick, sawed-off trunks and braced against another enormous tree. A long, rising walkway leads to the front entrance.

The result, however, is far from whimsical. The house is crudely built, with wood that looks like it's battled a hundred thunderstorms. The frame looks sturdy enough, but there's no trim on the windows, no shingles on the roof. It's as though the builder lost interest halfway through the project.

"Charlie lives here?" I ask, my mouth dry.

"Yep." He opens the door and hops down from the Tahoe. "For at least the last decade."

I should follow him out of the car, but I don't. Thoughts whirl around my head like a tornado. I have to kill a person. Not just any person, but Bandit's *uncle*. The person we just drove two hours into the woods to see.

My heart rams against my chest. I have no experience at this. This mission. This *murder*. Let's say, for the sake of argument, that I even get the opportunity to point a gun at Charlie. Will I be able to pull the trigger? Can I single-handedly be responsible for ending a person's life?

I don't want to do this! I want to find a brook and listen to the water gurgling past the rocks. I want to be a girl whose only goal is getting to know this intriguing blue-haired boy. I want to forget I ever heard a voice in my head.

A set of knuckles raps against the car window, and I jump. Bandit peers through the glass, his brows furrowed. "You coming out?" Hastily, I slide the backpack over my shoulders and step onto a field of overgrown weeds that tickle my ankles.

The long trip up the walkway feels like I'm marching toward the gallows. My breathing doubles with every few steps. By the time we reach the front door, I'm a sweating, knee-trembling mess.

Charlie better not be in a violent mood, because I'm not overpowering anyone in this state.

Instead of knocking on the door, Bandit turns to me. "I didn't mean to brush you off before," he says. "Back at the house, when you asked me who made me feel worthless. I said it was none of your business, but the truth is…I was glad you cared enough to ask."

My pulse downshifts to a more even rate. "It's okay. The question's personal. I get it."

"My parents," he blurts. "It's funny, really. The rumors couldn't have gotten it any more wrong. In order to bribe *anyone*, they would first have to care. And the truth is, they never wanted me."

"I'm sorry," I say softly. "It's tough when parents put their work ahead of their kids."

"No, you don't understand." He rubs his neck. "My dad's just a distracted person, but my mom actually doesn't *want* me. She tells me all the time. She accidentally got pregnant when they were starting their business, and Khun Ta threatened to disown her if she got an abortion." His words spill out in a rush now.

"She's never told me she loves me. Not once. In the third grade, I brought home a Valentine, a big red heart I'd made in art class, with the words 'I love you, Mommy' across the front. Do you know what she said?"

"What?" My stomach clenches involuntarily.

"She said never to call her *Mommy* again. I was to refer to her as the formal *Khun Mai*, and that's it."

The ache in my chest is so tangible, I could hold it in my hand. Your parents are supposed to love you above all else. And when they don't, you can't help but question your worth. I should know. The doubts started when Mom left. But every instance of Dad's indifference reinforces those insecurities and makes them real.

"It's her loss if she doesn't value you properly," I say fiercely.

"Maybe." He moves his shoulders. "Anyhow, I just wanted you to know. You flew to my defense, even though we just met last week. And that means something. I didn't want you to think otherwise."

I lick my lips. I'm glad my words mattered to him...but why is he telling me now? "Are you, uh, saying all this because you think we're in some kind of danger?"

He laughs. "Why would we be in danger?"

Oh, maybe because I have a gun in my backpack. And we're about to knock on the door of the person I'm plotting to kill.

He faces the door again, and prickles of apprehension cover the fullness of my heart.

Nobody answers the first knock. He tries again, trading in his knuckles for a fist, banging instead of tapping. Still nothing.

He cranes his neck to peer around the cabin. "His car's not here. Weird. He never goes out. Even his groceries are delivered once a week. Plus, he was expecting me."

He tries the knob, and the door swings open. A scent wafts out, dank and musty. Instantly, the hair on my neck stands up. I have no idea what the smell is. I just know I don't want to be here.

Indecision wars across Bandit's face. A light breeze blows over us, and in the bright light of the late-afternoon sun, I can see goose bumps pebbling his skin. "What do you think?" he asks. "Should we go in?"

No! I want to scream. *Let's leave now, before I commit a crime that will lock me up for the rest of my life. Before the situation goes terribly wrong and* he *ends up killing* us.

But the Alice I want to be isn't a coward. And I didn't drive all this way just to turn around and go home. I take a deep breath. "Let's go grab the papers you were sent here to fetch."

I sound 500 percent braver than I feel. Too bad my teeth start to chatter. So much for my swagger. To cover up, I stride past Bandit...and bite back a scream as *something* scrabbles over my sneaker.

"Oh," I gasp. "A cockroach or rat just ran over my foot."

"You don't know which? They're not exactly the same size." He steps gingerly beside me.

I don't want to tell him that this *something* was closer to the size of cat.

His fingers brush against mine ever so slightly. That's all the invitation I need. I grab his hand and hold on tight.

We move farther into the house. I take in the simple layout. Living room in the center, kitchen to the right, bedroom and office to the left. The meager pieces of furniture—bookcase, table, couch—are spare and utilitarian. A layer of dust coats everything, almost as thick as the blanket of leaves outside, and a pile of gray fluff is swept against the wall.

But no Charlie.

My shoulders droop. Oh, thank goodness. Maybe I won't have to use the gun today.

"Is it always like this?" I ask, covering up my relief with a sneeze.

"Charlie's never been tidy," he says. "But this...this is next level. Sometimes he gets so preoccupied with his work that he forgets to clean. I guess this is one of those times."

Charlie's obsessing over a project *now*, right when the Voice started showing up in my head? The timing's too coincidental. Whatever this research is, it's got to be related to the virus.

"Can we take a breather?" Bandit asks faintly.

His tone makes me snap up my head. He's looking around frantically, as though we might be trapped inside.

"The balcony," he manages. "Can we go outside?"

"Of course." I usher him through the double glass doors.

The view is breathtaking. The world is bisected into two colors: the heartbreaking blue of the expansive sky and the lush emerald of the tree line. A breeze lifts the hair off my shoulders, and I can see the appeal of living in a tree house, shoddy housekeeping and all.

My fingers actually ache for my camera. But the gun took up too much room in my backpack, so there wasn't room for the Canon Rebel.

Bandit, however, is not appreciating the view. He's not even looking at it.

Instead, his palms are braced against the railing, and he's lowered his ears between his shoulders, breathing hard.

Uh-oh. Does he suspect what's inside my backpack, amid the dried-flower-infused lip gloss and cell phone battery pack?

I place a hand on his shoulder. "Bandit, are you okay?"

He pauses for an inordinately long minute. "I'm fine."

"No, you're not. Talk to me." Dropping my backpack, I wiggle my way in between his arms so that he has to look at me.

He lifts his face, and his expression is both sheepish and miserable. "I kinda have this thing about germs."

I let out a breath. So he doesn't suspect me. Suddenly, I remember the small mountain of sanitizer he squirted into his hand when I vomited in the bushes. I guess he wasn't concerned about *my* germs, in particular. He just doesn't like anybody's.

"It's more than a *thing* if you're out here trying to catch your breath," I say.

"First time that's happened," he admits. "The level of filth is just over-the-top. I could feel myself getting sick just standing there." He shudders. "'Phobia' is too strong a word, though. I'm not a fan of germs. That's all. I don't even like to touch people."

"You're touching me," I point out.

We both look down at our bodies, which have somehow become nestled against each other.

The air practically bristles with energy. I'm wedged in between his legs, my back up against the railing. A pulse beats at his neck. His lips are parted—and inches from mine.

I detect the moment his eyes change, shifting from panic into…something else. Something that warms me from the inside out.

"See, that's what I like about you." He places both hands at my waist, and my nerves sizzle through my T-shirt. "When I'm around you, I hardly think about germs."

"You held my hair back when I threw up in the bushes," I say, my voice wobbly. "That had to be challenging."

"It wasn't my favorite moment." He brushes back my hair, and his fingers skate along my ear. "But to be honest, I was just focused on helping you."

I'm trying really hard not to go up in flames, right here on the balcony. It would be such a shame. With so much wood, I'd turn this entire house into an inferno.

"You make me want to try all sorts of things I've been too afraid to try," he murmurs, staring at my lips.

"Do you mean kissing?" I ask, trying to string together some brain cells. "Are you saying you've never kissed anyone before?"

I'm stunned, honestly. Bandit's *really* attractive, and his abs are a hot topic of discussion among the girls—and a few guys—of the junior class. In all that talk, I swear I've heard rumors of him making out with *someone*.

My own kissing experience hasn't exactly been vast, since I don't date. But there's been the mashing of lips in the darkened gym during homecoming. Some amateur groping at a party.

"Not for lack of opportunity." He touches my cheek, one of his fingers lingering on the corner of my mouth. I almost scream. "With the right incentive, I could get over my fear. I just haven't had the right incentive yet."

"I don't blame you," I babble. An army of ants is trying to push its way out of my skin. The red fire kind, which create a burning sensation when they sting. "I mean, I heard that a person's mouth is dirtier than a toilet bowl."

He raises an eyebrow, in that annoyingly superior way of his. It just makes me want to press my lips to his brow.

"Alice." His voice is stern. Faintly amused. "Are you trying to dissuade me from kissing you?"

"Is it working?" I whisper.

"Nope," he says. "If you don't want me to kiss you, you're going to have to be a little clearer."

"I want you to kiss me," I say, so fast it's almost embarrassing. "With every beat of my heart. With every breath that I take."

He rewards me with one of his hard-earned smiles. "Now, *that's* the right incentive."

CHAPTER 27

Bandit doesn't lower his head, though. He just stands there, hesitating.

Clearly, I need to be more proactive.

I tug him down so our foreheads are pressed together and splay a hand on his chest. Underneath those well-defined muscles, he goes completely rigid.

Great. He's in shock. Can't say that I blame him. Because I'm scared, too. Scared my not-so-expert kissing abilities will disappoint him. Scared to open up my heart to this sweet, complicated boy.

Still, I have to try. I brush my lips against his in the lightest contact. A monarch butterfly would exert more pressure. Once… Twice… Three times. His lips are soft. His warmth, enticing.

But obviously, I'm not going to make him do anything he doesn't want.

I begin to pull back, but his hands wind around my neck, keeping me in place. And then his mouth moves against mine.

Wow. Oh *wow*. I forget about the weapon in the backpack.

I blank on the Voice that's been appearing in my head. A different kind of electricity shoots through me. So *this* is what a proper kiss feels like. It's light-years away from the tongue Marcus stuck down my throat under the gym bleachers.

Bandit angles his mouth until it fits against mine like adjoining pieces of a puzzle. His lips caress mine with infinite care. He tastes good. Really good. Like cinnamon toothpaste. I'll have to ask him what brand he uses.

He moves his hand to either side of my face, and my heart swells to twice its normal size. So full that it might burst.

He makes me feel…cherished.

And that's a feeling I'd travel to the end of time to find, over and over again.

Minutes or hours later, Bandit eases back and snuggles me against his chest. No pillow has ever cradled me so comfortably. No blanket has ever made me feel safer. I would gladly stay here until the sun sinks behind the trees, enveloping us with the night, but a particularly strong breeze buffets us, reminding me of where we are…and what I was supposed to do.

"I think I'll be able to face the disaster inside now," Bandit says.

"If a mess was all it took for you to kiss me, maybe I should lose our broom," I tease.

His lips twitch. "I could forget to put away the dishes after they're cleaned."

I raise my eyebrow. Is that the best he can do? "Don't shower for a month."

"Leave rotten fruit on the counter until it's crawling with ants." A smile spreads across his face.

Challenge accepted. "Let your baby cousin take off his poopy diaper and smear it on the walls."

"Oh, man," he groans. "I'm getting light-headed again."

Giggling, I pull him into another hug. I like this guy. I really, really do.

He laces his fingers through mine, and for a moment, we just stand there, grinning at each other. "Thank you for being here with me today," he says.

"Anytime," I promise. Is that really my voice? Since when did it get so low? So husky?

He kisses me on the cheek, and we head inside, hand in hand. But not before he picks up my backpack—with the gun inside—and slings it over his shoulder.

My heart stutters. He's just being chivalrous. Right? He didn't try to carry my bag before, but maybe that's because I was clutching it so tightly. I shouldn't overthink it. I *won't* overthink it.

Still, anxiety replaces the glow in my stomach as we speed-walk through the living room and into Charlie's office.

It's warmer in here, probably from the wood furnace that's burning in the corner. Less messy, too. Three neat stacks of documents line the top of the massive oak desk, with only a few loose sheets on the floor.

Dropping both my hand and the backpack, Bandit picks up a piece of paper. "The only thing Charlie is meticulous about is his research. He asked me to take home the pile on the right."

Casually, I nudge the backpack to the wall with my toe, just as "Cat's in the Cradle" blares from Bandit's cell phone.

He grimaces. "That's my dad. I should take it. Sorry."

He lets go of the paper and strides out of the room. Idly, I pick up the sheet. It appears to be a letter from Charlie.

I bite my lip. Should I read it? I don't typically snoop, but if Charlie is my target, then the Voice—the very future—made his correspondence my business.

Decided, I skim the text, my eyes snagging on words like

"contagious" and "infected." Swallowing hard, I start at the beginning.

Dear Chubbs,
Allow me to share my vision with you. Imagine, if you will, an invisible agent that can infiltrate the human body.

I suppress a shudder. I can just imagine Charlie's voice, smooth and strangely melodic. I wouldn't be any more creeped out if he were standing next to me, whispering in my ear.

In the first stage, the agent interacts with your cells, changing them thoroughly and irrevocably, but with little symptoms, little harm. Creating exactly zero alarm. The victim experiences what they consider to be a mild cold. This highly contagious, airborne agent passes on to the next victim and then the next. Until most of the people in the state, the country, maybe even the world, are infected.

I'm vibrating like a timer. Holy Christmas flaming monkeys. He's describing *the virus.* The one that will be invented ten years from now. And this letter is addressed to *Bandit.* Why? What can it mean?

This dormant period lasts anywhere between six months to a year. In the second stage, the virus alters the body's cell, so that the victim is allergic— no, damn near defenseless—against a substance that used to pose little danger. A substance at once ubiquitous and necessary for our survival: the very sun. Chaos will ensue as people begin to drop like flies.

By the time the world's leaders understand why, it will be too late. Half the world's population will already be gone.

My lungs won't fill. My breath comes faster and louder, like an ocean wave gaining momentum. I hoped for a clue, a subtle piece of information.

I didn't expect an outright confession.

Of course, the crime to which he's admitting has yet to occur. It won't be committed for another ten years, by someone other than Charlie.

Someone who goes to my school.

Someone who could very well be the boy I was just kissing.

I sink to my knees next to the scattered papers. *No*, damn it. Bandit can't be the Maker. He's terrified of germs. Why on earth would he invent a virus?

Unless this very obsession leads to a study of viruses, something inside me whispers. *Unless this research leads to the breakthrough that turns Charlie's vision into reality.*

I shake my head, trying to knock the voice out of my thoughts. Instead, electricity zaps across my skull.

Trust my older self to choose this moment to come back.

CHAPTER 28

"I'm mad at you," I blurt. "So mad. But there's no time to yell right now." I glance over my shoulder. Bandit will be back any second. "What do you want?"

"Burn Charlie's research," the Voice says, jittery energy coursing through her words. "The paper in your hand. The stacks on his desk. Destroy them all."

My jaw drops. "You think they won't be able to invent the virus if we get rid of these papers?"

"That's the plan. Charlie's old-fashioned. He hasn't backed up his research anywhere. Now move, Alice, move!"

She doesn't have to tell me twice. Half a second later, I'm sweeping up the sheets and shoving them into the furnace, one by one. The embers catch the edge of the papers and light up, spreading instantaneously. Turning Charlie's equations into ash. I have no idea if these documents contain his research about the virus or a precursor to it. All I know is that watching his genius go up in smoke—literally—makes me feel like I'm finally getting somewhere.

Plus, now that I'm killing Charlie's research, maybe I

won't have to kill him.

One stack down. Two more to go. From the next room, I hear the mumbled garble of Bandit's words. He's still talking to his dad.

Come on, come on. I feed more paper into the furnace. *Hurry up and burn.*

Bandit's voice gets stronger. Either he's raising it in excitement or he's walking closer to the door. I move faster, shoving the sheets four or five at a time into the fire.

One stack left.

His voice gets louder still. He's *got* to be right outside the office. I stuff the rest of the papers inside.

OWWWW. The flame singes the side of my hand and several fingers. At least all the documents are burning now.

I slam shut the furnace door just as Bandit comes into the room. "Hey," he says, taking in my flushed cheeks and my position by the furnace.

My stomach tightens. Here we go.

But instead of hurling accusations at me, he looks at the now-empty desk. "Where are the papers?" he asks, confusion ringing in his voice.

I lick my lips. He hasn't so much as glanced at the furnace. Maybe I'll actually get away with this duplicity. "I don't know. Didn't you take them with you when you left the room?"

"Maybe. I can't remember. I have no idea what's going on anymore." He shoves his hands into his hair, eyes wild. "Charlie's in the hospital. The car came out of nowhere, ran straight into him." The sentences come out haltingly, as though he's speaking words from an unfamiliar language. "I don't understand why he left the house in the first place."

A series of emotions rolls through me—shock, excitement, relief—none of which I can reveal. I move forward and touch his arm. "I'm sorry, Bandit. I know he means a lot to you."

His eyes find mine, loss and confusion swirling in their depths. "My dad says he's in critical condition. He might not make it through the night. Alice, he might..." His voice cracks. He takes a deep breath and tries again. "Uncle Charlie might...die."

I tighten my grip. My mind spins with a million thoughts, a million conclusions. This car "accident" is highly suspicious. No doubt, a person with a mission similar to mine lured Charlie out of his home when he had an appointment with his nephew. That same person probably plowed their car into Charlie's.

Bandit looks dully at my hand. "I'd better go look for those papers," he mumbles and trudges out of the room.

I watch him leave, my triumph growing with each departing step.

"We did it," I whisper as soon as he's out of earshot. "We stopped the virus from being invented. And I didn't have to kill anyone!"

Charlie's in the hospital. He's in critical condition. He'll probably even die.

Whee! I whirl around, my hair flying out in an arc, my lips taking over my cheeks.

Okay, so maybe I shouldn't be feeling so victorious at the thought of someone in the hospital. But Charlie's out of commission. I contributed to the future by destroying the research. I probably just helped save millions of lives. How else am I supposed to feel?

"Not so fast, little girl," the Voice says. "You haven't earned the right to celebrate yet."

"Why not?" I demand. "I stopped the virus, and I didn't have to hurt anyone. Instead, I chose to get to know Bandit, to earn his trust. And that led to him bringing me *here*, where I could burn the papers. So, you see? Killing is not always the only way to make a difference. It's not even the best way."

"Oh, please." I can almost hear the Voice rolling her eyes. "You're so young. So *idealistic*." She says the word like she's eating an *umeboshi* sour plum. "Changing the future is not that simple."

"It *is* this simple," I protest. "You just don't want to admit that love is more powerful than hate —"

I break off as Bandit comes back into the room. His hands, predictably, are empty. "Did you find the papers?" I ask brightly, knowing full well that they're nothing but ash at the bottom of the furnace.

He shakes his head. "Where could they have gone? I know I'm distracted, but this is ridiculous."

I scoop up the backpack and link my arm through his, guiding him to the door. "I'm sure they'll turn up. Were they important?" I ask with an impressively straight face.

"I guess not." He turns and surveys the office once more. "Last week, Charlie asked me for instructions on backing up his research on his hard drive and the cloud, even though he's never been interested before." He looks at me as though I'm from another planet. Another time. "It's like he knew this day was coming."

I stumble on nothing. Backed up his research? Last week?

My brain explodes with keyboard symbols, and I've lost all semblance of speech. Doesn't matter. The Voice articulates my thoughts for me.

"That's what I've been trying to tell you," she says. "The Virus didn't disappear from my future. You're not off the hook yet. You still have to kill someone."

CHAPTER 29

An hour later, I stare into the distorted "mirror" in a gas station bathroom. In fact, it's not a mirror at all but a piece of warped metal with a faintly reflective surface. Still, I can glimpse the lingering shock in my eyes. I can make out the slump of my shoulders.

Did Charlie know? About me? About the mission? He must. He backed up his research *last week*. When he's never been interested before. The timing, once again, is too coincidental.

The Voice said there are several missions occurring simultaneously. Does the Virus Maker also have voices traveling to the past? Did one of them warn Charlie? What does this mean? Who am I up against?

I take a deep breath, and my sneaker squeaks against the concrete floor, sticky with unidentifiable liquids and darkened with dubious stains.

If only I had someone to discuss these questions with—someone smart and insightful, like Bandit. But not only might he be a future mass murderer, but we haven't even spoken for the last forty-five miles. Me, lost in my thoughts. Him, in his grief. The only reason we stopped was because the Tahoe needed gas. Where our silence before was soft and comforting, like a beloved bathrobe, it now resembles a scratchy turtleneck sweater.

Electricity skates across my consciousness. I gulp, instantly on edge. Two visits in a single afternoon? This can't be a positive sign.

"I've got bad news," the Voice announces.

My stomach sinks. "Of course you do. Not once have you ever come to me with anything good."

"Well, excuse the future for being so dreary," she snaps. "You know, none of us *like* living in a world surrounded by death and despair. That's why we're trying to prevent it. This isn't a game, Malice. Millions of lives are at stake."

Maybe it's the disgusting smell of gasoline mixed with urine. Maybe I'm sick of only knowing bits and pieces of the truth. Whatever the reason, my temper flares. "I know that! Why do you think I've done everything you've asked? Even though you never bother to tell me anything!"

"You want information? Fine. I'll give you information." Her thoughts get louder, too, as though we're having a shouting match that spans two decades. "You were right. Charlie's accident was caused by one of our people. But as you know, it didn't stop anything. The virus was still invented." She takes a big breath that fills up her lungs and mine. "The person whose mission was to crash into Charlie's car? He's maxed out on trips to the past. So have all of our other travelers. Which means you're our last hope. You're the only one left."

This stops me. I lower my arms, which are somehow on my hips, just as the door opens and another patron comes in. I skirt around the heavy door and slip outside onto the lawn.

The sun is good and buried behind the trees now, but the

blaze of the gas station lights means that no stars peep out of the sky's inky blackness. Thirty feet away, Bandit pumps gas into the Tahoe, his profile granite, his jaw precisely chiseled.

My heart bumps, and I'm not sure why.

"I don't understand," I whisper. "I'm just a high school girl. How can the future depend on me to save millions?"

"Because you're smart," the Voice says, her tone soft. It's not lost on me that she's talking about her younger self. But there's no arrogance in her words. No pride. Just a simple affection for the girl she used to be. "You're more resourceful than you know. You figured out that Charlie has a voice coming to him, too, preempting our every move. That's why he backed up his files. That's why he wrote clear and explicit instructions to his successor. He had to ensure that his life's work would pass on to someone else. A brilliant young man whom Charlie looks upon as a son. A man who will go on to complete what Charlie started."

She pauses, as though she has to gather the strength to continue. "I wanted you to figure it out on your own, but we only have a limited number of trips to the past, and we've run out." The words are regretful, resigned, and chock-full of sorrow. "Your target's not Charlie. It's Bandit. It's always been Bandit."

I freeze. My heart stops beating; my lungs cease to pump. Even the rush of blood through my veins comes to a standstill.

My eyes, however, continue to track the guy in front of me. Bandit, screwing in the cap of the gas tank. Bandit, who prepared me a bowl of fragrant boiled rice. Bandit, who kissed me as though time didn't matter.

I suspected him from the beginning. Hell, even Charlie's letter was addressed to "Chubbs." But now I've received actual confirmation. Even though the Voice refused to tell me his identity earlier. Even though she said I had to come to the conclusion for myself so that I could feel the unshakable knowledge in my soul.

Well, the unshakable knowledge is inside me, all right. But not in my heart. Never in my soul.

"You mean to say…" I can't speak the words out loud. They're too terrible to think, let alone utter.

"Yes. You have to kill Bandit." My older self has no such problem. How can she be so blunt? Is it because she's wiser than me? Or just harder?

"Killing him will take everything out of you," she continues. "It will test your very limits—of strength, courage, willpower. You'll have to draw on reserves you didn't know you had." I can almost hear her ragged breathing against my ear. Feel her racing heart superimposed over my own. "But you have to save us, Malice. You have to protect our world."

My kneecaps evaporate and I collapse, sinking onto the damp, muddy grass. My mind revolts as though it's a toddler throwing a tantrum, refusing reason, abhorring logic.

I don't want to. I don't want to. I don't want to. It's one thing for me to plot Charlie's death. If given the choice between two evils, would I take out unpleasant, skin-crawling Charlie, so that millions of people can live?

In a heartbeat.

But Bandit?

Maybe. I think so. I don't know!

My older self warned me. She told me not to fall for him. She said it would only make what I had to do later harder.

Did I listen? I tried. Flaming monkeys, I did try.

"Maybe I can talk to him," I suggest, clutching at water. "Warn him about what he'll do so that he can take steps to prevent it now. He's a good guy. He can't possibly mean to destroy the world."

"Don't you dare!" The words tumble out, one on top of

the other. For good measure, she zaps me with another wave of electricity. I'd cry out, but she's already served me with the most intense pain. I'm numb to any more. "There's no guarantee talking will do any good. He's locked into a certain mind-set, and he only hears what he wants.

"Plus, if you tell him now, you risk making the situation worse," she continues, more slowly but just as insistent, just as dire. "He could launch the virus sooner. The lead time could help him improve its efficacy. More people will die. Even more than the millions who have already perished."

I'm falling, sinking, disappearing into the ground. "I don't have a choice, do I?"

She pauses, and hope surges. Is there another way out? An action that could save the future without taking Bandit's life? Please, please, please. I can hear the words. I can almost taste them.

"You always have a choice," she says. Her voice gets softer and more distant, as though she, too, is being sucked away. "It's just that sometimes, that choice is between horrific…and worse."

CHAPTER 30

The headlights cut a swath in the darkness, showing us no more than a few feet of road. But that's okay because the car hugs the mountains, and I'm not sure we could see much beyond the curves anyhow.

I peek at Bandit. He stares straight ahead, both hands on the steering wheel, his lips a tense line. Who can blame him? To me, Charlie is an evil man who will one day help to destroy the world. But to Bandit, he's a beloved uncle who's just suffered a serious car accident.

We zoom around a corner, and my stomach flips. "Slow down," I order, not because I'm actually concerned but just to have something to say. The silence between us has stretched too long, too thin, and I'm afraid it might choke me. "You're going to get us killed."

"I would never put you in any danger," he says, even as he eases his foot off the accelerator.

The car slows, but I hardly notice. Instead, my last words echo through my head. *You're going to get us killed. You're going to get us killed.*

You're going to. Get. Us. Killed.

If only he did drive off the road. *That* would be an easy solution to my problem. I wouldn't have to use the gun. One hard yank of the steering wheel, and we would go careening off the edge. I wouldn't have to clean up the blood or dispose of the body. One jerk of the arm, and I'd be done. An entire world saved.

Of course, I'd die, too, but maybe that wouldn't be so bad. At least I wouldn't have to live with his murder on my hands. Maybe I would balance the scales of justice by sacrificing my life along with his still-innocent one.

"Like what you see?" Bandit arches an eyebrow.

Oops, I'm staring. Although I'm not sure how *he* knows that, since his eyes haven't left the road.

"Very much." I intended the words to be sarcastic, matching his tone, but my voice is too low. My tone too rough. I end up sounding like I did when I promised to be with him anytime.

His mouth parts, and he glances at me before returning his attention to the road. A few moments later, his eyes wander back again, as though he knows he can't divide his focus—but can't resist looking.

I wet my lips. I can just see the news story now. A dark, windy road along a cliff. Two teenagers, distracted by each other. Uncle and nephew, victims of separate car accidents on the same day. A sick twist of fate or something more sinister? The police will investigate. But by then, it will be too late.

Don't think, Alice. Don't let memories of your life run through your mind. Don't fling any goodbyes into the universe, not to Dad or Archie, not even to Lalana or Zeke. Just reach out and yank down that steering wheel.

When I was a kid, I used to be scared to go off the high dive. "You can't dwell on it," Dad counseled. "The longer you stand on the board, the harder it will be to jump. Just get up there and launch yourself into the air. No hesitation, no thinking."

That's what this situation is. The high dive. Higher—and more dangerous—than any fall I'll ever take.

I square my shoulders. And then before I can change my mind, I slide across the bench seat until I'm sitting right next to him, not thinking. My thigh presses against his leg, and I'm still not thinking. I reach for the bottom curve of the steering wheel. Not. Thinking. At. All.

His gaze dips down to the collarbone displayed by my T-shirt and then rises up and fastens on my lips. I stop breathing.

Oh no, I'm thinking again.

Would it be so bad to kiss him on the way to our untimely demise? We're already going to die. Shouldn't we enjoy the last few seconds of life?

I raise my mouth just a fraction of an inch. An instant later, his warm lips are caressing mine. This kiss is even sweeter, even more potent than before. How is that possible? I melt into the leather upholstery. His hand glides up my jean-clad thigh, over my hip, and underneath my T-shift, touching the bare skin of my waist…

The contact sends a jolt through me, yanking me back to my senses. Wait a minute. He's been kissing me—and not looking at the road—for entirely too many seconds. Why aren't we flying off the cliff right about now?

Pulling out of his embrace, I glance wildly out the windshield. We're not hurtling around a corner. The treetops in the valley aren't rushing up to meet us. Instead, the light beams, the yellow stripes on the road, the crumbling facade of the cliffside are all…perfectly…still.

He stopped the car.

I hiss as if burned. And I kinda am. By his presence. By

his proximity. By the lips that unwittingly saved us.

I should've known that he wouldn't lose his head enough to kill us, especially after what happened to his uncle today. Bandit's too responsible. Too conscientious. It was my own fault I got distracted before I could grab the steering wheel.

Scooting back across the seat, I press myself against the passenger door. The cold metal of the handle digs into my back, but I welcome the jab.

"I'm sorry, Alice," he says, his eyes earnest in the dim light. "I know we just kissed for the first time this afternoon. Was this too…fast?"

Fast? I wrinkle my brow, and then I remember his fingers on my bare waist.

"Oh, no. I liked it. I was just…" I flush, floundering for an explanation. "We're in the middle of a twisty mountain road. And, uh, I was thinking that you're having a rough couple of days."

"I have. First the damn cupcake. And now Uncle Charlie." He wrinkles his brow. "Speaking of which…I've been thinking. You said you didn't know the cupcake was poisoned. And I believe you. But you never told me why you gave it to me in the first place."

I raise my eyes to the ceiling. A long scratch winds right above my head. What credible lie can I tell?

Nothing. I've got nothing.

I exhale slowly. "Let's just say…something inside me made me do it."

When all else fails, go with the truth. Or at least a version of it. The Voice *is* inside me. She *did* control my arm. Even if I don't always understand her motivations, I have to trust my older self. Right?

Except…sometimes I don't.

Oh, I have no doubt that she's an older Alice. She sounds

like me, thinks like me. She knows all my secrets. We often breathe together, our actions synced across ten years. More importantly, I feel the truth of who she is in my very cells.

And yet I don't always recognize her. Sometimes, older Alice is frantic. Erratic. She's calm during some visits and angry during others. She occasionally repeats herself. Could the time travel be interfering with her mental faculties? Or is that just wishful thinking, because I don't want to kill Bandit?

"Please, Alice," the boy in question pleads. "Give me something. Anything. I'll take any explanation that makes some sort of sense. I just need some logic in my world, now that everything's been upended."

I can't tell him. I may not be happy with my older self, but I can't knowingly jeopardize the future. Not on a few fleeting tendrils of suspicion.

"I'm sorry," I say quietly. "I wish I could give you a good explanation." For more reasons than one. "But I just can't."

He continues to stare at me, a stripe of his cheek and jaw highlighted by the moon. When I remain silent, he sighs and turns the key in the ignition. The engine roars to life, and the car inches forward, slower than ever.

We travel twenty miles without speaking. I stay plastered against the door, giving up the notion of killing us tonight. First, I'm too frazzled. More importantly, the opportunity is gone. While I pressed my cheek against the window, willing it to cool, we descended from the mountain and got on the highway that will take me home and Bandit to the hospital to see his uncle. I can't take out the gun and shoot him any more than I can yank down on the steering wheel. Any accident now might involve another vehicle. Might end the lives of innocent bystanders. I can't take that risk.

Cars zoom past, their beams painting Bandit's face with dappled light. I collapse against the seat with the temporary reprieve. I'm glad I don't have to kill him tonight. I'm just not ready.

I will be. Tomorrow, or the next day, I'll gather up my courage and do what needs to be done. Or maybe...I'll find another way out.

Bandit is still innocent. He hasn't done anything wrong, not yet. There's got to be another solution to this mess. I just have to find it.

"Tell me this much," he says as he signals the turn onto my street. He hasn't so much as glanced in my direction since he started driving again, and he doesn't look at me now. "This afternoon, when we kissed. Did you mean it?"

I bite my lip. It's a difficult question. Not because I don't know the answer but because I do. Because my feelings for him are stronger and more genuine than anything I've felt in seventeen years. But I don't want to lead him on. Not when this can't possibly end well.

"I meant it," I finally say. "But I've told you before. I don't date in high school."

"You won't give me a straight answer. Now you're sending mixed signals." He pulls in front of my house and turns to me, his gaze searching my eyes, my cheeks, my mouth. "Are you trying to make me lose my mind?"

Again, I consider. I'm not in the sense he means, but my older self *does* want to kill him. So yeah, she probably wouldn't mind if his brains were splattered on the concrete.

"Yes," I whisper. To soften the blow, or maybe because I just want to touch him again, I put my hand on his cheek. The touch is brief. I barely feel the rough skin over his jaw before he jerks his head away.

His eyes blaze under the shine of the streetlamp. "You're succeeding."

CHAPTER 31

I dream.

I'm in a high-speed vehicle screeching around a curve, too fast, too wide. The car spins wildly into space and then free-falls in slow motion. My body strains against the seat belt, and my hair flies around my ears. Loose coins and paper clips float in the air, as though there is no gravity. Delighted, I turn to Bandit to point out this oddity. Instead of a muscular teenage boy, I find a little girl, dark ringlets shot through with gold, bark-brown eyes and burn scars decorating her forehead. "Mommy," she says, distinctly and clearly.

Then the dream shifts.

I'm stuffing the little girl into a wood-burning furnace, along with a stack of papers. I alternate, sticking in a sheet of paper and then ripping off a piece of the girl. I've burned her nose, both ears, and a piece of her cheek before I realize what I'm doing. By then, it's too late. An ember catches onto her hair and spreads through her body. She blackens and disintegrates into ash. Just like Charlie's research. Just like my future.

The dream shifts yet again.

I'm kissing Bandit, the way I did in the car. Hot, hungry licks of his tongue across my lips, inside my mouth, until I feel like I'm in the furnace, too, being burned alive. We're driving along a windy mountain road, but Bandit keeps giving me quick, appreciative glances. "I know I should keep my eyes on the road," he says, "but I just can't." And this makes me burn even hotter.

But then I'm kissing Charlie instead of Bandit. I struggle to get away from him, kick and fight to break free of his grasp. The car spirals down, down, down into a forest of trees, while Bandit watches from behind a set of iron bars.

The dream doesn't so much as shift as it melts away.

I'm in a black void somewhere, floating in ether, my limbs weighing nothing. No, that's not right. I have no limbs. I have no body. I have no head or mouth or lips. I'm just a consciousness, existing in the realm between times.

I'm no longer dreaming. That much I'm sure of. My mind is too sharp for that, my awareness too precise.

I look around. In front of me, a bright line unravels, wavering and fuzzy. Somehow I know if I follow it, I'll return to my own time. I'll exit from this void and reclaim my body in the present world.

I move forward, but then something makes me look down—if "down" is a concept that exists here. Instead of more blackness, streams of color run beneath me.

What is that? I peer closer. Dozens of threads weave in and around one another, of varying thickness. The biggest, shiniest stream runs directly down the middle. The main thread, I realize instinctively. The original one. Every other thread originates from this central cord, branching out before weaving back in again.

I drift lower. The ribbons of color aren't static. Rather,

they're made up of moving...photographs? Scenes? I focus on the moving colors, and they slow down, flipping by more and more leisurely until I see images of...me.

My face in different iterations. The round cheeks of my babyhood, the scarred nose from my toddler years, the acne of my adolescence. And older, too—my face as I have yet to know it, with crow's feet emanating from my eyes and fine wrinkles around my mouth.

Flaming monkeys. I'm watching the *literal* time stream of my life. I always thought the term was just an analogy. I had no idea it was an actual river, with moments of my life rushing past like a current.

Except...the central thread seems to be fraying. In the distance, the colors fade. And then just stop. Even as I look, the loose threads begin to organize around a new stream.

Time travel, I understand with a flash. Every time we interfere with the past, a new thread is formed. Most of the time, it weaves back into the main cord, but change the timeline enough and the threads will organize around a new stream. A new center. A new world.

If I had a mouth, it would be hanging open. Instead, I move even closer to the time stream, the big bright one that's fraying, the one that represents my original life...

...and then I tumble right in.

CHAPTER 32

The music is so loud, it beats inside me, replacing my heart rate, taking over my pulse. Bodies crush around me, and the scents of alcohol and sweat battle in the air. I don't mind the elbow in my stomach. The shoulders knocking into mine make me smile. Nothing can faze me today. Because today, I'm a college graduate.

I... Me... Mine.

There is no younger and older self in this moment. No separation between body and mind.

Why is this trip to the future different from my previous one? I don't know. But when I fell into this Alice's time stream, I also fell into *her*. I'm not simply observing her life.

I'm living it.

"Where is that hunky boyfriend of yours?" a voice says behind me. "Did he say where he was meeting us?"

I glance back. She's older. More black makeup rims her eyes; her top is cut lower than I've ever seen her wear. But there's no mistaking my best friend. Lalana.

My heart leaps, and I can't tell if the emotion belongs

to me or the older Alice. Our minds blend together like a milkshake, and it's impossible to distinguish one from the other.

"He said in the club." I rise onto my tiptoes. But with wall-to-wall people and arm-to-arm jostling, it's like trying to find the one pink grain in a Santorini volcanic sand beach.

Except…there he is!

Miraculously, I glimpse Zeke's beloved Silver Oak baseball cap, turned backward on his head. Four years since we've left high school, and he still wears that old thing.

"Be right back," I murmur to Lalana. I push through the crowd, ducking under limbs and skimming past backs.

I catch up to him and wrap my arms around his torso. Definitely more solid than before. He just started a new workout regimen, and holy wow, is it working. I make an appreciative sound in my throat and run my fingers over his abs.

He turns, and my blood runs still. Oops. It's not Zeke but a stranger with black hair and beautiful eyes that taper at the corners.

Cheeks burning, I snatch away my hands. Damn the long-sleeve collared shirt! "Sorry! I…uh, thought you were someone else."

He arches an eyebrow. "Apparently."

I nearly stumble. There's something familiar about that brow. That bored, bored expression. I know this guy; I'm sure of it.

"We went to high school together," I blurt. "You're that kid who used to have blue hair."

"And you're the girl who has the genius brother," he returns.

This, for some reason, hurts. "Is that all I'm known for?"

"I could say you were the girl whose attention I tried—and

failed—to catch," he says, the corner of his lips twitching, "but that would sound too much like a line."

I can't help it. A shiver moves across my spine, and I drop my eyes before I can stare too hard at his mouth.

A moment later, a hand closes around my arm. I look up. Same height as Bandit, same build. Just as gorgeous, just as smart. And that's where the similarities end. Zeke is African-American, while Bandit is Asian. Zeke is my boyfriend, while Bandit is a stranger. Just a boy who traveled in a different circle at my prestigious private school.

"Let's get out of here." Zeke twines his hand through mine and turns toward the door.

My heart sinks to the alcohol-slicked floor. An intense sense of loss overwhelms me. Why? Why do I have this reaction to a guy I don't know and barely remember? "Nice running into you," I say to Bandit. "Sorry, uh, about the accidental fondle."

Zeke tugs me into the crowd. I glance over my shoulder. Bandit winks at me. He *winks*. I've never known a guy to pull off such a corny move, but if the heat bubbling up my insides is any indication, it works.

Not that it matters. I'll likely never see him again. I grip Zeke's hand as he leads me through the crush of people, propelling me on to our future.

And leaving Bandit to his.

CHAPTER 33

I jerk awake. My pillow is soaked through, and the thin sheet is twisted around my body. I pant, trying to collect my thoughts, to remember how to breathe.

It's okay. It's okay. It was only a dream… Wasn't it? The earlier images fade and twist, becoming even fuzzier and more convoluted the longer I'm awake. But the scene at the club remains clear. Sharp. I can repeat my conversation with Bandit word for word. I feel as though I lived it.

Does that mean the scene actually happens in my future… or at least one of my futures? The original timeline, maybe, before the Voice interfered. Before she threw Bandit in my path a few years too early.

I groan and grab my head. The jellyfish in my mood lamp jump over one another, oblivious to my distress. What is happening? Why is my present and future getting all mixed up?

Suddenly, footsteps pound down the hall. Urgent, rattled—an emergency.

I raise myself on one elbow just as Archie bursts into the room. His hair sticks out in every direction, and he's wielding a wooden rod as though it were a baseball bat. He wears, of course, his Marie Curie T-shirt. Does he sleep in that thing?

"Are you okay?" he gasps. "Where is he?"

I lift my hands in the air. "It's just me, Arch. No one else is here."

He lowers the rod, his eyes narrowing on me, in my striped pajama pants and cotton tank, alone in my bed. "Are you sure?"

"As one of your proofs," I say.

He prowls the room, checking behind my desk, opening the closet, even lifting up my mood lamp, as though he's searching for a false bottom.

"Why do you think someone's here?" I rub my arms. Now that my heart rate is slowing, the sweat is drying on my neck, chilling me.

"I heard you scream." He drops to his knees to check under the bed, sweeping the rod in a wide arc. "I thought you were being attacked."

I shiver. If all goes according to plan, the only person who will be doing the attacking is *me*. And yet, nothing has proceeded like I hoped. Is Archie's concern an omen? Maybe the Maker's allies are organizing a strike on me, right at this very moment.

Archie collapses at the foot of my bed, and the wooden rod bounces harmlessly on the carpet. "I don't know what I would do if something happened to you." He hunches his shoulders, his breath weird and hitching.

I freeze. My brother is actually...crying.

"Archie!" I fly across the bed, throwing my arms around him.

"I have these dreams," he mumbles. "Demons chase me. Every night. No matter how fast I run, no matter where I hide, they always catch me. That's why I hate sleeping." He pulls away from our hug, his eyes blurry behind his glasses. "Tonight, they found you. They ate you up, crunching on your bones, spitting out your organs, and there wasn't a thing I could do to save you."

The shiver turns into a full-body tremble, and it's all I can do not to dive under the covers and take my brother with me. Dreams. Nothing but the unconscious mind processing the events of the day.

And yet, I know better than anyone else that dreams aren't quite so benign. Hell, I just had proof of that.

"I'm right here," I say, ignoring the prickles on my skin. "I'm not going anywhere."

But even as I say the words, I know they're not true. Just a few hours ago, I contemplated flinging myself off a mountain road alongside Bandit.

Archie must've sensed I was in jeopardy. Somehow, he knows that I might be ripped away from him. It's this strange connection we've always had, being born eleven months apart. Not quite twins but closer than regular siblings.

"Listen, Arch," I say. "About Maggie. I don't think we can trust what Lee says—"

"Don't." He takes off his glasses and rubs his eyes. "Even if Lee was lying to me, Maggie is sincere. I know it."

I twist the comforter into knots. "I just want you to be happy."

"I'm not happy," he says, so softly I have to lean forward to hear him above the *whir* of my mood lamp. "I've never been happy."

Guilt slices through the chills. My brother spends the bulk of his time in our basement, alone. I thought that was what he *wanted*. I must be as bad as Dad if I never bothered to make sure.

"You're the only one who's ever loved me." His eyes blaze.

"Do you know I've never had a real friend, ever? I have no idea how it feels to have someone like me for *me*. Not because I'm their brother. Not because of what I can do for them."

"Zeke's your friend."

Archie laughs. The sound could crack windows. "Zeke? I'm not sure you know him nearly as well as you think."

I frown. "What are you talking about? Clearly Zeke cares about you. He's over here all the time!"

"I'm pretty sure Zeke only wants to be my friend because of the brainpower I can lend to his research."

"What research?" I ask, but even as I say the words, my stomach flips. Because Archie already complained to me that Zeke didn't thank him in his acceptance speech. Because Zeke himself told me at the car wash that he needed Archie's help with a conundrum.

Is *this* the reason Zeke won the award over my brother? Because there were two minds working on his project rather than one? More importantly, can research on cell modification lead to the invention of time travel? Or...a deadly virus?

Bandit might be my target, but that doesn't absolve the others of all guilt. This web is too tangled for someone to weave alone. And I have a feeling that my mission can't end— won't end—by killing a single person. I lace my trembling fingers together. "What, exactly, have you and Zeke gotten yourselves into down in that basement?"

"Forget I said anything," Archie mumbles, picking at a loose thread on my bedspread.

"But I don't understand," I protest. "What you're saying about Zeke doesn't match anything I've witnessed—"

"I said, drop it!" My brother's tone turns sharp. He lifts his eyes to mine, and they're so vulnerable, so raw, that they steal the words from my lips. "I just...I want someone to talk to."

"You have me," I say helplessly.

He snorts. "No offense, Alice. But you don't understand half of what I say."

I shrug. Because he's right. I'm not the best companion for him. And even if I were, I can protect him only until the end of summer. After that, my brother's path will diverge from mine. He will go somewhere I cannot follow.

He stands and walks to the door, and I'm seized with a deep, dark certainty that I'm losing my brother. He began this slippery descent into loneliness six years ago, when Mom left. All my efforts to preserve our closeness have been about as successful as stopping the flow of the Amazon River with a toothpick.

"Hey, Arch," I call. "Remember my first day at preschool? I stood in the middle of the blacktop, bawling. And then you came up, took my hand, and led me to the tricycles. We spent the rest of recess chasing each other and laughing our heads off."

The corners of his mouth quirk. "Yeah. I remember."

"You were my hero that day. And every day after that."

He searches me like I'm a faded equation in an ancient textbook. "Your only friends back then were your dolls, squirt. So forgive me if I'm not impressed."

"I only owned, like, *one* doll," I protest.

"Exactly. Even among your pretend friends, you only had one." He smiles, which never fails to make my heart lighter.

And yet, I can't shake my uneasiness. His casual teasing reassures me that my brother is still there, underneath the loneliness. But it doesn't tell me what he's really thinking. It doesn't help me close the gap.

Archie adjusts his glasses and grasps the doorknob. "Be careful, Alice. There's so much evil in this world. I don't want you tangled up in it."

One blink later, he is gone.

CHAPTER 34

I don't go back to sleep after my brother leaves. I can't. My mind spins too wildly; too many emotions push and jostle at my heart. Anxiety over Archie. Dread at my upcoming mission. Confusion over my dream.

I'm more certain with each passing minute that the scene in the club happened in my original timeline. Does that mean I'll end up with Zeke? Is Bandit nothing more than a blip in my life?

At least I know that I'll find love and happiness, even if it's not with Bandit.

That should make him easier to kill.

I wince like I do every time I think about my mission. But that won't work. I need to desensitize myself to the words. Numb myself to the idea.

Kill Bandit. Kill Bandit. Kill Bandit.

A phrase to block out the soft feelings that threaten to arise. A mantra to turn me into a murdering machine.

I don't want to kill him. Every organ inside me rebels at the thought. I can't help but cling to the hope that there's another way. He can change. I believe in his goodness, and I just can't accept that death is the answer.

And yet…millions of lives are at stake. The Voice told me in no uncertain terms what I must do to protect the future.

Can I really defy my older self, and her hard-earned wisdom, on a whim? Can I risk all those people in a deluded attempt to save one boy?

I don't know.

Ping. Ping. Ping. The cell phone on my nightstand sounds with three successive text messages. Rolling over on my mattress, I pick up the device, almost afraid to look.

Sweetest Boy Alive: I'm not telling u what I'm wearing. This time I'm just gonna show u

The text is followed by an image of Bandit—more precisely, a selfie of his handsome face and solid body. In it, he peers at me through the blue hair flopping over his forehead, his eyes piercing and vulnerable. He's wearing khaki pants and a black T-shirt emblazoned with the words *Sorry, not sorry*. The last two words are crossed out with a thin strip of masking tape.

Sweetest Boy Alive: *Last night didn't end how I wanted. Can we talk? Plz*

My breath catches. He's apologizing…with his clothes? Even though *I'm* the one who won't give him answers? That's as cute as the baby hedgehog videos I watch on YouTube. Helplessly, I brush my finger across his face. The image moves as soon as I touch the screen, pulling me back to reality.

I shake my head roughly. What am I doing? I'm supposed to *kill* him, not caress him. The millions of dead people couldn't care less how adorable he is.

Sweetest Boy Alive: The rents r out of town. That's not a come-on, I promise. just...if u want 2 talk, I'm here

I drop the phone like it burns me. This is it, then. The perfect opportunity to fulfill my mission. His parents gone, the house empty. I can't put off this task any longer.

Tonight. I have to kill him tonight.

I take breath after breath, faster and faster. But I can't fill my lungs. I can't stop my panting. Bandit can no longer be the guy I'm crushing on. I refuse to think about him as a person, as the boy who drinks sweet chrysanthemum tea because it reminds him of his khun yai. I have to forget his smiles, pretend I never knew the feel of his lips.

He can only be one thing to me: the target I need to take out to save the world.

So I change into workout clothes and do what I always do when I need to not think: run. Down the street, through the park with the rusted playground, onto the wooded trail that will take me on a four-mile loop.

Kill Bandit.

The sun inches into the sky, sneaking fingers of light through the gaps in the leaves. The shade offered by the densely grown trees is cool and blissfully serene.

Kill Bandit.

My heart pounds, my muscles ache, my feet slap at the dirt path. I revel in the sensations, pushing myself harder. Faster. Longer.

Kill Bandit.

Is my soul sufficiently numb yet?

I slow to a jog as I round the corner back to my house. I can do this. I'll fire a bullet into his chest, just like I researched on the internet, and poof, he'll disappear from our world, taking with him unimaginable loss and sorrow. All I have to do is not think. Not feel...

My best friend sits on our front porch, her fingers laced loosely over her knees. Her hair is pulled back in a simple ponytail, and she's holding a blown-glass butterfly, with wings so fine they might as well be gossamer.

I suck in a breath. She's here. She's actually here.

"Lalana!" I launch myself at her, wrapping my arms around her back. "How are you?"

I'm almost sobbing, I'm so excited to see my best friend. But her spine is as stiff as a board, and she holds the butterfly as though it were a life preserver. She's not hugging me back.

I retreat, my hands dropping awkwardly to my sides. "I've been so worried," I say quietly. Part of her hood is tucked into her collar, and I have to fist my hands so I don't reach out and straighten it.

"Have you really?" She raises her eyebrows. Uh-oh. I know that expression. Lalana has the kindest, most generous heart in the world, but she doesn't put up with *anybody* mistreating her. Apparently, even me.

"Of course," I say helplessly. "You're my best friend."

She strokes a finger over a butterfly wing, not looking at me. "The school suspended me for a week. Since this is my first offense, the lawyer recommended we enter a guilty plea for possession and pay the fine. Not a big deal, in the larger scheme of things. But that's not all." Her fingers tighten on the butterfly. "As you can probably guess, my parents are shipping me out to California. They've had enough of my wild behavior, and they're putting an end to it, *diaw nee*. I'll finish high school out there."

"I'm sorry. I…" The words fade, as though they know how hypocritical they are. "When do you leave?"

"It hardly matters, does it, when this will be the last time you see me." Finally, she looks up. At last, those dark-brown eyes drill into mine. "I know the marijuana was yours, Alice."

My heart stops. "What… What are you talking about?"

"I thought you might be using drugs. You were acting so weird. Waltzing up to Bandit and telling him you loved him?" She shakes her head. "I can't believe I thought you were covering for me. Wow, was I deluded."

Her voice hardens with each word. Becomes so brittle, it might shatter. "I know you put the weed in my locker. There was a huge chip of your sparkly blue nail polish on the Ziploc bag."

"Lalana…" I swallow hard. What can I say? Other than the drug use, everything she's claiming is true. And I can't lie to her. Not when I've put her through so much grief. "I can't tell you how sorry I am."

"Why?" Her glittering eyes imprison me. "Why would you do this? Were you so desperate not to get caught that you'd rather sell out your best friend?"

"No! That's not it at all!" The need to defend myself, to explain, overwhelms me. "You're the best friend I've ever had. I would never… Not unless I had to. Do you understand? I can't explain now. But I will someday. I promise. When I can, I'll tell you everything—"

She stands, cutting off my babbling. "Goodbye, Alice." The words sink like lead to the bottom of my stomach. She shoves the butterfly at me. "Here, take this. You thought it was beautiful, and I'm not taking a present from some creepy secret admirer to California."

"Wait." I reach for her, but she's already walking away. "Why are you still moving? Aren't you going to tell everyone the truth?"

"No." She continues walking.

"Is it because of the future?" I'm pleading now. Straight-up begging. "How are you connected to this mess? You asked me to stay away from Bandit. Why? Are you on a mission, too?"

She turns. An expression I can't read crosses her face, which is ridiculous. She's my best friend. I know every one of her expressions. Annoyance when one of our ignorant classmates ask her "what" she is, rather than "who." Amusement when I claimed last winter that I was going to iron my clothes to stay warm. Shame when her parents argue in front of me. But this look—it's like a haunting mash-up of all the emotions she's ever displayed.

"I don't know what mission you're talking about," she says slowly. "But I told you to stay away from Bandit because he knows secrets about my family. Secrets I didn't want anyone to find out." Her cheeks flush red under the brilliant sun. "My dad cheated on my mom, okay? That's why he's there and we're here. Me finishing high school was just an excuse. And now, because of you, I screwed up my parents' plan of saving face."

"I'm sorry." I grip the blown glass, its sharp wings digging into my palms. "But you could've told me. My dad cheated, too. I would've understood."

She rubs her eyebrows. "It's not you, Alice. This carefully crafted silence is cultural. We keep dirty secrets to ourselves. Locked up tight in the family vault."

"Tell your parents it was me," I urge. "That way, you won't have to move."

She sighs, an exhalation that moves through her entire body. "I'm not going to do that."

"How come?"

"Because in sixth grade, when my mom said I had to put lettuce on my peanut butter sandwich, you didn't laugh at me. You even took a bite and said it was delicious." The words roll out of her. "Because in eighth grade you had a crush on Ryan Park. I know because you wrote his name over and over in your notebook. And still, you set me up with him. You stood by and were nothing but supportive when we dated for the next year." She takes a shaky breath. "Last semester, when I was flunking history, you tutored me every day after school. Even when you were sick. Even when you had to take the SATs the next day."

Her eyes catch the sunlight. They're more than glittery now. They're glossy with unshed tears—or maybe that's just the sheen of liquid bathing my own eyes. "I don't know why you put that marijuana in my locker, but you are—you used to be—a good friend. Up until a few days ago, the very best." She swallows. "The colleges will ask if you've ever committed a crime. One time, after an Avengers marathon, we were giddy from Tony's snark and Cap's smile—"

"And Thor's abs," I interrupt. "Can't forget those."

"Yes. Thor's incredibly ripped six-pack." She smiles faintly. "You confessed to me that your secret wish was to follow Archie. Your wildest dream, one that you never told anyone else, was to get into Harvard. A guilty plea will affect that."

"I was practically drunk when I said that!" I protest. "A shirtless Chris Hemsworth would scramble anyone's mind. Harvard's never going to accept me…"

"You have to try," she says fiercely. "Me? I'll be happy going to any old college. So I'm not telling my family. The authorities don't need to know. I just hope you find what you're looking for."

My heart is battered, each knock against my rib cage bruising it further and deeper. "Oh, Lalana, I don't deserve you—"

"No. You don't," she cuts in. "Which is why you don't get to *keep* me. We're no longer friends, Alice. I don't forgive you. I'm just not willing to screw up your entire future. Got it?"

I nod despairingly. I have nothing else for her. No words, no actions. Not a single way to make any of this better.

"Don't contact me again," she says with finality. "That wasn't my mom who texted you. It was me."

With this pronouncement, she walks away. This time for good.

I close my eyes. It's as though a lightning bolt has struck me, slicing off a piece of my heart. I know instinctively that this scar won't heal. The severed part will not be reabsorbed by the whole. Instead, the mutilated organ just sits on my chest, beating. Hissing. Hurting.

The Voice warned me this would be hard. She said I would have to compromise everything in order to save the future: my integrity, my character—my soul.

When I open my eyes, the butterfly lies broken in two in my hands. The Voice was right. Because with Lalana leaving, I've lost more than just a friend. I've broken more than a piece of art. I've sacrificed a piece of my soul.

How much more will I have to surrender tonight?

CHAPTER 35

'm back in the void. One moment, I'm lying on my bed after my shower, physically exhausted by my run. Emotionally wrecked from my encounter with Lalana. And the next moment, I'm here.

How I arrived at this place, I'm not sure. But I don't think about it too closely. There are too many things to wonder, too much space to explore. In front of me, once again, is the bright, fuzzy thread that will lead me back to my present. Below me is the never-ceasing, never-slowing river of my original life.

I could go back to my time, my present, my bed—or I could take another dip in the stream. Falling in the first time was an accident, but this time… This time would be deliberate.

Is this dangerous, what I'm considering? Maybe I have no business poking around in the original Alice's life. Maybe I'll learn something that will adversely impact *my* future.

But there's no question what I'll do, not really. I need answers, and now I know where to find them.

Decided, I steel my consciousness and jump back into the rushing stream of colors with both my metaphorical feet.

· · ·

Pain. Pain like I've never known it, pain like I've never imagined, explodes inside me, stretching my cells beyond their limits, snapping nerves beyond repair. It takes over my body, my mind, my soul, turning everything I know and everything I am into one unending wail.

"You can do this," a voice says in my ear. My husband. I grip his hand so hard, I swear I hear the crunch of bones. Instead of giving me a broomstick to hold, like he joked before I went into labor, he just takes my hand even more firmly. "This is the ordinary miracle, Alice, and you are nothing short of miraculous. You've shown that to me a million times. Show me again. Bring our daughter into this world."

I want to weep. I want to surrender. I want to collapse onto this narrow cot and disappear, because then I won't have to feel this pain anymore.

But instead of giving in, I focus on his words. I think about the first time I heard that phrase: the ordinary miracle. I remember a car wash, long ago, of a girl in cutoff jean shorts, the soapsuds wetting her legs. Of the boy for whom she yearned with every cell in her body.

They were so young, so innocent. As worthy of protection as the baby inside me now.

I wish they didn't have to grow up to live in this world. I wish my baby didn't have to be born into conditions so desolate.

But it's too late for wishes now.

An indescribable pressure rips through me—and then a baby swaddled in a cotton blanket is placed on my chest. I sob. It's over. I can't believe the pain has finally stopped.

Through my tears, I see that the baby is wrinkled and not terribly cute. Her skin is the color of an acorn, which is perhaps fitting because she looks more like a chipmunk than an angel. She moves her tiny fist through the air, bopping herself on the forehead, and I free-fall through zero gravity into love.

I will never abandon her, I swear to myself. *I will travel from timeline to timeline to keep her safe.*

I've already chosen her name. Hope. The thing with feathers, as Emily Dickinson said. She will help us transition from this world into a new one.

Heaven help us, may we all survive.

CHAPTER 36

That night, back in the present, I thrust up on the frame of a window outside of Bandit's house. It doesn't budge. Great. At least the latch doesn't appear locked. Instead, the glass seems welded shut by paint and old age.

The moon shines in the sky, full tonight, as though it's casting a spotlight on me and my upcoming crimes. The smell of budding growth mixes with the rich dampness of the earth, and the ground is hard and packed beneath my sneakered feet. My breath puffs into the air. There's so much vapor, you'd think I was sneaking into a factory.

I wish. Because then, my only offense would be burglary. And not murder.

I don't know how I keep traveling to the black void. Why I'm getting flashes of my original time stream. But like my trip to the underground tunnels, this latest vision is exactly what I need to propel me to act.

It reminds me of what's important. Hope. The baby girl I swore to do right by, since my mother couldn't, wouldn't do right by me. She's the priority. Everything else fades into the background. Even boys. *Especially* boys.

Zeke stopped by our house earlier tonight. He was visiting my brother, and I was relieved that Archie seemed pleased to see him.

Before Zeke descended to the basement, he gave me a present: a framed photograph of a Sevillanas dancer, whose flowing white dress was splashed with crimson polka dots. The picture is compositionally perfect, but my eyes filled because he *knew* how much I would appreciate the subject matter.

This boy gets me. He understands and supports my dreams, through and through.

"You didn't tell me it was your birthday a couple of weeks ago," he said. "I only found out because Archie mentioned it the other day."

I looked at Zeke, with his kind eyes and his brilliant smile, and tried to imagine him as Hope's father. The name fits, given our mutual love for Emily Dickinson.

It gives me comfort to think that my husband will be Zeke. Despite Archie's recent misgivings, Zeke is loyal, dependable, hot—I could do a whole lot worse. More importantly, the vision confirms that I'll be fine without a certain blue-haired boy in my life.

As much as I like Bandit, he's just someone I met a few days ago. He's not my destiny, not my fate. I cannot risk the life of my baby, of millions of people, on the hope that he will change.

I ease to the next window. I refuse to think, damn it. At least Bandit's house is a single, sprawling story. Still not thinking. I wipe my sweaty palms on my leggings—murder black, what else?—and position them under the window frame. The peeling paint scratches my skin. I take a deep breath.

One... Two... Three... *Push.*

This window actually moves, screeching and screaming against its rusty grooves. I hold my breath, hoping that the Sakdas don't have a security system. I didn't notice one last time I was here, but I wasn't looking, either.

Ten, twelve, fourteen heartbeats race by. No alarm blares. No angry voices demand to know what I'm doing.

I sag against the wooden ledge, limp with relief. As first steps go, this one's pretty minor. I'll have to take much harder, more permanent action before the night is over. But I rest a minute anyway. Catch my breath and repeat the mantra.

Kill Bandit. Don't think. Kill Bandit. Don't think.

Fortified, at least for the moment, I hoist myself through the window and stumble onto the thick carpet. It's quiet inside. A clock ticks softly, and a faucet emits a sporadic drip. And my heart. It's thudding so loudly, I'm surprised I can hear anything else.

I swallow. And immediately have to swallow again. There's no less than an ocean of spit inside my mouth. Here's hoping it doesn't drown me.

Judging from the shadows, I've landed in the living room. Couches sit across an entertainment center, and picture frames line the mantel. The light is too dim for me to make out the photos, and it's just as well. I don't need the ghosts of Bandit's younger selves mocking me.

Automatically, I pat my pockets. Gun taken from my backpack, check. Spindle from the chair that my mother flung at us, check.

The gun is self-explanatory. After lugging it to Charlie's cabin and back, maybe I'll finally be able to use it.

And the spindle? Turns out, that was the stick Archie carried into my room, the one he was wielding like a baseball bat. I grabbed it just as I was about to leave. The wooden rod is small but hard and sturdy. It won't kill anyone, but that's the point. If my night devolves into a fight, I'd like to have a nonfatal weapon, just in case.

Oh, who am I kidding? If I end up in a fight, I'm screwed. The only hope I have of taking out Bandit is if he stays asleep the entire time.

I sneak down the hall. So far, so good. Every few steps, the floor creaks, and my pulse accelerates. But the noises are nothing out of the ordinary. They don't even approach the particularly loud shriek, made during a sleepover years ago, that had me jumping so high I about hit my head on the ceiling fan.

Turned out, it was just Lalana returning from the bathroom in her squeaky ladybug slippers. I swear those slippers were a dog's chew toy, never meant to be worn. But Lalana, being Lalana, she insisted on wearing them anyway.

The thought of the ridiculous footwear makes me smile. And then frown as sorrow slips through the cracks of my memory.

This won't do. I can't let *any* emotion approach the walls I've erected around my heart.

Kill Bandit. Don't think. Kill Bandit. Don't think.

Four doors line the hallway. The first one on the right leads to a bathroom, narrow and tiled, with a porcelain tub and toilet. If I flipped on the lights, I bet I would see veins running through the granite countertop.

I don't flip on the lights.

The door on the left opens into a guest room. Stacks of unopened boxes are piled against a wall, and a twin-size bed boasts a pretty paisley comforter. Not Bandit's room, that's for sure. I doubt he'd fit on the bed, for one thing. And second, I just don't see him with that print.

I hit the jackpot on my third try.

Science medals and basketball posters jockey for space

on the walls, and a lava lamp sits on the corner of his desk, throwing iridescent blue light all over the room.

Bandit is sprawled on his back on the bed, one arm hanging off the mattress, the other draped over his eyes.

I freeze, my feet digging roots into the floor. My eyes, however, follow their own path. They start at his long and elegant toes and move up. Past the sheet twisted around his midsection to the well-defined planes of his abs and chest. The air gets stuck in my throat. He, uh…doesn't sleep with a shirt. Hell, maybe he doesn't sleep with any shorts, either. The sheet blocks my view, and I certainly won't be moving it to find out.

But wow. He looks good draped in blue light. Really good. Surprise, not at all surprised.

I release a shaky breath. Where is the Voice when I need her? I could use someone to order me around right about now. To prod me unmercifully with electric shocks until I comply.

Come on, Voice! Zap my brain. I don't know if I can do this by myself. I need you.

Instead of a wave of electricity, however, memories wash over me. Bandit's cinnamon toothpaste taste when he kissed me on the balcony. The way his eyebrows lift, haughty and aloof. His undisguised pain when he talked about my photo of the little boy and his grandmother.

I try to stem the tide of memories, try to recall the mantra. *Kill Bandit, don't think, kill Bandit…*

It's no use. So effective before, the mantra's now just a mouthful of words whose meaning I can't comprehend.

Can I really do this? Can I actually aim a gun at this guy's chest—and kill him?

I'm shaking now, trembling from head to toe. I'm not a murderer. But I never thought I would tell a stranger I loved him, either. I never dreamed I would frame my best friend.

Extraordinary circumstances require extraordinary actions.

I may not want to kill him, but I have to. The lives of millions of people are at stake. The life of my child, with her springy curls.

I swore I would go to the ends of time to keep her safe. Well, here's my chance to prove it. Because after I kill this boy, I will surely go to hell.

The breath flows out of my body until I'm completely, utterly still. Until my mind is devoid of all thought, all memory. I cross to the bed in three long strides and pick up his hand. So warm, so alive. But not for long.

I fumble in my pocket. But my brain's not working properly, and I reach into the wrong one with the wrong hand. Instead of the gun, I pull out the spindle, the one inscribed with my mother's customized words of wisdom. I look down just as a blanket of blue light washes over the room. The words carved into the spindle come into focus, and I read them for the first time.

Hope must be strongest when hope appears lost.

I frown. The statement jostles something in my brain. Not just because it contains my daughter's name but also because the saying is familiar. Too familiar. I've heard it somewhere before. Or read it...

My hand falls open, and the spindle slips through my fingers and thunks onto the floor. That's it. I remember how I know that sentence.

I read it in a note to Lalana from her secret admirer.

CHAPTER 37

My brain explodes with a million questions, a gazillion ramifications. I don't get it. How can the line from Lalana's secret admirer be engraved on this spindle? *How?*

I press my hands against my temples, but it does nothing to calm the tornado swirling inside. I almost can't think. I almost can't go down the rabbit hole to the logical conclusion.

But there's a gun in my pocket. I was seconds away from shooting Bandit. So I have to do this. I have to follow this path to see where it leads.

Tilting my face to the ceiling, I take a long, slow breath, focusing on the ballooning of my abdomen. And then another. And another, until I'm capable of basic analysis again.

Archie's been carrying around the spindle since my mother left…the same saying appears in Lalana's note… therefore, Archie must be Lalana's secret admirer.

Not Bandit.

And if Archie is Lalana's secret admirer, then that means the Voice was trying to separate her from *my brother*. So that he wouldn't feel so betrayed. So that there would be one less way for him to lose touch with reality. And that means…that means…

This is where I falter. This is where my mind shuts down, erecting a wall so impenetrable that my thoughts can't go any further.

I sway. The room spins dizzily around me, the blue light messing up my sense of direction. I stumble, and my knees crash into something hard and metal. I pitch forward and—

OOMPH.

I land in a heap on top of solid muscle and taut skin. Bandit.

He jerks awake, and then I'm flying through the air, my back slapping against the firm mattress. Within seconds, he's got my wrists above my head and the rest of my body pinned underneath him. Good instincts, this guy.

His mouth drops when he gets a look at me. "What the…? Alice, what's going on? What are you doing here?"

The sight of his bare skin sends a jolt through me, scattering my thoughts even further. There's just so much of it—on his chest, on his torso, on the legs nestled against mine.

His thighs press down on me, and the contact is too much. Too confusing. I put my hands on his chest and push with all my strength. Startled, he eases back, letting go of my hands.

He sweeps his gaze over my body, taking in the black knit hat. My long-sleeve black shirt. Black joggers. My sneakers— you guessed it: black.

Not exactly the outfit you would wear if your intent was to seduce.

The realization registers on his face.

"You have exactly ten seconds to tell me what this is about, or I'm calling the police," he growls.

My heart leaps into my throat, and my eyes dart all

over the room, searching for an escape. No exit materializes, unfortunately.

He can't call the police. But how do I stop him? I can't even untangle the thoughts in my own head. What can I spit out that will satisfy him?

"Five seconds," he says warningly. "Four… Three… Two…"

I have no other choice. Reaching up, I press my mouth against his. Warm, just as I remember. Soft, like I'll never forget.

His lips go still under mine, and then he's kissing me back, hard and desperate. My mouth parts, and that's even better. I didn't mean to enjoy this. I only intended to buy myself time. But he's kissing me like he's drowning, and I'm his one last hope for air. I might as well not have a pulse if I don't die a little, too.

I wind my hands around his neck. His fingers go to my waist, careful to stay on top of the cotton material. Impatient, I yank up my shirt, revealing my bare stomach.

I want. I want to stay in this bed, with our limbs intertwined, for the rest of our lives. I want to kiss him until we melt like a beeswax candle. I want to have never heard of the Voice, to possess no inkling of the future, to bear no responsibility for saving the world.

But even now, the future reaches its long, shadowy fingers into the present. The images of a flailing baby, of a little girl with pigtails, float at the edge of my consciousness. Somewhere on my original timeline, she's dying slowly, day by day. I can't ignore that just because Bandit Sakda is a good kisser.

The best, actually. His kisses caress not just my lips but my entire body, making me feel protected, now and for the rest of time.

Which is the biggest illusion yet. If I don't change the course of the future, then none of us is safe.

I want…but I can't.

He must reach the same conclusion because he wrenches away his mouth, and it's like pulling away from an electric current.

"Don't," he pants as we both sit up. "Don't kiss me because you're trying to distract me. Or because it's part of some master plan I don't know about. I want you to kiss me for one reason alone, and that's because you want to."

I do, I wish I could say. *This is what I want more than anything.*

But the gun jabs me in the leg, reminding me of why I'm here and what I meant to do, before I read the inscription on the spindle. Before everything that used to make sense all of a sudden didn't.

"Are you in love with Lalana?" I blurt.

He blinks. "Huh?"

"Lalana. Your old family friend, the one you've known since you were kids, peeling layers off your *kahnom chun*. Are you in love with her? Did you leave letters in her locker, proclaiming your undying devotion?"

He arches an eyebrow. Ah. His signature bored face. My heart actually squeezes when I see it.

"First, that's *still* how I eat my *kahnom chun*," he says. "And second, how could you think that? Lalana's like a sister to me. Besides, she's your best friend. I'd be kind of a jerk for falling for you both."

Now it's my turn to blink. "You're falling for me?"

The corners of his lips twitch. "Well, yeah. I assumed you knew that."

"I *assumed* you thought I was an untrustworthy girl who refused to explain anything."

"That too." His smile fades before it has a chance to bloom. "You never answered me. What are you doing here?"

I wince. Minutes have passed, and I *still* haven't come up with an adequate response.

"Well, it's not to ravish me, that's for sure," he says. "If it were, we wouldn't be talking right now." He searches my face. "That means you must be here because of this." Before I can react, he plucks the gun out of the pocket of my pants.

My jaw drops. "How did you know that was there?"

He blinks at the weapon, whose metal glints ominously in the moonlight. "I knew something was trying to brand itself on my skin. But holy crap. I didn't realize it was a *gun.*"

He rolls the weapon on his palm, weighing it. Considering it from every angle.

It would serve me right if he shot me. After all, *I* tried to kill *him.* He doesn't know I had a good reason, but so what? If I succeeded, he'd still be just as dead.

"What, uh, are you going to do with that?" My mouth is as dry as the Kalahari Desert.

He picks up my hand, smiles mock seductively…and then reaches past me to set the gun onto his desk.

"What did you think I was going to do? Shoot you?" He glances at the weapon and shudders. "Was that your intention?"

"Not anymore," I mutter.

He shakes his head. "Am I supposed to thank you for that? Or be annoyed because, *I don't know*, you planned to kill me?" His eyes pierce into me, cutting through the layers of my confusion, pushing aside my deception and my lies to the real me. The girl I am right here and now. In this present, this timeline. "I want to trust you, Alice. My gut says you're a good person. But you sure aren't making it easy for me."

The truth suddenly coalesces in my mind. The swirling questions, the ill-fitting puzzle pieces—all of it descends into one stark realization.

He's on my side.

"A voice in my head told me to kill you," I blurt.

His eyebrows jump. "You're hearing voices in your head?"

"Yes! I mean, no. Not multiple voices. Just one voice. My older self." I stop. Tilt my head to the glow-in-the-dark solar system on his ceiling. I have the same stars in my bedroom. If the situation weren't so grave, I might've smiled at the thought of the two of us lying under the same model universe all these years.

"Don't worry," I continue. "I'm not losing touch with reality. I promise this situation is much more rational that it sounds. My older self has been traveling from the future, whose population has been decimated by a virus. She said I had to kill you in order to save the world. I had every reason to believe her. Every sign pointed to you as the Maker. But then I read the inscription on the spindle…"

Scanning the plush carpet, I snatch up the wooden rod from where it rolled next to the nightstand. "And if you're not in love with Lalana…"

I look into his eyes. Dark brown. Tapered at the corners. Aloof but sincere. Confused as hell but still trusting. Always trusting. I'm probably not making much sense to him, but it doesn't matter. Every cell in my body, every filament in my brain, tells me I'm right.

I just need to say the words out loud in order to believe them.

"You're not my target. I don't think you've ever been my target." I swallow hard. And push out the conclusion I've reached. "My older self has been lying to me all along."

CHAPTER 38

Two, maybe three seconds pass, but I live an eternity in my mind. The conclusion I've reached feels too big for my brain. So epic, so all-encompassing, that it fills up this time stream and reaches its fingers out to another.

"I have to go." I leap up from the bed.

"Wait!" Bandit pushes the hair off his forehead. "You can't just drop this bombshell and take off. I have so many questions—"

"Me too," I interrupt, edging toward the door. "But I can't explain anything to you until I figure out the answers myself."

"But, Alice…" He stands and begins to move toward me.

"Later," I blurt out. "I have to get out of here."

I flee from his house, praying that he doesn't follow. My heart's pounding so hard that I wouldn't be able to hear footsteps, even if there were any. But when I arrive home, winded from the run, and I see that I'm alone, I stop to take a shaky breath.

I have only one destination in mind. One spot that makes any sense. One place where I hope to find my answers.

I head straight to the bedroom next to mine. The one that's been by my side ever since we moved into this house—and every house before that.

Archie's room is a mess: Marie Curie T-shirts and khaki shorts strewn on the floor, stacks of old textbooks burying his desk. The comforter hangs half on, half off the mattress, and the pillow is a misshapen ball shoved in the corner. Dawn is fast approaching, judging by the soft splashes of light dispersing the shadows in the room.

And my brother's not here.

I sink onto the tangled mess of his sheets, trying not to breathe in the musky scent of dirty laundry and old books. He was home last night. Right before Zeke visited, I went down to the basement to bring him a snack.

"Brother Bear," I said in the world's worst British accent. "May I interest you in some Oreos and a spot of milk?"

Archie dragged his eyes from the computer screen, blinking like I was a baffling line of code. "Huh?"

"It's from Berenstain Bears," I said, feeling faintly foolish. "You know how Mama Bear was always giving them milk and cookies? And in one of the books, she was teaching them manners?"

His blinks only grew more pronounced.

"They decided to be extra polite to dissuade Mama, and that made us go around for weeks, speaking in a British accent—" Cutting myself off, I sighed. "Oh, never mind. You don't remember."

Although I don't see how he could forget. My parents were always busy, and my genius brother started reading when he was three. So, guess who was in charge of my bedtime stories? Together, we systematically worked through a hundred Berenstain Bears titles, with him reading out loud and me tucked against his side.

The memory of it is indelibly imprinted on my mind. But I guess Archie's got more important things crowding his gray matter.

Turning, I began to trudge away.

"Why, Sister Bear, I didn't recognize you without your pink bow," Archie said in an affected, posh voice.

I stopped in my tracks, delight spreading like honey across my face.

"And look! You *bought* these cookies instead of making them. My stomach and I thank you."

I puffed out a breath to feign annoyance. "Ha-ha. Brother Bear the comedian."

"Could be. Those bears learned how to do *everything*. How did I go so wrong as to not read you a book teaching you how to cook?"

I snatched up an Oreo and threw it at his head, but we were both grinning like forest animals sitting down to a feast of grilled salmon and wild berries.

The conversation rolls through my mind now, lodging in my throat like a section of honeycomb. I just need to see Archie. Talk to him once more, and I'll know that the thoughts buzzing around my head are ludicrous.

I grab two fistfuls of the loosened sheet. Now that I'm alone with my thoughts, I finally let myself remember the Voice's words:

Lalana's secret admirer grows up to be the Virus Maker.

There. She said it. An equation as clear as $1 + 1 = 2$.

But that doesn't mean I have to believe her.

She straight-up lied to me about Bandit. Which means I can't trust *anything* she's told me.

Maybe my actual target really is Lee Jenkins. He's cruel enough. He has access to time travel through his relationship with his old friend Cristela.

Or, hell, maybe it's Cristela herself. The poison that made Bandit sick didn't get into the cupcake by itself, and she admitted that time travel is her passion.

And then... And then...there's Zeke. I didn't want to entertain the possibility before, but he has the scientific expertise. Charlie even expressed interest in his research.

But Zeke's my boyfriend in the future. My *husband*. Does that automatically absolve him? Or is that the very reason the future chose me to go on this mission?

I gulp at the air, my pulse racing faster and faster. I feel guilty even working through this analysis. But in the future, people are dead. More are dying. I have to go down this path. I have to view the suspects objectively. I have to consider the possibility that the person I need to kill might...be...my brother.

NO! my mind screams. My stomach heaves. Every cell in my body revolts.

I dig my fingernails into my palm until I feel the pain at my core. *Just consider it. You owe the future this much. Is it possible that Archie is the target?*

He's always had a soft spot for Lalana. He would look at her whenever she was around, a small smile on his face. Add in the telling quote from the spindle, and it's pretty clear he's the one in love with her.

Does that mean he's the Virus Maker?

That's the million-dollar question. Or at least, the millions-of-*lives* question. I lean back on Archie's bed and look at the darkened ceiling. No glow-in-the-dark constellations for him.

Charlie and my brother met at the cocktail party, thanks to me being preoccupied with Bandit. Still, they don't have a relationship. Not yet. And they may never have one, if Charlie doesn't make it out of the hospital.

But what if they do? What if Charlie takes Archie under

his wing? What if they research together, side by side, first as mentor and mentee and then as equals? Would Charlie entrust Archie with his life's work? Is it *possible*?

Yes. I don't know! Maybe?

I leap off the bed, tearing at the sheets and flinging off the comforter, as though there might be evidence of the future hidden here. Rational? Of course not. Can I stop the desperate frenzy of my hands? No more than I can halt the beating of my heart.

A few minutes later, I collapse on the carpet, wadding up pieces of my brother's bedding. The mattress is naked, its sweat stains exposed, its potential secrets locked inside.

Who is Archie Sherman?

He's the brother who once gave me a dog biscuit disguised as a cookie and then cracked up when I took a bite. He's the boy who gamely handed over his spinning, light-up pinwheel when mine broke. He's the guy who tore down the hall, wielding a wooden rod like a baseball bat, determined to protect me at all costs.

Who will he become?

That, I don't know. That, I can't answer.

Which means I'm not leaping to any conclusions. There are too many pieces of the puzzle that still don't fit. Too many parts of the equation I can't understand.

Resolved, I stand and leap nimbly over the crumpled-up bedding. Only one person has the answers to my questions. I'll be waiting when—and if—she ever shows up in my brain again.

And if she doesn't appear?

Then, I'll just have to go looking for her.

CHAPTER 39

A couple of evenings later, lightning flashes across the sky. Three seconds pass, and then the entire house rattles as though it's on the San Andreas Fault line.

My dad jostles the coffeepot, spilling the dark-brown liquid onto the tile. "Toss me a towel, would you?" he asks. "I need to get back to work. Big deadline."

I throw him a dishrag that was hanging on a cabinet hook, and he mops up the coffee. "You're not supposed to use electronics during a storm," I say.

But he's already finished with the spill and walking out of the kitchen. "I'll take my chances." He lifts his mug jauntily as a goodbye.

"Are you going to work two days from now, too?" I call after his retreating back.

I'm not sure why I'm taunting him. Maybe I just need my father...or at least the few scraps he's willing to give me. I *thought* we made progress the night of the banquet...but any headway seems to have vanished. Who knows? With all the activity that's been swirling around my brain, maybe I just imagined our breakthrough.

"Saturday's the anniversary of the day Mom left," I say. "Or did you forget?"

He doesn't stop walking. Doesn't turn around. "What would not working achieve? It won't bring her back."

"Maybe you don't want her to come back," I mutter.

He pauses mid-step. "What was that?"

I shouldn't repeat my words. Dad's always telling me he's not comfortable with emotions—when I'm pretty sure he's just not comfortable with *me*.

Well, too bad. Because he's a parent, whether he likes it or not. I've spent six years keeping emotion out of our dialogue. Six years never saying how I really feel. Tonight, I'm done giving him a pass.

"You didn't love her," I say, louder now. More aggressive. "I know what you did at the end of your marriage. I know you had an affair."

He wheels around, his eyes wide. "Is that what she said? How old were you back then? Eleven?"

I nod, a little surprised he remembers my age. A lot surprised at the pivot in conversation.

"Oh, honey. I'm sorry." He moves forward, and his hands— the hands of my no-nonsense, all-business father—actually shake. "I had no idea you were dealing with that burden. If she wasn't already gone, I'd choke the life out of her. To think what she put you through…"

I expect him to retreat, like he usually does at the first hint of conflict. Instead, he plunks down his coffee cup on the counter.

"I swear, your mother could talk herself into anything," he says. "I was always devoted to her, Alice. I want you to know that. Not once did I stray from her physically."

"What about emotionally?" I press. "Did you cheat on her,

emotionally, with someone else?"

"I had no idea she saw it that way." He shakes his head. "But I guess she must've, if she told you about it. She got so upset when she overheard us talking. But I didn't know she was jealous. I mean, that's absurd."

"It's not absurd, Dad," I say heatedly. "If you were invested in somebody else, it's natural for her to be hurt."

"It wasn't someone else, though. That's the thing!" He slaps a hand on his forehead and looks at the ceiling. But if he expects the stars to help him out, our skylight is a few feet to the left. "It's an interesting philosophical question, I suppose. Are you the same person now as you will be ten years in the future?"

I freeze. "What did you say?"

He starts. Looks at me slack-jawed, as though he's just realized what came out of his mouth. "N-Nothing, sweetheart," he stammers. "I'm tired. Overworked. I have no idea what I'm saying."

"You're talking about time travel." I'm sure of it. As positive as I am that the Voice is lying. "You're saying Mom was jealous because you were talking to...*her older self*. Is that right?"

A horrified look crosses his face, and he stumbles backward, crashing into the wall. "I'm sorry," he gasps. "This was a breach in protocol. I've said too much."

"But I know about the future," I say, my mind spinning. "A voice has been coming to me, too."

"We can't...talk...about it," he wheezes. "Your mother and I discussed it so much that it changed the future...and then she left. I will not lose you, too."

"Dad, wait." I reach out a hand to stop him. "Don't go. I need your advice."

But it's too late. He turns and runs from the room as

though a pack of wildebeests is chasing him.

I blink. I knew it! Dad's involved with the future. Those peculiar turns of phrases weren't coincidental. But if I'm right, then Mom was incensed at…herself? She accused my dad of having an emotional affair with her older self, ten years later? Is that even possible?

Massaging my temples, I try to wrap my mind around the concept. I suppose, yes. I mean, I have an older self tricking me. Clearly our selves at different times are separate entities, with our own agendas.

I have so many questions. What did Dad mean, he didn't want to lose me, too? And how was he visited by my *mom's* older self? I want to go after him, but it won't do any good. Dad doesn't talk until he's ready. I should know. Hell, I probably inherited my stubbornness from him.

So I'm left exactly where I started this night. Sick of my own company. Bored of hoping for the Voice to appear. Tired of the way my stomach twists every time I think about Archie.

More than two days have passed since I've seen him. Neither Dad nor Zeke knows exactly where he is, but they're not worried. He told Dad he was going on a research trip for a few days. I have no choice but to be wait. After forty-eight hours, however, I'm all out of patience.

I want answers. Now.

I tried reaching the Voice through my mind. Yelling at the top of my lungs. Even searching in my sleep for that black void outside time.

Nothing's worked.

But there's still one method I haven't tried. One avenue of contact that might actually be successful. Every time the Voice has spoken to me, she's been preceded by a *zing* across my brain. If I create a similar flash of electricity, will I somehow signal to my older self that I want to talk?

The idea might be completely out of left field. But I have to try.

I take a deep breath. Walk into the living room. And shuffle my socked feet across the shaggy carpet. The beige fibers are bleached in one corner, where Archie conducted one of his chemistry experiments. I circle that spot a few times, storing up loads of static electricity. And then I touch a metal doorknob.

A sharp, aching spark flies off my finger. My heart leaps. *I did it! I produced a shock!*

I hold my breath. Seconds pass. The space inside my lungs becomes tight and uncomfortable. But the Voice doesn't appear.

The air whooshes out of me. Of course it's not the same kind of electricity. Archie explained to me that static shock is created by opposite charges and a surplus of electrons. Whatever spark precedes the Voice has to be way more complicated.

But I don't need to re-create the identical electricity, I remind myself. I just need a spark strong enough to get my older self's attention.

I scan the room. Cords everywhere. Skinny black, medium gray, thick white. For the television, my laptop, the lamp. All disappearing into outlets hidden behind the sofa, bookshelves, and entertainment center. I wonder…

Okay, so this might actually hurt. But I've come this far. I can't give up now.

Before I can change my mind, I cross the room, reach behind the sofa, and plug and unplug the laptop cord. Five times. Ten times. Looking for that elusive electric shock.

Nothing.

I sit back on my heels, thinking hard. What else? What is equivalent to jumping up and down, waving wildly at the future, screaming, *Look at me! Look at me! Look at meeeeeee!*

An ear-shattering *crack* pierces the air, pulling my attention to the window. Fat drops of rain pelt the glass in a never-ceasing drumbeat. That's some storm out there.

Storm. As in thunder. As in lightning.

Goose bumps pop up on my arms. Every conventional wisdom on how to avoid being struck by lightning flits through my mind. I couldn't *break* those rules.

Could I?

Sweat pools at the nape of my neck. At the same time, I'm cold, so cold—the kind of chill that even a hot bath won't steam away. Can I really do this? Will I stoop to anything to get ahold of the Voice, even risk my own safety?

Clearly it's more sensible to just wait. It would be foolish in the extreme if I let my impatience lead to something fatal, such as electrocuting myself.

But if I put myself in jeopardy—and by extension, *her*— maybe the Voice will actually take me seriously.

Squaring my shoulders, I stride to the door. My older self won't let me get electrocuted. I'm sure of it. As she's so fond of pointing out, we're the same person. Anything I do to her, I'll have to suffer, and vice versa. She sure as hell won't want me to hurt myself. If I do, I'll never grow up to be her.

This entire time, she's been in control of our relationship. *She* tells me what to do. *She* decides what information to confide or withhold. *She* lies to and tricks me.

Well, I'm done letting her jerk me around. I'm not just a silly teenage girl without my own thoughts and opinions. I have power, too. After all, I hold the ultimate bargaining chip: our body.

So I'm taking charge of my destiny. Right here. Right now.

Maybe then, she'll understand that I'm not just a pawn to do her bidding. Maybe she'll treat me like an equal partner in our mission to save the world.

Maybe she'll tell me the truth.

I slowly let the air flow out of me, deflating my lungs. My shoulders. My mind.

"Here goes nothing," I mutter, flinging open the door and walking into the rain. The water assaults me. In half a second, my clothes are plastered to my body and strands of hair drip around my face.

I grab a rake from the tool bar outside the garden shed. Metal lightning rod, check. I jump on the generator and begin to climb onto the flat roof of our covered back porch. The highest point around, check.

Raindrops lodge on my lashes, blurring my vision. I shake my head to flick away the water, but more just take their place. My muscles strain as I push and pull, and the brick scrapes against my palms. I haul myself onto the roof, the sharp edge nearly bisecting me. And then the sky glows. Lightning zigzags around me, way too close for comfort.

But that's precisely the point.

I shiver. *Please let this work.* The Voice made me move away from the flying drops of wine. Surely she'll come to me before I do something irreversible.

"What's it going to take, older Alice?" I shout into the night. "How do I show you I'm serious about talking?"

I take a deep breath as the rain continues to pour down on me. This is a game of chicken between my older self and me. She doesn't believe I'll follow through. She doesn't think I'm brave enough—or foolish enough—to extend my makeshift lightning rod into the sky, awaiting, tempting, even *daring* the next bolt.

My insides churn like they're set on the spin cycle. *Watch me, older Alice.*

I straighten, slowly raising the metal rake. A bright light

flashes next to me, and the air sizzles—

ZIIIING.

Did the lightning get me? Am I electrocuted?

"Stop, Alice," the Voice shouts. "Stop it! I'm here, for goodness' sake. I'm here."

CHAPTER 40

She came. The Voice saw me or felt me or *remembered* me, and she's actually here.

I collapse on the roof, and the rake slams onto the siding. The adrenaline flees my body, turning me into a cold, wet noodle. On the top of a house. In a raging thunderstorm.

I won. In a game of chicken, she yielded first. She fell for my bluff.

At least, I'm pretty sure it was a bluff. I wouldn't have continued to tempt fate. I wouldn't have held my rake in the sky until the lightning found me. I don't think.

"Get inside," the Voice says wearily, as though reading my mind. "Dry yourself off, put on something warm. And then we'll talk."

For once, I'm happy to obey.

"Seriously?" the Voice asks a few minutes later. "What were you thinking? Don't you have better things to do than to hurt yourself?"

"I wanted to talk to you," I say weakly. And to show her that I have the upper hand in our relationship. But I can't admit that.

I'm perched on my bed now, wrapped in a fluffy robe, my damp hair pulled into a ponytail.

My jellyfish mood lamp sits on the nightstand. It reminds me of Bandit's lava lamp, although it emits pink, purple, and orange lights instead of the singular blue. The trajectory of the gelatinous creature is easy, mindless, soothing. Good thing. I need all the comfort I can get right now.

"You actually thought you could summon me by exposing yourself to lightning?" Her tone hardens "News flash. The only thing that will do is get you killed. I come on my own time. Got it? Just this once, I decided to accelerate my visit by a few hours—but I won't do it again, no matter what foolish stunt you pull."

I run my fingers over the glass of the mood lamp, not saying anything. Oh, she'll come again if I want her to. She proved that in our game of chicken.

The bravado she's displaying now is *her* move in the game. *Her* bluff. In fact, we've been playing a game of chess this entire time. I just didn't realize it until now.

The reason she's been so harsh? Her motivation for ordering me around like she's my boss? It's because *I* have all the power in this relationship. Not her. *I* decide what the future will hold. *I* determine whether or not she'll even exist. Not the other way around.

And she's absolutely terrified I'll figure that out.

"You lied to me," I say calmly. "Why?"

"On the contrary, I've *never* lied to you," she says. "At least not yet."

Not yet? I push up the overlong sleeves of my robe. "It's

only been three days! How can you have already forgotten?"

Four, five, six seconds pass. "Ah, but it hasn't been three days. At least not for me," she says finally. "You're used to thinking about time as fixed. Linear. But all those concepts go out the window when it comes to traveling through the fourth dimension.

"For *you*, three days have passed. For me, in the future, it could've been any amount of time. I could've squished all my visits into a single day...or spread them out over a few years."

I stare at my jellyfish, turning over her words. The fake sea jelly travels along the bottom of the lamp, its tentacles trailing behind. When it hits the wall, it arcs into the water above, sometimes returning to the beginning of the path, sometimes to the midpoint.

A thought niggles at the edge of my mind. Something big, even huge. I just can't quite grasp it.

"Don't question so much." The Voice takes on her now-familiar lecturing tone. "I'm not your adversary. We have a real enemy, one who will destroy—and has destroyed—the world. You need to focus your energies on stopping them, not dissecting my every word."

"Do you mean Archie?" I ask. "Or Lee? Zeke? Cristela?"

She sighs. "I told you, Alice. I can't tell you who the Maker is. You have to reach your own conclusions."

What? We're back to this *again*? But she *already* revealed the Maker's identity, albeit a fake one. Why is she still insisting that I reach my own conclusions?

Argh. I want to pull out my hair at the lack of answers. I want to wrap my hands around her neck—*my* neck—and shake until she gives them to me.

In fact, I do. Span my fingers around my neck and squeeze, until the pressure is uncomfortable but not quite suffocating. "I'm done with your evasion," I snarl. "You gave me the name of the target, but you were lying. Explain yourself. Now."

"I don't know what you're talking about," she says.

I tighten the hold around my neck. Heat rises to my face, and I'm gasping at the air, trying to fill my lungs. Is it possible to strangle yourself? I'm not sure, but damn it, I'm going to try. "Tell. Me."

"But I've always been truthful with you!" she exclaims. "There's nothing to explain."

I squeeze harder still. I'm light-headed now, and black dots dance in my vision. I'm going to pass out any second, but I don't let up. I'm *this* close to my answers. I just have to be strong enough, determined enough, to get them.

"Stop!" she screams. "Don't be mad at *me*. I haven't done anything to trick you. At least not yet."

My grip loosens, and I choke at the air, refilling my lungs, reclaiming my senses.

There's that phrase again. *At least not yet.* She's used it twice now, but the words don't make any sense. She *has* lied to me. She *has* tricked me. And yet she seems to believe what she's saying.

Snippets of conversation come back to me, crashing into one another. The moments when she's repeated herself. Her erratic behavior, the change in her personality with each visit.

The times when she called me *Malice.* Three separate occasions. The only conversations that were accompanied by physical pain.

In the first visit, she made me tell Bandit that I loved him. In the second, she tricked me into giving him the cupcake. And in the third, she named him as the target.

Bandit, Bandit, Bandit. The only times she ever mentioned him were the same visits she referred to me—to herself—as Malice.

That has to mean something.

I assumed that time travel was messing up her mental faculties. But what if I was wrong? What if there's another explanation for her strange behavior, one that I'm a hair away from grasping?

You're used to thinking about time as linear, she said earlier. *All those concepts go out the window when it comes to traveling through the fourth dimension.*

I glance at the jellyfish, at the arc it chooses to travel after it hits the wall. Like time travel, it can choose to go all the way back to the beginning of the path...or it can insert itself midway.

I've never lied to you. At least not yet...not yet...not yet...

The answer hits me like a bolt of lightning.

That's it. That's the huge something at the edge of my mind. But I have to be sure. I need one last confirmation.

"Why are you here?" I whisper. "You said in our very first conversation that you would go away, once and for all, if I did one thing for you. If I told Bandit that I loved him. And yet you continued to come back. Again and again. Why?"

She doesn't say anything. Because she has no response. Instead, she flees from my head, cutting short our conversation. Not because she's in control. But because she's panicked. Because she's scared.

That's when I know. I can taste the bitterness on my tongue. I can feel the aching in my heart. I understand the unshakable knowledge directly in my soul.

She's telling the truth. She hasn't lied to me about Bandit. She hasn't tricked me with the cupcake. Because in *her* timeline, that lie and that trick haven't happened yet.

All along, the Voice has been coming to me out of order.

The very first time she visited me...was actually one of her last.

CHAPTER 41

The world tilts. The jellyfish lamp, my desk, even the mattress on which I'm sitting slant, and I have to dig my fingers into the bedspread to keep from sliding off.

This is huge. If the Voice has been visiting me out of order, *everything* changes.

I take a deep breath. And then another. Okay. I need to clear my head. I need to think this through.

Five minutes of deep breathing later, I'm steady enough to go to my desk. To pull out a piece of paper and start writing. Detailing each and every time the Voice visited me.

I list the visits in order—with one key exception. I pull out the three times she called me *Malice* and stick those at the end. And then, I examine the paper with fresh eyes.

Holy moly. It's like those dot images where you step back and allow your eyes to un-focus, and presto, a completely different picture emerges.

Other than those three visits, when she targeted Bandit, she never mentioned the target's name. She was steadfast in insisting that I reach my own conclusions.

Is it possible that in all those visits, she was sincere? That she truly wanted me to stop the Virus Maker, that she had no intention of tricking me? This conclusion would jibe with her calm and collected manner.

The other three visits, she was frantic. Panicked. She insulted me and zapped my brain to coerce me to obey. She even went so far as to take over my body, shooting out my arm to give the cupcake to Bandit.

I lean back in my chair, lifting it up onto its two back legs. Something must've happened in the future. Something that made older Alice change her strategy midstream. Something that convinced her to come to her teenage self out of order, to try and rewrite the story she was telling.

The legs tilt back an inch too far. For a moment, I'm suspended in the air, flailing, and then the chair—with me in it—crashes to the floor.

Ow. My tailbone throbs, but I'm smiling as I rub my injury. Now that the hailstorm of my revelations has settled, I'm left with a few key conclusions.

The depth of my older self's trickery is even more complicated than I imagined.

If I want answers, I need to investigate without her knowledge.

And in order to do that? I'm going to need Bandit's help.

The next afternoon, I pull into the parking lot of our local hospital, next to a navy Tahoe. Bandit's car.

By now, my surroundings have stopped tilting, but my life and everything in it continues to feel surreal. Like I'm not truly sitting here, in my Honda Accord. Like the air doesn't smell damp and sweet from yesterday's thunderstorm. Like that's not a tall, good-looking guy hurrying down the sidewalk.

Except it is.

I snap to attention and get out of my car. Bandit scowls as I approach, dispensing with his signature bored face. I never thought I'd say this, but I kinda, sorta *miss* that aloof expression.

"How did you know I was here?" he snaps.

I suppose I deserve the surliness. Last time I saw him, I broke into his house, tried to kill him, kissed him instead, blurted out that I had a voice in my head, and then ran away.

I would be wary of me, too.

"I rang your doorbell, and your mom answered," I say. "She was suspicious that some *falang* girl was asking for you. But when I *wai*-ed to pay my respects and said I was a friend of Lalana's, she softened and told me you were volunteering at the hospital, reading to patients in the cancer ward."

"I'm surprised she even knows." He tugs at his hair, which is now back to its brilliant blue. "What do you want? Are you planning to stab me here, in front of everyone?" He scans the parking lot as a harried mom speed-walks past, a screaming baby on one hip and a wailing toddler in a stroller. "Not wise. Or maybe you want to invite me into the back seat of your car, in broad daylight? Tempting but also not wise."

I ignore his sarcasm. "I was going to bring you a peace offering. I make a mean bento lunch, you know. I roll up omelets, add a carrot beak, and voilà! It looks just like a duck."

"Mallard or Muscovy?" he asks drily, melting my heart a little. Okay, a lot.

I push forward. "But then I assumed you wouldn't eat anything I brought, since it could be poisoned. And probably wouldn't even taste good."

"That's a safe assumption," he agrees.

"So I decided to give you the one thing you've been asking for." I spread my arms wide.

"You?" he asks, blinking rapidly.

"No!" I flush, lowering my arms. "I meant the truth. That's what you want, right? What we *both* want. I couldn't explain before, but now I'm ready to tell you all of it." I stop, suddenly unsure. "That is, if you don't mind talking to a criminal."

"You're not a criminal, Alice." He pushes a hand through his hair, pausing while an elderly man clomps by with a walker. "I got rid of the gun. Buried it in the woods, after I wiped off your fingerprints. That doesn't mean I'm going to pretend you didn't sneak into my house, intending to shoot me." His eyes flash. "But I know you don't belong in jail."

Something squeezes inside my chest. Even after everything I've done, he still believes in me. My older self was right. I shouldn't have let myself get close to this guy. My feelings for him are way too soft. Too dangerous. If not for my physical well-being, then to my heart.

"I was wrong about you," I say softly. "You're not the most obnoxious boy alive. Not even close. Instead, you're the most loyal. The most true. And I'm sorry I didn't see it before."

I swallow hard. Part of me wants to weep at all the things that went wrong between us, but I can't indulge my regrets. Not yet. Not when the future still hangs in the balance.

"Let's sit," I say briskly and guide him to a wrought-iron bench.

A few drops of water still cling to the iron, left over from this morning's showers, but the sun is shining now, the air warm and breezy. I smell cinnamon. The scent wafts off him, stronger than usual, so he must've just chewed some gum or brushed his teeth.

I'm dying to know which, but I can't ask. I'm too scared he'll shut me down.

Instead, I tell him everything I know. About the Voice, about our future. From the highly contagious virus that will render people allergic to the sun, to the millions of people dying, to my mission of saving the world by killing the Maker.

I explain Charlie's role in developing the virus, how the Voice convinced me that Bandit was my target, my subsequent discovery that my older self was coming to me out of order.

As I talk, a chaos of emotions crosses his face. Skepticism, shock — and then belief. My account is too detailed; it explains perfectly my strange behavior and fits in with what he already knows. I see the moment his face changes, when he crosses the line from doubt to acceptance.

"I can see how you would believe I was the target," he says slowly after I finish. "Charlie *is* my de facto uncle. But I'm not going to invent that virus. He tried to mentor me years ago, but I refused. The truth is, as much as I love him, I've always found Charlie to be…unstable.

"When he asked me to pick up the papers, he wanted me to hold on to them. There will come a time, he said, when someone comes looking for his research. And I'll know to turn over his papers then."

"I read the letter with his instructions," I confess. "It was addressed to Chubbs, which is your nickname. That was one more mark against you."

"Oh," Bandit says, startled. "That's a generic nickname. In the Thai culture, *ouan* can be used as a term of endearment. Charlie loved this, so he adopted the English counterpart and calls everyone close to him *Chubbs*."

Oh. I didn't know that. Lalana probably could've told me, if we were still speaking. But we're not.

How many other things am I wrong about?

I look at Bandit, at the tips of his hair made even bluer in the sunlight. At his arched eyebrows that are both superior and adorable.

I now know why killing him felt so wrong. My mind was confused, my heart burdened. But I never felt the unshakable truth of his guilt in my soul.

"I know you're not the Virus Maker." Each word slices and scrapes its way out of my throat. Because if Bandit's not the inventor, then someone else has to be. Someone who might be…my brother. "The Voice wouldn't have had to resort to tricks if you were the true target."

Twin waves of panic and sorrow crest inside me, threatening to sweep me under. I shove every last drop behind my resolve. "I need to figure out why the Voice lied to me. Maybe then I'll discover who I'm really supposed to kill," I say, a thousand times more calmly than I feel.

"How are you going to do that?" He tries valiantly to erect his bored face once again. But it doesn't stand a chance against the interest gleaming in his eyes.

"With your help, I hope. I need to travel to the future, and I need Cristela to send me there." I twist my hands. I'm taking a risk that Cristela's not the Maker. But from my assessment, she's the least likely to be guilty. Besides, she's the only one with the expertise to push me forward in time. "I gave her my contact information, but I didn't think to get hers. The two of you are friends, right? Can you tell me where she lives?"

"I don't know if I forgive you. But given my uncle's involvement, I need to see this through. He's in stable condition, you know. He made it through the worst of his injuries, but they're keeping him in the hospital for a few more days." He clicks his tongue, as though coming to a conclusion. "Cristela's not in town this week. She's visiting her grandmother for spring break, a couple of hours away. I can take you there tomorrow."

"Thank you." Should I tell him? I've already confided so

much. Might as well impart the rest of it. "I appreciate your coming with me. I'll need backup."

"Backup?" he asks. "Why would you need backup?"

I take a deep breath. "Because we have to ask Cristela why she poisoned the cupcake."

CHAPTER 42

Cristela Ruiz, student scientist and premier researcher on sending the human consciousness through time, stares at me like I am her wildest dream come to life. In other words: like I'm a traveler from the future.

Perspiration dots her upper lip, and she lists to the right. My hands shoot out automatically. She's going to faint. My biggest hope for getting to the future is about to collapse right here at my feet.

What's more, her grandmother is out, which means it's up to us to save her. Bandit must have the same thought, because he steps forward and winds an arm around her shoulders.

"I'm so sorry, Bandit," Cristela says, guilt bubbling from every pore. "That cupcake wasn't meant for you. You were never supposed to get hurt."

Bandit and I exchange a glance. So I was right. Cristela was on a mission, too.

"You were visited by a voice," I confirm. "Your future self, perhaps, ten years older?"

She nods. "That's how I'll be able to invent time travel

later. Other scientists will come close, but something will dissuade them. Doubt. Finances. Competing passions. But not me. I'll stay the course because I *know* that one day, I'll succeed. My older self couldn't have visited me otherwise."

I guess I didn't have to worry about telling her that time travel existed. Instead of altering the future, the advanced knowledge only reaffirms her path.

"Who was the poisoned cupcake meant for?" Bandit asks, gently but firmly. "If not me, then who?"

Cristela shoots me a look that I can't decipher. "Can we sit down? I feel dizzy."

"Of course. Is this the kitchen?" He guides her through an open doorway into a sunny room. "Let's get you a drink."

He helps her onto a twisted metal chair that looks more fashionable than comfortable and fills a tumbler from a pitcher of filtered water. I perch on a stool amid the shiny steel appliances, trying to ignore the calendar on the refrigerator, with today's date circled in red.

It's Saturday, the anniversary of my mother's abandonment. My nerves already won't let me forget the day's significance. I don't need the extra reminder.

"Thanks for not hating me." Cristela accepts the tumbler from Bandit.

His gaze strays to me once again. "I have a feeling we'll all be doing a lot of forgiving before this is over."

I swallow. Does that mean he might forgive me someday? We barely talked during our entire car ride. I can hardly blame him. When all is said and done, I did try to kill him.

How does any relationship move past attempted murder? Can it?

He shifts his focus back to Cristela, and the moment—real or imagined—passes. "The cupcake," he prompts. "Who was the target, C?"

Again, she looks at me. Again, I can't unpack her expression.

"Archie," she says slowly. "I was supposed to give the cupcake to your brother."

I pitch forward. My feet hit the floor, stopping my body, my stomach, my brain, my heart. Every organ goes spinning into outer space, and in a realm without friction, without gravity, I don't know how they'll ever stop.

Oh. That's why Cristela wanted to sit down. Not for her sake but for mine. She placed that particular cupcake in front of Archie, I suddenly remember. But I switched ours because I wanted to photograph the lustrous pearls.

I think I knew the truth the moment I saw the inscription on the spindle, but I couldn't admit it. Not to myself, not to Bandit.

My brother, dearer to me than anyone on this planet, cannot be the culprit.

And if he is?

I will never be able to kill him. Not for a million lives. Not for my unborn child.

And yet… And yet… A sliver of hope lives in the most desperate part of my heart.

"That doesn't mean he's the Virus Maker." The words tumble out of my mouth. "My older self tricked me into believing the target was Bandit. Maybe your older self tricked you, too."

"Maybe," Cristela says. But I can tell from her peek at Bandit, from the pity in her eyes, that she doesn't believe it.

I jump off the stool and pace the hardwood floor. Adrenaline bubbles in my veins like the magma inside Mount Vesuvius. "You have to get me to the future. That's the only way we'll know for sure."

Cristela lifts the water to her lips, and I count her swallows, long and slow. Three, four, five. She's probably spent hours—weeks, months—thinking about this problem. If anyone can help me, it'll be her.

"I can't help you," she says. "You forget, I haven't invented time travel yet. I won't do that for another ten years."

I send Bandit a pleading look. Whether or not he forgives me, I know that in this instance, he's on my side.

Nodding, he drops his hands to her shoulders, massaging. "Please, Cristela. It would mean a lot to us. Could you try?"

She knocks his hands off her back. "I've *been* trying. What do you think I was doing for the last year? The world's scientific conundrums don't get solved just because Bandit Sakda turns up the charm!" She sinks back against her chair, expelling a breath. "Actually, that feels good, so keep massaging."

His lips quirking, he resumes kneading her muscles.

I sit in the chair next to hers. My heart and thoughts race, trying to outpace one another, but I have to stay calm. I need to convince her if I want to uncover the truth. "You haven't had *me* for the last year. I don't know much about the science, but I've actually traveled to the future. My experience should give you valuable insight."

Cristela purses her lips. "You, keep massaging," she says to Bandit and then points to me. "You, keep talking."

I recount everything I can remember about my trip to the future, from zipping up my consciousness with my older self's to residing inside her physical body. I describe the movie reel that flashes through my mind when I take an action that diverges from the original time stream. I even tell her about entering the black void and dipping into the original Alice's life.

As I talk, Cristela closes her eyes, and Bandit moves his long, capable fingers along her shoulders. I try not to stare. I can't be distracted by imagining those hands on *my* shoulders.

On my cheeks. On my bare waist.

"I got it!" Cristela announces. She leaps to her feet, away from Bandit's hands, away from me, as though she needs the extra room for her brilliance.

"When your older self traveled to the past, she opened a portal in your brain." She traces the same path I took across her kitchen. Before the sun sets, we'll wear a rut right into the hardwood. "And when she took you to the future, she wrenched this portal open even wider. Wide enough that you were able to slip into it accidentally while you slept. All you have to do is find this portal. And *presto*! You'll be back in the black void, on your way to the future."

"But I've been *trying* to return to the void," I protest. "I haven't come close to finding this portal again."

"You haven't been doing it right." She tosses her black hair over her shoulders, reminding me so much of Lalana that my heart aches. "You've been stumbling around your brain, trying to find the one cell that will let you enter the void. That's like looking for a four-leaf clover in a random field of grass. You could search for years and never find it!'"

The sunlight streams through the window, highlighting the dust particles around Cristela. Even those specks seem to dance, as though infected by her exuberance.

"You have to go back to a moment when you *know* the portal was accessed. Such as the first time the Voice visited you." Her words become faster, tumbling into one another. "This was also the moment she started tricking you, which corresponds to the point in the future where you want to travel. Correct?"

I nod. My mind hasn't worked this hard since my AP Calculus class. "I guess. But you said yourself: You haven't invented time travel yet. How am I supposed to return to last week?"

Bandit drifts to my side, his arm next to—but not brushing—mine. We haven't touched since he found out I was trying to kill him.

I get it. I really do. I wouldn't want to touch me, either. Doesn't stop my stomach from sinking to the floor, though.

"You're right. I haven't," Cristela says cheerfully. "And I'm certainly not going to do it today, in this kitchen. This is a hack that works *only* because your older self has been visiting you. The thing is, we all have a pseudo time machine, one that takes us to the past." She taps her temples. "Your memory is a powerful thing. Recall a scene forcefully enough, and you might be able to trick your brain into believing it's the real thing. At least, real enough to activate the portal. Think you can remember that moment strongly enough?"

"Probably." I dart a quick glance at Bandit, blushing. He stares straight ahead. He knows that the Voice's first appearance coincided with me telling him I loved him. Is he wishing that our meeting never happened?

"There's only one problem," he speaks up, his voice gravelly. "We're trying to outsmart Alice's older self. But she, by definition, knows everything that Alice knows, because she's already lived it. Won't she sabotage Alice's trip to the future before it even begins?"

My mouth drops. He's right. I never knew having your older self as an enemy could be so complicated. "We're doomed," I moan.

"Not at all." Cristela shakes her head vigorously. "Everything in my research indicates that when the future interferes with the past, there's a lag while the new action ripples outward to the succeeding time. Think about it. Your older self knows everything your *original* self does…but she can't know what actions your *new* self will take until you take them. You follow?"

"Kinda?" My brain hurts. Bandit's nodding thoughtfully. Clearly, he understands exactly what Cristela is saying. That makes one of us.

"You have a small amount of time where you can act without your older self knowing," Cristela continues. "From my calculations, it takes a few minutes for your actions to ripple forward. That's your window of opportunity."

"Let me get this straight," I say, my thoughts whirling. "I'll travel back to last week, when the Voice first appeared in my head. Once there, I'll intertwine my consciousness with hers, like I did before—"

"Except this time, you have to do it *stealthily*, so she doesn't notice," Cristela interrupts, pushing the long bangs off her face. "And then you'll hitch a ride to the future, to the exact moment that should give you the answers you want!" She looks from me to Bandit, as though she's expecting applause. "Well? What do you think?"

I swallow hard. It's a stretch. The plan could break down at any step. I might not be able to trick my brain into activating the portal. My older self might notice when I try to link my consciousness with hers. We could be missing several key elements that make travel to the future possible.

But...it's a plan. One we didn't have a few minutes ago. And if the events play out just as Cristela described, it might actually work.

I look at the girl in front of me. Her hands, forearms, and shoulders vibrate with anticipation. She's not just a student any longer but a bona fide scientist now.

"What do I think?" Amid the chaos of possibilities and thoughts, one lone opinion rises to the top. "Cristela, I think you're a genius."

CHAPTER 43

We move to the living room. Large windows usher in the late-afternoon sun, and spider plants grow in pots hanging in each corner. The dangling green tendrils stand out in sharp contrast to the yellow and blue walls, and the room smells friendly—lots of lemon, citrus, and a hint of earth.

I turn in a slow circle, awed. "This room is gorgeous."

"Isn't it?" Cristela runs a hand over a set of three brightly colored vases with holes in the shape of petals punched in the center. "I wish I could visit more often. My abuelita chose the bright colors that you find on the houses in Nicaragua. She said it reminds her of home. The whole family pitched in and helped her paint this room. My tío, my cousins. Mama and I even made the two-hour trip. It was a regular party in here."

I feel a pang at the thought of her extended family. Both my parents were only children, so it's just our small family unit. Another reason why Archie and I have always been close. We never had anybody else.

"Come." She pats the leather sofa. "Make yourself comfortable."

I lay down. The cushions are soft and yielding, but that doesn't dry the sweat on my palms. It doesn't drain the saliva pooling in my mouth.

"When did you say the Voice first came to you?" Cristela settles on the floor in front of the sofa.

"One week, two days ago," Bandit says, just as I begin to count on my fingers.

We both turn to him.

"What?" he says defensively. "What happened that day… I'm not likely to forget it anytime soon. Or ever, really."

I flush. His eyes flash at me, deep and dark. I'd drown in them if I could. Maybe, just maybe, I haven't ruined things between us. Maybe one day, we'll find a way to move forward.

"The scene should be easy to recall, then." Cristela tucks a strand of hair behind my ear. "Are you ready?"

I bite my lip. Am I? How badly do I want these answers? Am I willing to chase my older self through time in order to get them?

Yes, my heart roars. *Oh, I want these answers. More than that, I need them. I need to know the truth, in my heart, in my soul. I'll never be able to save the future until I do.*

My eyes drift to Bandit of their own volition. No matter where we're at or what we're doing, I will always look for him, again and again. "Wish me luck?" I croak.

"You don't need luck." He leans against the wall, crossing his arms. "In fact, I'm jealous of you."

"Jealous? Why?"

He raises an eyebrow. "If this experiment works, you'll get to relive that moment on the basketball court like it's the first time."

Now I do smile, his voice reaching across the room and giving me the confidence I so desperately need.

"Now," Cristela says. "Bring back that day. Every detail,

every moment. Make your brain believe it's real! This is the most vivid memory of your life. This — and no other."

I close my eyes and remember as hard as I can.

Blue ink spreads like ants across my brother's skin. He moves the pen over his palm, dipping into the hollow of his hand and rising up again. Never stopping. Never slowing.

I take a deep breath. This part, I remember. This image, of the blue ink spreading like a colony of carpenter ants, I'll never forget for the rest of my days. If I ever make it to the ripe old age of the Voice. If I live to be 101.

The next few minutes aren't so clear. I tried to get Archie to eat. I walked off in search of Lalana. The Voice came to me then, and a series of independent moments flash across my mind.

"Listen up," the Voice barks. She sounds feminine, but I can't tell if she's young or old.

A guy with electric-blue hair raises his hands to shoot the ball, and his shirt rides up, revealing nicely defined muscles.

The sharpest, most intense lightning bolt yet sears my brain. The world fractures into a dozen glowing stars, each one bigger and brighter than the last.

Is this enough? Am I recalling enough details, enough sensations? Have I activated the portal, so that I can move into the black void?

Apparently not, because I'm still here, in Cristela's grandma's bright and airy living room. I can still hear the low humming of the air conditioner. I can still feel the nails digging into my palms.

I wrench open my hands. The tangible bite of nails against skin is one more thing keeping me here. I need to sever all ties to the present, lose myself to the past.

"More." Cristela's voice urges me, but it's fainter now, and that's good. That means I'm detaching myself from my physical body. "Remember more. What were you doing? What were you feeling?"

"She was telling me she loved me." All of a sudden, Bandit is hovering above me. "Relive that moment when you first tapped my shoulder." His breath flutters against my skin. "I know I do. Every night."

I'm drifting now, on the wave of my memory. Because that's where I want to be. More than anything, I want to live that moment again, no matter how embarrassing it was. I want to be approaching this wonderful boy for the very first time.

Now what? Do I clear my throat? Tap his shoulder? Going for broke, I do both at the same time.

He turns and lifts his eyebrows, as though wondering how a mere mortal such as myself dares to approach him. He's tall—really tall. Almost a head above my five feet five. His jaw is chiseled, his shoulders broad. I'm so close that I can feel the heat rising off his body.

My brain scrambles. I forgot to check if I had any food in my teeth! Did I brush my hair this morning? Put on clothes?

The scene rolls forward without my participation, without my focus. I can't feel my toes. I'm no longer breathing. I don't have ears. This is good, all good. I've retreated to the space of my imagination, waiting for the portal to activate…waiting for it to show me the way to the black void…

And…here…it…is…

The portal flashes at me invisibly. Blares at me soundlessly. I don't know how I'm sensing its location, but it's right here, hidden in the gray matter of my brain. I move toward the beacon—and fall through a metaphysical door.

For an instant, I'm surrounded by inky blackness. In front of me, I see a bright wavering line. Below me, the colorful streams of time unfurl. And then the brain waves of my memory sync up with the vibrations of the past. The force would have my teeth clicking together, but I no longer have any in this bodiless void.

    I steel my consciousness...

    ...and then I'm hurtling backward through the blank nothingness of time.

CHAPTER 44

I come back to myself as though I'm waking from a deep sleep. Disoriented, foggy. And standing in front of someone. Flaming monkeys—my mouth is moving.

"I love you," I blurt. "That is all. Goodbye."

Except that's not me saying the words. That's not me wheeling around, ready to sprint, when a hand snags my arm.

Instead, it's my past self feeling these things, performing these actions. I can see, hear, smell, taste, and touch everything she does, but *she* controls our body. Not me.

Holy moly, we did it. We sent my consciousness to the past.

"Wait a minute," Bandit says, his eyes 2 percent less bored. "Are we in third grade? Do you want to give me a note asking if I love you back so I can circle yes or no?"

My cheeks burn hotter than the sun assaulting my skin. Hotter, even, than the flames that got me into this mess.

Oh, past Alice. That's not just embarrassment you're feeling. That flash of heat is also *me*—your older self by one week, fully waking up in your consciousness. You don't happen to notice because you're dying a slow death in the middle of the basketball court.

Which gives me an idea. I know how to attach myself to my older self's consciousness without her realizing it.

I spare my younger self one more moment of pity—*don't worry, past Alice; this humiliation, too, will pass*—and begin to sift through the space inside our mind, looking for a *third* consciousness, one that's from ten years in the future.

I search like I've never searched before. I don't use my eyes or my ears, my tongue or my hands. The five senses I've spent my whole life developing are useless now. Where I am, those senses don't exist.

Instead, I search for her with my mind. I feel for the contours that are nearly identical to—but not quite—mine.

Aha! There she is. Bright, sparkly. Shimmery on the edges and glowing in the center. A consciousness that is so young, so full of life, that it has to be the teenage Alice.

I mourn. Sorrow fills up my consciousness with no outlet for release, because I don't have eyes to cry. I don't have a mouth to wail. How can this be me from one week earlier? Just nine days, and I've changed so much. That's what a heavy knowledge of the future will do. That's the effect of bearing the burden of saving the world.

The object of my supposed affection smirks. "We can skip the note. Can't say I blame you for falling for me. I mean, I'm a lovable guy. But have we actually met?"

I'm running out of time.

I need to find my older self before that earsplitting whistle; I need to zip up my consciousness to hers at the exact moment that past Alice jerks back. *Stealthily*, as Cristela instructed. Without my older self's notice.

I start combing through the space again with renewed determination.

And…bingo! I feel her.

Instead of a consciousness overlaid on past Alice, my older self is chilling in the space *underneath* my younger self's mind. Very sneaky, although I doubt she's actively hiding. She's probably just hanging back so she doesn't interfere.

I fit together our jagged edges—carefully, slowly.

An earsplitting wolf whistle slices through the air, and I yank up the zipper.

Click. Our consciousnesses lock together, just as…

I jerk back, away from Bandit. Away from my disgrace. Without looking at him, I crash through the crowd.

Did my older self notice? Can she sense me here, attached to her consciousness? I don't think so. She's thoroughly distracted by past Alice fleeing the basketball court.

"Whatever you do, don't fall for this boy," the Voice warns. *"It'll only make what you have to do later harder."*

And then I'm hurtling through a black and bodiless void once again. Only this time?

I'm going to the future.

CHAPTER 45

roar back to myself. No disorientation this time. No fogginess.
I know exactly where I am. *Who* I am—and who I'm not.

My older self opens our eyes, and I see twisty metal coils
above our head. They're affixed to a curved, shiny wall that
goes all the way around our body, encasing us in a tube. We're
lying on a narrow surface that's slightly padded but mostly
hard, and I smell the cold, crisp scent of antiseptic mixed with
human sweat. There's no noise inside the tube, an absolute
silence you get only inside a vacuum. It's so quiet that our
ears begin to hum.

This must be Cristela's time travel device, the one she
invents in the future.

Panic surges. Last time I traveled forward in time, I didn't
wake up inside a tube. Did something go wrong? Am I not
in the future?

Calm down. Last time, the older Alice knew I was coming.
She was probably shielding me until she exited the machine,
in order to limit my knowledge of her time.

I force my attention back to our body.

My older self wiggles our toes. Swallows. Flexes our hands. Must be a routine check to make sure all our parts are still here, still working.

I hunker underneath her consciousness, not thinking a word. Just...waiting. Watching. Hanging back the way *she* did, so that she didn't interfere with past Alice's actions. I learned this stealth mode directly from her.

Luckily, she's not looking for another consciousness. Our brain is clogged full of thoughts; our heart is bursting with emotion.

"Malice?" A distorted male voice fills the tube. There's still no one here but me—us—so the man must be speaking through an intercom, which makes him sound tinny and slightly robotic. "You made it?" he asks, his voice weak with relief. "You're still...you?"

Our heart leaps. Hers, because she must be glad to hear from him. Mine, because I know who he is.

This must be the man who placed his warm hand on our shoulder the last time I came to the future. The one who squeezed ever so gently.

This man must be my future husband. He must be Zeke.

"Yeah," my older self says. Our voice is thin and patchy, like she's exhausted from a faraway adventure. But it's also warm and full of love. "I made it."

"Take a few minutes," the older Zeke says. "You're not invincible, you know. After eighteen trips to the past, even the great Malice will feel the ravages of time."

I don't realize it until that moment, but our body feels... tired. Our limbs melt onto the narrow platform, boneless, and our heart is racing too fast. Our head pounds, as though from a migraine but worse, because it comes from deeper. Way deeper.

My older self runs our hands down the hospital gown

we're wearing, pausing at our stomach. Soft. Old.

Or at least older. By approximately ten years.

"It's not like you would let me out of here anyhow," she says, still weary but lightly amused, the tone you use with someone who knows you better than you know yourself.

"Nope," he says. "Not after what you did last time. Honestly, woman. What were you thinking, jumping up as soon as you came out of the tube? These trips are wreaking havoc on both your body and your mind."

"I only have two trips left," she mutters, closing our eyes. "Two more trips before my mind starts coming apart."

"Thank goodness for that," he responds. "I'd like to enjoy some time with my wife, with my family, before we all fade away."

She doesn't respond, but a hot liquid pricks the backs of our eyes. Our heart, heavy before, seems capable of dragging our whole body through a deep black hole now.

I don't get it. I thought the whole point of this mission was to save the future. To save my future daughter. Why would they all fade away? What does that even mean?

The surface under our back vibrates, and then a rolling ball moves across our neck, shoulders, spine, kneading the muscles with a precise amount of pressure. A fine mist is sprayed into the air. It smells bright and fresh, like sunshine.

No, not sunshine, I automatically correct myself. Ten years in the future, the sun is associated with evil instead of good. I know this as well as our heart knows to keep beating.

Not because anyone told me. Not because I'm reading my older self's thoughts. But because the knowledge originates from our body's instincts. The fact of the sun's danger has been internalized down to our very bones.

She inhales deeply. These scents must not just be pleasant but also medicinal. Sure enough, I can feel the adrenaline rushing to our muscles. I can feel our mind becoming clearer.

"Your vitals are looking better already, Malice," Zeke says. I wish he weren't speaking through an intercom. His undistorted, familiar voice would be a comfort right now. "I'll let you out soon."

"I can't wait to see you," she says.

"*And* touch you. *And* lick you."

She laughs. "Don't be crude."

"You married me," he points out.

"You're right," she says. "And I would do it again, in every life, in every time."

She closes our eyes, and this time, the liquid does rush out, smattering onto our cheeks. Zeke doesn't speak for a moment, but the silence seems to reach out and gather us close. I've never experienced anything like it. How can he make me feel so loved when I can't even see his face?

"Was the mission…a success?" he asks, his voice a low rumble.

"Yes. I think so." She blinks our tears away. "It took some… convincing. But young Alice did it. She told him she loved him. You can bet they're aware of each other now."

"And you're absolutely sure she's not going to fall in love with him?" He clears his throat. "Young Bandit is awfully irresistible."

If I controlled our ears, they would perk. As it is, I'm listening as hard as I can, straining against the edge of my consciousness. This is it. The reason why I traveled to the future. If I'm going to get my answers, it will be now.

"Trust me," my older self says, her voice harder. A concrete so inflexible that it makes my consciousness shiver. "At that age, I was absolutely welded to my no-dating rule. She won't fall for him. She thinks he's an arrogant jerk."

"I hope so," he says gravely. "This is our last chance. And

it all comes down to your choices as a teenage girl."

Come on. I grit my metaphorical teeth. I know this already. Get to the good stuff. Explain *why.*

"It will work," she insists. "She'll have no problem killing him. She doesn't have any ties to him. No history, complicated or otherwise. She'll do it."

"She'd better. The future depends on it."

My older self wiggles on the plank, almost rolling off the narrow surface. "Get me out of here. I'm ready."

A noise fills our ears, a soft *whir* coming from underneath us, rising above the hum of the metal coils. The narrow plank begins to slide out. My older self rocks back and forth, as though to hurry the motion.

I, too, am about to jump out of my consciousness. I'm finally going to meet the older Zeke. The man who can comfort me without a word. The one who understands me, through and through. He loves me so much that I feel the depth of his affection even when I have no body.

We exit the tube entirely, and my older self blinks up at the bright light. A man steps into our peripheral vision, and she snaps her head in his direction, as though she can't delay seeing him a moment longer.

My consciousness freezes. Time, however you define it, comes to a complete stop.

I can't…I can't understand this. The man before me is older now. His shoulders are broader, although he's maintained his lean, strong build. There are lines creasing his features, but the eyes, oh, the eyes are unmistakable.

It's not Zeke after all.

I'm looking into the face of Bandit Sakda, ten years in the future.

CHAPTER 46

Does not compute. Does not compute. Does. Not. Compute. Bandit is my future husband? How can that be? The husband in my vision said that line about the ordinary miracle. Zeke's line. I assumed my older self would marry Zeke. Not Bandit. *Zeke.*

Why does my older self want me to kill the boy I end up marrying? Who clearly loves me? Why, why, why?

My consciousness zooms out of my hiding space. Crashes into one side of my older self's brain. Ricochets into the other. Bounces back and forth, up and down, and I can't control the motion. I can't rein it in, even though I know that I must. Even though I'm risking this entire mission.

I don't get it.

I don't get it.

I don't get it.

My older self gasps. "Bandit! She's here! Young Alice. Her consciousness. She must've snuck to the future somehow."

"Send her back," he says grimly. "Before she ruins everything."

Nooooooo!

I dig into this present with everything I have. Curl my consciousness into our physical body and hold on tight. The cold, hard rock underneath our bare feet, bits of dust pushing up between our toes. The air hitting the back of our throat as our mouth gapes in a soundless scream. This warm, loving man standing before us, looking at us with those deep, familiar eyes.

"Don't worry, Malice," he says. "I'll fix this. I won't let her mess up everything we've worked for."

I'm not the enemy, I want to say. *I'm only looking for the truth.*

But even if I had control of our mouth, it's too late.

ZIIIIP.

With a ferocity that makes her last ejection seem tame, my older self detaches my consciousness, drop-kicking me out of her brain.

I shoot into the void. The space between times, the one through which I traveled to get to the future.

But I'm not ready to go back. I still don't understand. I *need* more answers.

Gathering every filament and strand of my consciousness, I stretch into the void. In a realm with no gravity and no friction, I imagine putting the brakes on my forward motion. I *will* my velocity to slow—and then stop.

What do you know? It actually works.

I'm floating in deep black space, instead of being hurled through it. I have no limbs. My body and head and lips cease to exist.

Automatically, I look down. There! Underneath me. The colorful stream of my life. But I won't fall in randomly this time. I'll wait and watch for just the right moment. The time that will tell me the truth. The days that will explain everything.

The images slide by, faster and faster.

Alice breaks up with Zeke, the day after she accidentally fondles Bandit at the club. A week after that, she shows up on Bandit's doorstep, after hunting him down through the friend of a friend.

They become a couple, and on the day of his father's funeral, Alice holds Bandit close, repeating a thought she heard long ago, about ordinary miracles and ordinary tragedies. Bandit looks into the face of the woman he loves. Those words, couched in that voice, wrapped around those arms, give him comfort when he didn't believe comfort was possible. The saying resonates so much that he'll repeat it later, during another pivotal moment of his life.

Alice and Bandit get married at a winery in Napa Valley. They promise to love each other to the depth and breadth and height their souls can reach, in this timeline and every other, with children or without.

Baby Hope is born, and the small family moves into the caves after the second wave of victims fall, stuffing all their belongings into one meager carved-out space...

This is it! The moment I've been waiting for!

With the precision of a professional diver, I plunge into the river of my life at that...exact...moment.

CHAPTER 47

Archie looms on the holo-screen, larger than life. His hair is a wild bramble of brown strands, and the abnormally pale skin speaks to an existence of huddling inside a lab. He stands in the center of an unsheltered clearing, the sun beating down on him in his khaki shorts and T-shirt. He's not wearing a single protective layer. No helmet or shield. No sun suit. He's probably not even wearing sunscreen.

I stick my hand in my mouth and bite, hard. Bandit tugs at my wrist and manages to dislodge it, but not before my skin boasts a row of distinct teeth marks.

Along with a hundred other people, we're watching the holo-screen from an underground bunker. We descended into the earth a week ago, three months after the initial outbreak, but the air already smells used and stale. Sweat and fear cling to the crumbling tunnel walls, and I can almost believe we've lived here since we were born.

Easier still to imagine that we'll stay here until we die.

The first wave of victims dropped like murres on the beaches of Alaska. One moment, people were walking down the street, a child or two hoverboarding beside them, and the next, burns erupted on their bodies as though they had been set on fire. They clawed at their clothes, ripping them away to find open, gaping wounds spreading over their skin. In a single day, thousands of people broke out in burns—and died.

The government figured out right away that the victims became infected outside, so they sequestered everyone inside homes and emergency shelters. Society screeched to a halt, and half a million people perished before the scientists could discover the cause.

The sun. The life-giving, ubiquitous sun, nearly impossible to avoid. The deadly rays snuck in through the cracks of blinds, the edges of curtains, to infiltrate every inch of a building. People laid low, sticking to the darkest corners of their lowest floors. Existing, for the first time, in a world with no natural light.

As long as their food lasted.

People snuck outside then, but only at night. They wore as many layers as they could pile on: visors, hats, sunglasses, helmets, gloves, stockings, snow pants, long sleeves. Still, they became infected.

Still, they died.

That was when the scientists discovered that the allergy stemmed not just from the sun but from UV radiation in general. It was a hell of a choice. Stay inside and watch your family starve. Or venture outside and risk imminent death.

Another million people succumbed to the radiation before the first underground cities opened. Millions more passed before the last of the remaining population was invited under the earth. North America suffered the most deaths, since that's where the virus was released. But populations were also decimated in Asia, Africa, Europe. Not a single country escaped without extensive casualties.

Underground bulldozers worked, day and night, tunneling more space, pushing deeper into the earth. Building a new world with a third of the previous population.

And now my brother has limped to the security cameras in front of the underground city of the District of Columbia. The last time we talked, I begged him to retreat underground with us so that we would be together. So that he could be safe.

He declined. I didn't understand why, but even back then, my body knew. As it does now. Sweat courses over my skin, and both my heart and stomach think I'm caught in a storm on the Bay of Biscay: tilting, falling, somersaulting.

Except I'm not. I'm in a dry underground cave, my eyes magnetized to the screen.

Archie laughs, loud and braying, and holds his palms up to the sun, taunting us. Mocking the world.

"It was me." His eyes shoot all over the holo-screen, as though he might be searching for someone in the audience. Searching for…me. "I'm the one who released the Sun Virus. Not to punish the world, as you might believe, but in order to help you."

I press my hand to my heart in an attempt to hold together the shattered shards. *Oh, Archie. No. NO.* I can't accept this. Even here, even now, I cannot believe that my brother is the Maker.

"People have become cruel," he continues, indifferent to my denial. Oblivious to my pain. "You care only about yourselves. You've forgotten how to be kind. Unselfish. You no longer remember the things that were supposed to make us human. You haven't remembered in a long time.

"So I'm giving you a new start. By shrinking the world's population, I'm allowing you to think about what's truly important. How, and to whom, your time and energy and love *should* be allocated. I'm providing you with the opportunity, as you rebuild your lives, to avoid the mistakes of the past."

Tears fall onto my cheeks. For all the people who died. For the fathers and babies and spouses and best friends. For the dreams that have been cut short, for the lives that were never lived. For all the love that's been snuffed out, mercilessly, from this world.

Raising a shaky hand, I swipe at my face. I don't deserve to cry. Not when it was my brother who caused this wholesale destruction. Not when I should've, could've stopped him. Some way, somehow.

"I am the Maker," Archie shouts. "The Virus Maker but also the maker of the new world. If you have any doubt, witness my resistance to the sun. I — and I alone — ingested the antidote to the virus. I — and I alone — am immune to the effects of these rays."

He looks directly at us, which means he's located the security camera. "Make no mistake. This is not a cure. The antidote was created during the earliest days of the virus by a freak mutation that I haven't been able to replicate. And thus, I am the only one in the world of my kind." He lowers his arms. "I always was, you know. *You* made me this way. You made me different; you made me alone. And now, I literally am."

He laughs, wretched and miserable. The sound echoes in the empty space around him, in the oceans of crumbling dirt, in the waves of rippling fields.

My insides twist and fold, becoming a grotesque origami of their original selves. I reach my hand toward the holo-screen. This man...has lost all his humanity. He has killed millions and condemned the rest of us to live in a cramped, dark facsimile of our normal world.

This person is not Archie. Not anymore. He bears no resemblance to the brother I used to know. The one I've always loved.

And yet, I long to comfort him, like I've tried to do all my life. I want to reach the desperate, lonely boy inside. His pain started when our mother left. It grew with the taunting of our classmates. And then it exploded when, one by one, he lost us all. His best friend, Zeke, to a new research passion and other colleagues. The woman he secretly and then not so secretly loved, Lalana, when she couldn't return his feelings. And then me, when I married Bandit.

I feel his pain like a stake in my heart. And I *need* to make it better.

Something glints at the corner of the screen. Something silver, something reflective. My breath catches. There's only one thing it could be. A sun suit issued by the military.

My pulse roars. I dart my eyes over the holo-screen, skipping from the thick thatches of grass to the undulating hills. Archie's been on the security camera for ten minutes now. Plenty of time for the military to set up a mission. Plenty of cover for a sniper to take aim at the most dangerous man in the world.

Even as I recoil, a bullet whistles across the screen. My toes curl in on themselves, and Archie collapses to the ground, red blossoming on his chest.

"Alice," he pants.

The scream starts deeper than my veins. Further down than my core. It goes all the way back to the black void of a womb, where kindred spirits find each other. Where soul mates can be formed, even before they're born.

My brother. My protector. My best friend.

The people closest to me startle. They turn and stare, but they can't possibly know who he is. They can't possibly understand what we once meant to each other.

"You shouldn't have married him, Alice," he gasps. "I needed you, and you deserted me. Just like Mom. Just like everyone else." He lowers himself to the ground, as though he is lying down to go to sleep. "Well, I hope you found the happiness you were looking for. Because I sure as hell didn't."

His eyes close.

My knees go out, and my hands slap against the rocky ground. I taste blood, so I must've bitten my lip or my tongue. I don't know which. I don't care.

I tried to explain to Archie that I never left him. That my love for my husband occupies a separate compartment in my heart. I could continue to love them both—and I did. I do.

The words bounced off my brother like rubber balls from a wall. He retreated to the woods, to a grown-up tree house elevated twenty feet off the ground. The place where he created the virus that wiped out the world.

And now he's sprawled on the ground with a growing red flower on his chest. Eyes closed for the very last time.

The pain ripples out from my soul, and it doesn't stop until it pulverizes every last cell in my body.

That evening, Bandit and I sit cross-legged inside our unit, a woven mat all that separates us from the cold, cold earth. Our furnishings are simple, utilitarian. A single mattress on the cave floor, a small sink carved into the rock. Our dinner consists of a bit of rice and even less potato. I think of the bento boxes I made for Archie, once upon a time, and my hands shake.

I can't eat. My stomach growls, but I can't bear the thought of putting any food in my mouth, not when my brother will never take in sustenance ever again.

The six-month-old on my lap doesn't have the same

problem. Hope, we named her. Ironic for the offspring of parents called Bandit and Alice. Fitting for the cramped, desolate conditions in which we live.

Hope wraps my hair around her fists, and tears spring to my eyes. Not because it hurts. But because she never met her uncle. And now, she never will.

Bandit scoops up a spoonful of rice and feeds our daughter.

"He was a bad man, an evil man." I test out the words in the air. It's what everyone's been saying about the Maker. "He killed millions of people. Is it…wrong…of me to mourn him?"

"He was your brother," Bandit says simply. "You loved him."

"Still do," I whisper, patting Hope's mouth with a napkin. I bury my nose against her hair and breathe. She smells like everything that's fresh and clean. Laundry blowing in the breeze, a pot of flowers on the front porch. But those are analogies from the old world, the one we lived above the ground. Try as I might, I can't conjure up an equivalent in our new, tunneled life.

"I wish there was something we could've done," I say. "Maybe, if Mom never abandoned us, things would've turned out differently."

"Maybe if he never met Charlie," Bandit offers.

"Maybe if Lalana hadn't broken his heart."

"Maybe if you hadn't married me." Bandit picks up my hand and holds it against his heart. The familiar *thump-thump*, the one I've been listening to for five years, almost makes me break down again. "Maybe then, our world wouldn't be what it is today."

"No," I say fiercely. "If I never married you, then little Hope wouldn't exist. And I wouldn't trade her life for anything."

An hour later, after Hope is tucked into her crib, which is just a hollow boulder lined with a piece of mattress and the softest blankets we could find, a knock sounds on our unit. Bandit opens the door, and a strikingly beautiful woman walks inside. Her dark eyes are as luminous as the stars that we no longer see.

"You may not remember me," she says to me. "But ten years ago, we went to school together. We met briefly at the Newhouse awards banquet. Your brother was honored as one of the most brilliant young minds of our nation. So was your husband." She winks at Bandit. "And so was I. My name is Cristela Ruiz, and I'm brilliant. So brilliant that we may be able to help each other. Together, we can change the fate of our world."

She smiles, and for the first time since my brother closed his eyes on the dusty ground, an emotion rises in my heart. One tiny flutter, no stronger than a subtle stir. And yet it has the power to change lives. Futures. Worlds.

I know it's changed mine.

Hope.

CHAPTER 48

I'm back in the void, floating in deep space. I must be getting better at existing in this realm, because there's no disorientation. No flailing of limbs that don't exist.

I have confirmation now. More explicit proof than I ever wanted that my brother is the Maker. As much as that pierces my incorporeal heart with an incessant onslaught of daggers, I need more.

How? How did we get from stopping Archie to killing Bandit? Why didn't we dissuade him from going to Harvard? Why didn't we prevent Mom from abandoning us?

Why didn't we just…gulp…kill Archie himself?

I scan the images of my time stream as they slide by, faster and faster. I dip in and out of the river, and small pieces of the puzzle jump out at me.

Bandit and Cristela and I sabotaged his application to Harvard. We interrupted his mentorship with Charlie. We tried to convince Lalana to fall in love with my brother, and when that failed, we set him up with other women.

But my mom's abandonment—we couldn't touch. That

event didn't happen in the original time stream, Cristela explained. That branch was created by other forces, other actors from the future. For laws of science that I can't understand, that incident is off-limits to us.

And then I see it. The scene that addresses our attempt to kill my brother. This moment, I want to understand deeply. This decision, I have to live fully.

Taking a figurative breath, I leap into the river with both metaphorical feet.

"I will throttle her." I pace the tiny floor in our residential unit. My feet slap against the stone, threatening to wake Hope, whom I just got to sleep in her carved rock crib. But I can't bring myself to care. "So help me, I will reach my hands through the black void, wrap them around my younger self's neck, and choke her until there's no breath left."

"Now, now." Bandit steps directly in my path. "That's my wife you're talking about. One whom I love very much. No matter how old she happens to be."

I lower my forehead onto his chest, and for a moment, we just stand there, breathing.

"How was I ever that stubborn?" I mutter. "How did you put up with me all these years?"

"Believe me, it's been a challenge," he says, his lips twitching.

I smile—almost. Too much is unsettled. Too much is at stake.

"She just won't kill Archie." I pound my fists against his chest. "No matter how I explain to her. Not when we showed her the burn victims. Not when I told her that he was already dead, here in the future. Not even when I withheld the name of the target and let her reach her own conclusions."

"So we keep trying."

"We've *been* trying." I take a deep breath and look into his face. Deep circles rim his eyes, and his always handsome face is too thin. As a doctor, he's closer to the devastation. He visits the patients in the trauma bays every day, studying the disease in hopes of finding a cure. Witnessing that much pain, that much sorrow, day in and day out takes a toll.

My heart twinges. "I have three trips left. You and Cristela have both reached your limit, so this is it. Our last shot to save humanity." My shoulders droop. "I hate to say it, but our chances don't look good."

Hope cries out, and Bandit scoops her out of the crib, cradling her as he sways back and forth, a tuneless hum on his lips. The burn that originated on her forehead has spread to her limbs and covers her entire torso.

By now, we've all been infected with the virus, and our only recourse is to stay underground. But the caves aren't foolproof. Cracks form in the rock, and UV radiation seeps through. The walls of Hope's day care were tragically compromised—and now we're dealing with the consequences.

"She's worse today," I say. "She doesn't gurgle anymore. Hasn't smiled in a week."

"We can't lose faith." He fixes his eyes on her tiny nose, her delicate but well-defined lips. "That's all we have left."

How can I not?

Every hour that I walk with my daughter in our cramped living quarters in an attempt to soothe the shivers that wrack her body, I die a little more. My heart gets a little harder. When the day comes that I lose her altogether, all that will be left is a blackened mass that disintegrates upon impact.

"I don't know how I'll keep on living when she's gone," I admit.

Bandit looks up sharply. "Don't say that, Alice. You've lost her before, and you survived it. You can do it again."

I frown. "What are you talking about? I've never lost her. She's right here."

He doesn't speak. Hope has quieted, and he sets her in the crib, smoothing her sleep sack so that it lays unwrinkled beneath her. He then takes my hands solemnly, his callused palms scraping against my knuckles, and we sit cross-legged on the woven mat.

"When you travel through the black void, have you ever seen the twisted ropes of our time stream?" he asks, playing with my fingers.

"Yes, of course." I clear my throat. "They kinda smack you in the non-face."

"So you've noticed how the smaller threads break off from the central strand before weaving back in?"

I nod, in spite of my confusion. We're not talking about time travel. We were discussing Hope. Where is he going with this?

His fingers stop moving. "Every time we travel to the past, a thread breaks off the original time stream. So far, the disruptions have been small, the ripples so minute, that the thread eventually rejoins the central rope. What this means is that although some details may change, our overall world looks the same." He takes a breath. "What we *want* is for the threads to break off completely, to form an entirely new rope, because we need a world that is entirely different. A world where the Sun Virus doesn't exist, where two-thirds of the population hasn't perished."

I'm still following, still waiting to see where this explanation leads. Hope shifts in her sleep, her breath coming out in a soft sigh, and my eyes flicker to our daughter.

"There are some events in our central thread that are unshakable. Take, for example, our love." His thumb flicks over the back of my hand. "We've interfered with the past; we've tried to prevent ourselves from falling in love. But in every instance, we end up together. Even when we refused to officially marry, we become important to each other in a way that ultimately disappoints Archie. I believe, in every iteration of this timeline, that you and I will always find each other. We'll always love each other."

"That's a nice thought," I murmur.

Bandit drops his head. I want to hurry him along, to tell him to get to the point, but something stops me. A growing anxiety in the pit of my stomach.

"Other events are more fragile," he says eventually. "Less... permanent, I guess you could say. Such as the exposure to the sun by a little girl."

"What are you saying?" I ask faintly.

He looks at me, an unspeakable sorrow in his eyes. "Every time we travel to the past, we disrupt the universe enough that it changes the integrity of the cave walls. In a few lucky worlds, Hope manages to dodge the sun's rays altogether. Other times, she succumbs to the burns later in life. But in approximately half the worlds..." He stops. Swallows hard. "She's exposed earlier. And there's nothing we can do about it."

I yank away my hands, looking at the crib. A sliver of Hope's ear peeks out from under her knit hat. The most perfect lobe in the history of time. "Are you saying in some of those worlds, Hope doesn't survive?"

"Yes," he says softly. "Between the two of us, we've traveled to the past thirty-seven times. Thirty-seven times, we've disrupted the universe. Five of those times, Hope lives a long—albeit limited—life underground. Twelve other times, she grows up to at least see adulthood. And the rest of the time, she…dies. As a child. Before she ever gets a chance to live."

The truth crashes over me. I can't breathe. I can't claw my way to the top of this wave. Hope. My Hope. The candle of my heart. The breath and joy of my life. Gone. Extinguished.

I did this. By messing with the past, I destroyed the most important part of me. I did what I couldn't get my younger self to do.

I. Killed.

Even worse, I killed my own baby. Over and over again. I lift my eyes to Bandit, to the only anchor I've ever had in this chaotic world. He's crying. No, he's *sobbing*, in a way I've never seen, tremors rattling his shoulders, silent tears streaking down his cheeks.

No similar moisture flows down my face. It's like all my tears have been used up, erased out of existence with the deceased versions of my baby. "How do you know? How come…I don't remember?"

Except I do remember. I know that now. In the last few months, there's been a deep loss inside me, a void similar to that realm between times. I never understood it, but now, that hole has a shape. It has a name. It's filled with moments and laughter and lives—even if I've never experienced them.

He gulps at the air for several seconds before he can compose himself. "From the beginning, I had my suspicions, a deep foreboding that what we were doing could mess up our lives. The people we care about. But my worries were swept away with the urgency of our mission. Before my last jump, I confronted Cristela. She admitted the truth. She's known all along what could happen if we disrupted the past. She knew that our interference might save some lives and destroy others. But she thought it didn't matter because we wouldn't remember."

"She's wrong," I whisper, my voice cracking along with

my heart. "It matters. *Hope* matters, no matter which parallel world she's in."

"I agree." He wipes away his tears with the back of one hand. "That's why, during my last jump, I couldn't resist. I dipped into some of the alternate threads. The ones that broke off from the main time stream after our earlier trips."

I freeze. "You saw Hope?"

He nods once.

My world narrows down to a single point. "Tell me."

"It won't help. Seeing other versions of our baby doesn't allow me to sleep through the night. If anything, knowing makes it worse, because now I can put images to the nightmares that haunt me."

"I don't care," I say fiercely. Nothing will keep me away from my child. Not his flimsy need to protect me. Not even time itself. "She's my baby, too. I deserve to know what happened to her. What I did to her."

He nods again. He knows me so well. He always knew I would insist. "She was four years old in the first thread I visited. A beautiful little girl with a gap between her front teeth. We knew we would never be able to fix it, but we didn't mind. We thought the gap only added to her perfection. She had a pair of striped pajamas, with a shark on the chest, that she wore every day. That is, until the burns spread across her body. The wounds were so raw, so gaping, that even the brush of that soft fabric was too painful. She cried when we took them away. She thought she was being punished, and she promised that she would be a good girl again, if only we would give back her pajamas.

"In another thread, Hope was just a newborn when she was exposed. So small that she still fit on my forearm. You put those little mittens on her so that she wouldn't scratch herself, and you cried so much that your tears fell on her face like rain. She would never feel actual rain, you told me. On account of us living underground. On account of her life being so short. So you were giving her that experience, in the only way you could.

"And then, there was the time she was eight years old and understood exactly what was happening to her — "

"Stop," I say hoarsely. One of these days, I'll listen to all of Bandit's stories. I'll write down every detail. If some version of my baby had to suffer through those atrocities, then the least I can do is hear the specifics. Embrace them. Keep the stories in my soul where they belong. Where they live now.

But at this moment, guilt and sorrow lacerate my heart, and each word rips the gashes a little more. Each sentence sprinkles the salt a little more liberally.

"You're not to blame," Bandit says. "We did this together. We did what we thought was right."

I almost laugh. What is right, and what is wrong? In this world, morality doesn't exist. There is no good decision. There are only the choices that we made. The ones we decided were the less of two evils. The ones we'll bear forever on our souls.

"Say something, Alice," he begs, pain lancing his words. "I'm sorry. Sorrier than I can ever say. I need to know you're going to be okay. Please, Alice."

I snap up my head. "Stop calling me that. She doesn't exist anymore. Not after what I've done. Not after I killed Hope, over and over and over." My voice breaks and then shatters. "I don't deserve that name. Not now. Never again."

He takes a shuddering breath. "What should I call you, then?"

There's only one answer. Only one name that fits. Only one word I merit.

"Malice," I say. "You can call me Malice."

CHAPTER 49

I open my eyes. The exposed beams of the soaring living room ceiling stare down at me, and the leather sofa cradles my spine. Sunlight dapples over the lower half of my body, and a lemony-citrus scent tingles my nose.

I'm back in my seventeen-year-old body. Back where I have complete control over my limbs, where I'm the actor, not the observer, in my life.

Testing, I wiggle my toes. Swallow. Flex my fingers. Just as my older self did ten years in the future.

In an instant, the next events of Malice's life rush through my mind.

Panicking and desperate, Bandit hatches a plan so wild that it might actually work: kill his younger self so that he and Alice never fall in love. Never disappoint Archie. They'll break the chain of abandonments that Archie suffers, take away that final hurt that sends him over the edge.

They may have failed in the previous attempts to separate the two. But they would succeed if one of them was dead.

With only three trips left, however, they have to be

strategic. They have to return to a time where they've already laid the groundwork. They have to trick young Alice, so that it appears like Bandit was the target all along. And they have to accomplish all of the above without giving their younger selves a chance to fall in love.

Shouldn't be a problem, Bandit said. In high school, he was arrogance personified. She was closed off to dating. And then he said something that Malice would never, ever forget: "Sometimes even soul mates won't fit together if they meet at the wrong age."

They proceeded to execute their plan.

Only, I'm not there to experience it because I'm back in the present.

I zoom around my brain, searching in those little nooks, in the shadowed corners where a traveling being might hide. I even check for a consciousness crouching stealthily under mine.

There's no doubt about it. *She*'s no longer with me—the woman named Malice who tried to trick me. The mother who inadvertently killed her child, over and over again. The version of my older self who said goodbye to the man she loved across time streams.

It's just me in here. No one else.

Disappointment floods me, which is ridiculous. There's always *only* been me for the bulk of my seventeen years. Do I actually feel…lonely…now that I've reverted to my normal state?

Yeah, I do. Because for long moments at a time, while I was blended with Malice's mind, we merged into the same person.

And I *miss* her, in a weird, nonsensical kind of way.

"Well?" Cristela's impatient voice intrudes on my thoughts. "Did it work? Did you go to the future?"

I sit up so quickly, the room spins, and I have to press both hands against my temples until the furniture rights itself.

"Yes." That one word is woefully inadequate in capturing what happened. "How long was I gone?"

She glances at her wrist, bare except for a few freckles. "Two, three minutes?"

My stomach tightens. What will it be like to see Bandit again? *He* didn't travel to the future. He has no idea what we'll become to each other. To him, I'm just a girl he's kissed who tried to kill him. But to me, he's...so much more.

To me, he's everything.

Except he's not here, slouched against the brightly colored walls or fiddling with the dangling spider plants.

Only two minutes have passed. Where did he go?

"Spill it," Cristela demands. "I want to know everything. What you saw. How it felt. What you did."

Automatically, I start talking. This is her research, after all. She figured out a way for me to get to the future; the least I can do is give her information.

"I'm not sure why you lived the future, instead of observing it," Cristela admits when I've told her everything. "Maybe it's because you dove directly into the time stream, instead of zipping your consciousness to hers? One more thing I can look forward to in my research. That, and figuring out how Malice was able to control your arm when you gave Bandit the cupcake."

I scan the room as she talks, from the vases with the petal cutouts to the waist-to-ceiling windows, as though I expect to find Bandit's tall frame folded like a pretzel.

But I don't. Because he's not here.

Maybe it's just as well. My insides churn with a mix of sorrow, anger, and love. But a single piece of knowledge rises above all that emotion.

Do I dare share it with Cristela? She's little more than an acquaintance now, but in the future, she's my ally. More than that, she's my friend.

"In order to save the world, I need to kill somebody," I say slowly. "Bandit…or my brother."

She whistles, long and low. "That's quite a dilemma."

"Bandit was supposed to be the easy choice." I get up from the sofa, shoving my hands into my hair. "He was supposed to be just a student at school. A guy I barely knew. But that was before I traveled to the future. Before I understood how much he'll mean to me. Before I learned the truth."

She shivers, as though glad *she* doesn't have to make the decision. "Do you agree with what your older self has concluded?"

"I don't know. Once, I would've deferred every important decision to her. I thought, falsely, that just because she was older, she was also wiser. But I've seen her heart." I stalk the circumference of the cheerful room. The brightly colored walls do nothing to assuage my uneasiness. "The organ that beats in her chest is as black and hard as a lump of coal. There's no life left. No hope. How can I trust someone like that to make the right choice?"

I turn back to Cristela. "The future was right about one thing. I need to figure this out for myself. And I won't be able to do that until I see Bandit. Where is he?"

She frowns. "A minute after you closed your eyes, he bolted straight up, muttered something, and ran out of the room. I assumed he went to the bathroom."

We look out the double french doors.

"I'm sure he'll be back," she says unconvincingly. "I mean, where would he go?"

My heart leaps into my throat. What am I doing? Why am I standing here, talking to Cristela, when Bandit's been gone for entire minutes?

Something's wrong. It has to be. He wouldn't have just left. He would've wanted to know if my trip to the future was successful.

Anxiety strums through my veins, and I stride out the door. Cristela hurries after me. I check behind every door in the hall, and she slips past me to the two-story foyer.

"Bandit!" she bellows up the stairs. "Where are you?"

No response. There's no one inside the orderly office, the walk-in closet, or the flowery powder room, either.

Cristela and I meet where the hardwood joins textured stone tiles. "Does he like to wander around houses?" Her nail scratch-scratch-scratches at her thumb.

"I don't think so," I say, although the truth is, I'm not familiar with his habits. All I know is that one day, we'll be soul mates.

Unless I kill him first.

I dart my gaze from the thick wood banister to the wedding-cake chandelier. It lands on the stained-glassed windows…and then my heart stops.

"Um, Cristela?" I say faintly. "I don't think Bandit got lost on his way to the bathroom. His car is gone."

We both stare at the empty driveway. Both sides of the concrete are lined with beds of greenery dotted with little purple flowers. But even through the rose-tinted glass, I can't find anything to appreciate about the view.

"I can't believe he would ditch you," she murmurs.

My thoughts spin. "You said he bolted upright. Did he remember something? Or could he have heard…someone?"

She widens her eyes. "You mean, like a voice? From the future?"

The older Bandit's last words, a moment before I was ejected from Malice's consciousness, flash through my mind.

Don't worry, he said. *I'll fix this. I won't let her mess up everything we've worked for.*

I'll fix this.

I'll fix this.

I'll fix this.

The pieces click together. "The timing's too coincidental—one minute after I closed my eyes, when I was only gone for two. The future Bandit had already used all his jumps. Any more, and his mind will come apart." The words sprint out of my mouth, but my thoughts have been lapping them and then some. "But our older selves had already decided to kill him. So he has nothing to lose by traveling to the past one more time."

"Why?" Cristela's eyes are shiny black ponds. "What did he need to say to his younger self that was so important?"

"Bandit loves me." No truer words have ever been spoken in any time stream. When I was in the future, I felt his heart, and it was as unshakable as the laws of gravity. As inevitable as the rising of the sun. "I don't mean *this* Bandit, in *this* time. Who knows what he feels? But the older Bandit loves the older me.

"He would've been thinking about me. Only me. How he can help me. How he can ease my pain." I take a rattling breath. "I'm pretty sure he came back to tell his younger self to take the decision out of my hands."

She blinks three times. Stops. And then blinks three more. "You mean to say…"

"Yep." I look at the driveway once more, but this time through a shard of blue-colored glass. Same scene, new angle. The absence of his car now makes me want to howl, long and loud and never-ending. "Right at this moment, Bandit is either on his way to kill Archie…or himself."

CHAPTER 50

I fly over the highway, pushing the odometer to its limits. Seventy-five, eighty-five, ninety-five. And still, the car's not going fast enough. Still, it can't keep pace with the racing of my heart.

Bandit has at most a twenty-minute lead on me, but I have no idea where he's going. I'm not sure what he's planning. For all I know, he could've already flung himself off the road.

My knuckles tighten on the steering wheel. *Oh, please. Not that.* I have to believe he's still alive. I have to believe that he needs time to digest his older self's orders, that he wouldn't jeopardize anyone's life hastily, much less his own.

I swipe at the sweat on my forehead. At least I have a car. Cristela wasn't too keen on parting with her Mini Cooper, especially because I didn't know where I was taking it or when I could bring it back.

"But this is a matter of life and death!" I shouted. She agreed, although whose death, we weren't sure.

I urge the car faster, hoping there are no cops on the road. Wishing that for once, Fate is on my side.

Oh, please, I plead again. It's a refrain with no specifics, and I don't know what it is I want. I'm not sure to whom, exactly, I'm begging.

Do I want Bandit to live? Of course I do. But not at the expense of my brother. Does that mean I would choose Archie over him, this kind, strong-willed boy who will be... might be...my everything?

I don't know, I don't know, I don't know!

A conversation flits through my memory. Funny. I don't remember experiencing it, but I must've absorbed it during the hops I took through the original time stream. One more thing for Cristela to figure out and explain to me.

"I'm going first," Bandit says, his tone arrogant, his jaw chiseled rock. If I weren't so irritated, I might marvel at how I married such a handsome man. We're in Cristela's unit, and the time tube emits a low, constant hum as it warms up. "The younger me will be easier to convince. He already believes time travel is possible. He'll accept more quickly that the Voice is his older self, and he'll question less."

My temper flares. "Oh, because my *younger self is an annoying brat who won't listen to reason?"*

"You said it, not me." His mouth quirks. After five years, I've finally learned that means he's teasing me. He pulls me against him for a hard kiss and then leaves the room for his final prep.

Huffing, I join Cristela at the computer, where she's inputting the coordinates for Bandit's trip to the past.

"You're a lucky woman," she says, her eyes soft.

"Why? Because I'm married to the most exasperating man on the planet?"

"No. Because every thought that man has is to protect you," she says simply.

I sag against the wall as her words sink in. She's right. Bandit doesn't actually want to go first. He's not a reckless

thrill seeker looking for adventure in an untested time machine,
one that could as easily send his mind to a black hole as to
the target date.

He just wants me *not to take the risk.*

"You're right," I say. "I am lucky."

In the present, my eyes fill. Blinking quickly, I press my foot on the accelerator. The car rattles, as though it might come apart at any moment.

Good. Because I'm going to find Bandit in time—or die trying.

CHAPTER 51

Ninety minutes later, I arrive at my house. Pulling crookedly into the driveway, I'm out of the car almost before the engine stops running. I vault up the front steps and burst through the front door.

"Archie?" I call. "Are you here?"

Of course my brother's home. He was sleeping in his bed when I left this morning, and he never goes anywhere on Saturdays. It's his favorite day of the week because he can work uninterrupted.

I skip down the basement stairs two at a time, but he's not sitting in front of his computer. Huh. I go back upstairs and check the bathroom. Nope. The living area. Nada. The bedroom, in case he's sleeping—nothing, nothing, nothing.

Okay, this is weird. Déjà vu washes over me. Didn't I just go through these same actions, looking for someone else? For the one other boy who's vitally important in my life?

I swallow, but I can't budge the lump that's taken permanent residence in my throat. I shuffle my feet—and then I hear it. The scrape of a spatula against a frying pan.

Come to think of it, I also detect the greasy scent of something cooking in oil.

Archie! I race toward the kitchen. I suppose even my scattered brother can make an omelet when he's hungry enough.

When I fling myself over the threshold, however, I see not my brother but another man standing at the stove, one with the proud stance of a prodigy who graduated college at nineteen to start his own company.

"Dad." I screech to a stop, dismay seeping through my word. "It's you."

He lifts an eyebrow. "And you wonder why I'm not around more often. So pleased to see you, too, daughter."

"Sorry," I say, too distracted to be truly sorry. "I was looking for Archie."

"He already left for prom." He cracks an egg in the frying pan and then peers at me. "Which, frankly, is where I thought you were."

Prom.

I stumble backward. *Prom.* I can't believe I forgot. This is what happens when the administration schedules the most important dance of the year on the final weekend of spring break. Damn the exam schedule and budget constraints!

Bandit and Cristela didn't mention the dance, but I suppose it would've been awkward for Bandit to bring it up if he were attending with someone else. And Cristela and her girlfriend recently split, I suddenly remember.

The egg sizzles in the pan. Dad stares at me, even though he likes his yolks runny. "Archie was looking for you, too. You were supposed to go somewhere with him? He was banging around the basement all afternoon because you stood him up."

Aw, crap. The tux shop. I'm a terrible, terrible sister.

"Did he end up getting a tux?" I ask. "He must have if he

went to prom."

Wordlessly, my dad gestures to a garment bag hanging from a chair at the dining table. A piece of white paper is stapled to the plastic.

I snatch up the receipt and scan it. The line items include: a white tux with purple stripes. A satin top hat. White gloves. Even a cane.

I gulp at the air. No. He couldn't have. There's no way he thought this outfit was appropriate.

"Dad?" I ask in a strangled voice. "Did you see Archie before he left the house?"

"I did." He slides the egg onto a plate, the edges crispy and practically burned. It's no secret where I got my cooking skills. "I wondered about his attire. But I didn't want to crush his spirit. Goodness knows I'm not in touch with what's hip these days."

"Dad!" I yell, anguished. "It was a purple-striped tux! That's not hip in *any* time period. Someone…must've tricked him. Maggie, most likely. He's too smart to fall for it from anyone else. She must've convinced him purple stripes were the trendy look of the season. That he had to wear the tux in order to match her. And I wasn't around to tell him otherwise." I sway forward as the full horror of the situation sinks in. "They're going to laugh at him, and it's all my fault."

Dad whirls so fast that it almost gives *me* whiplash. His eyes are as wide as dinner plates, his skin the same color as his egg whites. "Are you saying he's about to be embarrassed in front of the entire school? Not just a few kids here and there but hundreds of them?"

I nod, a blast of ice hitting my core.

"This wasn't supposed to happen! Not in the original time stream. Not in any version of the future I was told about."

I don't even blink. Dad already admitted that he was being

visited by a voice, even if I'm not sure how much he knows about Archie or the decimation he'll cause.

"I put us on a new time stream," I say, my stomach hollowing. "These last few days, I've been investigating the Voice, and I enlisted Bandit's help. Neither of these things was supposed to happen. That's why I didn't go to the tux shop like I was supposed to."

"You have to get us back on track!" Dad surges forward. He wasn't this frantic when his company was the target of a hostile takeover. He didn't agitate this much when he discovered Mom had left us for good. "We don't know what will push Archie over the edge. In every iteration of the future, there was always one devastating event that made Archie lose touch with humanity. This one is occurring way earlier than the others…" He stops. Swallows. "If we lose him now, we'll never get him back."

His hands tremble. "Everything I've worked for these last six years will be for nothing. The sacrifices we've made as a family—for naught. That's why I pushed him to form connections with legitimate scientists, in hopes that it would shield him from Charlie's influence. That's why I held *you* at a distance. In the original timeline, Archie felt like you were the favorite child and hated me for it. We thought that if I favored him, it might prevent his slide into darkness."

I blink, hardly able to comprehend his words. Is he saying that his coldness, the distance he imposed between us…was all the result of a mission to save the world?

"That's why you stopped talking to me?" I whisper. My heart pounds, a time machine in its own right. Because all of a sudden, it's reverted to the frantic hop-skip pattern of the little girl who only wanted her father's attention. "It wasn't because you stopped…caring about me?"

"Oh, Alice," Dad says, tears in his eyes. "If you only knew

how much it destroyed me to push you away. I love you, honey. I'll never stop. But I hope you understand that I had no choice. I had to do everything in my power to keep Archie from inventing that virus."

Of course. It makes sense that the future would've approached not just Bandit and me but also Dad. They would've used every arsenal available to them. They would've tried every avenue of reaching my brother.

"You have to fix this, Alice." Dad straightens, morphing back into the hard man he's been these last six years, the one who's single-mindedly focused on one goal. "You can't let him be humiliated in front of the entire school. Go — now. Our entire future depends on it. Go, go, go!"

I have so many questions. About the voices that were visiting Dad. Whether they were working in conjunction with us in the future — or apart. Why our older selves weren't allowed to stop Mom from abandoning us. But there's no time. Satisfying my curiosity is a distant second to saving Archie. To saving the world.

For what I hope is the last time today, I race out the door and jump into a car.

CHAPTER 52

When I arrive at the high school, the sun is a fiery orange ball several inches above the tree line. But I don't appreciate its beauty. I can't. I'm too busy looking for a spot for Cristela's car. Parking space after parking space is full, which is to be expected on prom night. Everyone's here, from the attendees to their family and friends.

Finally, I find a space in the overflow lot and rush inside the building. Wall-to-wall people pack the front lobby. The dance itself is taking place in the gym, but the professional photographer has set up a studio out here, complete with dazzling spotlights, ornate columns, and elaborate backdrops. Black velvet ropes hold back the audience, and my impeccably dressed classmates form a line, waiting their turn to get their portrait taken.

The backdrop, at the moment, features a stunning sunset over crystal-blue waters. And the equally gorgeous couple posing in front? Zeke Cain and Kadijah Johnson.

Cameras go off like fireflies in the crowd, and the photographer slashes a hand across her neck, obviously frustrated. The flashes are interfering with her lighting. I should know.

I need to go—to find Archie—but I'm distracted by Zeke's magnificent smile. Involuntarily, I press a hand against my heart. A week ago, I would've been surprised, flustered—even envious. I had no idea Zeke was going to prom. He certainly didn't invite *me*, and I would've pictured myself by his side, holding on to his capable hands as we beamed at the camera.

Today, I don't know how to feel. So much has happened. Too much I've learned. In the original version of the future, I end up dating Zeke. And yet, he's not my soul mate. He's not the man I love across time streams.

I still have a soft spot for him. Maybe I always will. But right now, the only thing I want is for all of us to survive.

The crowd between the velvet ropes and me is six people deep, and I fight through a gap, trying to find Archie.

There! Purple stripes on white, impossible to miss. The getup is even more hideous than I imagined. The tuxedo is stiff and cheap, and the purple is so bright that it hurts my eyes. I'm pretty sure it's a Halloween costume, not an actual tux.

Archie's third from the front of the line. Looks like I got here just in time.

Except he's not alone. He's standing next to Maggie, and she wears a purple dress the exact color as his stripes. His hair is combed nicely, and they're talking together. Laughing.

I bump into the girl next to me, and she shoots me a dirty look. I mumble an apology, although I hardly register what I'm saying. Did I make a mistake?

Maybe Maggie didn't trick him. Maybe this date wasn't some elaborate setup, and purple-striped tuxedos are totally hot in some highly exclusive celebrity circles. Archie said he trusts her. Maybe I should, too.

I bite my lip. The next couple steps up to be photographed,

and a pair of people shoves their way to the velvet ropes. Overeager grandparents, it looks like, who have no concern about anybody's toes, even the precious pink toenails of the scowling girl next to me.

By the time I find Archie again, Maggie's no longer standing next to him. What? I only took my eyes off them for two seconds. Where did she go?

In my peripheral vision, I see a girl wearing a violently purple dress shove her way across the lobby.

My stomach sinks. Oh *no*. I wasn't wrong. This *is* a setup.

A person jostles me on my left, and someone elbows me on the right. First heat and then ice flashes through me, as disorienting as strobe lights. *Do something!* a voice inside me screams. And I try. Damn it, I do try. But horror has welded my lips shut. Panic has planted my feet to the floor. All I can do is watch the scene unfold before me, as helpless as a consciousness in my older self's body.

Archie steps up to the backdrop, his eyes scanning the lobby. The photographer's spotlight shines down on the lock of hair that will never lie down.

"Um, my date will be back in a minute," he tells the photographer.

The crowd titters. Someone pushes Archie from behind, and he stumbles forward, moving more fully to the center of the backdrop. Cameras go off, but the flashes are more than a few isolated bugs now. They're a swarm of golden sparklers, producing yellow-green light.

That's when the heckling starts.

"Hey, dude! You took a wrong turn. This is prom, not the circus!"

"Whatcha wearing under that tux, Archie? Your Marie Curie T-shirt? Never leave home without it!"

"Hey, Archie! Hypothesize this! What do you get when

you put a freak in a purple-striped tux? An even bigger freak!"

The laughter swells. Archie turns bright red. He stands, as frozen as me for a few endless seconds. And then, finally, he takes off. Crashing through the velvet ropes. Tunneling a path through the crowd.

My stomach tilts.

I'm too late. The words scroll through my head like a news ticker on a never-ending loop.

I'm too late. I'm too late. I'm too late.

CHAPTER 53

It takes me a full five minutes to make my way across the lobby. The crowd doesn't part for me like it did for my brother, since I don't have the cachet of the humiliated.

When I finally make it outside, a stiff breeze blows against my arms. Shivering, I look around. Jackpot! Twenty feet away, I spot our Honda Accord in the parking lot.

My heart pounds. Okay. That means Archie's still here, somewhere on the premises. That means I can still fix this.

I walk away from the main building, leaving behind the chattering of the crowd, the loud bass of the music. A few strides later, I break into a trot. Where would Archie go? What location in our school would give him solace?

I end up in the grassy area behind the annexed buildings. The spot where the upperclassmen like to eat lunch. The place where I presented Archie with burned chicken shaped into a caterpillar, a little over a week ago.

I take a shuddering breath, trying to calm my supercharged heart. Even if I find Archie...then what?

My rush to get to the school and Archie's ensuing

embarrassment have distracted me from my true purpose: Before this night is over, either Archie or Bandit has to die.

I still haven't decided who.

Before I can think about the dilemma too hard—and risk running into the street, screaming—I move farther onto the grass.

The sun is beneath the trees now, a bright glow behind the branches. The orb is so low that I know the descent's going to be fast. Any minute now, we'll be bathed in shadows.

"Archie?" I call. "Is anybody here?"

Nobody answers, but I didn't expect a response even if someone *were* present. The only sound is the continuous buzz of the crickets, deafening…and more than a little creepy.

The hair stands on my neck, and I rub my arms, trying to warm up. Where is he? Our car is here. So unless Archie's been dabbling in Harry Potter and has apparated with the help of a shoe, he's got to be somewhere.

I drift toward the back of the field, which backs up into the woods. He could've ventured in any direction. There are about a million spots where he and Bandit could be grappling with each other, even as I stand here.

The urge to tear through the woods, shaking down each tree, overwhelms me. But I can't dart into the night without a plan. I've already lost too much time. I have to be smart.

Come on, Alice. Where would he go?

I half hope the Voice will pop into my head and tell me what to do. But she doesn't, of course. She *can't*, since she's already taken her last trip.

Which means I'm on my own.

And it feels lonelier than I ever imagined. Malice was my adversary. She tricked me—she lied to me! But she loved me, too. Underneath her rage and exasperation, she only wanted to save us from a horrific future. We just didn't agree on how to do that.

Once again, I sweep my eyes over the lawn—and this time, I see a glint by the basketball court. My mouth dry, I head in that direction. Yes, there it is again. A flash that comes and goes, a shimmer that you'd miss if you blinked at the wrong moment. As though the setting sun were reflecting off something. A pair of glasses, perhaps. Or maybe a gun.

I'm running across the grass before I have another thought. A minute later, the hair is plastered to my head, and I'm sucking the air in large, openmouthed gulps.

But I've found him: my brother. A shadowy figure in the middle of the basketball court. His back is turned to me—his tux jacket off, his sleeves rolled up—but I'd recognize that slouch anywhere.

Once again, paralysis spreads, from my head to my feet, digging roots into the dirt. I'm...scared. Of Archie's hurt, of his potential devastation. Of what he might or might not say to me. Of what I might or might not do to him.

When—and if—I leave this basketball court tonight, I'll no longer be the girl I am now. I'll have made decisions that irrevocably alter me and—oh, please—the future.

Change is inevitable. The original time stream is fading; the foundational threads for the new path are already being laid. By traveling to the future, I set into motion a sequence of events that will lead to a brand-new world, for better or for worse.

Now, all I have to do is live it.

Straightening my spine, I stride across the basketball court and tap the shadowed figure on the shoulder. He turns, and I see his face—my dear, sweet, wonderful brother.

Relief rushes through my veins, as heady as any drug, and I throw my arms around him. "Archie, I'm so glad I found you—"

The words die in my mouth. Because my dear, sweet, wonderful brother is holding a gun.

And he's pointing it right at someone behind a clump of trees.

Even in fading light, I can see that the person's hair is dyed a brilliant blue.

CHAPTER 54

The curved, polished gun gleams, so foreign in my brother's hand and yet so natural in the way he casually grips its heavy weight.

I shudder, not because of the wind that blows through the space but because of the memory of a certain open cabinet in our basement. My mother's gun cabinet. Untouched until a few days ago, when I raided it for the weapon I took to kill Bandit. Archie must've grabbed its twin earlier this evening, before he left for prom. I always knew my brother and I were more similar than different. I just wish I didn't have additional proof right at this moment.

"What are you doing, Arch?" I ask, my voice low and soothing so I don't scare him. So I don't cause his finger to inadvertently jerk. "Put away the gun."

"You don't get to tell me what to do. Not anymore." He raises the weapon to shoulder height and advances a few steps toward the clump of trees, his tuxedo shoes scuffing across the blacktop. "It's your fault I'm the laughingstock of the school."

His voice crescendos. His hand trembles. Both are so

violent, I don't know if the gun will drop or go off. "You promised, Alice. You promised you would go with me to the tux shop. But you didn't. You forgot all about me. Because you were with him!"

I lick my lips. I've never seen him like this. So angry, nearly irrational. He bears much closer resemblance to the Archie in the holo-screen than the brother I know and love. "You don't understand. There were extenuating circumstances—"

"No, *you* don't understand!" he rages. His skin is pale, almost translucent, in the first pearly beams of the moon. "You have no idea how it feels to be me. The last one picked in every gym class. The guy who forever has an empty seat next to him in the cafeteria, on the school bus. I only have you, and you let me down."

"I'm sorry—"

But he doesn't let me finish. "Show yourself, Bandit!" my brother roars. "If you want to date my sister, at least have the guts to come out and face me."

A moment passes. I don't hear the screech of the crickets anymore, so either they've gone into hiding or my ears are too full of my thunderous heartbeat.

Bandit steps out from behind the clump of trees. He's holding a gun, too, and it's trained on Archie. Flaming monkeys. He must've dug up *my* gun, the one he buried in the woods.

My mind flits hysterically to the angles and filter I would use to best capture this shot. Bandit's arm is rock solid, his eyes watchful. The way he's framed by the dusk and shadows, he could be a work of art. The scene is oddly picturesque... and very, very wrong.

My brother tightens the grip on his own weapon. "Put it down, Bandit."

"No," Bandit says, his voice strong and certain. "We'll put

our guns down together. Or we'll both exit this life."

Archie sighs, and for a moment, I think he might actually comply. And then he swings the gun and points it in my general direction.

My heart stops. What is he doing? The aim's not directed at me, not yet. But it's way too close for comfort. "You w-wouldn't," I stammer.

He lifts his eyebrows, and they rise above the black frames of his glasses. "Wouldn't I? It's only right, don't you think, after all the times you tried to kill me?"

Every last drop of blood drains from my face. I'm surprised my feet don't start leaking red. "What did you say?"

"I never thought we kept secrets from each other." His voice is small, hurt. As vulnerable as a child's. "You didn't bother to tell me about the voice in your head, so I decided not to tell you about mine."

The blacktop lists lazily around me. Of course. I was visited by my older self. So was Cristela. And Charlie. And Bandit *and* my father. It makes sense that Archie would have his own voice, too. "You've been communicating with the future?" I confirm. "With your older self?"

"Yes." Archie's hand vibrates, and the gun shakes with it. "Your precious Cristela isn't the only one who will build a time machine. I know people, too, and they happen to be smarter. Unlike yours, my older self didn't keep me in the dark. He told me everything. How this one's trying to kill me." He jerks his head toward Bandit. "How you'll betray me. How you *are* betraying me, even now. How could you, Alice? How could you do this to me?"

I stumble backward, repelled by his rage, forced back by his bafflement. A gust of wind swirls around the court, and I scan the ground, searching for a sharp stick, a heavy pole. Anything that might function as a weapon. But all I see are a few basketballs lodged in the grass. Piles of jump ropes wound up like nests. And Bandit inching toward Archie.

"Your older self has it out for me." Archie blinks, his eyes wounded. Haunted by events that have yet to come. "What did I do to deserve her hatred? All I've ever done is be a good brother to you."

"You are, Archie." My face is hot. My throat full of gunk. "The very best. I'll never forget it."

He stomps his feet, and Bandit goes still fifteen feet away. "But you do forget!" Archie shouts. "Otherwise, you wouldn't try to kill me!"

"No!" I cry out. "My older self *wanted* me to murder you, in order to save the world. But I refused! They tried a gazillion ways to convince me, but they failed. Because of *me*. Because I was too stubborn. Because I loved you too much."

My brother howls, on the knife's edge of laughing and crying. He lowers the gun. "Is that what your older self told you?"

Bandit moves another few inches, and my pulse thuds erratically. I try to calm my breathing, try to focus on my brother. "It's what she believes. I snuck forward in time, and I overheard her."

"Well, she's wrong." The glasses slide down his nose, probably slippery with sweat, and he shoves them back up. "Your missions have failed *not* because of your so-called love for me. But because *I* was there. Every time. Informed by my older self, countering your every move."

My mouth parts, and Bandit slides an entire foot closer to Archie.

"That's right," my brother continues grimly. "You tore up my invite for the cocktail reception, so we had the future Charlie tell his younger self to give Zeke a note. You burned Charlie's research, so he backed up his work, in triplicate, the week before."

His eyes glint, strangely exposed through the lenses of his glasses. "More importantly, each time you thought about killing me, my older self instructed me to go to you. To remind you of a childhood memory. To prey on the feelings you had for the brother you always wanted to protect." His voice becomes rough, dripping with disgust. For me or for the boy he used to be. Maybe both. "Like a pawn, you fell for it. Every. Single. Time."

I squeeze my eyes shut. I want to break down. To despair at all the horrible things my brother's saying. But I can't give in to my grief. Not yet.

"Those weren't tricks." I wrench open my eyelids. "Don't you see? You couldn't have reminded me of memories that didn't exist. You couldn't have preyed on my feelings if I didn't already love you." Taking a chance, I walk toward him. "Did your older self tell you about the virus you're going to invent? Did he tell you about the millions you'll kill?"

Archie's breathing hard now, and his eyes zoom around the court like he's a cornered Siberian tiger, from me to Bandit, from the basketball hoop to the jump ropes. "They deserve to die," he says haltingly. "People are shallow and self-absorbed, and they don't care whose feelings they shred. They don't care whose lives they ruin, so long as they have fun." He looks back at me, and in the dim light, his eyes are no longer wild. Now, they're just hurt. "In all the millions of people on this earth, not a single one cares."

A smile spreads across his face. "Except for Charlie. He chose *me*. He saw me for who I am, for who I could be. To him, I was more than just a son to brag about, like I was to Dad. More than a brain to solve his research snares, like Zeke believes." His lips tighten. "I was even more than just some clueless guy who needs his sister to take care of him."

"That's not what I think!" I protest, even as my mind whirls.

When did he meet Charlie? Is this why my brother's been so preoccupied these last few months? Is Charlie's cabin where he goes for his research trips?

I glance wildly around the basketball court, as though my answers might be hidden in the shadows, and my gaze collides with Bandit's. He looks about how I feel, like someone just punched him in the gut.

Now what? I can't tell Archie that Charlie was using him, too, in his own way. That will really send him over the edge. I have to appeal to him the only way I know how—as his sister.

My skin prickles, coming alive with the force of my emotions. I will him to listen. I will him to *believe.* "I love you. With all that I am, with everything I'll ever be, I love you. That's never going to change."

Archie gazes back at Bandit, who's no longer moving, and then returns his attention to me.

The breath gets pent up in my lungs. He wants to trust what I'm saying. I know this to the core of my being. Archie's not interested in destroying the world. He doesn't wish to decimate entire towns and regions and countries. All he wants is to feel a connection with someone, and that's what Charlie gave him.

That's what *I* could give him. If only he'll let me.

The seconds tick by as we stand on the precipice of this decision point. The fork in this road could take us onto an entirely new time stream—or keep us on the same one.

"You've always been good at saying the right thing, Alice," my brother says sadly. "But it's no longer enough."

He raises the gun so that it's pointed directly at me for the first time. He might've been testing the waters before, when he swung the gun in my direction. To rattle my composure, to shock me into a confession.

To flirt with the idea of taking a life.

But this time?

This time, I can tell by the determination in his eyes, by the concrete in his voice, that he is committed and ready.

"It doesn't matter how close you get to me, Bandit," he rasps. "Alice will be just as dead if I pull the trigger. Put down your gun now, or I will kill my sister."

CHAPTER 55

My brother's words hang in the air, so tangible that they could be a physical object. A shiny red tricycle on the playground, a cutout face on a stick…or a knife straight through my heart.

Bandit shoots me a panicked glance. "All right, all right. No need to get testy." He lies the gun down on the concrete, his movements slow and fumbling.

"Kick it across the court," Archie demands.

Another pause. Another glance. And then Bandit obeys.

"You." My brother gestures toward me. "Tie him up with the jump ropes, around the basketball pole."

My heart pounds, the beats overlapping one another. If I follow his orders, if I render Bandit helpless, I'll cut in half our minuscule chances of besting him. And yet, the weapon in his hands takes away every choice I have.

"Archie, please," I say faintly, not certain what I'm asking.

"Wrists and ankles," he says in a bored voice. "Make it tight, Malice, or I'll have to do it myself."

My mouth drops. "Why are you calling me that?"

"Isn't that the name you've chosen for yourself in the future? That's what I heard."

I stare at this boy who looks and sounds so much like my brother. "In the future, you died before I took on that name. I watched you on a holo-screen inside a cave."

His face hardens. "Or did I? You shouldn't always believe what you're told. What you think you see. You're so naive, Malice. That's why it was so easy for the future to trick you. You have to believe the best in everybody. No wonder your older self was so disgusted by you." He shakes his head. "Now stop stalling and move!"

Quivering, I cross the lawn and scoop up the pile of jump ropes. Without my asking, Bandit positions himself in front of the pole and crosses his wrists around the length of metal. So thoughtful, this guy. Even now, every action he takes is to help me.

I wind the jump rope around his wrists, trying not to touch him. But my fingers graze his skin anyway, and my heart fractures with the touch.

"Hi," I whisper.

He twists around so that he can look at me, his lips turning up at the corners. "Hi."

Heat rushes behind my eyes. "Don't do that. Don't smile at me now, of all times. I can't handle it."

"These might be the last moments of my life," he says. "Would you rather that I frown?"

I drop my head because I can't bear to look into his finely chiseled face. My ponytail hangs by his now-bound wrists, and he flexes his fingers so that they brush against the tips of my hair. The fracture turns into a full-on break.

"You left me at Cristela's," I say around the lump in my throat. Crouching, I wrap another jump rope between his ankles and the basketball pole. Archie's lowered the gun and is watching us intently. "What made you leave? Did a voice appear in your head? Or did you think…I would try to kill you again?"

"The first one," he says. "My older self came to me. He asked me to help you." He reaches out his fingers again, this time grazing the top of my head. It's as though he's taking each and every opportunity to touch me. The pressure on my scalp is almost imperceptible, and yet I know I'll never forget the sensation as long as I live.

"Has he ever come to you before?" I whisper.

"Nah. This was the first time he's appeared. I think he visits me in the future? I'm not really sure." Bandit wiggles his jaw, as though he needs to shake the words loose. "He explained about the virus. The deaths. His and Malice's failed missions." He stops again. Swallows hard. "He asked me to ease your burden. To kill Archie…or myself. Obviously, I have a vested interest in staying alive. But my older self said either option would do." He moves his shoulders. "Too bad Archie knew I was coming."

I finish the knot and stand. My hands are chilled, but my heart is warm. So I was right. The only reason he's here now is because the future Bandit loves me.

"More, Malice," Archie calls. "Another jump rope each at his hands and feet."

Picking up another plastic cord, I repeat the process of tying his wrists. I try to leave some slack while knotting the rope tightly enough to make Archie happy. But it's hard to tell if I succeed.

"The future Bandit had already reached his quota of trips," I murmur. Archie's staring. He probably hears every word we say. I don't care. If this is my last chance to have this conversation, I won't back away because of a deluded desire for privacy. "If he time traveled any more, his mind would come apart."

"Yes." The word is as slow and reluctant as the sap dripping out of a Vermont sugar maple. "This was his last gift to you. His first and final request to me. At the end of our conversation, his consciousness...shattered. That's the best way I can describe it. It broke in a million pieces, and the light I felt in my head disappeared. Not like it traveled back to the future but like it was...snuffed out."

My breath catches. My heart stops. Time itself comes to a screeching halt. "He...died?"

Bandit turns his head so that he's looking directly at me. His expression is calm, although his eyes are freaked. "Yes."

I break down. Weeping for the man who loved me with every ounce of his heart. With every inch of his soul. For the person who took his last breath for me. The one who made his final sacrifice...for *me*. A stubborn girl whose insatiable curiosity ruined his plans. All because I will one day grow up to become the Malice of his heart.

"Alice?" Bandit sounds dazed. "He loved you very much."

"He did," I whisper, past the aching heart that sits in my chest, as useless as a broken toy. "He and Malice loved each other across timelines. No matter how they interfered with the past, they found each other every time. He said..." My voice falters, but I make myself try again. I need to make sure this boy, *this* Bandit, understands. "He said their love was an unshakable event in the universe."

Bandit squares his shoulders and faces forward. "Then I'm okay being tied to this basketball pole. Whatever the results, if this was his last wish, it is my honor to fulfill it."

My knees give out, and I fall. You'd think I'd feel lighter with this raw, open wound in my chest. But like a black hole, the emptiness sucks all the goodness from my life, all the happiness and joy, so that I'm pulled to the ground with a force stronger than gravity.

He was right. My future husband, when he was assessing how his younger self would react. Bandit doesn't need to ask questions. He simply trusts—in his gut, in his instincts. It's a sign of his steadiness, and it's one of the reasons I love him. *Him*, the guy standing before me now, not the man he'll become in the future.

I pick myself up just as Archie approaches to check the knots. Satisfied, my brother jabs me in the back with the gun, urging me forward. I lumber in the direction of his prods, my mind stunned and my heart numb.

"Tell you what," Archie says, as if he's come to a long and hard decision. "I think you're being sincere. No matter what you feel for him, I think you *do* love me. I *want* you to be telling the truth, more than I've ever wanted anything, really. So I'm giving you the chance to prove it."

He lifts the gun and offers it to me. I stare at the glinting metal of the barrel. "You're…*giving* me your weapon?"

"If my older self is right, I'm not in any danger." He licks his lips. "You weren't able to kill me in order to save millions of people. In order to protect your own child. You're not going to hurt me now.

"But that guy?" He jerks his head toward Bandit. "Kill him, right here, right now. And the action will bind us together. You'll be a murderer, and I'll be your accomplice. Me and you, Malice. Brother and sister, forever and always."

My heart stutters. Bandit yanks desperately at the restraints, but it's Archie's expression that destroys me. Picks me up and smashes me against the blacktop. Hope. Even now, all my brother wants is to be loved.

"This is what Malice wanted. Even what *his* older self desired. So much that they tried to trick you into making this decision." My brother's eyes drill into me. Beg me. Plead with

me. To choose him, for once. Just like Charlie did. Just like
no one else ever did. "But you were too smart for them. You
found out the truth. Doesn't change the wisdom of their plan.
Killing Bandit is still the right choice. It always was."

He takes a shaky breath. "The only question is: Will
you do the right thing? Will you kill this boy and save your
brother? Save the entire world?"

I can't breathe. I pant and pant, but it's like all the oxygen
has been sucked out of this time stream. How can I make this
decision? How?

But I know that I have to. The entire week was leading
up to this. Every thread on every timeline culminates here,
in this moment. What I choose now will change everything.

I turn to Bandit. Our eyes meet for one searing moment.
And then my heart rate slows. My breath becomes still. I look
from him to my brother. Both so important to me in different
ways. Both of whom I love, present and future.

I know what I have to do.

CHAPTER 56

Moving quickly, I cross the blacktop in a few large strides, putting distance between my brother and me. Between Bandit and me.

Then I press the gun against the underside of my chin.

When it is precisely lined with my brain, I look up. Both Archie and Bandit are gaping at me.

"Alice, what are you *doing*?" Panic whips into Bandit's voice, and he strains against the bindings. But he's too far away. Even if he could get free, he won't be able to reach me in time.

The acid climbs my throat. My neck moves. So does the gun. The metal is ice against the fire of my skin. But it's too late now. I stepped onto this path. I have to see it through.

"Holy crap, Malice." My brother's voice is a mix of awe and fear. Bandit can't comprehend my actions, but Archie… does Archie understand? He knows me better than anyone else. Will he be able to accept what I'm about to do?

"Archie." I lick my lips, trying to figure out where to begin. "In the future you will do awful things. So awful that the future saw no other way than to travel to the past and kill you while you were still innocent. Charlie used you. Is still using you. You're just too desperate to see it."

An expression I can't read crosses my brother's face. He starts forward, hands curled into fists. Bandit darts his eyes from me to him, and I pray that Archie lets me finish before he charges.

"Charlie would never use me. Those people deserve it—" my brother starts to say.

"I love you, Archie. I love you, I love you, I love you!" I repeat the words louder and louder until they penetrate his haze.

He halts, five feet from me. Five feet from the gun that's pressed at the juncture between my neck and chin. Uncertainty wars across his face, and I know I've bought myself a couple of minutes.

"I tried to show you with every conversation we had, with every meal I accidentally burned, that I love you. But my actions weren't enough." I swallow, and my throat moves against the metal. "And that's okay. That's not your fault. You haven't been treated well. You've been made to feel worthless. And so I don't blame you for not wanting to live in this world. I don't fault you for creating a new one of your own making. Even if you were manipulated into thinking that was the only way."

Perspiration gathers at my neck, drips down my forehead. "The truth is, if the future is right, if killing you is the *only* way to save all those people, I would do it. No single life is enough to justify all that death. All that pain."

I take a deep breath. "But I *don't* agree with the future. I don't think your death is the only solution. It's not even an effective one. So long as Charlie's research exists, the future will just find a way to pass it on to someone else."

Both of them stare. Bandit stops struggling, and Archie's hands hang limply by his sides.

"But he chose me," my brother says haltingly.

"Yes," I say. "Because you're brilliant. The smartest person I know. But you're still a pawn. If you don't invent the virus, he *will* replace you."

Archie's eyes flash. He's getting angry, which I don't want. He just needs to understand the truth. To see what he's been missing.

"My older self is jaded," I hurry on. "She's lost so much, she hurts so deeply, that she can't see the only thing that might save our world. Hope."

I close my eyes, remembering my future daughter. Remembering the black hole of despair that has replaced Malice's heart. "Every time my older self came to the past, her one aim was to destroy. Erase the research, damage a relationship, eliminate a life. Her pain narrowed her vision, killed off her idealism. Her only strategy to combat violence was with more violence." I open my eyes. Look straight at my brother. His shoulders are hunched, and he appears smaller than before. Younger. "Not once did she try to believe in you, to believe in humanity, a little more."

I fill my lungs. "Her final mission was to trick me into killing Bandit. She thought this was our last chance to save the world, but she's wrong. Because I have every moment for the rest of my life—however short—to believe in you. And I'm starting right now."

With shaking hands and a steady heart, I tighten my grip on the gun. "I won't choose you over Bandit. You are my brother. He will be my husband and the father of my child. Whether you like it or not, he matters, in every version of my future. You have to find a way to accept that."

Bandit makes a gurgling sound in his throat, and his eyes

bulge, probably from the news of our future marriage and child.

But my whole and undivided attention is on my brother's face, so pale that his freckles stand out like stars.

"Your fight for the future can end right here, right now," I say. "If I die, there will be no one to stop you from inventing the virus. No one to betray you because you think I've chosen someone else."

Bandit pulls so hard that his wrists pop free of the jump rope. Off-balance, he falls forward to his knees. It's a sweet gesture, but it's too late.

I run my free hand along the barrel of the gun. So smooth, so cold. "I believe in you, Archie. I will always believe in you, no matter what the future tells me. I believe you don't want millions of people to die. I believe you will remember what I do tonight, and it will remind you to be the brother I know. The one I love so much."

A thin teenage boy no longer stands before me. Instead, all I see is eight-year-old Archie's gleeful smile as we survey the platters of microwaved pizza rolls, the first meal we ever cooked. All I hear is his high voice as he chatters animatedly to our stuffed animals, preparing them for spaceflight. All I feel is his small hand gripping mine as we linger on our school's front steps, our mother late yet again.

"I've tried to protect you since Mom left," I say, my voice rough with unshed tears, tears that may never have the chance to escape. "Out of guilt, out of love. But now I understand that my approach was wrong. You never needed protecting. All you need is someone to believe."

With my final words, I swing the gun around. And then I shoot my brother directly in the leg.

CHAPTER 57

With an anguished cry, Archie crumples to the ground. My heart pangs, but I can't look at him. I can't mourn my actions. Not yet. My work here isn't done.

Without another glance, I take off toward the gym inside our school's main building. Toward the ever-increasing thumping of the bass. Toward Silver Oak's prom.

I make a brief stop at Cristela's car. There, in the trunk, I toss the gun under a pile of old blankets. Buried in the woods, drowned in a river…one way or the other, I'll get rid of the evidence later.

I run through the parking lot and across the front lawn. The moon has crept up the sky, bathing the high school in an eerie glow. In another time, another place, I might've stopped to soak in the atmosphere, take a few photos. Now I just dash through the double doors and past the fake backdrop of the setting sun.

When I run up the stairs, however, scenes of my past life flash by like a memory reel. Here, a skateboarder flew down the hall, shoving me into Bandit's arms. A few feet later, I stashed a baggie of weed in Lalana's locker. Farther still, I slouched in a plastic chair in the nurse's office, waiting for the lockdown to lift.

Finally, finally, I arrive at the gym. It's been transformed into a landscape straight from Van Gogh's *Starry Night*. Yellow disco balls, swirling white lights, blue tinsel that gleams like a nebula.

But I barely register the decor. All I notice are the students. My peers. Archie's classmates. The ones who made fun of him, who thought nothing of joining and perpetuating the mocking laughter. The very same people who can save him.

"Help!" I scream, dragging out the word, stuffing it full of power. A few heads turn toward me and then a few more. "My brother. He's hurt! Help me, please!"

Three, four, five people start moving in my direction. That's all I need. Mob mentality will take care of the rest. I run back the way I came, peeking over my shoulder every few yards. Sure enough, there's a stampede behind me, a veritable herd of most of the junior and senior classes.

Within minutes, we reach the basketball court, where Bandit's feet are still tied to the pole. Where Archie lies, panting. Blood blossoms on his thigh and pools on the blacktop, soaking through his pants and connecting purple stripe to purple stripe.

Five second later, the people descend on him like a swarm of honeybees. Annaliese curls up beside him and holds his hand, while Chelsea dabs at his face with her handkerchief. Zeke takes off his tuxedo shirt, ripping the fabric into strips, while Reggie, the heartthrob of the senior class and Lalana's former crush, fashions a tourniquet for Archie's leg.

At first, my brother doesn't seem to notice the attention. He hisses through his teeth, his face contorted with pain. But the shouts get louder. And the encouragement comes faster.

"Oh, Archie! You poor thing!"

"Breathe, buddy. Ambulance is coming."

"How can I help? Anything at all. Just say the word."

"We've got you, Archie. Just hold on."

My brother jerks up his head. He looks around, wonder in his eyes, at the ten, twenty, fifty people surrounding him. He shakes his head, as though their kindness is another trick. But there's no ulterior motive to their words. No hidden agenda behind their support.

The blood still flows from his leg. Pain still pinches his eyes. But there, at the corner of his mouth, I see something else. A smile, or at least the seed of one. With the right friends, with the appropriate care, it might grow and flourish into a real grin. A permanent one.

That's my hope, anyway.

I fade into the crowd, which surges forward to fill the spot I've vacated. Kneeling by Bandit's feet, I begin to untangle the knots I so recently tied.

My brother doesn't blink at my disappearance, and that's good.

That's right.

The solution was never about me. It was never up to *me* to save him or sacrifice him, no matter what my older self believed. Archie becomes who he does because of a long line of hurts, a long string of abandonments that started with our mother. We'll never be able to change the future because we eliminate any one event. Someone like Charlie will always find him and prey on his need to feel wanted. Accepted. All we can do is try to fill that void.

And hope that we succeed.

Bandit catches my chin in his hand. My skin is sweaty, his fingers grimy, but none of that matters when our eyes meet.

"Why'd you do it?" he asks.

I sip in air and release it. Suck in more and push it out again.

"Once upon a time stream, Archie Sherman invents a virus that will wipe out two-thirds of humanity," I say musingly. "There's only one thing that can stop him, one action that might wrench our world onto a brand-new thread."

"What's that? Shooting him in the leg?"

"No." My lungs are getting the hang of the rhythm again, bit by bit. "It's changing his relationship with that very same humanity." I take a full breath. The air fills me up, almost to capacity. "One step, one kindness, one moment at a time."

CHAPTER 58

*O*ne week later...
   The sun streams through the window, bright and cheerful. Safe. A sign of new beginnings, of better things to come.

We can only hope, anyway.

Archie came home from the hospital a few days ago, and already, his room looks and smells like a florist shop. Red roses cuddle with blue hydrangeas and orange poppies on his desk. Their scents swirl together, producing a heady mix that makes me want to sneeze.

Still, the intentions of the senders were good...all two dozen of them. I didn't think *I* had that many friends, let alone Archie. The rumors circulated around school in less time than it took for me to travel ten years to the future and back.

Apparently, a gunman descended on our school and tied Bandit to the basketball pole. Archie confronted him and managed to scare him off, but not before suffering a bullet in the leg.

The facts are close enough to the truth that we didn't

bother to correct them. Especially since they paint Archie as a hero. Especially since that gunman was…me.

After all, I'm still trying to convince my brother to shift his perspective. To understand that although people like Lee and Maggie exist in this world, there are other people as well. Nicer people.

Along with the events of that fateful night, I let slip that I was responsible for the weed in my best friend's locker. The confession is probably too little, too late. I received a suspension from school, which, all things considered, is the least of my worries. But Lalana's already left for California, and I doubt she's ever coming back.

As much as that makes me feel like pond scum, at least Archie won't be reminded daily of his unrequited love. If, in some small way, Lalana's cross-country move helps prevent my brother from becoming the Virus Maker? Well, I've heard that pond scum has its uses, too.

Lalana and I haven't talked, but she did send me a cutout of Captain America's head on a chopstick. The accompanying note didn't say much, just "heard what happened" and "hope you're okay," but I'm hopeful this means she's forgiven me a little. Maybe one day, when we're face-to-face, I'll be able to tell her the whole story.

In the meantime, I pin up Captain America on my corkboard, next to Thor and Loki. Underneath my collection of Avenger heads is the photograph of which I'm most proud, the one with a little Asian boy pushing his grandmother in a wheelchair. There was a time when Bandit looked at this photo every day. For that one moment, it helped him breathe more easily. And that's enough to motivate me to continue taking photos.

I've all but given up my foodie account. While I have the utmost respect for food photographers, it's not my dream, not my passion. I want to spend my time doing something I really care about: photographing people. Exploring culture. Learning about animals. And if I never make it to *National Geographic*? Well, maybe it was never my true path.

I let out a deep sigh. Maybe there's no one thing—or person—that remains unshakable across time streams.

I should know.

What does the love of my future do when he watches me put a bullet in my brother's thigh, right after I declare that he will one day father my child?

He stays away. Far, far away.

Who can blame the guy?

When we first went to the hospital, and I set up camp in the waiting room, Bandit never left my side. For twenty-four hours, we took turns picking stale snacks from the vending machine. We played a massive, best-of-seven tournament of Scrabble. And in the middle of the night, when I couldn't sleep, he read out loud to me from his favorite book, *Flowers for Algernon*.

Once we heard that Archie's operation was successful, however, Bandit was quiet. Contemplative.

"You said you loved me," he spoke up when Dad went to visit Archie in the recovery room.

I smoothed a hand over the bird's nest disguised as my hair. "Did I?"

"Yes. Before the ambulance came. You were practically delirious, and you said you loved me. Not the man I'll become but who I am now." His tone was almost accusatory, and I blushed. Because he wouldn't sound so upset if my confession were a good thing.

"You said it yourself: I was delirious."

He shook his head, not letting me off that easily. "Is it true?"

I wasn't ashamed of my emotions. If there was one thing I learned from the Voice, it was to embrace my heart. Time can make all things transitory, even love.

So I looked right into his solemn eyes, and the universe clicked into place. It was all the evidence I needed of our rightness. If only such proof were sufficient for him.

"Yes," I said quietly. "You have to understand that when I went forward in time, I lived Malice's life. I saw what she saw. I felt what she felt. Maybe our emotions got mixed up, I'm not sure. But I do know that I can't isolate the future from the present. So yeah, it's true. I do love you."

He bent his head over his hands, and minute after awkward minute ticked by. I shifted in the hard chair, the plastic hot and sticky against my palms.

Finally, he lifted his face, and the discomfort in his eyes gutted me. "I'm sorry, Alice. But I didn't travel to the future. We've known each other for little more than a week. And I'm just not there yet." He paused. Took a deep breath. "I don't know if I'll ever get there."

He bolted soon afterward.

We haven't spoken since. He hasn't texted, although I obsessively check my phone, hoping for something, anything, from the "Most Wonderful Boy Alive."

He can tell me what he's wearing, right down to his socks. I'd gladly hear about his oral hygiene routine, if it meant he was talking to me again.

I tug out a rose I "borrowed" from one of Archie's bouquets, accidentally pricking my finger on a thorn. A spot of red blooms against my skin.

Ten years in the future, the best man I've ever known said, "Sometimes, even soul mates won't fit together if they meet at the wrong age."

I'm terrified, down to the very last drop of my blood, that

this is one of those times.

I wipe my finger on a tissue and walk into Archie's room, where he's sitting on the bed. An old textbook is open on his lap, and "Look What You Made Me Do" blares from his cell phone.

"Hot date with T-Swift?" I ask innocently.

He mutes the music, shrugging. "At least she serenades me. Which is more than I can say for your paper cutouts."

"I'll have you know that Thor always has time for me." I toss my hair over my shoulder. "He's captivated by my stories. Best listener ever."

"Captive audience is right." My brother smirks. "He doesn't have any legs, so he can't run away."

I roll my eyes—or pretend to. Inside, my grin is so big that it practically splits me in two. I'm just glad Archie's teasing me again. Relieved that he sounds like his old self, the brother I know and love.

For a few hours each day, Dad and I make a point of hanging out with him so that he's not alone. So that he doesn't get too much in his head, especially during this all-important recovery period.

My small family hasn't spent this much time together since Mom left. Since voices appeared in Dad's head and asked him to keep me at a distance.

Now that I know the truth, now that we suspect that closeness—rather than coldness—might be the answer, we're trying, both Dad and I. You don't erase six years of remoteness in a single conversation, however. But with each squeeze of the shoulder, each shared bark of laughter, we're getting there, bit by bit. Day by day.

Sometimes Zeke joins us for a board game or two. Archie eyed him suspiciously the first couple of times, but he's slowly relaxed as Zeke continued acting the same way he always has.

They never talk about their research, though. I have a feeling that part of their friendship is over.

And yet, I appreciate Zeke's steady presence. His solid kindness. He's dating Kadijah now, and I laugh when he tells me about their antics. Smile when he says her name, his features soft.

He doesn't appear to have been visited by a voice—at least not yet—but the jury's still out on Lee. The school bully just appeared at the wrong place too many times. And if his nastiness is a result of a mission, rather than a defect in personality? I suppose we'll find out, sooner or later.

I incline my head toward a stuffed bear that's the length of my torso, the newest addition to Archie's bedroom. "Another present?"

"Nah. This one's for you. I ordered it online." Archie passes me the stuffed animal. It has an oversize head and a cream-colored belly and reminds me of a bear he used to have.

"His name is Fu Fu," the six-year-old Archie had said authoritatively.

I, being a lowly kindergartner, was terribly impressed. "How'd you come up with that name?"

My brother shrugged loftily. "Made it up."

It wasn't until I graduated into the first grade that I realized he had lifted the name straight out of a classroom book.

I smile, about to remind Archie of the story, when he gestures toward the plush toy. "I picked this one because it has a pouch in the back."

Sure enough, I flip the bear over, and a zipper runs from its neck to its bottom.

"Look inside," Archie instructs.

Lifting my brows, I slide down the zipper and pull out a plastic bag.

The baggie holds a gun, one that looks very much like the one he pointed at Bandit and me. Like the one I eventually used to shoot him.

I drop the bag, and the gun bounces harmlessly on the mattress. The last time I saw this weapon, it was buried under some old blankets in Cristela's trunk. I can't believe I forgot to get rid of it.

An ocean roars in my ears. "Why…why are you giving this to me?"

"I've been thinking." He pushes the glasses up his nose. "You put all of humanity at stake for me. It was, arguably, a decision that was too risky, and I got shot in the process." He looks ruefully at his bandaged thigh. "But your belief means a lot, and I don't want to let you down. So I asked Bandit to search for the gun, and he found it in Cristela's car." He pauses. "I want you to have it as collateral."

I wrinkle my nose. "You want me to shoot you again?"

"Of course not," he says. "But we all know the sudden interest in me isn't going to last. I'll do my best not to sink back into my head. Maybe I'll even go back to the therapist. In the meantime, Charlie's been released from the hospital. He's on his way to a full recovery—for the time being. Five years from now, in one of the future's failed attempts to stop me, Bandit will fire this gun at Charlie and kill him."

I gape. There's a lot to process in his words, but I can't get past the image of Bandit killing his uncle.

Archie clutches the bear, six years old once more. "Maybe that won't happen anymore. Maybe you've succeeded in wrenching us onto a new time stream. Maybe our lives will unfold in ways we can't predict." He moves his shoulders. "We won't know for sure until Cristela invents her time machine. In the meantime, we can destroy Charlie's research. Every last bit of it. Bandit's already started the process. But if that doesn't work…"

He swallows. "If I'm foolish enough to invent the virus, if we can't stop the future from barreling down these tracks… Well, I want you to turn in this gun to the authorities. I've wiped off your fingerprints and pressed mine in their place. When and if the time comes to kill Charlie, tell Bandit to wear gloves. To not smudge my fingerprints. And this gun will be your insurance policy." He peers at me through his glasses, his eyes desperate and young. Oh, so very young. "If I'm in jail, then I can't hurt anyone, right?"

A chill runs up my spine. I made my big move, but it might not be enough. I always knew that. There was never any guarantee. All we can do is try, every moment of every day. Try and love and believe.

"Oh, Archie, I hope so." I squeeze his hand.

He leans back on the pillow, as though the conversation has exhausted him. "I'm going to take a nap. See you at dinner? We're having chicken *tikka masala*."

I raise my eyebrows. "Dad's cooking?"

"Do we really care, so long as it's not you?" His lips twitch. "Just kidding. We're getting takeout." He pauses. "If you want to know the truth, I don't actually mind your food. Much. So long as you don't burn it."

A lump forms in my throat. "Thanks, Brother."

"No problem, Sister Bear."

I blink, the moisture in my eyes refracting the rays of the sun. I'm being silly. A name derived from *The Berenstain Bears* is a little corny and a lot childish, but I like it. As nicknames go, it's way better than "Malice."

In fact, I could live a full and happy life without anyone calling me "Malice" ever again.

CHAPTER 59

One month after that . . .

Cristela wraps a strand of my hair around a hot iron, transforming my unruly waves into long, springy ringlets.

"Gorgeous," she says, running her fingers through the curls. "In this time or any another."

I smile, even as a part of me mourns. I always insisted that I would never date in high school, and Lalana always countered that she would get me to break my rule, some way, somehow. I guess she was right, even if her slashing cheekbones and straight eyebrows aren't the ones looking back at me from the mirror.

I'd like to think that in a different future, on a different thread, she'd be the one curling my hair, the one hooting with laughter as she tries on spandex and ends up chucking it at the wall.

But in this timeline, she's not. And that's okay, because I have a beautiful and brilliant Nicaraguan scientist by my side.

I don't know how I would've survived the last month without Cristela. We talk on the phone multiple times every day and text even more. In some versions of the future, she'll see me at my worst and yet, she'll love and support me anyway. That's about the highest recommendation you can get for a true friend.

We descend the stairs arm in arm, one minute before our dates are supposed to arrive.

Archie's tucked comfortably in the basement, his leg nearly healed, and Dad, of course, is at work. But this morning, he gave me a photo of him and my mom on their first date.

"I don't know how your mother would feel if she were here," he said. "Frankly, she's not the sentimental type. But I'm proud. So proud of how responsible and grown-up my little girl has become." Blinking rapidly, he ducked out of the room.

"Are you nervous?" Cristela asks me now.

"A little," I admit, smoothing the dress over my hips. I've only talked to Bandit a couple of times in the last month. Both conversations were…distant. Awkward. I have no idea why he wants to see me tonight. Even less sure why he suggested a double date with Cristela and his cousin.

"Have faith." She checks her hair in the hallway mirror. "He'll fall in love with you eventually. He has to. It's his destiny."

I bite my lip. But what if he doesn't? I've never confessed to Cristela the fear that keeps me up at night, chewing through my intestines.

Bandit is the love of my life. My soul mate across time streams. The man to whom I returned, again and again, no matter what obstacles were thrown in our path.

Or at least, he used to be. Before I changed the future so drastically that I (hopefully) wrenched us onto a brand-new thread.

What if in the process of trying to stop the Virus Maker, I've also shaken up the unshakable? What if, in this new time stream we've built, I fall for Bandit…but he doesn't love me back?

The doorbell rings.

I freeze, my palms turning into ice. My spine into petrified wood. I might've stood there for the rest of eternity, a redwood tree reaching for the sky on the California coast, but Cristela nudges my shoulder.

"Your life will happen, with or without you," she says.

My breath rattles free. I don't know if her wisdom comes from her glimpse of the future or from her natural genius, but she's right. Before I can second-guess my decision, I open the door.

Two strikingly attractive people stand, one with an adorable pixie cut and a metal bar in their eyebrow, the other with an athletic build and brilliant blue hair, freshly dyed.

I only have eyes for the latter.

Bandit steps over the threshold, his mouth solemn, his expression serious. My hands twitch. I want to run them over his lips, to tease them into a smile. But I don't have that right. Not yet. Maybe never.

"Hi," he whispers.

"Do you, uh, need to introduce Cristela to Mali?" I gesture at Bandit's cousin.

"They seem to be doing just fine on their own."

I peek over his shoulder. Cristela is shuffling her feet, already laughing, and Mali grins so broadly, I can count every one of their teeth. Instantly smitten.

Unlike some other people I know.

I turn back to Bandit, and he hands me a flower garland. My breath catches. It's a *puang malai,* like the ones I've seen from time to time at Lalana's house. Tight jasmine buds are threaded together to form a wreath, and half a dozen strands dangle from the circle, comprised of red roses and bloomed jasmine flowers. It is intricate, exquisite, and it smells just like my favorite perfume.

"It's gorgeous," I say, my throat tight. "Where did you get this? I know Lalana's family special orders garlands from a Thai florist for special occasions."

"I made it," he says, his voice gravelly. "Khun Yai owned a flower shop back in Thailand, and we've always had potted jasmine plants at our house. I grew up threading jasmine buds onto needles as long as my forearm."

My heart stutters. "Oh, Bandit. You didn't have to—"

"No," he says. "I wanted to."

Suddenly, I can't look at him. I run my fingers over the tight flower buds. "I'm sorry. I put you in an uncomfortable position. I shouldn't have blurted out my feelings like that. It's too much pressure."

He slips a finger under my chin, tilting up my face. "I'm not going to lie. It was a lot being informed you were my soul mate, witnessing my older self come apart. For a while, I just wanted to hide from the world, present and future. Pretend none of it existed. Do you know what happened instead?"

"What?" I whisper. My mouth is dry, and I'm dangerously light-headed. I hope to the stars I don't faint before I hear his answer.

"I couldn't stop thinking about you." He moves his fingers to my lips, touching them softly. "I would hear echoes of your laugh at the most random times, or I'd see your face in my mind, looking at me and not blinking. Those flashes made me want to give you everything. I don't know where these feelings are coming from. I don't know if they're mine or his or—" He breaks off, panting.

"I want to do this right," he begins again. "I don't know what the future holds. I can't make any guarantees. But I want to get to know you better. My older self is a pretty smart guy, after all. Most would say a bona fide genius." His lips twitch as he offers me his arm. "So what do you say, Alice? Wanna go on a date with me?" He winks. "Half the junior class would *kill* for this opportunity."

I burst out laughing. I can't help it. He's so ridiculous, so arrogant. So Bandit.

I tuck my hand through his arm, holding tightly onto my *puang malai*, and we glide into the night. I don't know what will happen in the next days, months, or years. But I'm hopeful. Even optimistic.

The future can't come soon enough…

Just as long as I don't have to kill anyone.

ACKNOWLEDGMENTS

Any acknowledgments of this book must begin with Liz Pelletier, my editor, publisher, and co–story developer. Quite simply, *Malice* would not exist without her. Liz, thank you for entrusting me with this story idea, and thank you for pushing me to utilize every last bit of my creativity. I'm proud of this thing we created!

My gratitude, as always, to the phenomenal team at Entangled, especially Heather Riccio, Stacy Abrams, Jessica Turner, and Curtis Svehlak. Special shout-out to Heather Howland and Madison Pelletier for their extremely insightful comments on the manuscript.

Thank you to the amazing Beth Miller for being by my side and helping me navigate the bumps and contours of this publishing career.

Big thank-you to Yanfeng Lim (and to my dear Anita for connecting us) for sharing her brilliance and scientific expertise. It was so much fun to brainstorm ways to wipe out half the world with you!

I am immensely grateful for my author friends—especially Darcy, Meg, Brenda, Denny, and Vanessa. Publishing can be fickle; it loves you one minute and loathes you the next. Lucky for me, you all are the opposite of that—as loyal as the time stream is long. This adventure is so much easier because I get to share it with you!

The one area in my life where I am truly blessed is my family—and this includes my lifelong friends who I count as part of my family. I often write about unconditional love, about ties that are so deep and abiding that my characters would travel to the end of time in order to preserve them. These stories would not be possible if you didn't show me, every day of my life, how it feels to be so loved.

To Antoine, Aksara, Atikan, and Adisai. You are truly the A^4 of my world. One day, I may even get a tattoo to prove it.

Last, but never least, to my wonderful readers. Thank you for reading my stories, and thank you for reaching out with your kind words and enthusiasm. You'll never know how much I appreciate each and every sentiment.

Turn the page to start reading
a sneak peek of

CROWN of BONES

A.K. WILDER

In a world on the brink of the next Great Dying, no amount of training can prepare us for what is to come...

A young heir will raise the most powerful phantom in all of Baiseen.
A dangerous High Savant will do anything to control the nine realms.
A mysterious and deadly Mar race will steal children into the sea.
And a handsome guide with far too many secrets will make me fall in love.

My name is Ash. A lowly scribe meant to observe and record. And yet I think I'm destined to save us all.

MARCUS

Morning light blasts through the woods, making me squint. "There! To the south." I urge Echo, my black palfrey, on to greater speed, the hunting dogs falling behind. We gallop hard, neck and neck with True, my brother's mount, careening around giant oaks and jumping fallen logs. Autumn leaves scatter in our wake.

"They're headed for the meadow," Petén calls over the pounding hooves. His dark hair streams behind him, revealing a high forehead, an Adicio family trait. I've got it, too, but not quite as pronounced as his.

We're alike in other ways—same tall, broad build, brown eyes, and olive skin, though my hair is the color of brass, not black. Also, Petén's nineteen, two years older than me, and non-savant—he can't raise a phantom. It's a blow to him, because I *am* savant and therefore Heir to the Throne of Baiseen, a fact that turns everything between us sour.

"Head them off." I signal toward the upcoming sidetrack.

"So you can beat me there and win all the praise?"

I laugh at that. Father's not going to hand out praise for

anything I do, even catching Aturnian spies, if that's what the trespassers really are. Besides, palace guards are coming from the south and will likely reach them first, so I don't know what Petén's talking about. He's right, though, I wouldn't mind being the one to stop them, just in case Father is watching. "Race you. Loser takes the sidetrack," I shout.

He nods, and our mounts tear up the path for a short, breakneck sprint. Echo wins by half a length, and I stand up in my stirrups, victorious, waving Petén off to the right. On I gallop, a downhill run toward the meadow. When I reach the open grass, there's a clear shot at the three men who race on foot. "Halt in the name of the Magistrate!" I fit an arrow to my bow and fire it over their heads, a warning shot. I wouldn't actually shoot anyone in the back, but they don't know that.

"Halt in the name of Baiseen!" Petén yells, bursting into the meadow from the north.

The hunted men veer to the left and keep running. Petén lets loose his arrow, and it lands just short of them, another warning.

I'm close enough to pick off all three. "Halt!" I shout, hoping they do this time.

My brother and I barrel down on them, and in moments we've corralled the men, trotting our horses in a tight circle, arrows aimed at the captives in the center. The dogs catch up and bark savagely, ready to attack.

"Stay," I command the two wolfhounds, and they obey, crouching in the grass, tongues hanging out to the side as they lick their chops and growl.

"Drop your weapons," Petén says just as Rowten and his contingent of palace guards, three men and two women, gallop into the field from the other end. Chills rush through me as Father appears behind them, riding his dark red hunter. The captives unbuckle their sword belts and raise their hands as the guards join us, further hemming them in.

"To what purpose are you here?" Father asks as he rocks back in the saddle. He turns to Petén. "Search their gear—if you are sober enough for the job." To me, he says, "If any move, kill them."

Sweat breaks out on my brow and a tremor runs down my arms. The problem is my brother's not all that sober. If he provokes them...

But Petén swings out of the saddle without falling on his face, and I keep my arrow aimed at each man in turn while he goes through their packs. They have a distance viewer and a map of Baiseen marking where our troops are quartered, the watchtowers, and the Sanctuary, with numbers in the margin.

"Scouting our defenses?" Father asks.

Officially, we're not at war with the neighboring realms of Aturnia to the north. I sat through a long council meeting just yesterday where U'karn assured us of this, but relations are strained, and Father suspects breaches on the border. Like this one.

The captives remain silent, which doesn't help their case.

"Answer." I try to sound authoritative. "Or do you not know who questions you? Bow to Jacas Adicio"—I nod to my father—"orange-robe savant to the wolf phantom, Magistrate of all Palrio, and Lord of the Throne of Baiseen."

The middle one lifts his head. He's not dressed in the robes of a savant or an Aturnian scout. He wears traveler's garb, leggings, tunic, riding coat, and high boots without a hint of mud. Their horses can't be far away. "We're lost, your Magistrate, sir. Meaning no harm or trespass. If you just set us straight, we'll be on our way." It's a fair attempt at diplomacy, but unfortunately for this poor clod, his accent betrays him.

"All the way from Aturnia? You are indeed lost." My father turns to me. "Did you track them down, Marcus?"

My chest swells as I start to answer. "It was—"

"I led the chase," Petén cuts in as if I wasn't going to give him half the credit. Which I was, probably.

"Fine," Father says, though he doesn't seem particularly pleased. I can't remember the last time he was anything but frustrated with either of us. But then, it's no secret he's not been the same since my eldest brother was deemed marred. Losing his first son changed Father...irrevocably.

While I blink sweat out of my eyes, the nearest captive makes to drop to one knee.

"Savant!" I shout.

"*Shoot!*" my father roars in command.

He means me.

I have the shot, ready and aimed, and I should have taken it by now. But the man is ten feet away. If I hit him at this range, with an arrow made to drop an elk, it'll stream his guts all over the meadow.

As I hesitate, my father is out of the saddle in an instant and touching down to one knee. The second he does, the ground explodes, a rain of dirt and rock showering us. The horses' heads fly up, ears pinning back, but they hold position as Father's phantom lunges out of the earth. The size of a Dire Wolf, its mouth opens, lips pulling back in a snarl. Still not clear of the ground, it begins to "call," a haunting, guttural sound that can draw weapons from a warrior, water from a sponge, flesh from bone. Before the phantom lands, the men's chests crack open in a spray of blood. Three hearts, still beating, tear out of their torsos and shoot straight into the phantom's mouth. It clamps its jaws and, not bothering to chew, swallows them whole.

Entranced by the brutality, my fingers spasm and the arrow flies from the bow. Its distinct red fetches whistle as it arcs high and wide over one of the guard's heads, a woman who gives me an unpleasant look. The arrow hits down, skipping through the grass to land harmlessly a distance away.

No one speaks as the horses settle and Rowten signals for the dogs to be leashed. I breathe heavily, staring at the corpses, blood welling in the cavities that were, moments ago, the bodies of three living men. Aturnian spies, aye, most likely, but living men just the same.

"Peace be their paths," Rowten says, and we all echo the traditional saying when someone dies. It refers to the path to enlightenment, the ones we savants are supposed to be so much further along...

But what if I got it wrong? What if the man had simply gone weak in the knees and wasn't dropping to raise his phantom at all? What if he really was non-savant, lost, virtually harmless to us? I cried out the warning that lead to these deaths. What does that say about me and my path?

When I look to Petén, I find him staring at the bodies, as well, until he turns away and throws up in the grass. Somehow that makes me feel better, though I don't think it has the same effect on our father, judging by his expression.

Father examines the dead men's weapons. "Aturnian," he says, and lowers gracefully to one knee, his phantom melting away as he brings it back in. It's a relief. Phantoms don't usually scare me, not those of our realm, but this one's different, more powerful, better controlled. Merciless. If Father wasn't already Magistrate, he'd be a red-robe, High Savant of Baiseen. I shudder at the thought.

Before mounting up, he turns to Rowten. "Take the dogs and find their horses. Then call for the knacker to deal with this mess." In an easy motion, he's back on the hunter, shaking his head as he turns to me. "You raise a *warrior* phantom, Marcus. When will you start acting like it?"

Heat rushes to my face, and Petén, wiping his mouth

on his sleeve, chuckles. Any warmth I felt for my brother moments ago vanishes.

"Ride with me, both of you," Father commands.

The road home is short and agonizing as we flank Father, one on either side.

"Petén, if I catch the reek of alcohol on your breath again, I'll take away your hunting privileges for so long you'll forget how to ride."

"Yes, Father," he says quietly. "Sorry."

My lip curls until Father turns to me.

"Marcus," he says, his voice a newly sharpened knife. "You know war is inevitable, if not now then certainly by the time you are *meant* to take the throne."

A subtle reminder of my failings. "Yes, Father." But war between the realms is something I want to prevent.

"If you can't master your phantom soon, you'll lose your vote at the Summit as well as your right to succeed me."

"Yes, Father."

"You know this?" His eyes narrow.

"I do."

"Then why are you acting so bones-be-cursed weak?"

I couldn't choke out an answer if I had one. Even Petén looks away. My eyes drop to Echo's mane as it ripples down her neck. When I look up, Father's face turns to stone. He cracks his reins over the hunter's rump and gallops away.

Petén and I trot our horses back toward the palace, cresting a gentle rise to come out on the hill overlooking the expanse of Baiseen. The view takes in the high stone walls and gardens of the palace, the watchtowers and bright green training field in the center of the Sanctuary, all the way down the terraced, tree-lined streets to the harbor and the white-capped emerald sea beyond. It's beautiful, but no matter where I look, those three dead men seep back into my mind. "If they were spies, then war's coming sooner than we thought." I ease Echo to a halt. "But if they weren't, we'll have to—"

"We?" Petén cuts me off. "Keeping the peace when Father tempts war is your problem, little brother, not mine." He chuckles. "If you make it to Aku in time, that is." His face cracks wide with a smile. "This year's your last chance, isn't it?"

I open my mouth to answer, but he's already pushing past me, loping the rest of the way down to the stables.

Yes, it's my last chance to reach Aku for training. If I don't train my phantom, I can never hope to have a voice on the council. And I fear my voice may be needed soon—because I know my father. He'll not let this incident go. His actions may bring the realms down upon us.

And if our enemies are infiltrating our lands, I may already be too late.

New York Times bestselling author Tracy Wolff will give you something new to crave...

Everything he craves dies...

crave

NEW YORK TIMES BESTSELLING AUTHOR
TRACY WOLFF

Find out what all the buzz is about...

Black Mirror meets Ally Carter in this futuristic tale of social media gone bad, and the teens determined to save the world from ruin.

KEYSTONE

by

Katie Delahanty

When Ella Karman debuts on the Social Stock Exchange, she finds out life as a high-profile "Influencer" isn't what she expected. Everyone around her is consumed by their rankings, in creating the smoke and mirrors that make them the envy of the world.

But then Ella's best friend betrays her, her rankings tank, and she loses—everything.

Leaving her old life behind, she joins Keystone, a secret school for thieves, where students are being trained to steal everything analog and original because something—or someone—is changing history to suit their needs.

Partnered with the annoyingly hot—and utterly impossible—Garrett Alexander, who has plenty of his own secrets, Ella is forced to return to the Influencer world, while unraveling a conspiracy that began decades ago.

One wrong move and she could lose everything—again.

Fans of Veronica Rossi will love this thrilling
The Count of Monte Cristo retelling that sheds
light on the dark struggles of humanity.

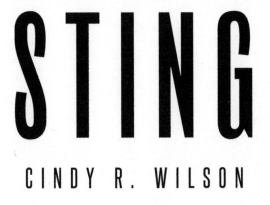

STING

CINDY R. WILSON

They call me the Scorpion because they don't know who I really am. All they know is that someone is stealing from people with excess to help people with nothing survive another day.

But then a trusted friend reveals who I am—"just" Tessa, "just" a girl—and sends me straight into the arms of the law. All those people I helped…couldn't help me when I needed it.

In prison, I find an unlikely ally in Pike, who would have been my enemy on the outside. He represents everything I'm against. Luxury. Excess. The world immediately falling for his gorgeous smile. How he ended up in the dirty cell next to mine is a mystery, but he wants out as much as I do. Together, we have a real chance at escape.

With the sting of betrayal still fresh, Pike and I will seek revenge on those who wronged us. But uncovering all their secrets might turn deadly…

This dark paranormal romance is perfect for fans of
Maggie Stiefvater or Leigh Bardugo.

keeper
of the **bees**

BY MEG KASSEL

KEEPER OF THE BEES is a tale of two teens who are
both beautiful and beastly, and whose pasts are entangled in
surprising and heartbreaking ways.

Dresden is cursed. His chest houses a hive of bees that
he can't stop from stinging people with psychosis-inducing
venom. His face is a shifting montage of all the people who
have died because of those stings. And he has been this
way for centuries—since he was eighteen and magic flowed
through his homeland, corrupting its people.

He follows harbingers of death, so at least his curse only
affects those about to die anyway. But when he arrives in
a Midwest town marked for death, he encounters Essie, a
seventeen-year-old girl who suffers from debilitating delusions
and hallucinations. His bees want to sting her on sight. But
Essie doesn't see a monster when she looks at Dresden.

Essie is fascinated and delighted by his changing features.
Risking his own life, he holds back his bees and spares her.
What starts out as a simple act of mercy ends up unraveling
Dresden's solitary life and Essie's tormented one. Their
impossible romance might even be powerful enough to
unravel a centuries-old curse.

Let's be friends!

 @EntangledTeen

 @EntangledTeen

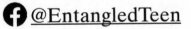 @EntangledTeen

📰 bit.ly/TeenNewsletter

entangled teen

an imprint of Entangled Publishing LLC